✳ A Novel of the French and Indian War ✳

THREE THOUSAND
DAYS ⊰AND⊱ NIGHTS

BENJAMIN W. FARLEY

[signature: Ben W. Farley]

LYDIA INGLETT, LTD
PUBLISHING
MMXII

❋ A Novel of the French and Indian War ❋

THREE THOUSAND DAYS AND NIGHTS

BENJAMIN W. FARLEY

Other Books by Benjamin W. Farley

FICTION

Beyond Homer

Quilly Hall

Of Time and Eternity

Corbin's Rubi-Yacht

Mercy Road

The Hero of St. Lo

SCHOLARLY

Jesus as Man, Myth, and Metaphor

John Calvin's Sermons on the Book of Micah

Son of the Morning Sky: Reflections on the Spirituality of the Earth

In Praise of Virtue

Calvin's Ecclesiastical Advice

The Providence of God

John Calvin's Treatises Against the Anabaptists and Against the Libertines

John Calvin's Sermons on the Ten Commandments

Three Thousand Days and Nights

Copyright 2012 by Benjamin W. Farley

ISBN: 978-0-9831519-7-5

Front cover painting used with permission: *The Death of General Wolfe* by Benjamin West. 1776, retouched 1806, oil on canvas. Courtesy of the Royal Ontario Museum.

Published by Lydia Inglett Ltd. **LI LTD**

www.lydiainglett.com

To order more copies of this book: www.starbooks.biz

for
Alice Anne,
John and Bryan
Cole, Mae, and Wren

Nous Sommes Tous Égals:
A Writer's Preface

If asked where and when the French and Indian War began, one would have to say, *"Alors! Je ne sais pas.* Only the historians know." But that is too easy an answer.

One could say it was inevitable, its origins embedded in the sole marks of Frenchmen like Cabot and Champlain, or Jolliet and Marquette, or the will of their Kings, from the time of Louis XIII on.

As for the English, do we begin with Jamestown or Plymouth? Or for that matter, with the Dutch and the founding of their colony on Manhattan? And Spain? Are we to leave out Spain, or De Soto's slaughter of native peoples from Florida to Mississippi? Did memories of this distant carnage make their way to Shawnee wigwams?

All Europe's powers were at war, vying for bullion and furs, markets, tobacco, slaves, and riches unimaginable. Lands for the grabbing, continents for the taking! And all with the blessing of the Church, whether Catholic, Anglican, Protestant, Quaker, or Puritan.

And who were these savages anyway? And what right did they have to lands, to "property" they never tilled, cities they never built, living in hovels as primitive as Mesopotamians before biblical times? Were they not to be conquered, converted, or eliminated to make way for a more civilized man?

Perhaps the war really began with Champlain's invasion of Mohawk territory in July of 1609. The Iroquois never forgave him; in that very year, Henry Hudson was also sailing up a river he would name for himself. How close the three parties came: Indian, Dutch, and French. Or certainly by the time of King Philip's War and the Puritan attempt to eradicate the Abenaki and Algonquin tribes of New England. Nor are we to forget the fate of the Lenape, Shawnee, and American tribes of Pennsylvania, Virginia, or the Carolinas. By the 1700s, all were being driven west of the Blue Ridge and the dark Alleghenies beyond.

At least the French seemed to understand. Yes, they wanted their pelts, furs, allegiance, and women. Above all they needed access to their rivers, their lakes and streams, and markets for their French goods of blankets, tobacco, kettles, pots, knives, hatchets, and even guns. For the Frenchman, it was a paradise, a land of adventure, of becoming an *homme naturel* as Rousseau himself had dubbed the savage.

As for the *sauvages*, except for the Iroquois, the French presence seemed to offer their best hedge against the alarming erosion of all they had cherished and loved. To whom else could they turn? Not to the British, or the Dutch, or even the noblest frontiersman. None of the latter cared or could be trusted.

Too simple! Too biased? Too prejudiced? Too wed to a sentiment that only a novelist could invent? I don't know. But I have tried to tell this story as best I know how.

And so, where to begin? I have chosen the year 1751, which I find as realistic a beginning as any one might select.

- Benjamin W. Farley

Acknowledgments

Three Thousand Days and Nights began as a dream inspired by a number of historical projects published during the two-hundred-and-fiftieth anniversary of the French and Indian War. Most compelling was Robert Leckie's *"A Few Acres of Snow": The Saga of the French and Indian Wars.* Once I read his coverage of the era I knew I had to create a story told through the eyes of an imaginary spectrum of characters: French, Indian, British, and Colonial American, who suffered and endured that struggle. I wanted to write something of their dreams and hopes, sacrifices and spirit commensurate with the period.

Before listing the principal sources I found most helpful, it is to Lydia Inglett that I owe the dream's fulfillment as a publication. Without her acceptance of the original draft, the time she dedicated to proofing and editing the story, plus her artistic design work, the novel would have never seen print.

In addition to Leckie"s fascinating account, I an indebted to the scholarship of the War's premier American historian, Francis Parkman, and his *Montcalm and Wolfe* and *Musket and Tomahawk;* also Fred Anderson's *Crucible of War;* Walter R. Borneman's *The French and Indian War;* Willard S. Randall's *George Washington;* James Thomas Flexner's *George Washington: The Forge of Experience;* and Thomas E. Crocker's *Braddock's March.* Many other sources were perused for particular nuances and personalities. Of central importance is Christopher Gist's own account of his surveying party's journey into the Ohio country in 1751 and George Washington's report to the Lt. Governor Robert Dinwiddie of Virginia, describing his rendezvous with French officials at Ft. Le Boeuf the winter of 1753-1754. René Chartrand's publication: *Monongahela 1754-55* was also beneficial.

The Internet provides numerous articles on almost all the historical personages associated with the era. In addition, it offers succinct follow-up bibliographies for readers who desire more. I found the Wikipedia's notes on the major French participants highly useful and wish to express my gratitude to the writers of said entries.

I alone am responsible for any misrepresentations of actual histori-cal facts or persons. Such was not intentional. In many instances, I could not find an in-depth account of some of the historical events I wanted to fictionalize. But then, this is a novel, not a history of the period.

Again, I am most grateful to Lydia Inglett and her staff of Lydia Inglett Ltd. Publishing. I am also indebted to Dr. Norma Kirkland for her assis-tance in proofing the final text.

- BWF

PART ONE

Beyond
the
Alleghenies
1751-1753

Chapter One

VIRGINIA'S LIEUTENANT GOVERNOR stretched himself to his full height to appear as tall as possible in his mirror. He liked what he saw in its ornate, oval-shaped disk. He turned sideways to admire his full-length, bright-flaxen dresscoat, along with matching hose and shoes of emerald green. Though short in stature, Robert Dinwiddie knew he cut an enviable pose when he had to, especially at galas and the mansion's reels. His dress and demeanor were also essential in his role as Governor over the quarrelsome House of Burgesses and its tobacco-smoking gaggle of aristocratic planters and wannabes. But his elegant attire could not override the profound disappointment Gist's message conveyed.

Travelled as far as the Miami. Numerous tribes loyal to the French. War parties to move south come spring. Have split from Burke and returning by alternate route. Have a full journal of surveyors' plots marked and described for the Company to consider. Burke carries a pack of his own. Should be in Williamsburg by May.

Yours faithfully, Christopher Gist. March 11th, 1751.

"Damn! Damn! And Double Damn!" the Governor snorted. When would the Colony ever be rid of the damnable French!

Far to the north in Quebec, a tall figure staring out the window marveled at the sudden, spirited snow shower. Pensively, he reached out to catch a flake. Slowly, its icy crystals melted into a soft web in the palm of his warm hand. For a second, he could have sworn it looked like a *fleur de lis*. Strange, he thought. With first a smile, and then a frown, Jacques-Pierre de Taffanel de la Jonquière, the Governor General of New France, rubbed his hands together and returned to his desk. His secretary, Jean Dugard, closed the window, latched it, and stood politely beside the Governor.

Monsieur de la Jonquière took his seat and glanced up at the lean man. "It isn't good," the Governor grimaced. "And such a brief note!" he handed the hand-inscribed, leather patch back to the servant. "Better file it."

"Monsieur, please don't be so troubled," the secretary consoled him. "What have we to fear from the English, anyway? So, they're back on the River. What are so few against our mighty bateaux and allies? And what did the note say? Only, Monsieur, that the prying Gist was handing out wampum belts to the Delaware and Shawnee. They are nothing, *rien* Monsieur, in comparison with our Ottawa, Wyandot, and Huron."

"*Oui*! 'Tis true! But Joncaire's no fool. His note's a warning. What did he write?" he pointed to the scrap.

Alors! Attendez! Gist is on the river again with belts and whiskey. Promises and lies. No less than eight travelers in his party. Coup de Sang and I will continue to track them.

> *Your servant, Capt. Joncaire, 17th of February 1751. Salut!*

"Don't you realize what that means? More troops, more supplies, more forts! More everything. And what is worse: more correspondence with His Majesty's Court. And where is François? I trust him far, far more than Joncaire, though the latter is never wrong. *Mon chèr ami, nous avons nos tâches à faire!*"

"Ah, but you forget one thing." Dugard smiled, as he placed his hands on the Governor's desk. "With the mountains and their gorges and forests, there is not a road in, nor a road out. Only trails and rivers. And to the north, our Algonquin. To the south, New Orleans and forts in between: Rouillé, Beauséjour, Beauharnois, and Le Jonquière. Maybe one more fort somewhere along the river would do."

"Would that I knew or could draw comfort from your words," de la Jonquière sighed. "I am proud of the forts," he smiled. "I ordered them built myself, you know. They should keep the English at bay for a while. But who's to say? *Non? C'est bon, Je crois!* You always make me feel better."

Farther to the south, Langdon Burke looked out across the Ohio. He had managed to avoid every contact possible with Indians. Skirting their villages, hanging back in the forest, and minimizing his horse's imprints, he had surveyed two hundred miles or more without detection. He knew such luck, however, was bound to turn. At that very hour, somewhere along the river, or in the meadows of Kentucky, Joncaire's savages were tracking him. They'd been doing so since Gist had dismissed him. "You'll make it," the swarthy guide had smiled. "Just don't fire your gun lest you have to."

Langdon dismounted, tied his horse's reins to a birch sapling, and searched for a thicket of reeds. Finding a shelter amid a patch of crimson sheaths, he sat down and faced the river. As he cradled his flintlock across his lap, a sudden sense of isolation swept over him. In truth, the silence and solitude of the forest had encoded themselves in him since childhood. If anything, the wilderness was his companion. Always and everywhere it alerted him to its wonders and dangers. What unnerved him, however, was an ambivalence far deeper. He loved the wilderness, but if Dinwiddie's Company had its way, its woodlands would fall victim to the axe and its grasslands to the planter's iron plow. He hated that, but what was he to do? He had his own fate to ponder.

Attempting to draw back the huge hammer of his flintlock, Langdon's thumb was too stiff from the penetrating cold to cock the mechanism. He shivered, in part from the frigid temperature, but not entirely. He had never feared for his life. But if discovered, he knew the horrific possibilities Joncaire's allies would exact. The muscular twenty-eight-year old took in a deep breath, then exhaled forcefully, snorting as his nostrils flared. He shook off his anxiety and regained his senses. There was no need to cock the gun.

Leaning forward, Langdon sensed more than saw the mauve shades of dusk creep quietly into the forest, the deepening stages of night all but concealing him. Turning his collar up against the cold, he studied the weaving silhouettes of dancers on the bluff below. How ghostly they appeared in the glooming twilight. A camp fire was too risky, so he concentrated instead on the sounds of tom-toms and drumbeats as the natives stepped in cadence about their circle of flames. Beyond them lapped the waters of the Ohio.

Aside from Gist and a handful of others, no one else knew of Langdon Burke's whereabouts. Langdon could not stop thinking about what Gist had said to him: "Don't let them see your compass or journal. Backwoods gentry or not, be careful, sir. Lookout for Joncaire. He's a devil in disguise. I'll wait for you along the Appalachians, near the headwaters of the James and, if not obstructed, I'll leave a cache for you." Gist had patted him on the shoulder before taking leave, a gesture that, at the time, had felt brotherly. But now, alone, he could not cease thinking about what the guide had uttered.

Langdon Burke had drawn a similar conclusion about Joncaire – Captain Philip Thomas Joncaire, Sieur de Chambert, to be exact. Still, in truth, he admired the man. Where did Frenchmen like Joncaire come from? Without hesitation, their forebears had left elaborate estates in France to take up residence in the remote hamlets along the tributaries and frozen bays of the St. Lawrence. Yet, at the same time, he feared Joncaire and his cohorts. They were not like the English, or his own family of modest descent, poised to cross the Blue Ridge Mountains with dreams to carve out hearths along the Holston. Instead, the French vied for adventure, for a life among the savages, for furs, guns, liquor, wealth and skirmishes beside their noble "*enfants.*" Many had been reared by Indians themselves.

As he huddled under his blanket with his flintlock in his arms, he searched the Indian encampment for the Captain. If the man were present, Langdon could not spot him. A French officer's white tent was visible, but he could see no sign of Joncaire. Perhaps it was the tent of the young lieutenant who had accompanied the Captain. Two months earlier, the lieutenant had sat with Langdon under the glow of a fire's blaze the night four Indians tortured and clubbed an old woman to death. It had been a horrid and senseless act. Even the host chief was disturbed, but he had sat in silence since the four Wyandots were his guests. The woman was their captive, not his. Etiquette was etiquette, even for the sachem. The old chief, Torn Ear, the Half-King, had sat with stiff dignity, his long gray hair tied with blue ribbons, embossed with yellow lilies – gifts from the French. His square shoulders, robe of badger fur, and large nose gave him an air of royalty all his own.

Since that night, Langdon had learned that many Wyandot tribes considered themselves allies of the English, but a scattered few supported the French and their leagues of Ottawa, Miami and Huron. The old chief favored the English, but had become agitated when the following day two white traders entered town and asked to see him alone. Their names were Croghan and Montour. They were dressed more like Indians than white men.

"You see I have guests," he had motioned toward Gist, Langdon Burke and the others. "You have been trading with the French. I have seen your canoes before. I am not pleased with this. But come into the council house. We will hear you."

Langdon had followed Gist, Half-King, and the traders into the council lodge. Warm red embers had filled the bark-shingled house with a soft oak redolence, glowing rouge and copper off the men's faces and hands. Croghan, the leader of the traders, waited for the chief to extend the pipe. After the participants fulfilled the time-honored requirement, the short, coarse-haired trader rose politely and began.

"We have come from the Wyandots, who have always been our friends. We are honored to be your friends, too. They have warned us that the Ottawas have sided with the French and have ceded to them all the branches of their streams that feed into the lakes. Those that drain into the Ohio, they claim for themselves. They disfavor their friends, even the French, and all English invaders and their allies from hunting, trapping, fishing or settling lands north of the Ohio. In the spring, when the snows melt and the corn turns green, they plan war parties against any who violate their claims. They intend to plant hatchets in your braves and wives' skulls, if you trade with the English or let them pass down river."

The old chief smiled and gestured with humor toward Langdon. "You have much hair," he pointed to Langdon's black ponytail. "Not good, I think. Mine is stringy and thin," he pulled on his gray matted mane. "You have come in peace," Half-King continued, as he addressed the traders. "Nourish yourselves before you leave. My people bear you no ill will."

It had been the brief visit of Joncaire's party that had created the most awkwardness, however. Traveling with them was a young woman of twenty-five or so, half-Indian, half-French, whom the lieutenant obviously prized. Her long black hair lay in braids across her breasts, her silk white blouse concealing her shapely bosom. Her skirt of deer hide descended to the tops of her fur-lined otter boots. A younger woman of similar dress and dark brown hair accompanied her. The younger woman's black eyelashes and engaging oval-shaped brown eyes had captured Langdon's glances from the start. From what Langdon could surmise, she was white.

"And how are you called?" he asked her in French.

Her deep brown eyes and red lips hinted at a passion that struck Langdon's loins. "Louise," she said softly. "*Louise-Marie de Touloine. Hélène est ma cousine. Et vôtre-même, monsieur, comment vous appelez-vous?*"

"Langdon. Langdon Burke."

"*Viens ici,* come on!" The older young woman seized her arm. "We cannot stay here. Until later, Monsieur," she shot a suspicious look at Langdon. "We've far to go."

"Yes!" interjected Captain Joncaire. "With surprises for the hapless." Joncaire's demeanor of disdain was not lost on Langdon.

"Perhaps we shall meet again," said the lieutenant, shaking Langdon Burke's hand. The lieutenant was dressed in a French officer's white coat, with broad blue cuffs, cinched with a tan belt, and bleached deerskin leggings, protected by gaiters about his shins and ankles. His wavy black hair and gray eyes complemented the broad smile on his pale lips. He was slightly taller than Langdon, but shorter than the sinewy Joncaire.

After their party left, Gist requested his own council with Torn Ear, the Half-King. "We have much to say from our Father across the ocean and his Son in Virginia. Will you hear us, Sir?"

"Yes. But do not flatter me. Our homes once dotted the meadows and forests of your lands. Now we are forced to find sanctuary in these colder climes and are caught between you and the mettlesome French.

But, come! Let us speak to each other in truth. Perhaps we can honor our words."

Torn Ear guided them once more into the Council Lodge. "Speak, for we are your brothers. What is the message your Great Father sends?"

For the next several hours, Gist launched into a long parley of Dinwiddie's desire to provide guns and gifts, if Torn Ear's people would side with the Colonists over the French. Pipes were smoked, wampum belts exchanged, and promises of peace extended.

The old chief eyed the presents with a knowing silence. He knew what acceptance entailed. His warriors' guns needed repair. It was not a time for pride to rule or for weakness either. He cleared his throat and spoke in his native tongue for Gist to interpret. "Many of our braves are out hunting. Our chiefs are with them. Perhaps in the spring, when the meadows flower and corn stalks grow tall, we shall come. I cannot promise more."

"We know your offer is true and your words straight," Gist said.

The old chief stood and extended his hand, first to Gist and then to Langdon. "So may our words bear fruit. We shall see."

Throughout the next month, it seemed to Langdon that they visited an endless collection of sordid villages, each time rendering similar speeches. Often the chiefs warned of French vessels, heading up the rivers, bearing arms and boatloads of soldiers and stone for new forts below the lakes. Just as often their hosts, especially the Delaware, reassured them of their loyalty to their English Father. As one chief had put it: "Brothers, we the Delaware pledge you our thanks and assure you that we will not listen to another voice or accept the wampum strings of the French. We shall look forward to the spring and joining our brothers in council with your King's great Son."

Sometimes Gist and his men crossed the Ohio on rafts, or swam with their horses through the freezing waters. Ice floats were common; sudden snow showers and days of unending rain kept them in camps longer than they wished to stay. All the while, Langdon and Gist took readings with their compasses. Rich bottom land, forests of oak and cherry, the swiftness of currents, the depth and composition of soil, the presence of salt licks, the extent of clover-covered meadows, cane fields, rye and

bluegrass, along with the abundance of turkeys, deer, bear, and buffalo —
all was noted and entered into journals. Governor Dinwiddie's commission had made it patently clear: the Ohio Company needed an accurate
depiction of the lands across the Allegheny Mountains, along with the
native populations' numbers and towns, friendliness or allegiance to the
French. Parcels of land were to be granted or sold as early as Gist could
submit his report. Movements of the French were to be recorded as well.
And all this kept secret from the Indians. Dinwiddie hoped to beat his
Pennsylvania rivals at the same game. The glory of the journey had lost
its appeal for Langdon, but not the adventure or intrigue.

Langdon took a deep breath. The cold air stung his lungs. He glanced
one last time at the white tent and the camp of dancers along side the
white waters of the rapids, then pulled the blanket over his face, his
ears intent for sounds in the darkness. He heard his horse snort. In the
distance an owl hooted. How he wanted to fall asleep, but he knew he
mustn't. Would he still be alive at dawn? Somewhere out there he knew
that Joncaire's *maudit sauvages* were tracking him.

Chapter Two

FRANÇOIS-PHILIPPE, le sieur Gabelle de Robert, warmed his hands by the fire's heat and stared up into the night. He had not seen so many stars in weeks. Snow, rain and overcast skies had dampened their journey from its inception.

In the darkness beyond the fire, François caught the figure of Coup de Sang crouching in the grass. With measured sweeps, the oily, half-clad native cleaned his hunting knife in the grass. He was tall, sizeable of frame, with three black tattoo pin-point-pricks under each eye. Coup de Sang was Joncaire's macabre nickname for the copper-skinned warrior, a disgruntled Seneca with a talent for fighting and a penchant for blood. To François' knowledge, his real name was Tekacayah, or Handsome Dog, but no one seemed to know for sure. As François stared, the Indian glanced across the glowing space with guarded indifference. After replacing his knife in its sheath, he produced a palm-sized mirror and began applying ochre lines to his face. "You want to come?" he smiled toward the lieutenant. "Or do you sleep?" he nodded toward the tent.

"Should I come?" François replied. "Whose scalp are you after tonight?"

"Come and see, if you have the stomach!" the Indian challenged. "Coup de Sang has not taken this path to talk. Your Captain pays much for English scalps."

"I doubt that you'll find them. They're far across the mountains by now."

"Do not be so sure. Their horses are thin, their shirts in rags. They are wet and cold. They must hunt to live. I will hear their guns. I will find their tracks. They will split up when desperate. I have already found the tracks of one," he nodded toward the bluff in front of them. "I will follow them home, one by one, and leave their women widows. You have much to learn, Frenchman."

François resented the indignation but let out a deep breath. "*Très bien!* I will come."

Handsome Dog rose to his feet, surprised. He said something in his Iroquois tongue and motioned for François to follow. "*Vite!*" he waved him forward.

The lieutenant returned to his tent, retrieved his gun, pouch and a wolf fur to cast over his white coat, and strode quickly after the Seneca. Bending from his waist, Coup de Sang slipped into the night, weaving from one side to another, up the bluff, until he and the lieutenant were standing in the semi-darkness of alders and underbrush. The Seneca moved as if he knew exactly where to go and what he intended to do. Without making a sound, he crept deeper into the undergrowth, and rested momentarily beside a scaly hickory. Silent slivers of starlight illuminated a path. The bronze figure bent down and touched the earth, then rose and picked his way slowly through the dark.

François did not speak or whisper. When Coup de Sang stopped, François halted. When the native sniffed the air, or examined the ground, François observed in silence. Suddenly, a button on one of François' gaiters caught a twig, breaking the stillness with a faint snap. From somewhere in the forest, wings stirred. The Seneca held up his hand for François to stop. Both men crouched and listened. Seconds passed, perhaps a minute. Without warning, the Indian suddenly stood, let out a bone-chilling "Whoop!" and sprang into the thicket to his right. He raised his knife, ready for blood. But no one was there. In the darkness, a horse whinnied, as its hooves sank into the rustling leaves. François could hear the squeak of a saddle, as the animal galloped off. The savage plunged his knife into the warm reeds where Langdon had lain. "Next time, I will come alone!" The Indian turned his face toward François. It was filled with contempt. "I wish all white dogs were dead."

"You are free to rejoin Joncaire. You may leave now if you wish."

"No! I will stay here and watch you," he smiled. "Then I will kill the young English."

Indians were still dancing about the flames when François returned to his tent. Some lay inebriated in the grass; others rolled in the sand, or moaned from the effects of the large keg of brandy. François had not consented to its distribution, but the officer in charge, a relative of Joncaire's, had provided it in order to numb the Indians' displeasure with having failed to catch Gist's party. They had waited for them along the Miami, but, sensing an ambush, Gist had redirected his band through the sullen woods farther to the east.

Hélène had awaited François' return with grim curiosity. "*Alors!* Did Tekacayah find the English?" the half-savage girl asked him. "Did he lift his scalp?" She spoke with equal measures of disgust and enthrallment. "Let's go back to Frontenac. To Montreal. Do we have to continue down river?"

François gently pressed his index finger to her lips, then took her in his arms and pressed her against his chest. He had not removed the wolf skin and its dried ears poked against her chin. He brushed the fur aside, smiled, and kissed her lips. "Where's your cousin? It isn't wise for her not to be here."

"She's fine! She's with one of the squaws, trying to learn her language. Why do you ask? Have your eyes found something in her that I haven't given you?" She drew back slightly and looked up at him, running her fingers under the wolf skin.

"Of course not. I simply feel responsible, as any good man would. Let me take you now, before she returns," he whispered, as he slipped off his coat and took her by the hand to lie down on a mat of dried reeds and woolen blankets.

Afterwards, holding Hélène close, François remembered the evening he first met her. Her long black hair, silver-lined braids, glistening eyes and native beauty had appealed to the deepest core of his *virilité*. Joncaire had accompanied her from Frontenac to meet Louise, her cousin, whom François had been selected to escort to the intendant's house that evening in Montreal. "*Eh, bon!*" his superior, Gaston de Soisson, had explained. "I envy you the duty! Two beautiful women in one fell swoop! This Hélène is a woodsman's dream. Coquettish as a brazen consort, worthy of his majesty's entourage! And her cousin, Louise, don't let her plain appearance fool you! Her father was a renowned officer who served the King's cavalry. You will find the girl bright, witty, and ever so gentle, as pure as a rose in the wilderness. And as out-spoken! *Et bien!* A sensuous task awaits you, my young friend."

François smiled and rolled sideways to admire Hélène's beauty again. "We will leave for Frontenac in the morning," he kissed her. "My commandant assigned me to this trip, only to observe the Captain and how he operates. I know that now, all too well."

"Yes! He's a strange one, isn't he? Half-savage, half-French; half noble, half knave! His father was a bush-runner, they say. His mother, Ottowa. He grew up on trading posts around Frontenac and Niagara. He joined the Marines at age eighteen. Or so he boasts. He was once engaged to a French girl in Montreal. I knew her, but she jilted him in favor of a bookkeeper. I don't think he ever quite got over it. But he's something of a legend extraordinaire for the lords of Montreal."

"That I can well attest!" replied François. "How did you ever meet him? Were you lovers once? You've never said," he fondled her braids.

"No, no!" she laughed. "But he did rescue me from Frontenac. He knew my father. He knew I was too French to be left behind in Ottowa and Chippewa villages. I owe him that much. Whatever you might think of him, *il est de bon courage.*"

"Of that, I have no doubt."

"This country's changed him." She stared into François' face with her dark black eyes. "I love it, but I don't want it to change you."

"It won't. I love it, too. Its rivers and forests and savages! And it belongs to us." He touched Hélène's warm hands and kissed her again. "Hélène," he addressed her anew. "I've something I've been wanting to give you, since that night in Montreal. It's all that I have that is dearest to me, save you." He lifted her blouse and kissed each breast and chestnut-toned nipple.

She lay back and stared at him with her gleaming black irises and soft brown cheeks, reddened by the cold. "My proud *homme!*" She ran her fingers across his lips and chin. "You are the only *beau don* I need."

"No! Please! Cherish this for me," he whispered as he searched the pocket of his white coat and, fumbling while he kissed her again, presented her with a palm-size brooch, picturing a maiden, resting beside a woodpile, adorned in a white blouse, lavender skirt, red vest, and yellow shawl draped across her lap. "My father gave it to my mother," he said rubbing it with his rough hands. "Now, it's yours."

Hélène clasped it softly and held it up in the pale light of the tent. Her eyes fixed momentarily on his, then she shook her head from side to side with strange dispassion. "No!" She returned his kiss and brooch with a warm smile. "It is too French and too fragile! Kiss me once more! That's all I ask of thee." She pressed the delicate brooch into his numb fingers, and, sitting up, kissed his hand.

François slipped it back in his pocket and clasped her to his breast, kissing her lips and chin.

His thoughts wandered to his father. Perhaps his father had overstated his achievements, but whatever the reality, the memories he recalled strengthened his sense of worth for himself and the Crown. Count Jean-Daniel de Robert had been tall, muscular, agile and blessed with esprit de corps. A shrewd financier, his father's acumen with money had earned both the allegiance of the Majesty's court and the respect of Richelieu's successors. He was also a great advocate of the hunt and loved to gallop along the trails of the King's forest at Senlis. Time again, his father had strapped young François behind his back and trotted his horse up the steep sandy ridges of the lanes and down the needle-littered paths between the pines and great oaks. François could still recall the sound of his father's neck sash snapping in the wind and his long gray and black hair caught by the wind, whipping across his shoulders.

Memories of his mother were less grandiose. Née Henrietta Marguerite de Gabelle, who descended from the House of Henry IV, had captured his father's heart while visiting cousins in a relative's chateau near St. Germain-en-Laye. With a complexion the color of milk offset by her curly black hair, small lips, inquisitive eyes, and dainty nose, she interested Sire de Robert as much as he did her. They married at Versailles in 1722. But her health deteriorated after François' birth and, in 1731, while giving birth prematurely to a second child, she and the newborn died. His father's death five years later left him at the age of 11 to be reared by his aunts and a Chippewa girl named Two Moons. The girl, who had been brought to France by a relative, was named for the refulgence of the moon over the small lake near her lodge. Later, he lived in the house of his archbishop uncle who had envisioned for him a life in the church. He had almost become a priest.

But his desire for adventure overpowered whatever interest he had in following in his uncle's footsteps. When he learned the French court was searching for volunteers to make the voyage to serve his majesty in New France, he told his uncle of his interest in petitioning the court and asked for his blessing and his support. His uncle was reluctant and tried to convince him that he would have a grander career in France against those still opposed to the Austrian House.

"You'll never have that opportunity again," he had said.

"Perhaps, but I'm tired of his majesty's court. I'm repelled by its petty lords and all those fawning messieurs clawing after favors and paper titles, and coquettish affairs."

"It's an endless parody, isn't it? *Bien*! I'll see what I can do. You're unmarried, and the King prefers the unattached, or peasant couples, to married lords and ladies abandoning home."

"Would that he might learn from the British! Their New England colonies and Carolinas attract the best. *Mais*! What do we do? We send knaves and the inebriated, along with the greedy and dumbest bureaucrats. They say the governor general of Montreal is as corrupt as they come."

"If proven, he'll be brought home. But our wars of succession are more in vogue than Nouvelle France."

"Yes. Sadly."

"His majesty's minister of foreign affairs is worried about the same. Perhaps they'll design a new strategy. I should love to see New France someday, the parishes of New Orleans, or the ramparts of Quebec. I understand its walls are impregnable. But I think it will only be through your eyes." The old man struggled to quell his quavering hands, as he helped himself to a second glass of wine.

Suddenly, François' reverie was disrupted when he heard Louise-Marie at the flap of the tent. "I'm entering?" she called. "You didn't kill the young guide, did you? The one with Monsieur Gist?"

"And if we did?' François replied, as he raised himself up on his elbows. A wide smile spread slowly across his lips. "Does someone care about this English? No?"

"Don't be so cavalier!" Louise snapped.

"No, we didn't. Or, I should say, Coup de Sang and I were too late. We could hear the young Monsieur fleeing on his horse."

François and Hélène both struggled to their feet. He slipped on his coat, while she smoothed out her skirt.

"You must forget him," enjoined Hélène. "There are many suitors at Frontenac and Montreal, and many, many more at Quebec. And some are quite splendid, no?"

"Yes, but most are old and fat. And their whores even uglier!"

"Well, I would never have thought you'd have accommodated yourself so quickly!" Hélène retorted.

"Hélène is right!" François concurred. "Tensions are mounting. The English colonists are spilling across the mountains, and we've too few forts to stop them. Joncaire's forays may be terrifying, but they've stemmed the tide south of the forks."

"We're returning to Frontenac in the morning," Hélène confided. "We'll be going alone, with a few Ottawa. You will need to come with us. We can't leave you here."

Louise's face showed her disappointment. "I should have stayed at home in France," she mumbled with tears in her eyes. "Yet, I do love it here."

"Don't we all," François sought to comfort her. "Perhaps we shall meet this young guide of yours in a happier time. Come, smile for us. Sorrow is not a French virtue, nor bravery a vice." He took her hand and kissed it.

"You're right!" Louise acknowledged. "I'll be ready in the morning. Come Hélène, help me pack my things, and I shall help you." Her smile belied her worry. Would she ever see the young frontiersman again?

Chapter Three

VAPOR FROM LANGDON'S horse's nostrils formed lacy mists before evaporating in the frigid air. He guided his horse across an icy stream and up into a meadow. Bluegrass and brown cane undulated along the stream and out into a field. Far off, the grasses disappeared into a frosty haze.

He halted the animal and dismounted. He had been traveling south by southeast for the past three hours. It was time to mark his bearings. The land was perfect for grazing and even farming, but what a shame to sink a plow into this sea of wind-blown grass. Patties of fresh buffalo chips were evidence the herd had passed earlier in the morning. He reached into his surveyor's pouch and slipped out a quadrant compass and his journal. As he raised the compass lid the black needle swung north. He faced south by southeast and determined his position to be S 30 E, 15 miles now from the Falls. The tract of land that rolled outward on all sides would bring a fine profit to the Company. Gist had instructed him to maintain that bearing for a hundred miles or more, before turning due east to head back into the mountains. He marked the location in his journal and replaced both compass and diary in their pouch.

Langdon patted his horse's thin face and ran his fingers through its mane before remounting. "You're a good one, Pellas," he called it by name. The animal had borne him through snow and flood since their departure on the Potomac, surviving only on dry grass and an occasional handful of corn. In the distance, he watched a line of deer slip out of nearby woods to feed in the frosty grass. How he wanted to fell one, clean it, and roast its meat for dinner. But he knew he could not chance it. Somewhere following him were Joncaire's savages, ever on the prowl.

Toward late afternoon, he dismounted for a second reading, then looked about for a safe campsite. The meadows had given way to hills of hickory, walnut, locust, cedars, maples and oak. The red tips and fuzzy twigs provided ample food for the ubiquitous herds of deer. As evening drew near, horse and rider sauntered along an old game trail that led into a copse of pine, honey locusts, and a dark clearing. It was the entrance to a shallow cave, with an overhanging ledge: the perfect place to spend the night and light a fire. If only he had something to cook. Instead, he would have to sup on meager rations of tea and a few kernels of corn. Tomorrow, he would hunt. After tying Pellas to a maple sapling, Langdon gathered handfuls of dry litter and began placing frail twigs and short limbs about it. He built the fire small, just inside the cavern's opening, but at an angle that concealed it from the outside. From a clamshell ember box, he dropped a spark onto the hairs of a small mound of dry moss, blowing on the spark. Slowly the moss began to smolder, and a fine line of white smoke drifted up. Instantly, the litter took blaze.

Langdon prepared a tin cup of tea. He fed Pellas what remaining corn he had, down to the last kernels. "Tomorrow, we have to find food," he rubbed the horse's neck.

Langdon spread a semi-circle of locust branches about the cave's entrance. Anyone attempting an ambush would have to jostle the twigs, which were loaded with thorns. One of the branches sported a strand of dried pods. He broke them open. The seeds inside were moldy and the gum about them hard. Nevertheless, he crunched down on the seeds to extract their sweet fiber. He fed the pods to Pellas.

As he lay under his blanket near the glowing embers, Langdon tried to sleep but his mind would not let him. He wondered where Gist might be. Gist had hoped to explore the lands southwest of the Forks of the Ohio and follow a compass bearing of due south, along the hills west of the mountains. He had heard of the area's richness, of its well-drained soil and abundant game. Langdon wanted to find that area, too. With a packhorse, traps, sufficient lead and powder, a man could earn two years' wages in a single season of hunting and trapping. Perhaps he could find a partner to share the expenses and risk. Shawnee and Cherokee both hunted the environs and skirmished with each other, as he well knew.

He rolled toward the entrance and imagined Louise as that partner. "Smitten!" he whispered to himself. The thought of her created a warm smile on his unshaven face. That would never do, he concluded.

How he wanted to fall asleep. Would he be as lucky as last night? He reckoned he had traveled a minimum of twenty-five to thirty miles. Indians on foot would find that easy to match, if they were traveling light and in a war party. He should be safe. Still, his senses were keen to every inflection of the night – creaking limbs, the dank smell of the woods, the rustling of an owl's feathers. His eyelids grew heavy. His brain felt feverish. It longed for rest. His cave was secluded. The fire's embers were surely opaque to anyone outside. Somewhere, wolves howled in the distance. He clutched his gun in both hands and fell asleep.

Twice during the night he awakened. A faint sound crept through the forest. Light sleet fell. He could hear the clatter of ice crystals sifting through the branches. A cold breeze accompanied it. He stirred the embers and placed more wood on the fire. Each time, he fell back into a deep sleep.

When he awoke the next morning, sleet coated the trees and patches of grass. He rose, flailed his arms to keep warm, and rebuilt the fire. After a breakfast of hot tea, he bundled his belongings, saddled Pellas, and rode out of the copse. Beyond the woods, a cold wind whipped the dry tips of rye and bluegrass. He halted, dismounted, and took a compass reading: The arrow pointed N 10 E. In his journal, he wrote: "~30 miles from Falls. Good land, water nearby, many deer, heard wolves." Moments later, he and Pellas renewed their trek southeast.

Less than a mile out, Pellas snorted lightly and pranced to one side avoiding something in the icy mud. Langdon glanced down at the innards of a rabbit. Puffs of white fur caught his eye, then the ominous sign of moccasin footprints. Langdon counted at least four distinct heel marks. The party must have killed the rabbit with an arrow. One of the heel marks showed traces of blood. The party was headed in the same direction Langdon had chosen. He would follow them at a distance.

Perhaps their overland trail would bring him to their hunting site and an opportunity to exchange knives and hatchets for food. On the other hand, they might be a war party, looking for white trappers and scalps. By noon, the sun had melted the sleet, and warm shafts of light created wavy mirages ahead. Thrice, Langdon dismounted and described the land and its bounty in his journal. He jotted down the compass bearings and estimated miles he had traveled. In the process, he lost the Indians' trail. It ascended through a patch of woods, only to disappear on a gentle knoll, covered with shale and dried leaves. From the top of the rise, Langdon could see higher hills far off in the distance. They were to the southeast. All the land would qualify as proscribed in Governor Dinwiddie's commission to Gist.

Toward late afternoon, he picked up the Indians' trail anew. Dark blood glistened in the sunlight. In one place, Langdon could see where the person had fallen near a puddle of mud and then clearly had been dragged through the slop. Was the injured individual of the party's own or a captive? If a captive, was he white or savage? And why in this direction? Perhaps they belonged to a hunting encampment, and this poor devil had been captured for their sport.

He wondered if Joncaire, or his own Indians, were involved. If they had been following him, why hadn't they attempted an ambush by now? Clearly, they could have done so. Langdon concluded that this must be a different group and decided to follow them – far better to surprise them than for the latter to spring a trap on him. If it were Joncaire or his assassins, it was better to know it now than later. Whichever, he was on horseback and they on foot. Besides, this land was far south of the Ohio valley; its wealth totally unknown to the Governor.

Suddenly, he detected the faint odor of smoldering wood and spied a wisp of white smoke rising just to the south of an approaching tree line. He guided Pellas into the woods, dismounted, and with his flintlock in hand, crept toward the smoke. Three Indians had tied a fourth to a pole, his wrists overhead. With jeers and mocking chuckles, they waved hot brands across the Indian's face and torso. It was Coup de Sang, Handsome Dog! A broken arrow shaft dangled from one thigh. His captors were Shawnee. He knew they had no love for Senecas, or any member of the Iroquois Nation. Langdon stepped into the clearing.

"Ho!" he called. "Listen, my brothers! He is bad medicine! A bad spirit! It is best to let him go."

The three savages glared at Langdon, stunned. Their faces had been painted for their captive's death.

"What you do here?" the leader barked in coarse English. "We are three. You alone."

Langdon raised his gun, while loosening a hatchet at his waist. He pointed his flintlock at the apparent leader. "Let him go!"

Suddenly, an arrow sang past Langdon's hair and struck the leader in the chest. Only its feathers protruded. A gun discharged, and the closest second Indian dropped in a heap. The shot obliterated the Indian's left eye, mouth and lips. The third Indian howled and turned to flee. In a hissing blur, an arrow thumped into his back, heart level between his shoulder blades. The man fell.

Langdon turned just as an Ottawa, face painted yellow on one side and black on the other, rushed toward Coup de Sang and cut him loose. The latter seized the Ottawa's hatchet and buried it in the fallen Shawnee's skull. The thud sent shivers down Langdon's neck. Handsome Dog grimaced and ripped off the Shawnee's scalp. The Ottawa had not come alone. Langdon took in a sharp breath when he recognized the man with the gun.

"*Alors, mon anglais!* We meet again!" It was Joncaire. Instinctively, Langdon braced himself for battle. Joncaire nodded with a broad grin, then, with a courtly sweep of his hand, he bowed before Langdon. "Your petite Marie will be overjoyed, I fear. Another time. French gallantry requires I let you go. Please note that I have exercised the liberty of taking your journal from your saddlebags," he smiled, as he held it up for Langdon to see. "Tell your Dinwiddie to give up his Ohio dream. *N'est-ce pas!* But I have left you your compass. You may need it, but your mountains lie straight toward the sunrise," he pointed east. "Go there and do not come back."

Handsome Dog eyed Langdon in silence. He raised his hand with reluctance, as if to signal something unintended, too deep to express or communicate in words. His face remained unchanged while the Ottawa lifted the scalps of the other two Indians. Joncaire motioned for Coup de Sang to approach. The Frenchman heated his knife in the coals of the fire that the Shawnee had lit until the blade tip was white-hot. Then, without words, he cut into the Seneca's leg and dug out the shaft. Handsome Dog remained silent, even as Joncaire dipped the blade into the coals again and seared the black wound. The smell of singed flesh permeated the cold air.

"*Ah, bon!*" Joncaire stated. "*C'est toute!* It's done. The three searched the mutilated dead for valuables, seizing knives, tobacco and a prize hatchet made from flame-hardened ironwood. "Remember," said Joncaire as he and his comrades slipped into the forest. "Go and do not return!"

Now I can hunt, he thought. He returned to Pellas, mounted the animal, and cantered back toward a clearing where he had passed a buffalo earlier. A young cow raised her head as Langdon approached. He dismounted, knelt in the grass, and fired his gun. Pellas whinnied, as smoke encircled the horse's head. The cow dropped to her knees and coughed. Moments later, it collapsed in a ragged mound of hump, hide and fur.

After two days of work, Langdon broke camp with hunks of meat hung in skins from Pellas' hindquarters. A pouch of jerky dangled from the saddle-horn. Langdon turned due east and headed toward the hills that rose gently along the horizon. One week later, he crossed a broad trace that ran north and south. He surmised it was the route Indians used to hunt in the dark forest. The next day, he surprised two bears and managed to kill the larger of the two. Langdon pitched camp and decided to render the bear's fat and skin it for its fur. The effort took two days. Early the next morning, he packed up and began ascending the wooded slopes of the foothills toward the Allegheny range. He made his way high into the mountains, up steep ravines and down dark coves swathed in rhododendron. Wet snow fell heavily for two days. Exhausted and disoriented, Langdon decided to hole up until the weather improved.

He guessed that it was April, but spring had yet to arrive on the high ridges. If they didn't descend to warmer shelves of grass, Pellas would soon starve. That night he camped along a gushing stream, flanked by steep rills of pine, rhododendron and oak. Caves provided shelter, but he hadn't the slightest idea where he was. Wolves stole in around them; their slinking eyes glowed green and yellow in the night. With barking howls, they crept ever closer on their stomachs, hungry for Langdon's meat and Pellas's flesh. All night he remained by the fire, twice having to hurl flaming clumps of wood at the wolves. When morning broke, he was exhausted. Chills swept over him. He was too young to die this close to the frontier. Or so he told himself. Mounting Pellas, he descended the mountain along the stream. Soon it widened into a rocky gorge, where another creek joined it. He had stumbled onto the headwaters of the James. Where might Gist have hidden a cache? He studied the river's banks. Several miles down stream a large hemlock caught his eye. The initials "CG" had been carved into its grooved trunk. Langdon guided Pellas toward the tree. There, upslope, under a shelter of broken boughs, lay something dark, obscured in the dead leaves under a pile of loose rocks and dried ferns. After dismounting, he clawed away the debris. It was a bearskin, filled with a horn of dry powder, pouches of corn and jerky, tea, and a pewter flask of brandy.

Grateful? Yes, he was grateful. But how would Dinwiddie react once he learned that Gist's partner had lost the second journal? And that he, Langdon, was responsible?

Chapter Four

ANNA ASHBY, YOUNG WIDOW of Lord Ashby of Dunswell, stole one last glance at her coiffure of blonde curls. She dusted her bosom of small breasts with a quick flurry of pink powder, adjusted her green silk gown with her right hand, while fluffing her black velvet shawl with her left. Pleased with her mirror image, she left her spacious bedroom of hardwood floors, woven carpets and gold satin drapes, and descended the spiral staircase to greet her guests.

Numerous members of the House of Burgesses were present, several distinguished planters from Fairfax, along with a splendid manly figure attired in his regiment's bright red coat. One of the planters' wives had gossiped about him earlier. "They say his ancestors are descended from the House of Henry V and one of them fought beside the King at the Battle of Agincourt in 1415 – three-hundred-seven years ago. What a lineage! They say the Grahams, his mother's side, hated Cromwell – don't we all."

Anna's eyes had lit up as she listened. Now she was standing before him.

"Captain, I am so pleased you could come," she said, as she presented him her hand. "I think you will find the Tidewater much to your liking, though a bit muggy on an August night like this." She fanned herself slowly in order the better to assess his looks.

Sir William Graham Tillson bowed slightly and kissed her gloved fingers. His tall erect posture, graceful nose, sturdy chin and blue eyes – all under a lightly powdered wig – would have caught any woman's eye: colonial born or English. "I'm not used to it yet, I must confess," he said.

"Won't you have some punch? It's made from pears picked this afternoon, with a dash of who-knows-what-else? I can never trust the servants when it comes to spirits," she nodded toward a silver bowl. "The brandy's made here, too." She couldn't tell if she had made the impression on him that she desired.

"I'm confident I shall adjust," he said. "I had no idea the homes here were so elegant." Tillson gestured toward the high ceiling, its sparkling chandelier, and tall glass windowpanes. "Forgive me, but I've been told there's a guide present who knows the trails west. Is that true?"

"You must mean Mr. Gist. Unfortunately, he's already returned to the Ohio."

"Is there no one else? I hear there's a young major on the Potomac who has surveyed across the mountains."

"Mr. Washington. Yes! His brother Lawrence recently died, just this past July. Lawrence was involved in the Ohio Company, along with my late husband. Mr. Washington is in the process of overseeing his brother's plantation."

"I've heard of it and would value a meeting with this Washington."

"Perhaps you shall. He'll be in Williamsburg soon, surely by the fall."

"I was hopeful he might guide me over the mountains. They say the Shenandoah is beautiful in the fall."

"They do, but I've not seen it myself. My estate's as far west as I've wandered."

Tillson stared at her with bewilderment. How could she not have ventured up the James or into the interior of so vast a commonwealth as Virginia? "Is there anyone else I might engage to take me west?"

"That I don't know, sir, but a young man somewhat refined: part gentry, part surveyor, and part hunter, is here tonight. He's speaking to that portly gentleman, right there."

"Thank you, my Lady," Tillson bowed with a tilt of his head. He touched her hands with his. "Would you introduce me?"

"Yes, of course. They say he speaks French as well. That would be quite a boon if you cross the mountains."

The short planter's face lit up with a lusty smile as they approached. "And what honor you bring us!"

"Gentlemen, allow me to introduce Captain Tillson, recently arrived from," she turned toward the tall figure, "from ..."

"Boston, actually," he replied. "My pleasure, gentlemen." Tillson offered his hand to each.

"Welcome to Virginia, Sir. I'm Carter B. Wright, tobacco planter," the older man introduced himself. "As you may know, we colonists don't often feel comfortable around his majesty's officers. You must excuse us, sir. But you do seem an exception. The crown won't let our militia mingle with your soldiers. At least not on equal grounds. No offense."

"I've been advised the same," Tillson said with genuine embarrassment. "Our troops are battled-hardened and quite disciplined. Please understand my own unease."

"You won't find better men than our '*milishy*,' as you call them," Langdon interjected. "Indian fighting isn't done in the open, with drums and fifes. Allow me to introduce myself. I'm Langdon Burke."

"You must be the frontiersman I've heard of. Is that true?"

"I suppose so," Langdon replied. "But the best of them is Mr. Gist."

"That's what Lady Ashby has confirmed."

"Well, I must let you three talk," she smiled. "I'd best see to others."

"Thank you," nodded Tillson. As Anna turned away, Tillson's eyes were not alone in watching her make her way through the crowd. After a moment, he said, "My full name is William Graham Tillson, and I'd be much in your debt if you could guide me across the mountains to your Shenandoah Valley. I can pay your wages and will provide all needed supplies. His majesty's minister of foreign affairs is eager for more forts to be built across the mountains. I should like to see the land for myself and draw my own conclusions. Just the two of us would go."

"Very well! Let me know when you're ready. I can secure what's needed, if the Governor consents."

"I will see that the Commissioner of Commissary is duly informed. When might we undertake such a journey?"

"It should be soon. The weather will be turning colder in another month. I could be available in two-to-three weeks. I'm hoping for news from the Governor's office concerning land interests of my own. My grandfather received a promissory grant in 1710, but our family – my sister, half-brother, and I – have yet to be awarded any parcels. We've asked for acreage along the Holston, south of the Big Lick, but west of the Yadkin. The land's gentle and fertile, they say, but at present inhabited by Cherokee and occasional parties of Delaware."

"Perhaps a fort should be considered there, as well as north of this Big Lick, you mention."

"I wouldn't know," replied Langdon. "Forts seem to complicate matters and only stir up the French and their allies."

"I've been informed as much. His majesty's officials have been told that the French have been cruising the Ohio, planting lead stakes at the mouths of rivers to the north. My assignment is to investigate and reinforce the Governor's commitment to halt this action."

Langdon hesitated to reply. He feared the man's resolve would postpone his own plans for the fall and plunge him once more into the wilderness north of the river. He had so wanted to return west of the Alleghenies to hunt buffalo and come back with bearskins. Yet, a delicious thought played in the back of his mind: *Louise-Marie de Touloine!* Her phantom image inflamed his fantasies. He could not let go of her. "Yes!" he uttered, as he thought of her.

Tillson repressed a smile, pleased with the young guide's enthusiastic muttering. Whatever his motives, Tillson concluded his own were noble. "Let's say a fortnight from now? In the parade field in front of the Governor's mansion? The 17th? Will that do?"

"The 17th, yes. Please provide your own mount and personals, but keep the latter to a minimum. Contact the commissary, and I'll see that all else is assembled and ready to go."

The Dog Days of summer waned. The fortnight passed all too quickly. Seasonal showers settled the dust along plantation roads and scented the forests with the musky odor of decaying leaves.

What a prelude for so perilous a journey into the colony's dark interior on the backs of two men alone, Tillson thought. Still, he knew the risks. Whatever hesitation he harbored, however, was surely trumped by the

Governor, whom he knew was driven by nothing more than avarice and self-glory. Tillson could imagine him, pacing the rooms of his mansion, sipping on his brandy, eager for his and Langdon Burke's adventure to begin.

Cold dew covered the grass in front of the capital's arsenal, as Langdon awaited Tillson's arrival. Langdon could see the Captain making his way slowly from the Governor's mansion. He was mounted on a large gray and pepper-spotted mare. Tillson's brass buttons caught a ray of the morning sun and illumined his white canvass britches. A white fluffy jabot, gathered about his throat and down the front of his shirt, flopped against the chest of his red coat. He would learn quickly enough, Langdon hoped. Tillson's highly polished saddle and black boots gleamed in the morning light. Langdon felt chagrined, however, at the packhorse behind the rider. It was laden with boxes of tea, boots, extra clothing, a small folded writing desk, assorted pistols and two muskets. Langdon's own pack animals — two in all — carried similar goods, except for the table. In addition, Langdon had secured a long rifle for the Captain, horns of powder, an axe, a small barrel of bacon, one of rum, two sacks each of corn, beans and flour, two rolled blankets with a square of tarp, tobacco twists and gifts for the natives they would encounter. That meant five horses in all, twenty hoof prints, enormous packs and a laborious drag on time.

"I am an officer and will be in command," the Captain said curtly, preempting any rebuff. "However, I shall accept your advisement," he smiled. "Is that clear?'

"I won't have to be told twice," Langdon responded.

"We'll make a striking force. In truth, *I'm* at *your* command."

Langdon nodded with appreciation, as both men smiled.

For the first three days, the two riders and their horses plodded slowly up the peninsula, until they crossed the James several miles above a series of falls. Two days later they re-crossed the river at a ford, where light rapids and mud-dried outcroppings afforded sound footing. The river ran low, but hidden pools twice claimed boxes of the Captain's goods.

In the evenings, they lay about a fire, listened to the eerie howling of wolves, and ate fresh turkey that Langdon shot and roasted over coals.

Tillson was particularly eager to probe Langdon for what he knew about the Ohio Company, his trip with Gist and his impressions of the French.

"I admired most a Lieutenant François de Robert," recalled Langdon. "His superior is a Frenchman named Joncaire. He and his Ottawa savages are rather daunting, especially a Seneca he dubbed 'Coup de Sang,' or 'Bloody Coup.'"

"Yes, the one you rescued! Why didn't you let native justice run its course?"

"I can't say. I was shocked at the time. I knew he was after me, yet, there he was, a victim of his own game. I'm not sure what I was thinking. But it was just as well. Joncaire would have killed me had I not intervened. Plus, I kept thinking of de Robert and his woman's cousin. It was strange. I can't explain it."

"That lovely creature you've mentioned. On assignment in Boston, I had a few of my own. But, all the same, do you think the natives Gist appeased will ally with the King? How swayed are they by the French? You colonists are committed to expansion. Since the treaty of Aix-la-Chapelle, nothing's changed. The French got their port back, and we ours.[1] But the French have wasted no time. What do you think?"

"I can't say! I marvel at their pluck, especially Céloron's!"

"Yes. They claim he's planted a number of plates. Imagine, claiming all the lands north of the Ohio as French possessions, guaranteed by treaties and rights of discovery?"

"All I know is that the land is magnificent beyond the Alleghenies. Only a few axes have been laid against its trees. Not an inch of sod turned by the plow. It's a land of rivers, of tall grasses and cane fields, and dark and foreboding forests. Buffalo, bear and deer roam everywhere. But that's south of the river. The woods north of the Ohio abound in oaks and hickories. Cornfields and open meadows border the rivers. But it's peopled by numerous tribes with different languages – all resentful of the French and us. Their chiefs aren't fooled. They

---

[1] The War of Austrian Succession, or King George's War, ended in 1748. The peace treaty signed at Aix-la-Chapelle returned Louisbourg (New France) to the French crown and Madras, India to the British. The War produced no lasting peace among its heads-of-state.

know what we're up to. The sorrow is they're dependent on us for arms and supplies. I came back sad."

"I find that quite empathic for a frontiersman. Curious, really. Anna said that you speak French. May I ask about your lineage or education, if that's not an imposition?"

"No, that's quite all right! I was born in 1723, three years after my sister, Sarah. Our mother was Jane Lawton, a descendant of the Nesbitt family from London. She and my father were married before leaving England. Along with my grandfather, Robert Burke, they landed in Portsmouth and worked as surveyors and hunters in Isle of Wight County. I grew up along its Blackwater River, near the Dismal Swamp. My grandfather and I fished and hunted together until yellow fever killed him in 1730. After that, my father, Caleb, acquired some abandoned property where we live now. We were still waiting on the title to the grant Queen Anne promised. Since her death, though, many of her grants have fallen through, or so we've been told. Nonetheless, we still have hope."

"What happened to your father, if I may ask?"

"He died as a result of a hunting accident near our farm – his musket exploded in his face. That was in 1745. I was with him and remember the gruesome wound. I fashioned a travois to drag him out of the woods. Sarah saw me coming across the cornfield and ran to help us. My father was still alive but unconscious. He had lost much blood. When Sarah saw his mutilated face, she grabbed hold of his hand and held it all the way to the house. By the time we got there he was dead. When my mother saw my father, she became hysterical and collapsed in the front yard. Sarah was magnificent. She pushed aside her own grief to steady my mother. It was Sarah who washed our father's body and dressed it for burial. I know no woman stronger than she.

"I would be honored to meet her."

"She is magnificent, but be warned she also can be stubborn," Langdon replied.

They both laughed.

"Where did you learn French. Anna said you speak the language quite well."

"From a defrocked Protestant minister and his concubine mulatto wife. Three months out of the year, I attended the minister's school. The couple spoke French with one another and I tried to eavesdrop as much as possible. Soon enough, the language became natural to my lips and ears. When we moved to the Blue Ridge, I continued studies on my own with English readers, a book on Roman civics, a collection of botanical sketches, military manuals and Bossuet's 'Discourse on the Universal History,' in French. Thanks to my father, I learned surveying from the time I was old enough to drag a chain."

Tillson stared at Langdon and shook his head from side to side. "And we've been taught to regard you colonists as backwoods heathens! If only they knew the truth back home! My apologies, sir."

"None needed," Langdon laughed.

"Nonetheless, thank you. I must say I am fascinated. Sometime, I must tell you about myself."

Before unrolling his bedding each night, Sir William set up his writing table to record their conversations. The first five nights, he changed into a long white flannel nightshirt; after that, following Langdon's example, he slept in his clothes.

Some eight days later, cloaked with dust, they finally completed their journey through the dry September woods. Before them rose the foot-hills of the Blue Ridge Mountains. On the evening of the 30th, Langdon departed from the narrow road, marked by an axeman's blade, and led Tillson to a log cabin on the edge of a cornfield that looked west toward forested ridges, rumpled and hazy in the distance. The first hints of autumn drifted in the air. The dogwoods shimmered purple. Most of the poplars had lost their yellowish-brown leaves.

"That's my home," said Langdon.

Tillson stared at the simple cabin, its windows covered with stretched deerskin, and chimney made of cross-logs, chinked with red clay. Of all the things he and Langdon had shared, he had forgotten to ask about his family's grant. "Have you received any hopeful word about your land?" Tillson asked as he dismounted, and walked directly to the pack mule.

"Five grants have been recommended to the King, one for eight thousand acres to a Dr. Kingsmore, the others for three-to-four thousand each along the Great Wagon Road near the North Carolina border. My family's one among those. Once we return, I hope to survey the land and select a home site, provided we receive the grant."

Sir Tillson pulled a cloth from the pack and vigorously dusted his saddle, then his boots and buckle. He removed his dusty coat and replaced it with another, just as the cabin door opened. From inside emerged an attractive woman. She was young with flaming red hair and a white apron tied about her waist. A white silk string held the woman's bright hair in place, and her shoes, though worn, possessed a hint of one-time elegance. She exuded energy. Next to her was a tall young man. His demeanor stood in contrast to the woman – he was wane, his complexion waxy, and when he walked, he limped. But Tillson's eyes were on the woman. This had to be Sarah. He could not help but smile. Her earthy poise penetrated the facade of his peerage. His face betrayed a surprise he could not conceal. "My Lady," he addressed her with deep courtesy, "you must be Mr. Burke's sister. And you, young man, his brother. It's an honor to meet you both."

"The honor is ours," the woman smiled, as Sir William reached for her hand and lightly kissed it. Tiny freckles twinkled about her eyes. Her nose was slender, her lips a full pale rouge.

"We've been expecting you," she said.

The boy nodded in agreement.

"Please let me introduce my sister," said Langdon. "Sarah Nesbitt Burke. Sarah, Sir William Tillson, Captain of his Majesty's privy services. And this is my stepbrother, Jonathan Weir, whose father was killed near here."

"Yes, I feel like I know you both," Sir William smiled. "On our journey, Langdon regaled me with stories of your family." He extended his hand to Jonathan. "Langdon told me about your parent's death. I thought Virginia was a civilized land."

"Only the Tidewater," Sarah exclaimed. "Jonathan will guide you to the stalls and help you unload. Gentlemen, when ready, do come in. A dinner of venison, sweet potatoes and cornbread awaits, with some grapes and cider."

She turned toward her brother with an exaggerated grimace. "And wash! Leave your clothes at the washstand and Jonathan will collect them." She rolled her eyes at Tillson. "And, yes, we *are* civilized, here!"

"Yes, ma'am!" he instinctively replied.

Suddenly, both laughed.

Tillson followed Jonathan and Langdon toward the stalls. Though dark and narrow, the outbuilding impressed him. Its bark roof and palisade of logs – sunk evenly in the ground – rose to create a draft-free barn, complete with a loft. All the animals appeared to fit in it. He noted a cow as well. Though exhausted and grimy, he had not felt so unencumbered and relaxed since departing Williamsburg. Whatever might lie ahead, he hoped they would rest here a few days.

Chapter Five

FRANÇOIS-PHILIPPE RAISED the south window of the castle's palace and gazed out across the clay chimney pots of Ft. Niagara. Since the spring, he, Hélène and Louise had been residing in a gray stucco house, attached to the fort's quarters. As cramped as the cottage's rooms where, it provided a restful view across the tiny bay. Their stay in Ft. Frontenac had been endurable enough, but the jagged point's exposure to the ice and winter winds had underscored their sense of isolation. Nonetheless, he had enjoyed the rough and tumble demeanor of the various bush runners and trappers who passed by way of the fort's location on their long journey upstream to Lake Ontario and Canada's interior. Still, François felt pleased that his duties centered only about the river and reaffirming alliances with its tribes. Pioneers from Pennsylvania were continuing to immigrate across the mountains. Now Mingo, Delaware, Shawnee and lesser confederations were begging the French to supply them with powder and arms, if not, interfere directly. Negotiating with them was no simple matter.

For all that, a part of him missed Ft. Frontenac, with its bold stone walls, deep snows, drunken Indians, stocks of furs, and sequestered existence. Indeed, there was something appealing about the fort's primitive location.

Philippe closed the window. The *intendent* of the Fort had issued clear orders.

Proceed to Lake Erie and then south, bypassing the Iroquois nations. Plant new marker claims along the Allegheny's banks, wherever you deem appropriate. Informants report that English traders have removed half of Céloron's plates. Visit every encampment and village of Indians possible. Reassure them of their Father's love, etc. Take gifts of tobacco, knives, and rum with you, along with wampum belts. Ten soldiers will accompany you, in addition to Algonquin and Huron guides. Travel with one or two squaws and your own Mademoiselles Hélène and Touloine. Women signal a peaceful mission. Carry extra fleur de lis, along with medals for chiefs. Be on the alert for M. Gist. Stir up trouble, if you find him. Warn all English settlers and traders to leave immediately. Place slashes on trees indicating where such transgressors have built cabins. Joncaire's orders are to find them and burn their houses. I have already dispatched him to the area. Your actions are to initiate peace.

> *By order of his Excellency, le Roi, Louis Quinze,*
> *avec son intendent de Frontenac,*
> *le Sieur Claude Deauville de Pondonvjeue,*
> *cet troisieme jour d' Octobre, 1752.*

On the 25th of October, François and his party reached its first village near the Mahoning River. François instructed Yellow Hawk, his guide, to place a lead plate into the bank of the northern side of the river. From this vantage point, Yellow Hawk could see the large Delaware cluster of wigwams ahead and alerted François, who signaled for the trailing canoes to come ashore behind him.

A brave with scars on his arms and face met them at the river's bank and escorted the party of François, Yellow Hawk, Hélène and Louise toward the largest council house. Two liegemen followed, carrying a *fleur de lis* and a small chest of gifts. A third soldier rapped a flurry of drumbeats behind them. A handsome chief, clad in a British soldier's red coat and leather leggings, stepped out of the lodge and opened his arms in a gesture of friendship.

"*Mes chèrs pères, bienvenue à notre petite assemblage. C'est toute nous avons. Entrez, s'il vous plaît et buvez et mangez avec nous.*"

"*Mais, alors!*" replied François. "I am surprised to see you wearing a red jacket. Your Father has a blue one for you," he nodded toward one of the soldiers, who immediately produced an officer's coat for the chief.

"*Merçi, mon père!*" said the chief. "I am Tall Moon, once great warrior of our proud nation. But, yes, this English coat is wearing thin," he pulled on its frayed cuffs. "I took it with my hatchet!" he grinned. "Please enter and let us parley. We are in need of many things. Our wives will care for your women."

François, nodding toward Hélène and Louise to follow the women, entered the lodge with Yellow Hawk. Two warriors carried in the chest and set it before the chief and several elders. When all the parties were assembled, François motioned for Yellow Hawk to address the Delaware in their own tongue. Yellow Hawk affirmed the French Father's love of the Delaware. After a prolonged silence, the chief turned to François. "Your brave's words are lofty. We wish to hear what lies in your own heart."

François rose and glanced about the lodge. All the figures seemed past their prime. Perhaps, their younger chiefs and warriors were hunting. Or were these solemn men, wrapped in their moldering red blankets all that remained of their harassed band?

François cleared his throat, while working to clear his mind. "My brothers of the great River, our King in France and your Fathers on the Lakes know of the English devil. Already, his traders are in your land. Be warned! They want more than your furs. They want your homes, your waterways, your corn, your game, and fields for their own. They bring you great quantities of goods from their own Father, but it is all a ruse, a trick to steal your land. Your true Father wants only to please his children, to care for you with goods you need in exchange for your furs. We sail your rivers, but only to protect you and our own lodges on the Lakes." He paused and reached into the chest. With great ceremony, he held a heavy belt of white tremulous shells before the chief. "We offer you this great wampum string as a sign of our lasting goodwill. Will you accept it and bid our English enemies to go home? That is all we ask." François placed the belt in the chief's hands. Then he seated himself beside Yellow Hawk.

The chief adjusted his bearskin cape and rose to his feet. "You speak wisely, Frenchman. Our enemies, the Iroquois, are your enemies, too. Now the English have banded with them. The Great Nations of the north sold our lands to the English. They considered us nought. I will fight with you. Many of our braves have lost home and family. As far as the sun climbs before noon across the river, they stole our land. Revenge is in our hearts. Our young men want blood. I counsel peace, but I have pledged to run no more. We accept your belt and present one in return."

An elder handed the chief a narrow belt of white beads. It appeared old. Many of its leather lacings were worn or missing.

Philippe accepted it with a formal half-bow. "We shall be friends with Tall Moon from the sun's rising to its setting far beyond the forest's edge." He turned toward Yellow Hawk with a nod.

The Algonquin opened the chest for the elders to see inside. Then he slid it forward toward the chief. The chief glanced down, bent over, and picked up a pouch of lead and one of powder. He also helped himself to a small mirror and a tin of paint. He handed twists of tobacco to the old men behind him. "Drink? Where is your dream water that makes one crazy and full of sleep?" he stared suddenly at François. A half-jesting, half-surly tone commanded his voice. "We have come to accept your ways."

"Let us rejoin our women, and we shall drink with you, and dance about your fire," François responded.

"It's a good idea. We were hoping you would. Come, let us do so," the old chief smiled.

Many young women gathered about the fire to dance. When one approached François to enter the circle, Hélène hopped to her feet. *"Non, non!"* she blurted. *"Voilà!"* she pointed to a soldier seated beside her. "Take him," her dark eyes insisted.

Yellow Hawk smiled when a second woman reached out for him. He rose with reluctance to join her, though the look in his eyes was one of pain. When after the dance, he slipped off with her into the woods, it seemed to François that his face filled with sadness. Later, when the Algonquin returned, François asked cautiously: "Is Yellow Hawk's heart not here tonight?"

Yellow Hawk sat down and ran his hands across his face. "Frenchman mean well. Have Hélène and young French woman. Yellow Hawk has chosen to walk alone."

"May I ask, Why? *Pourquoi?*"

"Frenchman asks too many questions. This I tell you only once. Her name was Leaping Fawn. Long black hair. Dark eyes. Slender face and high cheekbones. She came here, to my chest," he struck it with his fist. "A Mohawk killed her the night of Eau Froid raid. I found her in frozen snow next morning. Our mothers had planned for our marriage. I had gathered many pelts. We were young." He held his head erect. "I wish to say no more. *Rien! Vous savez, je crois?*"

François studied Yellow Hawk's eyes, hands and face. He knew so little about this man. He realized how much there must be to learn about him, savage or not.

Two days later, as Philippe's party continued down river, an advance scout waved from his canoe on the river's left bank. François ordered the flotilla to swing east. The scout's canoe approached and swung around beside. "English ahead. Two rafts with many goods. Five men. *Voilà!*" he pointed. "You will see *bientôt. Oui!*"

Moments later, they spied the two large rafts, laden with supplies, bound north. Two men guided the first, three the second. Upon realizing they had been discovered, the five directed their crafts toward a sandy bank and pulled ashore. François' party swung to and beached their canoes just out of gun range. Yellow Hawk, François, and the canoes of his soldiers disembarked. Yellow Hawk waved his arm and set out into the woods. Four Indians followed him silently into the thickets.

"We ain't here to cause trouble!" shouted one of the raftsmen in English. "Ain't no cause to stop us. This here's a free river. We've got licenses from his excellency, the Governor of Pennsylvania, hisself."

François and his group drew closer. His liegemen raised their arms to fire, if necessary. The men ahead stood still and glanced uneasily to their right. On the bank above them, stood Yellow Hawk and his warriors.

"Ain't no way to treat us!" continued the lead trader.

"Louise!" called François. "Disembark and tell him why we're here. Your English is better than mine."

Louise climbed out of her canoe and came to François' side.

"Don't waste words on them," he whispered. "Tell them to turn about and we'll let them go. We'll keep one of their rafts and all their goods. I suspect they are bound for the Iroquois, or settlements deep in the woods."

Louise approached the surrounded men. She could see the fear on the faces of the grisly bearded men. "You must turn back. This is French territory. You may keep one raft, but that is all. No supplies. The Lieutenant, Monsieur Gabelle de Robert, will keep his word and grant you a safe passage. Do not come back. Warn others there are those behind us with orders to kill and burn your English settlers' houses. Please, go! Otherwise there will be bloodshed." She glanced down at her hands. They were trembling. Her face felt hot; perspiration trickled inside her blouse and down her rib cage. She glanced about toward François and her cousin Hélène. She stepped back, behind the encirclement of soldiers on the bank.

"Hog spit!" replied the leader. "We ain't goin' nowhere! Sit down here and parley like real people. We got supplies we can trade. And whiskey!" he shouted in a loud voice for the natives to hear.

"*Ce n'est pas possible!*" retorted François. "Leave! Go while you can!"

The bearded man turned toward his companions. Their rifles were in hand. Slowly, they edged toward their rafts. "You ain't gonna do nothing!" he said. "We got rights to be here!"

Philippe hesitated to command his soldiers to fire. His mission was one of peace. But he couldn't let *ces anglais* bully their way past him. "In the canoe," he ordered Louise. "*Vite!*"

Just then, Joncaire and his braves emerged from the woods. In seconds, his warriors fell upon the traders with hatchets and war clubs. The attack lasted only minutes. Three traders lay dead. Two moaned with limb and head wounds.

Handsome Dog dragged one from the water. He wanted sport. A gauntlet for the captives!

"Can't we let them go?" François turned toward Joncaire. "I had no idea you were so close."

"My orders differ from yours! Remember? We have been following these *anglais* for close to a week. Wherever they stopped, we took notice. We have already burned two houses and driven out three families. Our Wyandots spared no one. Leave now! It is better for you to go! Take the women and go! We will follow you in a few days. Go! This is not for Hélène or Louise to see."

By now, Yellow Hawk and his braves had boarded the rafts. They were helping themselves to whatever they deemed of value. Once they found the rum or brandy, it would be too late. François turned to his soldiers. "Fire in the air. We have our orders. We need to press on."

The five soldiers aimed their weapons toward the sky and fired. The Indians whooped and fired their own guns in reply. This was their time of glee. They ignored François and continued to search the vessels until they had accumulated what plunder they sought. One had hacked open a keg of rum. In his excitement he had struck it too hard. It slid off the raft and began to float downstream. Two Algonquins dove into the river, but the swift current bore the keg beyond their reach. Soon it sank. Eight of François' liegemen had secured the rafts. They pointed their muskets at the natives. Yellow Hawk raised his right arm aloft. It was his signal for his scouts to desist. Without a word, they leapt from the rafts and returned to their canoes. The two would-be keg rescuers swam ashore, cold and wet. They had their plunder and were satisfied. "It is time to leave!" François ordered. "Back to the canoes." His voice was heavy and shaken. Finally, in a flurry of paddles and high-pitched shrieks, his party pushed off and sped down river.

François looked back over his left shoulder. Already Joncaire's braves had formed a line. The two wounded traders were forced to stand. It was the unspoken law of the wilderness. How long they would torment them, he could only guess. Louise sat hunched forward in the canoe behind his, her hands to her face to veil her horror and tears. He glanced down at Hélène, seated in the rear of his own bark. She held her head erect, her eyes focused on his. Throughout the skirmish, she had not once wavered. He looked at her lips and smiled. She smiled in return. He released a pent up breath and allowed her strength to renew his own. Suddenly, the toll and glory of France struck him with its concomitant savagery! The contradiction lingered long in his mind, as the flotilla raced downstream toward its next rendezvous with fortune or fate. His heart thumped in his chest, exhilarated and terrified.

Chapter Six

WARM SUNLIGHT ILLUMINATED the ravine as Langdon and Tillson guided their horses down slope toward the tumbling waters below. In the distance, the Ohio rolled slowly past, its deep current brown and frothy, too dangerous to cross. They halted their horses by the water's edge and gazed out across the river in the red glow of the late October sun.

"We would need boats to cross this," Tillson said. "How far are we from the nearest Indian village? Perhaps we could trade our horses for canoes and buy them back later."

"Half-king's encampment is still another four-day's journey," Langdon said, pointing to the east. "Torn Ear would sell us canoes as well as give our horses back, if we threw in a gun and powder."

"We've yet to see the first Frenchman, or their allies! This is the Ohio?" he said with uncertainty.

"Yes. Somewhere over there is the Little Miami. And farther upriver, the Scioto and Muskingum. Give them time," said Langdon. "It's fall. Most of the tribes are hunting. It's a wonder we haven't heard their guns. The Shawnee can be very fickle. Some have never seen white men. Not even French! They've bartered with their half-breeds and Hurons for years. Remember, they're savages. Many tribes still fight among themselves. They crave scalps and women. And we are on their land."

Tillson expelled an impatient moan, perhaps more out of disappointment with himself than with his guide. "We should have come straight for the river, rather than through that backcountry. Still, it was worth seeing. Once we reach this Half-King, perhaps we should turn back. I want to see the Monongahela and where it forms the river. If any fortifications are to be built, perhaps I'll know then." He glanced past Langdon, then back across the forest and the miles of endless grasses they had traversed. He looked up and then down the river. Even from a distance, he could see the autumnal hues of browns and gold that tinted the trees along the river's banks. "I had no idea it was so vast! This Ohio country, is this where it begins?"

"Yes," Langdon nodded, "and all the way to the lakes. It's watered by myriad rivers and gurgling springs, covered with oaks and maples, sugar trees and willows, as far as the eye can see."

"No wonder the French desire it."

While preparing to make camp, Tillson spied canoes in the distance. Nine to ten! "Look, Mr. Burke!"

"They're French!" said Langdon. "They travel like that, in groups of liegemen and Indians. They're headed our way."

"Good! They need to know the British are here!"

"All the same, we're the transgressors in their view."

"There are women! Two squaws and two whites. Or half-whites."

Langdon strained to make out the figures in the dusk. Why were they traveling so late? Why this side of the current? Who were the women? Chippewa squaws? His heart skipped in hope! *Mon Dieu*! It was Louise, her cousin and François! Plus six or seven barks of Indians and soldiers. Their birch canoes caught the last colors of the sun – red and yellow, pink and purple, above the muddy ribbon of the river. As the soldiers and Indians drew closer, Langdon, without hesitating, stepped in front of Tillson. "I know these people!" he waved. "It's the girl I've told you about!"

"What, in God's name?" he exclaimed.

"We'll soon find out," Langdon said. "Here! Help me catch their barks as they glide in."

"*Alors*!" greeted François. "You are a long way from home! We almost shot the *rouge coq*!" he feigned in French. "Does your peacock speak *français*?"

"Not that I know of."

"Louise and I shall have to trim his comb!" he smiled.

"I guess so," Langdon replied. He liked the cockiness about the officer, doubtless acquired from his mentor Joncaire. Still, the Lieutenant appeared apprehensive, if not disoriented. "What brings you here? And so late in the day?" asked Langdon.

"Help us disembark. A party of Iroquois is somewhere behind us. They attempted an ambush two nights ago, but failed. Most are in canoes. A few are on foot. They are in league with the Devil and your English rivermen! It isn't good!"

"What is he saying?" asked Sir William.

"They've been harassed by a party of Iroquois. Some may be in the woods above us now. He doesn't know."

"We will bivouac with you tonight. And hopefully parley." François turned toward the Captain. "Does he know the danger?"

"Yes! He's been ordered to reconnoiter the river and trade with the Indians."

"*Mon vieux.* We must be honest." François replied, with raised eyebrows. "*Je suis confident qu'il est plus.* It's more than that, isn't it?"

Yes! Langdon thought, much more, but better for François to discover it on his own.

Langdon watched Tillson assist Louise and Hélène ashore. Embarrassed, he hastened to their side and offered Louise both hands. Her hair was disheveled, her clothing ruffled and soiled, and odorous with perspiration and fear. To his surprise, she embraced him.

"I have often thought of you," she smiled. "That's shameful, isn't it?"

"Not at all! I have thought of you, too!"

"You sound like our Montreal Frenchmen: half-*sauvage, mais tout français!* So elegant in the midst of this uncivilized land!"

"Come!" said Hélène, embracing Langdon in French style, with her cheek first to one side of his face and then to the other. "It has been an ordeal."

"Steady! *Attention!*" ordered François, as the entourage disembarked and dragged their craft ashore. "We are with friends, even if enemies," he smiled. "Yellow Hawk, see that no one is harmed. Post a scout in the brush. The liegemen will guard the camp. Tonight, we will eat and sleep *ici.*"

Yellow Hawk eyed Tillson with suspicion. "Perhaps, I take his coat. Then I shall be like Tall Moon."

"No!" barked François. "There are many more of those, and many opportunities to come. Bide your time."

"You are too meek, Frenchman. *Trop doux*! I have sworn to guard you. We will see." He turned toward his Algonquins, singled out two, and sent them into the brush above the bank.

After lighting several small fires and eating a meal of dried venison, salt pork, and corn, François passed a small keg of brandy among his liegemen. He allotted his guides a smaller quantity in a pewter flask. Then François rose. It was time to address Tillson, which he did in civil but subdued voice. "Let us plant both our flags tonight side-by-side. The Iroquois will not know what to do. Your English masters have cowed them with guns and supplies. The English colors will numb them. But our French scalps, I fear, will reap rewards in Albany. Isn't that so? *Oui!*"

Langdon translated for Tillson. "We haven't much of a choice," he whispered. "When he finishes, you'll need to speak. The Indians will be listening with keen ears. They respect authority and despise weakness."

Tillson nodded with understanding.

François-Philippe continued. "We French have long been here!" he gestured toward the river. "We know our English messieurs regard our rights. These hunting grounds to the south, we have not claimed. They are not ours. They belong to our children, the Indians," he gestured toward Yellow Hawk's small band. "We may be attacked tonight. We must act as brothers. We are our own nation tonight."

As François sat down, Langdon could see the pleased countenances all around. He translated François' words.

Slowly Tillson rose. He pulled down slightly on the hem of his jacket and braided sleeves. With erect posture and a firm chin, he began: "My dear Monsieur and each of you. We have been at war, and now that war is over. We come to the Ohio to admire its potential. Yes. But we also come to trade and to build friendships. We seek alliances with all. We have no quarrel with your King in France," he said, directing his words toward François, "nor do we bear animosity toward our Huron or Ojibwa and Algonquin neighbors to the north. We pray the horror of King Philip's War lies in the past and regret that your war with the Iroquois lingers. Our New England colonies live in fear of the Abenaki. Great wrongs have been done on both sides. We must bury our hatchets for the night and lay aside our guns. Tonight, we are brothers; we are one. Let us hope for accord, but remain vigilant and brave. I speak as a soldier, as an English warrior."

"*Ah, bon!*" declared François. "The Captain has spoken well."

With that, the assemblage retired for the night. The Lieutenant lay down beside Hélène, and wrapped her close in a blanket. The Indians and squaws sought a place near the fire. The liegemen huddled as close as they could to the fire's warmth, while each guarded his area of the perimeter. Langdon lay with his back toward Tillson. Louise lay within view, just beyond his reach.

As the fire burned low and sputtered out, the air became damp and brutally cold. A milky moon rose above the river's bank. All was still save the river. Langdon could not sleep. First minutes, then hours passed. Eventually, he nodded off, only to sleep fitfully. He awoke at the sound of an Indian snoring. Fog had formed. Its spectral blanket lay gray and thick upon the river. Langdon could hear the water lapping against the canoes. All else was silent. Still. Too silent! Too still! He felt a hand on his shoulder. It was Yellow Hawk's. The Indian was staring into his face. His right hand was raised in the form of a hush! He pointed to the river. "They are coming!" he whispered. "No time to leave. The Spirit of the river has covered us with his blanket. It is a good omen. Awaken the others. Tell them to keep silent."

One by one, Langdon and Yellow Hawk nudged the sleeping party awake. The liegemen had already positioned themselves. François, his soldiers, and natives clenched their guns against their chests and pointed them toward the river. Hélène and Louise sat together against a fallen tree trunk, hunkered under a blanket and François' coat. Tillson crouched beside Langdon, his pistol in hand. His red jacket lay open. Several buttons were missing.

The fog grew light, then heavy again. The faint swish of a canoe and the sound of paddles cutting the water rose above the ebb of the river. The bark passed. Others sloshed behind it.

One, two, three! Then a fourth, fifth, sixth and seventh. And then another canoe. Langdon estimated their distance as less than thirty yards from the shore. Yellow Hawk crouched nearby. Langdon could barely distinguish his form in the fog. Voices could be heard high on the bank. The voices grew louder. A branch snapped. A grunt broke the silence. Then all was calm again. The voices resumed, but farther away. Then, silence.

"We must leave!" Yellow Hawk whispered to François. "We must cross the river. The fog will protect us. What you call the Little Miami is near. We can hide there." He turned to Langdon. "English! Take your British and go! One day I take his coat. Tell him. And his scalp!"

"Nonsense!" François brushed him off. "Mount your horses and ride!" he warned Langdon. "Do not look back!"

Someone pressed against Langdon's side. It was Louise.

"Take me with you!" she pled. "I don't want to go back to the river." There were tears in her large oval-shaped eyes. Her hair lay matted against her face. With trembling hands, she clutched his deerskin jacket and homespun shirt. Her nose had turned red from the cold.

"What are you saying?" demanded Hélène. "Do you realize what you're saying?"

"Yes," she replied, in a whisper. "I want to go. Will you take me?" she asked Langdon a second time.

"Yes!" he replied.

"Hurry, then!" urged François. "Get your things and go. We must leave, too!"

He pressed her against his shoulder and kissed her neck. "We will look for you in the meadows at Turtle Creek." He turned toward Langdon. "Bring her when the dogwoods are white and their centers yellow. We will look for you. Do I have your word?"

"Yes! I'll bring her."

Tears swelled in Louise's eyes. Hélène leaned forward and gave her a hug.

"*Alors*! Godspeed! *Que nous allions*!" said François.

Tillson reholstered his pistol in his belt. "I have my things. Quickly, to the horses! I'll gather up what I can." Suddenly he turned and stared at François. An awkward silence filled his face.

François stopped and extended him his hand. "Adieu, Monsieur. I wish you well!"

"Come, Louise, help me find the horses," said Langdon, "before the fog lifts."

"Good-bye!" François waved, as the last canoe slipped into the water and vanished into the fog.

Chapter Seven

ANGDON DISMOUNTED PELLAS and glanced back over his shoulder. He had circled the meadow twice. From every side, the roar of the rivers created a mournful cacophony. Budding alders, yellow birch, and slender willows caught the soft light of the morning sun and filled the plain with sparkling shadows and beads of dew. It was the 11th of May 1753. All around, the dogwoods had unfolded in full bloom, their petals white and centers yellow, crested with beads of red, but François was nowhere in sight. Of course, anything might have happened. Turtle Creek ran especially high. Its cold waters cascaded blue and white before converging with the Monongahela. He had selected a site for his camp, protected from the raw winds of the west, hidden from view, yet with a vista west toward the nearby Ohio. Numerous circles of blackened rock bore witness to the countless travelers who had passed this way. He searched for the site that Gist's own party had made two years ago. He could not locate it, however.

He longed for Louise! She was five months pregnant, weakened from their trek across the mountains.

"Oh my goodness! What have we here?" Sarah had exclaimed, upon seeing her on horseback.

Louise had smiled, before sliding off and all but falling into Sarah's arms. "You are as lovely as your brother said. I promise I'll be helpful and not get in the way."

"You're the lovely one!" Sarah chortled. "A rider passed through less than three days ago, telling us you were coming. He thought the three of you were French," she looked up at Langdon, "until he saw Sir William's jacket. He was returning with furs, but kept out of sight." All the while, Sarah had not taken her eyes off Tillson. Nor he his off her.

The Captain dismounted and bowed politely. He held out his hands. She took them and the two smiled.

"I guess it's bath time again," he laughed.

Langdon hobbled Pellas and began to gather wood for a fire. Perhaps the smoke would attract François-Philippe, le sieur Gabelle de Robert. Of course, it might attract the Delaware, or even Shawnee. He didn't fear them, however. It was the young braves who unnerved him. You could never relax your vigilance. Bands lurked everywhere in the forests. Plus Joncaire's parties were encouraged to bring back prisoners to torture before ripping off scalps. It was a lucrative business. It kept the natives dependent on the French, a perfect outlet for their aggressive nature. Langdon hoped he would be spared their presence.

Two days later, Langdon paced the river's bank, still waiting. He had not seen an Indian, trader, or frontiersman. That evening he debated what to do. As darkness settled, he saw a light on the Monongahela. It was a lantern, swinging from a raft. The men saw his fire and poled their barge ashore.

"Ahoy, Lad! May we join you?" the wiry of two oarsmen asked. "Ran into trouble. Had to turn back."

Langdon caught their line as their empty raft scudded in.

"Lots of Injuns, drunk! Fired up and hungry for scalps. The French done got 'em wild. Buildin' forts on Beaver Creek and fu'ther north! You're lookin' mighty perk. Ya huntin', trappin' or lost?"

Langdon couldn't help but smile. "No! Just waiting on someone."

"Well, if'n you're expectin' them from the north, they ain't comin'. Nothin' but Indian canoes on the river and them riff-raff Frenchies that act like 'em. They ain't a one of them civilized."

So it was. For the next two days, no one else came up the river. The morning after the raftsmen departed, Langdon spent hunting. He bagged a bear and a deer. He skinned the bear, butchered the deer, and packed what fresh meat he could in the bearskin. After sprinkling the bear's meat with salt, he rendered out its fat and saved that, too. He waited another day. That night he listened to the lonely howling of the wolves. As soon as the sun sank behind the hills, their chorus of nocturnal wails began. It rose and echoed through the black wilderness above the rivers. He spent his last night tending large bright fires to protect himself and Pellas, relieved that Louise had not accompanied him. Finally, Langdon saddled up to head home.

Four days earlier, just south of Lake Erie, François sat in the cramped cabin belonging to Captain François Le Mercier and listened while Mercier and another captain, Paul Marin, discussed the fort Montreal had assigned them to build. Outside, a freezing rain pelted the cabin with tiny granules of gray sleet. He clutched his long coat about his neck and walked toward the fireplace to warm his hands. François' orders were to assist the two men. At the same time, it grieved him that he might fail to make the rendezvous with Langdon at the Creek. Surely Burke would understand. In New France, time and distance repeatedly fell victim to factors no one could control.

Of the two captains, François admired Marin the most. Paul Marin de la Malgue was descended from a prominent Montreal family and had earned his laurels in the Wisconsin wilderness, credited with a keen understanding of Indian culture and for conducting successful negotiations among warring tribes. The Captain had traveled throughout the Ohio country and knew its rivers well. François judged him to be in his early fifties. He wore a shabby coat and trousers and limped when he walked. Despite his relaxed posture, he could express his ideas with solemnity and graciousness. The tiny yellow and blue bead adornments on his calf-high moccasins caught the fire's glow.

Mercier, on the other hand, evinced an air of formality. Tall and lean, almost gaunt, with a long nose and extruding chin, he rose from his chair to examine Marin's drafts one more time. Long black hair fell across his visage, whose strands he swished back with a flip of his head. "This bastion here near the entrance – shouldn't it have a more protruding platform than the others?"

"Not necessarily. It affords more rifle slits for repulsing frontal attacks. I urge you to keep it."

"You're probably right!" Mercier replied. "Lieutenant Gabelle, what do you think? It's your project in the long run since your men will be building it and responsible for logs. Take a look!"

François walked to the table to study Marin's plat once again. The plan looked perfect to him. The fort was to be built on the south fork of the French Creek with water on all four sides. The design showed four houses, one at each corner, with overhanging second stories for firing on attackers below. The plan reminded him of Fort Frontenac. Twelve-foot high palisades finished with sharp points connected the houses with platforms accompanying each cannon. The plan called for eight six-pound cannon on each bastion with a four-pound cannon at the entrance gate and numerous loopholes for small-arms fire. Inside, the plan included a chapel, guardhouse, supply stores and commander's quarters. Outside, three log barracks for the soldiers, stables, a smithy's shop, and other buildings completed the design.

"Gentlemen," Mercier stated, "all this is to be constructed by mid-fall, or, at the latest, before winter. Captain, your men should start selecting logs soon. *Que pensez vous? C'est extraordinaire? Non!*"

"Yes! *Sans doute!*" François replied. "What's its name to be? How will it be called?"

Marin rose to his feet and struck the sketch with his knobby right hand. "*Le Fort de la Rivière au Boeuf,*" he stated proudly. "I've been given the honor of naming it myself. 'Fort Le Boeuf!' Named for the bison that used to water here. I like it, *non*? Don't tell me you disagree."

"*C'est bon!* It's perfect," Mercier concurred. "As soon as the rains let up, we'll begin. Once the ships deliver the cannon on the Erie, it'll take us several weeks to muscle them across. Lieutenant, that'll be your task, too. Understood?"

"*Bien sûr!* I'll see it's done!"

François stepped back to the fireplace. How he wished Hélène were by his side. And her cousin, Louise? Was she still alive? Hélène was so eager for word, though she had not voiced it. François could see it in her eyes. Reticence and solitude were endemic to Hélène's nature. Joncaire!

Where was he? Or Yellow Hawk. Could he be trusted? Was it worth the risk? Would he get there in time? Why not go? It was time to put the question to his commander.

"Captain Mercier, I request a leave for a fortnight before securing the cannon. *J'ai un ami* near Logstown I'd like to visit. I'd take Yellow Hawk with me as a precaution. I'd not ask if it weren't urgent."

Mercier turned and eyed François with puzzling curiosity. "I don't trust your Yellow Hawk. He's too eager to kill red coats. We don't need an incident like that. This whole thing is delicate, especially the matter of building forts. That needs to be kept secret. Why not take Tekacayah? He's at Ile de Presque, recovering from a wrist wound. We can have him here by tomorrow."

François thought for a moment. He didn't trust Handsome Dog anymore than he did Yellow Hawk, but braves of their cunning were hard to find. A savage was still a savage, and Coup de Sang was loyal only to Joncaire. "Yes, sir," he finally replied. "I'll prepare to leave. Incidentally, where is Joncaire?"

"No one knows. That's a secret, too. He'll be assigned to Venango once the fort is complete."

At dawn, Langdon scattered damp ashes from the campsite and glanced once more down river. He hated the thought of returning home with no message to comfort Louise. She had been so companionable, eager to please, eager to help, so valuable to Sarah. She'd worked miracles with Jonathan. She'd applied a gummy poultice of tobacco and lye to his ankle, and the remedy was slowly drawing the arrowhead up. Soon, it might yield to surgery.

"Darling, I promise we'll marry soon. There's a preacher in Culpepper who makes the circuit every summer. If our baby has arrived, we'll have him conduct a bastismal, too."

Louise brushed his hair back and pressed herself against his chest. Langdon had added a room to the cabin, though it had no fireplace of its own. A black thick goatskin hung from the doorway between theirs and the main room. "I wonder how Hélène's doing?" she whispered. "I wonder where she and François are. I don't think they'll ever marry, but they love each other to the bone. You know, she's part Algonquin, part Ojibwa, and two parts French. Her father, my uncle, was posted at Frontenac and took an Indian wife; or at least she was his squaw until he was killed. But I want ours to be legal and acknowledged by the church," she said.

Langdon steadied Pellas and swung up into the saddle. He turned the animal around to lope across the meadow before descending the bank of the Monongahela. He caught sight of a canoe, laboring its way upstream. In the stern rowed an Indian, struggling to guide the canoe ashore. In the bow, a white man raised his paddle in signal fashion. It was François-Philippe!

Langdon dismounted and tied Pellas's bridle to a young willow. He waved in return and prepared to drag their canoe across the grainy scree. Both men's faces broke with smiles. Handsome Dog looked up, emotionless. He had decorated his cheeks with red marks, just below the tattoos under his eyes. The big Indian held the canoe steady for François to disembark.

"*Bonjour, mon anglais!*" François greeted Burke. "I see we made it."

"Just in time. I was on the verge of leaving. Where's Hélène? I know Louise will want to know."

"The same here. Hélène is with child. Too risky to bring her. And Louise? How's she? *Ou habitez vous?* We fear for you. Tensions have mounted along the river. Joncaire's braves have fired up a swarm of others. Captain Beaujeu has joined them, too."

"My campsite's still good. You look like you could use a respite. There's much to talk about. Louise and I are together. She is with child."

"*Merveilleux!* Help me with my pack and I'll follow you. Coup de Sang will hide the canoe. *D'accord?*" he turned to the Seneca, half-ordering, half-motioning to him what to do. He wondered if he would ever gain the Indian's trust. Since the night at the falls, François had endeavored to act and speak with a rigueur that commanded mutual respect. One had to be elegant and savage, master and brother, brave and courteous, all in one. Yellow Hawk was just as difficult to handle.

Handsome Dog acknowledged the request and set about to secure the canoe. He hid it under a growth of yellow birches and high weeds, picked up François' heavy pack, and followed the two men up the bank.

After a dinner of roast bear and rum, Langdon poked the coals and leaned back against his blanket. "May I ask about these forts, and rumors about the Indians? Two men passed by here on a raft several days ago and warned me about hostilities along the Allegheny. They had either sold or stashed their goods or they had been stolen. They seemed to be running scared. They mentioned forts, more than one."

"I can't reply to rumors. Yes, things are different on the river. The Crown wants all the lands drained by the Ohio and those that flow into the lakes claimed for His Majesty's empire. Efforts are under way to entice bachelors and peasant girls to leave *la belle France* and settle along the coves *de la grande rivière de St. Laurence*. The process is well under way, though not without setbacks. The forest terrifies most of the newcomers. Many are not prepared for its brutal winters and heavy snows, or months of isolation. Louise wasn't. But Hélène was born to it. Tell me about our Maria de Touloine. We miss her. How is she? Is she happy or sad?"

"Happy! Happy as anyone can be, I suppose. We've few amenities in the foothills. But this last year, George the Second granted us three thousand acres in the Holston Valley. It lies near the Carolina border in a fertile plain, still wild and forested. We could use a Frenchman like you to clear the stumps and fight off the Indians that come up the Great Warrior Path."

"You flatter me," François replied with a rye smile. "No! My heart belongs to the river, to the great lakes and endless forests that hug their shores. I am a savage now, perhaps a bit nobler, or something of Rousseau's rustic forebear of nature. I feign to think I am self-made and liberated from the lusts and greed of society. Tell me more. Is she as *jolie* as ever?"

"Yes! Beautiful and fair! Like your Hélène. Hopefully by August she'll have our first *enfant*! I plan to clear the land, start building a house and till the soil. It's rich in red clay and blessed with silicates and iron. And springs and salt licks, too, I've been told. Plenty of game, bear and turkey, with wolves thrown in too."

"You'll be a landed gentleman like my father. Eligible for your House of Burgesses, no?"

"I suppose so. But the Governor and Crown dictate what we do. I'm content to leave it there."

"I fear our two sovereigns are leaning toward another guerre. It's an age of grievances no longer resolvable. I am French and proudly so. You are English, colony born. Our paths are bound to clash. I wish it weren't so. I can't reveal what I know. We may not be able to meet again. You are not offended, *j'espère!*"

"No! I feel it, too. I long for the Ohio myself. But for the southern part, across the Appalachians. Bison roam in its meadows and deer hide and feed in the tall grass. Already hunters from the Yadkin trap and wander there. I itch to join them."

"What of your Captain, Monsieur Tillson? What are his aims? I find him rigid, without humor or élan."

"I don't know. Like you, he serves his Crown—His Majesty King George. War is a pathway for his career. Without engagements, he can't rise to Major or Colonel. His ambition is high. But he likes my sister. I see it in both their eyes. Who knows what will happen?"

For a long while, silence absorbed the two men. Throughout their discussion Tekacayah had listened. He seemed to smile at the thought of war. "I know this Beaujeu," he said, squatting near the fire. "Very tall brave. Many scalps hang from his belt. I will join him soon." Abruptly, he stood erect, glanced about and chose an isolated clump of brush for his nightspot. Without another word, he unrolled his blanket, spread it out, and lay down on his side. Soon, he was deep in sleep.

Toward midnight, the cry of a panther broke the opaque silence about their campsite. Its shrill cry startled Langdon. He could hear Pellas snorting and pawing the ground. The moon slipped behind a series of black clouds. All grew dark. Moments later, shadows rushed across the meadow. Langdon leapt for his gun, aimed and fired. The roar of the long rifle echoed off the trees and down the bank. White smoke obscured the view. Slowly, the powder cloud drifted away. In the clearing lay a long black panther.

François and Handsome Dog had sprung to their feet. The Seneca raced toward the animal with his hatchet raised. He kicked the dark object; then brought his tomahawk down with a swift blow. The hollow "tunk" of a skull cracking sounded in the night. Handsome Dog held up the animal's pelt. Beneath it lay a dead Indian.

"Mingo!" Coup de Sang grunted. "Not panther."

Langdon and Philippe remained silent. Both listened as Coup de Sang tore the scalp off the Indian's head. Langdon reloaded in the darkness, while François recovered his gun. Coup de Sang disappeared into the brush. Minutes passed. Footfalls, then someone floundering in the river. Langdon raced toward the bank and peered down. An Indian was paddling with all his might, but his canoe could not escape the lunging savage behind him. Coup de Sang rose out of the water, raised his hatchet, and split the man's skull from top to neck. He towed the canoe ashore and harvested the Indian's scalp. Blood dripped from his hands and elbows. Two bloody hairpieces hung in his belt. He threw the canoe ashore and waded back up the bank.

Neither François nor Langdon said a word. This was the wilderness they feared and loved, respected for all its grandeur and violent terror. Langdon lay back down but could not sleep. He rose and walked out in the meadow to peer at the disfigured savage at his feet. The Indian's body lay face up, its eyes open and staring through a film of silver mucus. It was the face of a boy, no older than Jonathan. Around his neck dangled a French silver coin, pierced and strung with a string made of raw gut. A large "L" appeared on one side, a crown and the *fleur de lis* on the back. It bore the date "1740" and read "REX LUD XV." No doubt the youth had been encouraged to earn more. Langdon would have sought the second body, but it had floated down river after Coup de Sang butchered the man. He returned to his bedroll, but could not fall asleep. Thunder rumbled in the distance. Moments later, the first drops of rain pummeled the meadow. Langdon sought shelter under a cottonwood near Pellas. Soon François and Coup de Sang joined him. The rain fell in glistening sheets, heavy and cold. As dawn burst bright and yellow over the Monongahela, Langdon saddled Pellas, swung his venison and bear meat packs across the horse's rump, mounted and rode east. If only he could have said "farewell" to François, but the Lieutenant and Coup de Sang had slipped away while he was still asleep.

Chapter Eight

A COLD SEPTEMBER WIND SENT chills through Langdon as he waited in the yard and observed the parson dismount. There was no doubt as to the man's identity, as word of his coming had spread quickly. Plus, his black coat, broad-brimmed black hat, and soiled but tailored black jacket easily identified him as circuit preacher.

"I'm Reverend Renwick Martin" the rugged, dark-skinned cleric introduced himself. "I hear there's a weddin' and a lass's baby to be baptized. Ya wouldn't know whose, would ya?" he smiled. "Is it yours, lad?"

"Yes. It might be," Langdon smiled in turn. "I'm Langdon Burke. My wife is Louise. The baby's a girl, Helen Marie. Please come in? Your persuasion, sir? You aren't one of those enthusiasts, are you? Like a Methodist, or a Baptist?"

"Well, now, lad, if I were, would it make a difference?"

"No, sir. I was reared Anglican. My father and mother were good Englishmen, 'til they came here."

"Won't matter a wee bit, lad. I'm a stolid John Knox *supralapsarian*, if that means anything to ya? Part Scot and All Irish!" he bantered. "Presbyterian, through and through! A lover of God's own plan! *'Those whom he foreknew, he predestined to be one of his own, and those whom he predestined, he called, and those whom he called, he justified.'* Romans chapter eight. Verses twenty-nine and thirty. We mustn't doubt the Word of God. Shall we go in?"

"Now aren't we gifted with a lovely lassie here!" he exclaimed, as he entered and met Louise. "And you, my dear mum," he addressed Sarah, taking off his hat, "no doubt the mother of this fair one?" he nodded toward Louise.

"Good Heavens, no! Do I look that ancient?" she laughed. "Won't you have a cup of brandy to break the chill? Goodness!"

"That I will," he smiled, as he handed his coat to Langdon. "May I stay with ya tonight? I've more to go in the morning and I want to cross the gap before dark."

"Of course, Reverend. We've expected as much."

"Then let's see to the weddin' and baptize that wee one you're a holdin' in your arms. But, the brandy first. My throat's a wee tight and my chest loose."

Jonathan brought his saddlebag in and placed it by the table. Soft firelight illuminated the room as they stood by the hearth. It sent its defuse glow of mingled reds, yellows and gold across the cold spaces of the room. After the parson had downed his cup of spirits, he opened his leather-covered service book and began.

"Come together," he addressed Langdon and Louise in his mellifluous voice. "And hold the baby between you," he nodded toward Louise.

"Dearly, beloved, God Himself 'ath assembled us here in His Holy presence to join this Man, and this Woman in the sacred state of marriage … God 'ath instructed ye who enter to cherish a mutual esteem and love; to bear with each other's infirmities and weaknesses; to comfort each other in sickness, trouble, and sorrow; and to provide and to pray for each other … Now, Langdon, wilt thou take this lass to be thy wife, and wilt thou pledge thy love to her, in all purity and honor, duty and service, in all faith and tenderness, to live and cherish her all the days of thy life? And Louise, wilt thou pledge the same to this lad, and take him as thy husband, in all love and honor, and duty and service, as long as ye both shall live?"

"I do!" said Langdon.

"I too!" pledged Louise.

"Then I pronounce ye husband and wife! Ye may kiss thy bride, Mr. Burke! But from the looks of it," he smiled, "ye two are long past the kissin' stage."

Louise's eyes swelled with tears in the fire's sheen. She reached up and kissed Langdon, while clutching her infant to her breasts.

"And now for this wee one," Martin continued. "Can ya bring me a cup of water for the sprinkling' of this child properly?"

Sarah brought him a small wooden bowl, into which she had ladled a half-dipper of water.

"What is the Christian name of this child?" Martin asked, as he took the tiny bundle in his arms.

"Helen Marie," Louise whispered, as she slipped the warm flannel cloth off the baby's head.

"Helen Marie Burke," Martin stated, as he dipped his hand in the bowl, "I baptize thee in the name of the Father, and of the Son, and of the Holy Ghost. And may our heavenly Father bless thee and keep thee and guard thee all thy life, in His Son's precious name, Amen!"

Lieutenant Governor Robert Dinwiddie sat in his green and gold satin-covered armchair and fondled with delight the letter freshly received from London. The King's own signature fed his ego and sense of importance. Before him sat the distinguished members and financiers of The Ohio Company, plus Captain Tillson and the youthful adjutant of the newly organized Boutecourt District, Major George Washington.

"Gentlemen, the news we have all anticipated is in our hands!" the paunchy, ex-merchant announced with solemn satisfaction. His thin lips, elongated nose, grey eyes and powdered wig seemed the perfect match for the well-groomed, business-minded governor. His pale red silk jacket complemented his dapper deportment. "This means that at long last we are free to act."

"And how is that?" asked Carter Wright, shifting his own portly frame in the uncomfortable couch on which he sat. "I've invested all I can. I must see some beneficial yield soon."

"Yes?" queried Nelson Custiss, another member and merchant beside him.

"Gentlemen, allow me to read his Majesty's orders.

To my illustrious sires and proprietors of Virginia, God's blessings be upon you. In recognition of the perils posed by Versailles' interventions west of the Alleghenies, I herewith implore you to seek the truth as to their intentions. Survey the land, make alliances with the natives, establish forts, and found settlements in the Ohio region. The Crown supports you. We will not surrender our claims to this duly recognized territory of Virginia. Inform the French to depart. If they refuse, remove them by force of arms. By order of my own hand, His Excellency, George II, King of England, this 20th day of October, in the year of our Lord, 1753.

"Distinguished sirs, is that not good news?"

The men nodded their heads with approval and rose to congratulate themselves. Servants brought in distilled brandies and garnet wines, along with arrays of vintages and meat raised on the Lieutenant Governor's own lands.

"Only one thing," Dinwiddie continued. "The House of Burgesses knows nothing of this. It is our secret, until we need their support. Do I have your word?"

"Yes," the assembled members agreed.

"May I ask, sir," Captain Tillson addressed the Governor, "why the need for privacy of such a matter of so great a monetary significance to the Burgesses?"

Carter, Custiss and others, including the tall young Washington, snickered politely in their sleeves. "Because, sir," the Major explained, "the Burgesses have never seen the need to cross the mountains. Their interests are limited to their own lands and wealth, debts and grievances, tied up therein, of which we have plenty. We bear our own expenses for raising the militia, you know, and rents and fees go but a few yards."

"All this is very well," interjected Custiss, "but who's to lead this expedition to extend the surveying beyond what Gist and Burke have already accomplished? And whose strong arm will protect them as they make these so-called alliances, while spying on the French, and – God help them – inform the French and their savages to desist and depart? Whom, may I ask?"

"He's standing beside you!" Dinwiddie smiled. "Major Washington, and Captain Tillson as my spy," he patted the Captain on his right shoulder. "I commission you both and pledge you to secrecy. Plan to contact Gist, whom you'll need, and any others. No one must know. I'll prepare orders and a communiqué for the French, which you shall deliver, of course, with the utmost diplomacy and *firmness*." Then, he turned directly toward Tillson. "And you, Sir, dear Captain, shall garner the truth about their forts. You shall suggest any actions appropriate upon your return. Do we understand?"

The assembled group expressed its affirmation.

"Very good. I shall keep you informed. Let us chat now and enjoy the fruits of our investments. Please indulge and drink as much as you wish. We've plenty of beds upstairs. And a wench if you need one."

The late October sun warmed Tillson's cold face and bathed the lane with soft shafts of citrus light. All but a few oaks had lost their foliage. A carpet of brown, rust, beige and sienna leaves crunched under his horse's hoofs. Tillson nudged his horse off "Tree Notch Road" to head south for Burke's farm. In his saddlebags, he carried gifts for Sarah, Louise and Jonathan. At his suggestion, Lady Ashby had invited the Burkes to a formal ball, and Tillson wanted the women to look their best. His heart felt torn, however, because he loved both Sarah and Anna Ashby. Since his return from the journey with Langdon, he had whiled too many hours happily at Anna's estate. Williamsburg lay less than twelve miles inland and upriver. Far too often, he had visited her. He had not displayed the propriety he ought. Gossipers had whispered. He would have to ask for her hand, disappear, or request quarters farther away. Dinwiddie's assignment could not have come at a more opportune time. But, first this visit and the ball. Somehow he would survive.

"Oh, William," Sarah greeted him. Not a hint of his peerage dimmed her outburst of excitement. "They are perfect!" she ran her hands gently across the silk and linen bolts of cloth. "And matching threads and bodice lace, too! Wherever did you procure it?"

"Don't ask," he smiled politely.

"Louise, what a pleasure to see you again," he bowed. "I should say, 'Mrs. Burke.' And your tiny one! Boy or girl? I can never tell."

"She is Helen Marie, named for Hélène and my mother. And yourself? How are you? Have you any word from François, or his fate on the river?" She had pulled her long dark hair back and tied it with a fragile cord, made of leather and interlaced with homespun thread.

"Come, let's go in," Langdon offered. "It'll soon be dark. Tell us more about this invitation."

"I shall, plus some other news, too." Tillson said. "But that can wait 'til later."

Langdon glanced at William's eyes. The officer had turned his face down, but Langdon could sense that his "news" implied something urgent, if not unsettling.

After a supper of yams, dried apples, biscuits and cider, Tillson pushed his chair back. "Ladies, you are wonderful! Langdon, when do you plan on settling your estate? You've not mentioned it at all. Is the grant still valid?"

"Indeed. Perhaps as early as next spring, or this winter. Plus," he turned toward Louise, "the baby needs more time. Here we're sheltered, safe and have plenty."

"Kindly walk out to the stalls with me," suggested Tillson. "I finally met Major Washington. I should like to know more about this young man."

"Well, don't linger too long," said Sarah. "You haven't told us what to expect at Lady Ashby's. I haven't been anywhere special since father died."

"My pleasure," he smiled. "As soon as we return."

The two walked silently toward the barn. A dark bank of rouge clouds capped the peaks of the Blue Ridge. Langdon glanced westward. Winter would soon arrive. He wondered what Tillson had to say. "Well?" he finally asked.

"Dinwiddie's sending a party to meet with the Indians west of the mountains. Washington's to lead the party. Imagine, such a young officer with so little experience."

"He's had more experience than you know. Alone, he's surveyed much of the land north of the Big Lick. He is muscular and self-possessed and can handle himself in the woods. He's part of the Ohio Company. He's ambitious, too! You don't have to worry about him"

"We're to meet up with your Mr. Gist somewhere on the Ohio. He's to guide us to the Indians and find the French. I'm to report on their forts, if any, and otherwise keep quiet. I'd feel more comfortable if you were my guide in case anything goes wrong, like that night on the Ohio."

"When do you leave?"

"Dinwiddie hasn't said, but he's hinted at the 15ᵗʰ."

"If we accept Lady Ashby's invitation, that won't give us time."

"The ball's still a month away. Won't that be sufficient?"

"I can't let Louise and Sarah miss it."

"I wouldn't want you to."

"It's going to be awkward, isn't it?" Langdon said. "She's sweet on you, the Lady, isn't she? Along with Sarah. She's always asking about you."

He glanced uneasily at Langdon.

Anna Ashby had worked with Williamsburg's leading dressmaker to create a most inspiring gown. Thousands of silver beads had been stitched into the mauve brocade, adding a dynamic dimension to the dress under the light of the chandeliers. The dress was finished with a long hem of soft velvet, which brought a touch of royalty that even the introverted Dinwiddie noted. "My Lady! The King himself would abandon his damsels for thee, if not his entire boudoir. Enchanting, no less."

Surveying the room, the Governor spotted the Captain. "It appears the Captain has brought guests," he said to Lady Ashby. "It's Mr. Burke. You know he lost an entire pouch of valuable maps. Who are the others? Do you know them?"

"Yes. The ladies are his wife and sister. But I haven't introduced myself," she said with more of an edge in her voice than she intended to reveal. "Perhaps I should. Excuse me, your Excellency."

"Not at all. I need to speak with Mr. Burke, myself. But later," he said, his eye on the bowl of brandy and its mixed spices. "You do have taste, my dear!"

Anna smiled and made her way toward the Captain and the handsomely caped woman at his side.

"Yes! Lady Ashby," the Captain said, reaching for her gloved hand.

"Permit me to introduce Sarah Burke, her sister-in-law, Louise, and her husband, Langdon, whom you know. Mr. Burke and his family will soon be departing for the Holston to establish their estate there."

"How nice to hear!" Anna said with a measure of enthusiasm. "Dr. Kingsmore has already left, I've been told. It must be a dazzling sight! A jewel in so infinite a wilderness. I'm so pleased you could come. Sir William never wearies of singing the Burke family's praises! Now I see why!" she gazed at Sarah with a hurt only a woman can feel. "Please enjoy your visit. The musicians should begin soon. Captain, I do hope you'll save a reel for me." Her gaze plummeted into the irises of his steely eyes. He had been so joyful and adventuresome in her presence. Now, she could not fathom his heart, or even her own. Surely, his kisses by the well had been genuine! Now, she was not sure.

Tillson put forth his best smile, bowed slightly, and kissed her gloved hand. "Yes, I will dance with you," he replied.

"And, don't forget me!" Sarah spoke up. "I haven't skipped to the reel in years. You won't mind, Lady Ashby, will you?"

"Why, of course not! I'm honored that you journeyed so far to be with us. We shall all enjoy the night!"

Enjoy they did. Still, Anna could not help but envy the Burke woman's natural beauty, or her sister-in-law's simple grace. Down and back Anna skipped with William to the Virginia Reel. She felt so secure and wanted in his arms, a vital woman again. His temper had mellowed since his arrival, and his formality soothed by the soft caress of the warm Tidewater days and nights. Suddenly someone bumped her! Her mouth fell open. Of all things! It was the Major himself, tall, youthful, rugged, smiling and dancing with Sarah Burke at his side. It was their turn to skip between the rows of gay dancers. The fiddlers played loudly; the booted men lifted their heels and stomped. The bloom of youth flashed with smiles. Cigar smoke drifted in yellow layers beneath the chandeliers. Ladies fanned their powdered faces and fought to conceal their sweat. The Major asked for her hand. He was so young! So handsome! Mr. Carter asked next. The honorable Governor remained seated by the bowl, rising occasionally to warm his backside by the fireplace. His wig had tilted back and his high forehead glistened pale under a mantle of perspiration. He spoke only briefly with Burke. The two had shaken hands after slight bows.

The urges of time, want, loss and desire throbbed in Anna's heart. Perhaps, perhaps after all, Sir William would be hers. She struggled to remain poised, ebullient and hopeful. God only knew if there were more she could do. Sir William came to her side and danced with her one last time. But his eyes kept drifting. Please, please don't let it be so! "William, take me upstairs," she whispered, "before you say 'Good night!'" He kissed her cheek and bowed. When he lifted his face, Sarah and Louise were gone. Only Langdon remained.

"Anna, I must chat with Burke briefly, then I'll come up,"

"I'll be waiting," she whispered.

Tillson eased slowly toward Langdon. "Sorry about all this! I do hope Sarah and Louise found the evening enjoyable! I am at a loss to say more."

"Nothing needs to be said. I've considered your offer. I'll go. But I'll scarcely have time to get the ladies home."

"Where can you meet us?"

"There's a place called Willis Creek. It empties into the Potomac, on the edge of the mountains. I'll wait for you there. I'm eager to see the Big Meadows again, and what the French are up to. Maybe we'll encounter François, or, God forbid, Joncaire!"

"That might not be so bad. At least we'd know what he's up to. Willis Creek. I'll remember and wait," he paused. "Please excuse me, now," he glanced uneasily toward Anna's stairwell. "Where are you lodging, if I may ask?"

"At the Framington Inn not far from here. We came by wagon and will be leaving in the morning. Louise had to return when she did, since Jonathan's keeping our baby at the Inn. Good night, Sir William."

The Captain shook Langdon's hand, lowered his gaze, and walked away with a despondent cast in his eyes. He was drawn to Anna and craved her embrace and kisses. But where his heart was, he could not tell.

Chapter Nine

THE WILD TORRENT OF WATER that rushed past the bend in the Potomac made crossing it treacherous. On the opposite bank, Willis Creek flowed into the swollen river. It was November 19th. Langdon raised himself in the saddle to search for Washington's party. At first, there was no sign of barge, canoe, horse or person to confirm his gaze. Then he noticed a pale wisp of gray smoke rising skyward on the western bank of the creek. Nearby, a tethered horse shook its mane. A man waved a cloth, tied to a long branch. It was Tillson! Langdon acknowledged Sir William's presence with an energetic wave of his hand. He glanced over his shoulder and rode along the river's bank until he came to a mass of driftwood. The tangled heap created a logjam, but below it a natural shallow ford appeared between the rocks. With extreme caution, Langdon led Pellas into the water. Deeper the two sank until horse and rider swam the remaining rills of the swift current. Quickly the two emerged and galloped toward the waiting figure. Once across Willis Creek, Langdon hailed Tillson with a genuine smile.

"Can you build that fire higher!" Langdon greeted him. "I must be late."

"True! But you made it. I told them I'd wait at least two days. They've gone ahead. Three days ago. That's when we arrived. Gist was already here. I have no idea how far up the gap they've traveled." Beyond the forest, a bleak outline of dark mountains climbed steeply to the west. "It took us a week to get here. You'd best get down and change. I'll build the fire higher."

Early the next morning, the two rose, downed a breakfast of hot tea and dry bread, saddled their horses, and turned west. Washington's party had left a distinct trail. In places, the horses' hooves had sunk six or more inches into the mush. A brisk wind ruffled the wraps of the two as they followed the wide path upward into the gap. The sky grew dark. Menacing clouds descended the slopes enveloping them in a white fog. Soon freezing rain fell. For the next several hours, they trudged on in the biting cold. By sunset they had crossed the first gap. Ahead of them stretched ranges of lonely hills and steep climbs, all cloaked in winter's landscape of barren trees, black and wet.

"Tis only my third journey," Langdon acknowledged. "It's at least sixty miles to Turtle Creek. We may catch them day-after-tomorrow. But in this weather, who can say."

Tillson shivered under his woolen cloak. "The winters in Boston were just as bad. Gist told the Major he had a cabin nearby. Maybe they'll rest there."

"His cabin's on the other side of the Alleghenies. We'll reach it in another day or two, if lucky. Any safety we enjoyed, we left at Willis Creek."

"What tribes live here? Are they friendly?"

"Most just hunt these mountains. Groups of Delaware and Torn Ear's people want peace. The Mingo, Shawnee, Miamies and Ottawas don't. You never know. The sooner we join Gist, the better."

Mid-morning the next day, they crossed the Youghiogheny. The following night as dusk approached, they trotted their exhausted animals into a frozen clearing. Beside it hunkered a squat log structure. No smoke escaped its chimney, but its odor piqued the air. An icy woodpile glimmered between the house and a primitive privy. A shed for horses stood at the side of the cabin. The men dismounted, hobbled their horses and knocked at the door. No one opened it. With caution they entered.

Red embers glowed in the fireplace. "They aren't that far ahead of us," said Langdon.

For both of them, the warmth and shelter of the cabin were more alluring than the prospect of catching up with their party. While Langdon gathered wood to refurbish the fire, Tillson sorted through his saddlebags. "Shad from Anna's," he announced, as he held up a cured, brownish-gold filet. "Her servants put up pounds of this every spring, she says, when the shad spawn in the tributaries."

"It's very good. We used to seine for them on the Blackwater. My father baked them on planks of oak. We'd cover them with butter and salt and let them baste near the coals. That was when my grandfather was still alive. Best we save that for the trail. Let's see what we can hunt on the premises."

Langdon set out with his rifle loaded with buckshot. Black squirrels were prevalent in the area and he was determined to bag as many as he could. While Langdon hunted, Tillson tended to the horses, rubbing them down with the saddle blankets, trying to warm their flanks. Their stores of oats were limited and had to be carefully proportioned as supplements to the foraging along the trail.

"I wonder how Washington's party is faring?" Tillson said.

"We'll know by tomorrow. We're less than a day's ride from Turtle Creek. Its banks provide an excellent campsite. They'll have to pause there, like it or not. Beyond that point, nothing but Indian villages and forest, snow, ice and frozen rivers greet the traveler. And maybe a hundred Frenchmen, scattered about, settled in for the winter."

"It's time to meet them. Now the surprise will be theirs!"

In all likelihood, Langdon thought, the French already knew of their presence. Their informants were as plentiful as the leaves of the forest. If there would be any surprises, it would be theirs.

As he and Langdon supped on squirrel meat cooked with wild onion and salt, settling into the comfort of warmth and nourishment, they heard the horses agitate. "Can't be a bobcat or wolves," Burke said in a low voice. "They'd be neighing and kicking."

The rap at the door came just as they both reached for their weapons. Langdon nodded for Tillson to open the door, aiming his weapon at the door. Outside, stood a young black boy with a blanket wrapped about his shoulders, trembling from the cold. His cloth trousers appeared stiff with ice. Langdon recognized him as Gist's servant, Isaac, his houseboy and camp mate on the trail.

"Isaac! What's happened?"

"I heard you comin' and hid in the woods, sir. That's all. Didn't know who you was. Indians passed through here last night. Delaware. They was returnin' home. They left a mess. Drank a whole jug of Mr. Gist's brandy. They snooped around, once they seen the horses' tracks. There's no way the Major's party ain't been seen."

Concern spread across Langdon's face. "I'm not surprised. Sorry we frightened you. Best get into something warm before you freeze."

"Yes, suh! There's brandy hidden. Jerky, flour and corn under the floor 'neath the bed! I can fetch you some, if'n you hungry!"

Tillson's face flushed at the thought. "A stout draught would be nice."

"Yes, suh! I'll have some with you, if you won't tell."

Langdon studied the youth's cold face. "We'd be honored to share that with you."

Early the next morning, Isaac prepared fresh bread and hot tea for them. He gave each a handful of smoked jerky. "Mr. Gist can't be too far ahead. It rained here hard before yous arrived. The creek's froze and the ground's slick. The men with him looked pretty miserable."

"Thank you, Isaac. We'll keep our secret," said Tillson.

"Yes, suh!"

It was close to sunset before Langdon and the Captain caught sight of Gist's horses. A cold drizzle had plagued them since leaving the cabin. The route had been slippery, the mud deep and caked with ice crystals. More than once, Langdon had observed moccasin tracks crossing the party's trail. Turtle Creek lay still a half-day's ride to the west. Now, in the distance, Langdon could make out the group of grim riders setting up camp. Close by, the Monongahela's waters roiled. Fortunately, he and Tillson already had crossed the Youghiogheny. With scarcely a nudge, they hailed the mix of traders and camp servitors as their horses plodded in.

"Well, well, Mr. Burke!" a swarthy Gist greeted him. "Your Captain said you was a comin'. I see you made it back! Did you find my cache?

I assume you did. It's good to see you. I'm delighted to have your company. The Captain did the right thing," he said, glancing up approvingly toward Tillson.

"Where is the Major?" Tillson asked. "I trust he's not ill."

"Oh, he's fine. A bit eager, but he'll learn. Went ahead with van Braam to scout out the headwaters. Can't cross the river here," Gist pointed toward a cabin on the south bank. "The young Major's not one to waste time."

"And whose is that?" asked Tillson, nodding his head toward the log building on the opposite shore.

"Mr. Frazier's. He's a trader with the Indians. Our eyes on the Ohio. This is the last outpost, where civilization ends and the forest begins. A wonderful life he has. He sees it all."

"Who's van Braam?" asked Langdon.

"A Dutchman from Fredericksburg. An interpreter. Speaks impeccable French, they say. He's the Major's negotiator, once we meet the French."

"Mr. Burke's quite fluent himself," the Captain interjected. "I should know. He saved our lives – his and mine – on the Ohio last year. He's quite well spoken with their officers, at least the one we met."

"That I know. I can attest to his gifts myself. But he ain't the one the honorable Governor chose. It's Mr. van Braam. And we're not to forget that! My advice is for us to stay out of the way. My role is the Major's guide. That's all. And to parley with the Indians. Most of the chiefs know me. 'Sides, I'm the one who carries the peace belts. Torn Ear understands. And I do, too. I've been trying to explain all this to the Major since leaving Willis Creek. He'll do the right thing. But Burke, you best listen nonetheless. As for the Major, he's one, lean sinew of a man, as skilled with an axe and gun as most of us in the wilderness. It's just that the French know how to bend the Indians' ears in ways we don't. They've got them convinced they know what's best for their wild children, and the English only want their land. I just wish it weren't so damn cold! What a hell of a time to deliver a message!"

"Mr. Gist, you make me feel at home," Langdon laughed.

It was not until the following afternoon that they spotted the Major.

He was returning in a canoe to the campsite where the group waited. Van Braam and a young brave paddled with him. The brave's arms were muscled and bare, blood red in the cold sunlight, while a wolf-skin covered his shoulders and chest. Osprey feathers hung from a large knot of braided black hair and a necklace of bear claws and river shells completed his upper attire. Leggings and moccasins protected the rest. To Langdon's surprise, Major Washington wore clothing much like his own: a long bearskin coat tied at the waist, with thick woolen shirts beneath it. He wore a black cap of inverted beaver fur, leggings and knee-high leather boots. Rabbit skins covered his hands. Van Braam's attire was similar. Gist and another man dragged the canoe ashore. The young Major said nothing, but Gist seemed to know what to do.

Washington took Gist's extended hand as he worked his way out of the canoe. Once on land, the Major repeated the gesture and extended his hand to van Braam. The Indian steadied the canoe as they disembarked. Washington glanced up and recognized Langdon.

"Welcome, Mr. Burke. The river's deep but its flow is calm. Right now it's impassable, swollen with rain and floes of ice where the Allegheny enters it. I must say, the Ohio is a mighty river!"

"That it is!" Langdon shook the Major's hand.

Impatient, Gist probed the Major for a progress report.

"I didn't get to Logstown, but Shinglis's village is just ahead. His grandson here volunteered to come back with us. Shinglis will accompany us to Half-King. He's eager to know what the chief will do."

"Well, let's set up camp and parley later," said Gist. "Sir, you know that Shinglis is the chief of the Delaware in these parts? But if Torn Ear sides with the French, so will he."

"I didn't realize that," Washington averred. "I should have waited for you."

Langdon smiled with a bit of surprise. Here was Dinwiddie's own diplomat respecting Gist as his equal. In wilderness, yes. But otherwise, no. Langdon knew how crafty and sometimes crude Gist could be. But as a guide, none surpassed him. Much of what Langdon knew of navigating the wild, he had learned from Gist.

With darkness upon them, the temperature dropped. Langdon,

Tillson and Gist shared the Major's tent while Washington elaborated on his dash to the headwaters.

"The land in the forks provides an absolute command of both the Ohio and Allegheny. At its point, it rises twenty to twenty-five feet above the water's surface. A considerable body of flat timbered land stretches all around it. The rivers must be a quarter of a mile wide, each of them. The waters of the Allegheny tumble with rapids and swift currents. Shinglis's village lies to the southeast of the junction. Captain Tillson, once you've viewed the point, I believe you'll confirm my judgment. It surely constitutes the ideal location for a fort, precisely the kind Mr. Dinwiddie has urged us to consider."

"Major, this whole area might qualify! Could vessels with cannons reach its walls?"

"That might be its drawback, since the French have such vessels. But if engineers raised a mound of ten feet or so, built the fort on that, and cleared the trees about, I'd say no cannon could reach it. You'll be able to judge for yourself when we pass it. Shinglis will join us when we arrive. Then, we need to ride toward Logstown. I've estimated we've come close to a hundred miles from Willis Creek, and Logstown lies another twenty or so up the Allegheny. December's coming. The tributaries are already bloated with ice."

"Sir, you can't rush the wilderness! It'll do what it damn well wants. But we'll make it," assured Gist.

Early the next morning they broke camp, and two hours later arrived at Shinglis's village. Langdon could sense Shinglis's disappointment when Washington sat forward in his saddle, but did not dismount.

"Chief," Gist began, "the young Major has great urgency to reach Logstown before dark. Please join us and guide our journey."

Shinglis wrapped his British robe tightly about his shoulders and spoke. "I Shinglis, chief of the Delaware, covet the honor of holding council. We are brothers, no? I too have wampum belts to exchange. We welcome you and your gifts of tobacco, and maybe rum. It is not good to move so quickly. There are many ears in the forest. Here, we meet alone."

"This I know, sir," replied Gist, "but the wind is wicked, the sun sets too soon and shortly the snow will blow. Perhaps on our way back, you will renew your welcome."

The old chief stared hard at Washington, then called for two braves to bring horses. He mounted the tallest of the horses and, flanked by his braves, head held high, he led the party through the frozen woods toward Logstown.

As soon as they arrived, Mr. Davison, a friend and interpreter for Gist, dismounted and spoke briefly to an elderly sachem. After introductions, he turned and translated for Washington. "His name is Monacatoocha. He's serving as chief during Torn Ear's absence. He bids you enter his long house, along with Shinglis and your leaders."

"Tell him we are most grateful," replied the Major.

The group dismounted. Respectfully, Langdon followed Gist, the interpreter, the Major and Tillson toward the chief's house. Davison stopped, signalling to van Braam to remain outside. "I prefer," said Davison, "to talk with the chief in his own tongue, not French. Please don't be offended."

The big Dutchman narrowed his eyes, his mouth contorted in a sneer. Still, he stepped aside.

After they entered and took their seats, Washington turned to Davison. "Tell him that I have been sent by the Governor of Virginia to bear a message to the French commander of the Ohio. Furthermore, that I am instructed to share this message with the sachems of the Six Nations, and all their sub-chiefs in the region."

Davison nodded and translated the Major's orders to the chief. The old gentleman sat stoic and erect throughout the translation, then, addressing Washington, directed the following: "Torn Ear, the Half-King, is not here. He lodges at his cabin on Beaver Creek. He has just returned from Venango. The Captain there is chief of the French. His fort is small but strong. Torn Ear will decide what to do."

Langdon whispered to Tillson to encourage Gist to assist the Major. "Sir," Gist said. "Let me present the chief with a string of wampum and a twill of tobacco. Then ask him if he'll send for Torn Ear, so we can deliver our message to the French commander. He must be the one at Venango."

The Major studied the faces of his companions and nodded to Davison to deliver their request. He gestured toward Gist to present the belt and tobacco. To Langdon's relief, Gist handed the chief a large twill of tobacco and a shiny strand of white shells, decorated with a peace tree, pipe, and the British colors. "It is our great honor to bring you this gift, dear father, from our own great Father and his Son in Virginia."

Respectfully, the old man accepted the offerings. "At first light, I will summon Torn Ear and send runners to inform the other sachems."

Langdon could tell Washington was pleased. It represented his first test as a negotiator with the Indians. Washington glanced toward Langdon and Tillson but said nothing.

"Thank you, Mr. Gist, Mr. Davison, and Honorable Chief," he bowed toward the aging sachem.

The members of Washington's party rose to their feet, excused themselves, and retired to their tents.

In the fading glow of twilight, a disheveled line of figures appeared on the village's edge. They were Frenchmen, a squad of soldiers seeking shelter from the cold.

"Mr. van Braam!" Washington called. "Interrogate them, sir! They look like stragglers. Ask if they speak English?"

"*Alors! Mais amis!*" van Braam addressed them. "You are lost? Hungry? What goes? *Que ci passe?*"

"We're lost, you could say," the highest in rank replied in French. "We were to rendezvous with a large force coming down from the lakes. We number one hundred and have sailed up from New Orleans. With our commander, we have escorted eight canoe loads of provisions for wintering the quarters along the river. We have already supplied four forts between the mouth of the Mississippi and *les isles noires.*"

Van Braam immediately translated their words.

"Good!" said Washington. "Ask how many men are garrisoned in each fort? And what artillery pieces they have?"

Van Braam pressed the question.

"Many, many!" the leader boasted.

Monacatoocha and Shinglis waved for the Frenchmen to approach the lodge.

The French soldiers stepped closer toward the crackling blaze in front of the council house. An old squaw offered the men gourds of hot soup.

After warming his hands and supping from his bowl, the leader continued: "Thirty-five companies of forty men are stationed at the fort near New Orleans. Its stone walls mount eight carriage guns. *Les isles noires* possesses six guns and is guarded by three companies of forty men each. Our strength is great on both rivers and stronger still on Lake Erie."

"Damn liars!" whispered Gist to Washington. "They're trying to scare the Indians. A cannon can do a hell of a lot of damage to wigwams and bark houses. Bastards! Tell 'em that!" he said in a raised voice to van Braam. "Or you tell 'em, Burke."

"No!" said Washington. "Leave them be! Their ruse works to our advantage. They're not the ones we need to see. It's their commander up the river we have to challenge. Desist, Mr. van Braam! And thank them."

"Yes, sir!"

Washington appeared disconcerted and retired to his tent.

Shortly afterwards, one of the Major's servants approached Gist, Tillson, and Burke, where they huddled before low flames in front of their own tent. "Sir," said the servant to Gist, "them soldiers, the Frenchmen, they've plumb disappeared. Ain't a one in sight. Gone! Just like wisps in the night."

"Damn! I thought as much. They were spies! Mr. Burke, see if they left a trail. Follow it if you can."

Chapter Ten

THE LONG TREK IN THE SNOW from Venango to his lodge at Beaver Creek left Torn Ear panting – this in spite of a remarkable physique for a man of fifty- two. Though considered old by his people, he could still outwalk younger braves who sought the glory of the hunt but not its discipline. The two men with him were his sons. Harsh winds blew against them, slowing their progress. They paused to tighten their snowshoes and catch a breath. Even to them at times the forest seemed threatening, filled with spirits and the fear of the Frenchman's allies — the Huron, Seneca, and Algonquin. Half-King wiped cold snow from his lips. Soon, they would be home.

As they resumed their march, Torn Ear relived Joncaire's mocking rebuke of his request of the Captain's commander. He had spoken openly and not minced words. His words burned in his chest like a firebrand.

"Fathers, I have come to remind you of your own speeches. This is what your own mouths declared. In former days, you set silver basins before us, with legs of beaver and bear. You desired of all nations to come and eat. You promised peace and plenty. You denounced all rude talk. We agreed that if anyone acted as a disturber, we would lay down the rod — you on yourselves and I to scourge our own.

"Now, Fathers, it is you who are the disturbers. You build forts and towns. You fill our rivers with thunder canoes and take our pelts for less than value. What you want you take by force. Our bows and arrows are no match. Your cannon and guns kill without mercy. Blood is everywhere.

"Fathers, hear me! Long ago on the *rivière de St. Laurence,* at your place called Montreal, we wished you to stay. We acquiesced and you took the land. Now, I ask you to leave our forests. Leave our land. Take your forts with you. We must learn to live again as our fathers taught us. You have made us weak and dependent on your goods. Our women laugh at us. Our young warriors crave your poisonous drink. The English are no better, though their guns and charity make us slaves, too.

"Fathers, look above you. Count the many shining stars. Look around you. See the hoary forests and our streams. All, all, belong to the Great Being above. It is He who gives us this land. Not you! He made it for our residence. Not yours! Fathers, we want you to leave. We want the English to leave. You are white. We are red and brown, deep copper and tan. Must we use force of arms? Be equal sharers with us, but no more. Trade, yes! Build forts and towns, walls of stone, No! My message is done! I, Torn Ear, have spoken. My sons will not forget! Will you?"

Angry, Joncaire rose and spat on the ground. "We have given you life! The English give you death. Our forts protect you. Not us! Our trade is what they protect. The English want your lands. We, only your furs! You whine like a dog after its master has fed it. Shame! Shame on Half-King and his sons! Enough of you! Our allies are not afraid. They hunger for your scalps. Remember that! The Huron, Ojibwa, Ottawa and Mingo are numerous too. Are you so silly? I fear you are! Are your braves a match for Handsome Dog? What am I to do? Throw our black belts in your face?"

Torn Ear lifted his head into the wind. It howled and cried in his ears. Swirling snow swept around him and enveloped his sons. O, Great Spirit above! Do you not care for your children, the red ones anymore? Whose voice do I listen to? My own, Joncaire's, or that of the English? You have put us in a snare! We are like the fleeting rabbit. Pity your people, O Spirit above! My face is cold; my body grows numb; my sons, will they live to bury me? Will I live to see them be chiefs?

Gradually, the wind dropped to a whisper, to the sound of tree limbs cracking like knuckles in the fading storm. Evening died in a streak of cold orange flame. Torn Ear was home. His hunting lodge welcomed him with the sound of a drum, its tom-tom signaling unrest. Evening was not over. Tasks remained. A runner waited outside Torn Ear's wigwam. The Half-King recognized him as Monacatoocha's older son. "English have come to our lodges," he greeted the chief. "They wish to speak to you. Their leader is young, from Virginia. He says he carries an urgent message for the French at Venango. He requests your help. He does not know the way. Shall I tell him you are coming?"

"It is too cold to run again tonight. Leave early in the morning, while it is still dark. Tell him I will arrive by middle sun. Perhaps his presence will save us from our French fathers. They are angry and fearful, both of us and of the English. It is good and not good. Our road is not easy. Stay now and be warm."

On that same day, just as dawn broke through the numbing mist at Logstown, Burke and Tillson mounted horses to follow the soldiers' trail. Though snow covered much of it, Langdon was able to discern where the stragglers had dragged their packs. Their trail led deeper and deeper into the woods, ever turning east. Then at the base of a pine-covered hill, their footprints converged with many others. They had mounted horses and ridden north.

"Spies, all right!" surmised Tillson. "I wonder where they're from?"

Torn Ear did not arrive at Logstown until late afternoon the next day. Many Indians had gathered in the commons to greet the chief and stare at the visitors. The Half-King could sense that all was not well. He glanced about at Gist, the tall young leader in buckskin, Tillson, and the brave Burke, as he thought of him. He trusted the two brothers. But why these other men? Who were they? Why were they here at this time of year? He did not want to see hatchets red as they had been when the Iroquois sold the English Delaware and Shawnee lands. Blood still was being shed. It was a dark time. Did the Great Spirit not understand? Why was He testing his people so?

"Hello! Chief!" Gist greeted him. "We've much to parley. This here's Major Washington, sent by his Father in Virginia. He bears communiqués for your people and the French. Please, let's enter your house and speak."

Torn Ear eyed Washington carefully. He was not dressed like the British in their bright red coats with sabers swaying from their hips. He liked what he saw. "So it shall be!" he replied. He turned toward Langdon and smiled. "I see we both have our hair," he tugged on his own. "Gist has taught you well." He pointed toward Tillson. "He is one of them, isn't he? Let us go inside."

The warm fire emitted a friendly air. Gist presented Torn Ear with a twist of tobacco.

"I have come," began Washington, "because the Governor of Virginia is concerned for his people across the Alleghenies and worried about the continuing encroachment of the French. I don't know the nearest road to the French, or where they lodge. Nor does our guide, Mr. Gist. I need your guides to take us there. We carry wampum belts of peace for all the tribes. Our wish is for you to bring your chiefs and your belts to the French and exchange your belts for ours. That's a heavy burden, I know. But our Great Father across the Sea thinks it best for all."

Torn Ear, who understood English, but spoke better French, waited for Gist to translate. After Gist completed his task, Torn Ear replied: "It is no easy walk to assemble all our chiefs. It is winter and many are hunting for furs and meat for their own lodges. Besides, there are four peace belts scattered among the sachems. I guard one; the others are protected by our brothers east, north, and across the river. I will need time. Three days! You must wait."

Gist translated, word for word.

Washington sighed and faced his interpreter directly. "Can you not urge him to see how important this is? Ask him what he knows about the forts? How many? Where? How well garrisoned?"

"Not too fast, Major!" Gist warned. "Give 'im time. Maybe the weather will break. We still have plenty of provisions. We need to rest, anyway."

"Sir, you're my guide. But Tillson needs to see their forts. Winter's only just begun. We could be stranded here for months. If the French are building forts, my orders are to command them to leave, even if by force of arms."

"And just whose 'arms' are you speakin' of!" Gist retorted. "Sir, we ain't but eight all told, including the Captain and Burke. Plus, we ain't out of here yet! We ain't there, and we're hundreds of miles from home! Think of that! And it's cold as hell and getting colder, sir!"

"Gist is right," said Washington. "What do you think?" he asked Sir William. "We have to go on."

"If you deem so, yes! The Governor's orders were simple and clear. 'Observe, communicate, inform, and threaten with arms.' Were those not his words?"

All became silent.

"Mr. Gist, ask the chief to assemble the sachems and belts as early as possible. Ask him if he is on our side. Mr. Gist, present the Half-King, Shinglis, and Monactoocha with gifts. Whatever you deem proper. Thank them and beg them to act with dispatch."

Mr. Gist delivered the Major's words. After the Indians replied, he said: "They insist it will take three days to retrieve the wampum strings and chiefs here. In the meanwhile, a guard of Mingoes, Shannoahs and Delawares will prepare to lead us to Venango. We will have to go overland, as the river is impassable. So says Torn Ear."

"Very well. Three days," sighed Washington. "Perchance the weather will break. Let's go to our tents and rest. Perhaps a little rum for the chiefs would be in order. But only a little. Mr. Gist, do you mind?"

"No, sir! I might snitch a nip myself!"

The men smiled and retired to their tents. They had scarcely settled in when a brave from Monacatoocha's house came to their camp and shook the Major's tent flap.

"Mr. van Braam, can you see what he wants?" asked Washington.

The Dutchman rose and stared at the brave. It was Shinglis's grandson. "What is it, lad?" he asked. "Can you speak French?"

"Yes!" he replied. "A runner has arrived from Venango. Monacatoocha has sent me. The runner says their Captain, a man called Joncaire, has called for all Mingo, Delaware and mixed braves to gather to him. In the spring, he charges them to descend the Allegheny and make war on all tribes that will not fight the English. His words are harsh. 'If you do not fight for me, your French Fathers will crush you. If you fight with the English, we will crush them and you and take away all your lands. If the English withstand, we will divide what is yours with them. So, fight! Or we will fling our black belts at you.' Very hard words! A terrifying speech! And with him, a terrifying chief, Coup de Sang! I go now to my father's house."

Washington waited for van Braam to translate the native's French. In the lull, however, Langdon had already deciphered it. His heart beat with uncertainty, but his thoughts were of Louise, their child, his sister and brother, and his grant along the Holston. He wanted to be home. Yet, this was his home, the cold reality of the wilderness with all its perils and promises.

Chapter Eleven

WRAPPED IN A HEAVY CLOAK, François-Philippe stood on Le Boeuf's bastion that overlooked the fort's entrance mesmerized by the large snowflakes falling from the heavens. Against the dark pines and scaly birch, it created an intoxicating splendor.

He glanced about the completed construction. Neither Mercier nor Marin was present to admire it, but their plan had produced a formidable fort. Just in time, too. Word from Joncaire that *anglais* were ascending the river, led by their guide Monsieur Gist, did not bode well. Spies had confirmed that a young Virginian was asking disconcerting questions. How many forts? How many cannon and troops? Where? A man of military bearing, possibly a British officer, accompanied him.

Why couldn't they stay on their side of the mountains? Why did they insist on spoiling it for all? His government had struggled assiduously to create their new empire in this hostile, vast, and tremulous world!

Le Boeuf's new commander would be arriving soon. Perhaps he would promote him to Captain. He had been Lieutenant François-Philippe Gabelle de Robert far too long. Or so it seemed. Had he not done all that was required? Executed every command? Even checked Joncaire's darker side when serving with him? The *intendent* at Montreal had personally commended him, yet, in a moment of gauche humor, had said: "*Alors*! De Robert! Joncaire is precisely the man we need. His savages are the unspoken key to our success. He is our wilderness commander, par excellence! Never forget that! *Jamais!"*

Legardeur would be different. Any day, the new commandant should arrive. The very sound of his name held gravitas: Jacques Legardeur de Saint-Pierre! For his bravery in action, the King had awarded him the Cross of St. Louis. His knowledge of Indian affairs, their languages, and his skill of conducting business at trading posts were unmatched. Since his days in the Wisconsin wilderness, he had united tribes as diverse as the Ojibwa, Cree and Sioux. He had served in numerous posts under different commandants and knew the Ohio region better than Mercier. Only six years ago he had fought with Louis de la Corne against the British and their Mohawk allies in Lachine. Rumors circulated that he had traveled as far west as Saskatchewan and had interrogated natives from the distant lands of *Les Grands Tetons*. Now with Captain Marin dead, Montreal had promoted Legardeur to be the new commander of Fort Le Boeuf. François was eager to meet him.

Gabelle, still transfixed by the falling snow, was suddenly jarred by a flicker, then a movement amid the shadows beyond the creek. Into the clearing loped Yellow Hawk with a deer looped across his shoulders. The animal's head bobbed as the Indian slowed his pace before kicking off his snowshoes.

As he paused to look up at the gates, a rush of pride surged through the Indian's heart again. The slain deer felt heavy on his back, but killing it in the deep snow had renewed his once sense of tribal happiness. Resting for seconds only, once again, Yellow Hawk was young, racing with a group of village hunters after the wounded moose. Floundering in waist deep snow, they chased the bleeding animal until its labored movement grew slower and slower. He watched as it collapsed in the dense brush and died in frost-laced breaths, head down in the red-smeared snow. He was the first to slash its throat open and gulp a handful of rich, dark blood. Soon the women caught up and gutted the great beast; then building a fire on the spot, they boiled its meat in their new iron pots, traded for furs from Montreal.

Yellow Hawk sniffed in the cold air and shuffled toward the gate. Once inside, he dropped the deer by the cook's quarters. A group of squaws scampered out and began the process of butchering the carcass.

The Indian stopped and peered up at François. "Red coats come soon. Already their spies approach Venango. Yellow Hawk will get his jacket one day. You will see."

"Of that I am sure," Philippe replied. "But you will be their target, too. Remember, many redbirds fly in the forests. Not all of them die from arrows!"

Yellow Hawk turned away and ambled toward a wigwam, where the fort's braves preferred to lodge.

François, shivering under his cloak, descended a ladder beside the bastion. As he entered his quarters, Hélène came to his side to help him remove his cloak. "You'll freeze out there waiting on the new commander. We'll know when he arrives. This blizzard can't last forever. *Oui?*"

"Tis true! But I want him to find me at my post. Our worst defeats have come in the snow when we least expected our enemies to strike."

"You don't have to remind me." A shiver went through Hélène. "I was at the village of Saint Croix the night the Mohawks crept through the snow and barbecued the women and children at Eau Froid. They skewered them like pigs; roasted them alive." Hélène's dark eyes filled with sorrow. "I know I'm half savage, but they are the true savages! No wonder Yellow Hawk can't forget. Imagine. They barbecued his own family! Sent by the British, too! He will never know peace until his knife drips with revenge!"

"*C'est vrai!* But there's a vast disparity between vigilance and revenge. Joncaire's like Yellow Hawk and Coup de Sang. They relish the knife and blood. I want to see the wilderness become that paradisiacal realm that Rousseau extols, while retaining its faultless soul."

"Ha! My Love! This is not your Rousseau's garden or some elegant chateau bordered by a tree-lined *bois*! *C'est la Nouvelle France*! The only home I know! Come, let's enfold ourselves in our bearskin rugs and make love," she pulled on his hands. "I want another baby. One that will live and not die like our first. I wonder if Louise's baby is alive."

Sarah winced as the large splinter tore into her numb hand. Wind whipped her bonnet, causing her red hair to stream like a comet's tail on fire. She lay down the axe, blood oozing from her palm. With her teeth, she clenched the jagged end of the oak splinter and pulled it out, then bent down and scooped up a handful of snow to quell the bleeding. She gathered up the kindling and firewood she had split and carried it to the house. Inside, Louise cradled Helen Marie in her arms.

"Can you help me with my hand," Sarah said, setting the firewood on the hearth. The fist of snow in her hand was red with blood, but the cold had stopped the bleeding. Louise blanched, but quickly came to Sarah's aid.

"I know I should do more," she said, wrapping Sarah's hand with a clean rag. "I feel so weak. Surely I'll regain my strength soon."

Sarah tried to smile. "Langdon should be home in another month. Maybe Sir William will come with him."

"I'm worried about Jonathan," Louise said. "He should have returned by now. The Weir's place isn't that far. I thought he'd be back by now. Didn't he take the horse? Maybe it slipped and broke a leg."

"Ole Red's a fine horse. Plenty strong. Sure footed."

"Why did he go to the Weir's anyway? I thought he was going to cut wood."

"He was carrying venison and salt in exchange for gunpowder and lead. Langdon made the arrangement before he left. They also card wool. They give us whatever we need in exchange for whatever they need. Mr. Weir's not a good hunter, says Jonathan. Thank heaven he and Langdon are."

Both women expelled their pent up fears. "It's already dark." Louise noted. "I've got to feed Helen again," she cooed to her baby. "Oh, Langdon, do come home! Jonathan, don't scare us like this."

"He'll be all right, I'm sure. He's probably almost here. On these moonless nights, it always seems darker."

Suddenly, a noise from outside caught their attention. Louise clutched Helen in her arms. Sarah moved for the rifle. The door opened. There was Jonathan with a lamb in his arms and a ewe and ram tied to a long rope, fastened at the saddle.

"They weren't very cooperative," he grimaced. "Now we can card our own wool. The Weirs still want me to hunt for them as often as I can."

As Gist, the Major, Captain Tillson, van Braam and others rode heads-down into the blowing snow. Langdon marveled at their advance, as slow as it was. Shinglis, Monacatoocha, Torn Ear and still another sachem, White Thunder, rode ahead. Younger braves followed, bringing up the rear, all but two loping on snowshoes through the soft grey drifts. Washington had pressed the chiefs the night before, imploring them to speak with one voice. To place before the commander at Venango black belts, to signal with resolve that each chief's break with the French expressed unanimity. "So shall I do," Torn Ear vowed.

The somber woods whispered back their own warning. Icy limbs groaned and creaked overhead. The darkened trunks of endless forest, of wind-whipped and snow-laced oaks created a foreboding canopy about them. All but the forest's faintest outline loomed obscured in the swirling world of falling flakes.

The horsemen ahead halted. Rising vapor from an icy stream signaled their arrival. Across the creek a large cabin wavered in the bleary snow. A cluster of wigwams and bark covered longhouses emerged in the downy shadows. The French had hoisted their colors beside the house. Gist turned in his saddle. "Venango! That cabin there's Mr. Frazier's. I've heard him describe it many times. The Frenchies drove him out. This here's French Creek."

Carefully, the men and horses entered the stream and crossed it. A group of Indians awaited their approach. One was Handsome Dog. He motioned for the others to assist. "You will find leader in lodge," he gestured toward the cabin. Just then, Joncaire came to the door. "Come in!" he called in a casual voice. "We've been expecting you. First eat something; then we'll talk. I see *mes bons frères* of the river are with you," he smiled toward Torn Ear and the other three chiefs. "Good! We will spread wampum together and smoke, renew alliances and share our wine. *Oui! C'est bon! Non?*"

No, it's not good, thought Langdon. He will shame the chiefs into keeping their white belts. "Sir William, be wary," he whispered. "This man's a charlatan, a cunning master of deceit!"

It was not until five o'clock that Joncaire, turning casually toward Washington, asked: "And what brings our *anglais* guests to my quarters?

To drink our wine, only? *Non*! I think not! Word has reached us of your urgent communiqué. You may speak freely. Note that I have sent the sachems away to lodge in their own wigwams. Even we must exercise secrecy. *Non*?"

"Ask him," the Major instructed van Braam, "if he's the commandant of the region. Tell him nothing more, if he isn't."

"Mr. Washington may only deliver our communiqué to the commander of the whole region. Are you he, Monsieur Captain?"

Joncaire eyed the interpreter and his guests with dismay. A rueful grimace glowered briefly in his eyes. "Tell him that I'm the commandant of this region, but above me is a general who resides at Ft. Le Boeuf. He alone speaks for his Majesty. Nevertheless, I control the river here. I decide who passes and who stays. Why must he see our general? Does he bear a message from his own king? From George II?"

"I can't answer that," replied van Braam. "I only interpret and relay words."

"Then, do so!" said Joncaire, pouring himself a third tankard of wine. "It is very good, *non*?"

Van Braam relayed the Captain's words.

"What do you think?" the Major turned toward Tillson and Gist. "He's stalling."

"I agree," Tillson answered. "This isn't much of an outpost, but would make a strong fort. Let's not alienate him."

"My sentiments, too, Major," said Gist.

"Very well," sighed Washington. "Tell him we come bearing no malice, that our Governor values trade relations, and expresses concern for the transfer of captives, since such exigencies occur all too frequently."

Van Braam did as told.

"Surely your 'Major,' as I heard you address him, is more experienced than that! The evening is long. The darkness lurks with danger. One freezes in an instant in the cold. I will be meeting with the chiefs in the morning. They are too innocent to lie."

"Major, he suspects our mission. What do I say?'

"Hint that we claim rights here, that the Lords of Virginia believe the King's lands extend to the far lakes. But nothing more."

"Yes, sir!" replied van Braam. Then he translated the Major's message.

Joncaire ruminated. Several ensigns entered and joined the debate. One by one, Tillson, Gist and Langdon excused themselves to retire to their respective tents. "Stay with me," Washington nudged van Braam. "Tell me what they say."

The Captain and his ensigns laughed among themselves. They offered the Major and van Braam as much wine as they cared to drink. Joncaire's men slowly emptied one flask after another.

"Ho, Mr. van Braam. Tell your good Major that we French have traversed this area longer than his English can know! We have undoubted rights to the River. LaSalle claimed them for us over sixty years ago. All the Mississippi, Ohio, and rivers and streams that feed into them are ours! We have numerous forts and liegemen garrisoned across the forests. Our allies, the Huron, Ojibwa, Ottawa, Fox, Miamies, Delaware and Shawnee outnumber you! It's best for you to return to your own side of the mountains. This side of the Alleghenies belongs to us. General Legardeur will inform you the same. If you march past Le Boeuf, the forts on Lake Erie and elsewhere will block you. Your supply train will succumb to attack, and your soldiers will be butchered with hatchets. It is wiser to return now. You will only waste your time at Le Boeuf. Besides, you will need guides. Does your Mr. Gist know the way? I think not. If you insist, I will provide one. Come, let's drink more wine! It comes from Montreal and Quebec. True, not as sweet as wines from the Loire, or the warm vineyards of Bordeaux; nonetheless, it's good."

Washington feigned a stupor. He raised his tankard and sipped at the wine. On and on the officers bragged, laughed and drank. Finally, he staggered to his feet, smiled, waved a thankful hand, and hurried to his tent. He wanted to consult with Torn Ear and the other sachems, but snow was falling afresh and the night bitter with cold.

Early morning came in waves of heavy sleet. Snow mingled with an icy rain coated the tents. Joncaire sent an ensign to invite Langdon, Sir William and van Braam to the warmth of his quarters.

To Langdon's surprise, the chiefs were all in the cabin, drunk and heavy with sleep, having spent the night there.

"Joncaire hosted them last night after the Major left," whispered Gist. "I heard him come out and round up the sachems for tobacco, parley and rum. They ain't worth an asshole's kiss in the wind. Just wait and see."

Washington appeared alarmed, Tillson wary. Joncaire rose to his feet and paced the large room. Bright red flames blazed in the fireplace. The smell of bacon drifted across the room, redolent of hot tea and bread. The Frenchman paused with a knowing smile. "*Alors! Mes chèrs!* I trust you slept well! Torn Ear, you awaken, isn't that so? Nudge your sycophant chiefs. You have something to say? Is it black or white wampum? Your allies," he sneered toward Washington, "will soon be gone. Who will be your fathers then? Think! Have I not been your father across these years? Has my rod ever failed? Has my word once been crooked? Have I not always walked straight with you? Speak! Tell the English the truth! Who are your real fathers, and where are their loyal lodges, if not in Montreal and Quebec? Whose canoes have never failed you with bounty and good? White or black! Which wampum belts shall it be? My children, return home, and let us live in peace. Have you words of your own to say?"

Torn Ear looked down from where he squatted. So did Shinglis, White Thunder, and Monacatoocha. Washington stared at each. No one spoke.

"*Et bien!*" Joncaire addressed the Major. "You have your answer. My guide will lead you to Le Boeuf. You are free to leave whenever. The creek is impassable by canoe. You will have to break through the snow. Your horses will be close to useless. But, still, you should take them. It is less than fifty miles, but the ground is swampy and overflows with ice. Your servants may stay here until you return. The winter is harsh now. Your way back to Logstown, risky! Hear my word. Do not delay! *Savez-vous?*"

"Yes!" replied van Braam. "The Major understands."

Assembling his needed party, the Major chose Burke, Tillson and van Braam to accompany him. "Mr. Gist, I entrust the others and our horses to you. We will be swift, I assure you. Thank Captain Joncaire," the Major said sadly to van Braam. "We must trust him till we return." He glanced out the cabin's front window. Its panes of wavy blue glass ran streaked with water. The sleet had morphed into a heavy rain. The noisy downpour glistened with crystals of ice. The way to Le Boeuf would be miserable. "Gentlemen, let's go!"

For three days they sloshed through sleet and snow. Creeks over-flowed with run off; slick, rotting downfall reduced progress to a crawl. At night, the rivulets froze. Thick ice caused the horses' fetlocks to bleed. Without fire or hot food, they emerged on the banks of French Creek, opposite the fort. It was December 11th.

"At last!" sighed Tillson. "It's a formidable fort! I should build one so well! We must try to equal it at the forks of the rivers."

"We will have our chance," mused Washington, "as soon as we re-turn. I am confident Dinwiddie won't hesitate."

"Look!" pointed Langdon toward the bastion to the right of the gate. "It's François. We're in luck! The Captain and I know him. His wife's my wife's first cousin!"

"*Bonjour!*" Gabelle hailed from his post. "Messieurs, rest and enjoy some wine. Then we'll meet. We've known of your coming since you crossed the Potomac at Willis Creek." A sardonic frown spread faintly across François' face. It seemed to Langdon that it signaled a change of attitude, however slight. "Our winters are severe. *Non*? Nonetheless, *bi-envenue! Nous sommes prêt*! Our commandant will receive you soon. But, come now. It's too cold to banter like this."

Once inside the fort, Philippe turned to Langdon with an apologetic air. "You are in danger here. Yes. Not from us, but from Joncaire's half-breeds. When you leave, you must slip away. After your return to Ve-nango, we can't safeguard your flight home. And 'flight' it will be. Orders from Montreal call for an additional fort near Logstown and one between French Creek and there. As for Legardeur, he's a sterling careerist. He will welcome you with fulsome French courtesy. And so will I. Hélène longs to see you, as I myself. You and the Captain will stay with us, in our own quarters, but we must be *très, très* discreet. Your Major and his interpreter will room in separate quarters."

"What's he saying?" asked Tillson, equally happy, but disturbed by Philippe's whispering. Tillson extended his hand to de Robert, who shook it with polite courtesy.

"Welcome, *chèr anglais*," Philippe smiled, speaking in English. "You are free to roam about, my friend. We fear nothing here. This fort is not my design, but I built it with my own men, my liege officers and troops.

We are all very proud. Please, look around, all you wish. And come this way and settle in."

Hélène rose from her deerskin-covered stool with controlled emotion at the sight of Langdon. "Langdon!" she reached out for his hands. Her long black braids hung forward about her white shirt. "Tell me all about Louise! She has a baby, *non*? Boy or girl? Ours died!" she held her voice in check.

"I didn't know," replied Langdon.

"I see you are still tall and strong and ever the same. Isn't that so?" She studied him thoughtfully. "Sit and eat. The post butchered a steer from a herd brought down by the commandant himself. He's an elegant man. All military. You will see."

As evening drew near, fires blazed in all the hearths of the separate quarters, especially in the larger maison of the commandant's. His house was constructed of logs and stood two stories high, with stone fireplaces heating its rooms. Candles burned in lemon shapes from sconces on the walls. A large oak table dominated the central room; wooden armchairs sat in the corners. A fine tapestry hung above the fireplace. Cloth cushions covered the chairs. Decanters of wine, brandy and rum lined the mantle. Tall, grape-stemmed, silver goblets were arranged in a tray on the table. So too wedges of meat, cheese and honey-soaked squares of bread. The commandant rose to his feet as Langdon and the Major's party entered. Tillson had donned his red British jacket and fancy shabbot. Dinwiddie had ordered he look his best. Only one man was missing — van Braam. Upon arriving, he collapsed with fever. The fort's own doctor prescribed hot wine, blood letting and rest. Langdon would have to translate.

Whatever Langdon expected Legardeur to look like, the man before him was quite different. He had anticipated someone lean, pensive, modestly arrogant, if not mustached, and elegantly vested for the occasion. Instead, a rather diminutive, ruddy and friendly man shook his hand. His leggings were of leather and he wore a blue officer's jacket with gold braid on the shoulders. Around his neck hung the Cross of St. Louis.

"So you are the translator? *Oui*?" the commandant spoke. "I have heard of this communiqué. Gentlemen, sit down. What is it about? Captain Joncaire's runners mentioned only your Governor's concerns. And those in the broadest terms. I must know the specifics. Please, ask your Major to speak."

A young ensign came into the room and filled each man's goblet with wine or brandy, depending on which nod he received.

"*Monsieur!*" Legardeur repeated. "Please, speak," he addressed Washington.

The Major glanced at Langdon, then at Legardeur. "I am honored to meet you, sir, and see your Cross of St. Louis. I know of your service, thanks to Lieutenant de Robert's report, which he shared with our translator and Captain Tillson. The honorable Governor Robert Dinwiddie of King George's Virginia Colony and claimant of Ohio lands has sent me to know your designs of the same. Proprietors and high men of influence wish to survey, sell or purchase, and settle claims. We view the French presence with no small alarm. Since the founding of the Colony, the kings of England and the Lords Proprietors have considered Ohio as theirs. We wish to avoid conflict at all costs, but my orders, sir, are to ask you to leave. Indeed, inform you of Virginia's resolve to settle Ohio as early as spring. Governor Dinwiddie wishes you out."

Langdon held his breath. What an affront, to say the least. And to all people, this experienced commander of forces and places beyond the young Major's wildest guesses. He choked at the lump in his throat but translated Washington's ultimatum. He emphasized that it wasn't so much the young Major's wish, as the wish of his Governor and the British crown. He tried to soften it as best he could. He concluded with the words: "*Mon Général distingué*, I trust you understand the Crown's concerns and desire to avoid conflict."

The commandant smiled and let out a droll sigh. "At least he hasn't come to assassinate me. You know, I believe he would. He's not overly polished, is he? No wonder they sent him. A less wise or more experienced man would have deserted before now. I forgive him. What more can be said. No! Thank him and share with him my own ambivalence over unsettled lands. Emphasize, however, that my nation and sovereign have no intention of abandoning what is ours. The Ohio belongs to us. And so too its natives and furs, its vast riches and wealth of natural bounty. It is good he has come. Assure him of my own felicities. It is wise that his governor should know the truth. We have no intention of leaving."

Slowly and carefully, Langdon translated Legardeur's reply. "He has no intention of leaving, sir. It is we who must leave."

"The Governor's orders are by 'force of arms,' if necessary. Monsieur Legardeur must be told. I have no choice. It must be said."

Langdon turned toward Legrdeur. "My commandant, the Governor's orders call for armed escort, if it comes to that. It will mean war, a *guerre de sang*, I fear. Those are the words of the communiqué, again, not our own."

"I fully understand. My answer has to be 'No.' Please tell your Major he is welcome to stay as long as he likes. But prudence suggests you return soon. Once my superiors learn of this communiqué, no English will be safe west of the mountains. You understand, regrettably, I'm sure."

"Yes, sir. I will repeat your words and sympathies."

As Washington listened, his face turned ashen. The big fire's glow filled the room with soft ambience. "What do you think?" he asked Tillson. "Van Braam will need at least another day to recover. Perhaps you and Burke should return on your own. I'll need to regroup with Gist at Venango. It doesn't look good, does it?"

"Perhaps the commandant could provide a guide for Langdon and me to cross the Allegheny and slip back into Pennsylvania. We could wait for you at Willis Creek, or you for us, or on our own, dash back to Williamsburg."

The Major stared briefly at Legardeur and his Order of the Cross. "Mr. Burke, thank General Legardeur for his hospitality and diplomatic grace. Both have made my task easier to render. Please explain that we bear him no enmity and that we must be off as soon as van Braam recovers. That you and the Captain would like to leave by morning, if possible. Can he trust a guide to escort you across the Allegheny? Perhaps the river will be frozen. Tell him that I'll journey back to Venango, and from there to the Governor's Palace with his answer. Our task is finished here."

PART TWO

Dinwiddie's Gamble

1754-1755

Chapter Twelve

THE GOVERNOR'S BODY SAGGED heavily in his satin chair. His pudgy shoulders slumped forward. With disdain, he stared at the small tea stain on the lapel of his rouge silk jacket. Before him sat Captain Tillson and Major Washington. In his lap lay the Major's formal report, along with Legardeur's letter of rejection. The Honorable Dinwiddie knew enough French to decipher the commandant's closing terse remarks. "*Sous rein conditions voulions nous quitter nôtre grande rivière marchande. Jamais, Monsieur! Avec cela dite, veuillex croire, chèr Guoverneur, à mes sentiments les meillerus.* "I guess that means 'No,'" he mumbled. "The foreign minister's office has ordered new forts for the frontier. This site you describe at the forks of the rivers, will that do? Can one be built there as early as May? Perhaps the French will change their minds if we best them at their game."

"It's a remarkable location," confirmed Tillson. "I've been sketching a plan since our return. I was deeply impressed with Le Boeuf's fortifications and believe we can construct one even better – higher, with bigger and stronger blockhouses, and adequate ramps for cannon and riflemen. It's the perfect spot."

"Do you agree, Major?" Dinwiddie looked up with a slight tremor of his hands.

"By all means. In my judgment, the sooner the better. The French won't wait, if I've learned anything at all."

"Well! Tidy your affairs at Belvoir, young George, and I'll see that the

Assembly appropriates sufficient supplies for the task. Choose a score of able-bodied men, and you, Sir William, create a workable draft as soon as possible. In the meanwhile, I've already sent a party ahead to clear trees and set up a rudimentary fort. You must have missed each other in passing."

"Yes, sir!"

"'*With that said,*' to echo the good Monsieur," Dinwiddie smirked, "it's a miracle either of you survived. It must have been one hell of an ordeal. George, yours is all here in the report. The flight from Le Boeuf, the dash to Logstown! The weather! My God, did it ever stop snowing? I hear van Braam and Gist suffered frostbite! And the native who fired his musket at you! Thank heavens it was a French one! You should have killed him! Whatever, you're back! And now you know the odds, the path in and out, the river, and the Indians! Can they be trusted?"

"I wish I could vouch, 'Yes.' Only time will tell. I do think Half-King will ally with us. His Delaware have been attacked all too often by a Captain Philip Joncaire and his Algonquin and Huron butchers."

"And you, Tillson! How in thunder's name did you escape this Yellow Hawk you refer to? What a treacherous savage he must have been!" The Governor's lips quivered. "I should be as brave! You know, I've only been to the mountains once. That's when I quoted Spotswood's silly pronouncement: '*Sic jurat transcendere montes*': 'Thus he swears to cross the mountains.' The Duke of Haroldsford was with me, and I knew he'd report our activities to the king. How did you evade this Yellow Hawk?"

"Only by courage and force, both being Mr. Burke's. The Algonquin wanted my coat, my red jacket! We hadn't traveled more than three miles from the fort when he lunged ahead on his snowshoes, turned, pointed at me, and hurled his tomahawk toward Burke. Langdon anticipated his move and threw himself and his horse into the snow. I could have shot the savage, but Langdon tackled him and placed his knife at the Indian's throat. 'Give him your coat, your jacket,' Langdon yelled. 'Just give it to him! We'll strip him of weapons and send him back.' 'Hell, no!' I replied. 'Only over my dead body!' Langdon released him, crushed his snowshoes, and said something in French. Then he remounted and we plunged into the forest. In places, drifts were shoulder high. Icy streams trickled everywhere. In other places, we had to dismount and wade through ice-covered bogs. Downfall proved almost insurmountable. At times it towered forty feet over our heads. It took us a week to cross the mountains. By accident, we stumbled onto the headwaters of a swift creek, and followed it back to the Monongahela. That night we met up with the original party, but George and Mr. Gist had already gone ahead. In hindsight, we were as lucky as the Major."

"Well, I'm sending you back. Major Washington, I'm promoting you to Lt. Colonel. You'll have to raise a militia. The men will have to provide their own arms, clothing and horses. I'll act as swiftly as possible. In fact, the Assembly has already appropriated 50 pounds sterling for personal expenses you've heretofore expended. I know! Parsimonious indeed! But better than nothing! I will impose myself on Carter and the others to help, whether they want to or not. If we lose the Ohio, we lose our investment, anyway." He paused and brushed crumbs off his jacket. His jowls appeared enlarged. "The only problem with silk," he muttered, "is it stains! In any case, Gentlemen, as soon as you've raised your army, George, march it immediately to the camp. And Captain Tillson, upon his notice, join him with due haste. By mid-April, I want both of you in place."

It was already April 5, so little time remained. Tillson longed to visit Anna, to steal up her staircase once more before departing to rendezvous with Washington. Yet, he wanted to race to Burke's cabin, to … to embrace Sarah, too. Would he have time for both? Anna promised everything an English Lord could desire: lands, beauty, servants, lineage, elegance, wealth, sophistication, loyalty, and a lady's proclivity for entertainment and banter. On the other hand, Sarah could offer none of that, save everything an officer of the field could crave: from her natural beauty, to her inner strength and poise, to her courage and fearlessness, candor and tenderness. It all sparkled in her eyes. Anna would probably tolerate adultery; perhaps even Sarah! He would court each and risk the gossip incurred. Such depravity startled his heart.

On that same day, Captain François-Philippe de Robert stood on the bow of the fifth bateau in line and glanced back at the others. Under the command of Claude-Pierre Pecaudy de Contrecoeur, Captain Louis Coulon, Sieur de Villers, his younger brother Ensign Joseph Coulon, and dozens of other officers, the massive armada of sixty boats and two hundred canoes headed steadily for the forks of the Ohio. François felt elated to be part of it. They numbered a fighting force of six hundred liegemen and two hundred Indians. Within less than three days, they had journeyed down the Allegheny from Venango and would soon disembark at the Forks. With them were engineers, stonemasons, carpenters and smithies, all under command to construct a fort twice the size of Le Boeuf. It would include high bastions for cannon and mortars and rifle slips for over two hundred marksmen. Except for the Half-King, most Delaware and Shawnee chiefs had raised their hatchets with them. Only Torn Ear threatened opposition. Joncaire's harassing tactics had outraged the old chief. "I will fling my black belt at his feet," the proud Delaware had proclaimed.

Ensign Coulon sat beside François on a bale of tents and fur skins. Kegs of powder and dry goods lay stacked in the center on the bateau's deck. Oarsmen guided the barge-like vessel through the tumbling waters. Indians struggled to pass them in canoes.

"Do you think our plan will work?" the young Ensign asked François. "You know these savages better than I. Will the English listen or fall back?" The short, black-haired man puffed on a clay pipe and stared wildly at the river. "I've grown too used to amenities in Montreal, I fear," he smiled. "And my papers, these official documents," he thumped his chest, "will they impress anyone, least of all Dinwiddie?"

"I've never met him," Gabelle replied. "Only the envoy he sent to Le Boeuf. The latter was a Major, tall, broad-shouldered, a rugged surveyor of the backwoods, yet the Governor's pick for so delicate a mission. *Incredible!* To think they could order us off the river!"

"Ah!" Coulon iterated. "Quite cocky, according to Legardeur. We will have to put him in his place."

"I suppose so," François half answered, his mind elsewhere, his heart cradled in the hands and warm lap of Hélène. Once more, she was pregnant. Would their baby live this time? Would it be a boy or girl? Did it even matter? Should he marry her? Should he one day return to France? Would she consent to accompany him? But why would he do that? Save for his uncle, what family was there to embrace her? He winced. No. Better to remain in New France, to cast his lot somewhere out here, among the hills that bordered the river: so rich in timber and furs, beauty and promise. Perhaps, if he failed to rise to *intendent*, his superiors would promote him to colonel. Or perhaps he might be transferred to the lakes of Wisconsin, travel inland like Legardeur, become an agent of Indian affairs, or a wealthy entrepreneur. "That the English actually think this region is theirs still mystifies me," he said to Coulon. "Incidentally, how well does your brother know the Marquis? After this mission, I'd prefer to see action on the lakes in the interior."

"Quite well! Duquesne has His Majesty's ear. My brother and I were at Versailles when the Duke of Chautange introduced him and us. 'My Excellency, permit me to present Sieur Ange du Quesne de Menneville, his Captain, Sieur Louis Coulon – just retuned from Montreal – and his brother, Joseph.' It was all quite affected, superfluous, if not bittersweet. One would think to meet the King an incomparable honor. But after weathering the crossing and fighting beside my brother in the woods of the Adirondacks, a man of powdered wig and flesh, vested in a blue and gold jacket, sporting rings of garnet and ruby, sickens a *vrai* man's heart." He looked up sadly. "Please don't share that! *Compris!*"

"Your sentiments are safe. As a child, I was told I met the king, but I have no memory of it. If I may paraphrase a new writer I've discovered – a Frenchman by the name of Rousseau – 'virtue never appears amid pomp,' he writes. 'Clothes may indicate an opulent man, but a healthy and robust one is recognized by his strength and vigor. He's like a wrestler who fights naked!' Will this Duquesne make a wise Governor?"

"Beyond doubt. His plans for the new fort are without parallel. The instant he arrived, he ordered its construction and assigned me to notify the British once we disembark. Will you and Yellow Hawk escort me to the place called Willis Creek?"

"Of course," said François. "If we are fortunate enough to be ordered. I know of this place, Willis Creek. It lies beyond the mountains and connects with the Potomac. From that point, runners can make it to Williamsburg in a week, they say."

"*C'est bon!* I'll be glad when we get off this boat!"

"I too," Philippe replied. Just then he reached into his leather pouch, opened the brass cover of his compass, and peered at its hands. Its eight compass points still fascinated him. Its maker had decorated each with a celestial design – from the five innermost planets to the sun and moon. The North needle resembled a gold *fleur de lis* in honor of the French monarchy. His father had presented it to him on his eighth birthday, two years before the elder de Robert was killed in a carriage accident. Although his father had never made the crossing to New France, stylized maps of North America hug in the hallways of his hunting lodge and above his favorite fireplace. Without saying anything to Coulon, François rubbed the crystal surface of the compass and closed its lid.

Tillson paused on the steps of Anna's gazebo to kiss her one last time. Pendants of purple wisteria fell about their shoulders and torsos. Her warm lips, arms and body aroused him with unmatched passion. To break the embrace struck him as a cruelty, undeserving of such a lover's innocence. "Anna, I do love you!" he whispered. "I hate to leave you like this. I am never my own free person, you know, as long as I serve the Crown."

"I know," she kissed him. "I shall await your return with longing."

"I will be back." With reluctance, he slipped out of her arms and, mounting his horse, trotted slowly down the shell-crushed lane. He glanced back to return her wave with his own. He did love her, he told himself. What man wouldn't?

His arrival at Langdon's cabin took Sarah totally by surprise. She was putting out laundry to dry in the warm April air. The wind tugged gently at her auburn strands, and her tanned face glowed with sunlight and vigor. A white cotton apron covered the front of her hemp-colored dress. A curve of her rounded breasts peeked lustily from the apron's top loop. "William!" she exclaimed excitedly. "How wonderful to see you! You're just what we need. Langdon's been gone a week. And there's chores a plenty for all to do. You do work?" she asked with a broad smile, filled with a woman's invitation to seek more.

"For you, Yes. But for you only," he laughed, as he dismounted. "Where's Langdon, anyway? Hunting, I suppose."

"How I wish!" she replied, as she pinned a last shirt to the clothesline. She dried her hands on her apron and approached him slowly. Her eyes glistened with inimical fire. "He's off north, helping the Colonel raise a militia. Washington sent a runner here and wouldn't accept a 'No.' So, off he galloped. I suppose you're on your way, too."

Tillson walked toward her, his eyes bright, measuring her from head to toe. Without hesitation, he bent forward, took her hand in his, and kissed it. Then he drew her toward him and held her against his chest. Sarah's arms clasped his shoulders and her hands felt for his neck. Their mouths met and lips kissed. "Forgive me, but I've been wanting to do that since I met you, when you scolded me at the barn," he laughed.

She smiled and kissed him again. "It took you long enough," she teased. "Tie up your horse and come in. Supper will be ready soon. Tell me about yourself. Langdon only said you both had a close call. That was all."

Inside the warm cabin, Tillson hugged Louise, her baby, and shook Jonathan's hand. "I always seem in transit," he began. "Always passing through. I realize one day you'll be gone, across the mountains to your grant along the Holston. I'll have to journey there just to see you. Perhaps, I'll be assigned to build a fort."

"That would be something," chuckled Jonathan. "I'd love to fight Indians like you and Langdon, if it weren't for my limp."

"Don't be so hasty!" William answered. "I fear a grave war is approaching. You at the frontier are most exposed. The French are amassing a great army and will no doubt unleash their savage brigades all along the border. You should be safe here."

"Can you stay awhile? A day or two?" asked Sarah. "We need to mend the barn, search for a missing ewe, and restock the woodpile. Let me see those hands!" said Sarah. "Look how calloused, scarred and harden mine are!"

"Not al all," Tillson responded. "Here, look at mine! They're the perfect match for yours! I've never beheld lovelier hands on a woman!"

"Ah, *bon Dieu!*' laughed Louise. "I thought only Frenchmen were charming liars! But the gallant Captain, I see, also knows the art. *Non?*"

"Two days!" promised William. "I'll stay two days, then I must be off! Who knows what awaits any of us! I am fearful and proud, all at the same time."

That night he slept on a straw-stuffed mattress in front of the dark orange flames of the fireplace. Sarah lay beside him. He held her hands and placed his arms around her. The room glowed amber from the warm soft radiance cast by the hot embers of the hearth. As the night deepened, they lay together, her back against his chest, his arm about her waist. For the next two days he busied himself with chores assigned by Sarah and Jonathan, to indulge again in evenings of bliss beside Sarah. The third day he rose, kissed her goodbye, and rode north for the Potomac. Sarah, Jonathan and Louise, with Helen Marie in her arms, stood in the yard and watched until horse and rider disappeared. Rain clouds rumbled across the Blue Ridge. Lightning flashed amid the thunder. It was time to go in.

Chapter Thirteen

ANGDON WATCHED FROM THE BANKS of Turtle Creek as men and supplies crossed the rising Potomac. Barge after barge ferried men and horses, wagons and goods, load after load, across the turbulent river. It had not ceased raining for four days. All told, Langdon counted thirty wagons, three cannon, and one hundred fifty-nine men, the sum total of Washington's militia. Langdon had recruited many of them himself. None wore uniforms. All shouldered their own rifles or flintlocks. Less than a dozen tents had been procured to shelter them. Only a score owned horses. Three teams of oxen had been driven up from Winchester to pull the cannon. A fourth team had drowned in the Shenandoah River during a flash flood.

Somewhere among the clammering throng was Tillson. But where? Langdon chaffed to recognize only three British officers, none of whom knew of the Captain's whereabouts, nor seemed to respect the Colonel, whose aides-de-camp the Governor had assigned them to be. Washington would have to command the group entirely on his own. The English officers saw themselves only as the King's observers.

As Langdon made his way through the pack of grumbling militia, he spotted Gist and others he remembered from the trek to Ft. Le Boeuf. They acknowledged each other with nods and waited for the Colonel to announce his orders. Seconds in command formed the groups of trappers and farmers into a semblance of an army. Washington approached on his horse, stopped in front of them, and signaled for the squads to stand at ease. "Gentlemen, we are under supplied, out-gunned, and out-numbered. The danger is imminent, but our duty is clear. At the forks of the Ohio, the French have assembled an army of eight hundred or more. Their purpose? To steal our future and unleash their Shawnee and Huron allies to attack and raid our homes. Our task is to stop them! Before us lie two hundred miles of pathless wilderness, with only an Indian trail or two to guide us. Mr. Gist, myself, Mr. Burke here," he pointed to Langdon, "and Captain Tillson," he raised his voice as the mounted officer rode through the ranks toward him, "have been there. All of you have lived in the woods most of your lives. We are taught to be loners, to endure silence, cold and hunger. But from this moment forward, we must act as one. The enemies' scouts will know of our coming, long before we arrive. Our own scouts will locate their camps in time. You must march with caution, obey your orders, listen and report anything unusual, and refrain from wandering off. Are you up for the task or not? Are you ready to march? Are you ready to fight if needs be? Are you ready to take the forks of the Ohio? If so, then let me hear it! Let me hear it, militia! Let me hear it for your homes and colony!"

Washington's words roused the assemblage of men and they lifted their voices and cheered for the cause of colony and home.

"Then prepare to march toward the mountains. Tonight we'll camp at their feet. Everyone with an axe, to the front! You with wagons and cannon, form a line!"

Tillson smiled and nudged his mount toward Langdon. "I believe this time it's for real! What do you think?"

"Pray that Yellow Hawk isn't among them!" he replied, restraining a smile. "If he is, I fear François will not be far behind. Engagements on paper are one thing. In reality, someone always gets hurt."

"I promise if I see the Captain, I won't fire."

"Nor I. But Yellow Hawk's a different matter."

"Indeed! He is!"

From April 18 to 20, the long, sometimes aimless, column worked its way slowly through the forest, through squalls of rain and hub-deep mud, crushing the tender may apples and blooming trillium beneath their feet. Langdon bent down to pick up a purple, green and white blos-

som and turn it in his fingers. How he wanted just then to gather a bas-
ketful for Louise and Baby Helen! On into the mountains they slogged,
up its ridges and through its gaps, dense with vegetation and profuse
wild flowers.

On the 21st, a runner overtook them. "A company of British Regular's a comin', sir!" he reported to Washington. "From South Carolina,
they are, under the command of a Captain James Mackay," he saluted
the Colonel before shrinking away. Washington returned the gesture and
waited with his exhausted militia for the Regulars' coats to appear. To
Washington's consternation, they marched in, four-abreast, to the rattle
of drums and the clank of harnesses and swords. Behind them lowed a
small herd of cattle. Tillson mounted his horse and trotted down the lane
to greet their commander.

"You're a glorious, welcomed sight!" he addressed Mackay. "We're all
at the point of fatigue. What a relief to see you!"

"Aye! And we you!" replied the erect Scotsman. "I'll be command,
now. No offense, sir, but your men will take orders from me. And you,
as well! My men are weary, too. If your Colonel is here, please summon
him forward."

"With all due respect, sir, the Colonel commands the militia. The Governor himself commissioned him. I serve as a liaison under him."

"Look about you!" Mackay leaned forward in his saddle. "You call *this*
an army," he whispered, nodding toward the mud-caked, leather-shirted
men before him. "I outrank the Colonel, whether he likes it or not."

"I wouldn't be too hasty, Captain," Tillson replied in a whisper of his
own, "as I hold the same rank, too. Our units need to support each other,
not quarrel over crown indignities!"

Mackay glanced about the foul-smelling dirty lot of the militia. Resentment burned in their eyes. They had stopped to rest beside their axes,
which were black with mud and slick with leaf litter. A horde of uncouth
drunkards, Mackay thought. But, perhaps the Captain was right. He
could see the Colonel approaching on his mount.

"I'm Lieutenant Colonel Washington," the proud Virginian stated.
"Your men are a welcome addition. Our march has been laborious and
difficult, as you can see."

"As a Regular officer, sir, I outrank you, Colonel," Mackay greeted him. "But I view it best for us to command our own *troops*," he offered, with a pejorative edge on the word *troops*. "Incidentally, you are no longer 'Lieutenant Colonel.' I am pleased to report that your Governor has promoted you to 'Colonel.' Our men will keep separate camps, as we do not dig roads or engage in manual activities. We, sir, are a fighting force and maintain the strictest of British discipline. You might bear that in mind with your own men, if I may offer a suggestion."

Washington's face flushed with anger, but he held his temper. What a hell of a way to be greeted as "Colonel!" As he sat on his horse, he took pleasure in looking down at the stocky Scotsman. Why did the colonies tolerate such insolent arrogant behavior? When it came to engaging danger, no Regular could best a frontiersman and his rifle! "*Colonel*! You say! I like the sound of it. Don't you? I'll take it over *Captain* any day!" he smiled. With a flick of his reins, he turned his horse about to face Sir William. "Colonel Washington!" he repeated to Tillson. "I've just been promoted to Colonel! What about that!"

Tillson suddenly wheeled his own mount about. "Let's hear it for the Colonel!" he shouted. "He's been promoted to Colonel!" he bellowed for all to hear. He smiled and waved his black hat. "Well! What are we waiting for?"

The long line of militia relaxed their grip on the axes. Some raised their rifles and fired! "Hooray! Hooray for the Colonel! We'll be damned, if it's not, Hooray!"

Thus resumed the march of the two separate "armies," one tired and filthy from hacking its way through the forest, the other composed in regimental glory, clad in scarlet and flour-white trousers.

Finally, on the day of the 25th, the two columns came within sight of a large clearing where Indians had burned the land for hunting purposes. A small encampment of riflemen had pitched a tent on the edge of the meadow.

Gist rode ahead at a gallop. Washington turned toward Langdon and pointed toward the leader. "That's Ensign Ward! Head of the garrison the Governor sent to the Forks a month ago. The French must have driven them out! I don't like what I see."

Mackay rode up beside them and joined the small party.

"Yes, sir!" the young ensign acknowledged. "Just a week ago we awoke to a river filled with boats, maybe a hundred or more, and hundreds and hundreds of canoes. Soldiers and Indians swarmed ashore, along with a bevy of officers. Oh, they were quite a sight! Bearing their colors and marching to drum rolls! I expected to be dead within the hour. But, their commander, a Captain Pecaudy de Contrecoeur, called for my presence and offered us terms of surrender. Sir, we hated to lose our fort, if you can call it that. And the surrender terms were all in their favor. 'You may keep your arms and lives,' was all a polite Captain promised us. He said his name was de Robert! Sir! We didn't wish any discord. They gave us three hours to depart. We were out in two."

"Disgusting!" blurted, Mackay, as he turned his horse about to rejoin his unit.

"I can't fault you," said Washington. "We're not to spill blood unless we have to. Were any chiefs with them? Delaware in particular?"

"Yes and no! Two chiefs Shinglis and Monacatoocha have taken up arms with them, but not the Half-King. Two of Torn Ear's braves are with us now. They bear you a string of wampum and a message from Half-King."

"Bring them here," ordered the Colonel. "Mr. Burke, if they speak French, will you translate for me? Van Braam won't be along for a while."

"Yes, sir!"

"Mr. Gist, take the lead if they speak their own tongue. Bring them up."

The riders dismounted and stood beside their horses. Behind them, the long line of militia began filing into the clearing. Muddy, tired, and hungry, they welcomed the unexpected pause. Mackay's Regulars filed out in a formation of their own. Two braves came forward. Washington sat on the ground, near a fire that Ward's men had built. Langdon, Burke, Gist and others sat with them. The Colonel nodded for the Indians to speak.

Langdon recognized one of the youths as Torn Ear's grandson. The lean brave presented a shiny belt of white shells to the Colonel. The youth had painted his face red and white on one side, black and yellow on the other. He had decorated himself for war. For scalps!

"Chief Torn Ear is glad you have come," the youth said in good English. "He welcomes his English brothers. He feared you wouldn't. He shakes his fist at the French. Twenty of us are following the French. They are coming for you. We know where they hide. Come with us to lift our hatchets together. Hear now Torn Ear's own words: 'Do you come or not? If not, we give white belts to French. They are many; we are fearful. How will our English Fathers respond? If you do not come, I think we will never meet again.'"

"Give me a moment," the Colonel replied. Quickly he turned to those at his side. "We can't afford to dismiss this offer. Perhaps with their help we can surprise these ambushers. What's your view?"

"I'd be cautious," warned Gist. "It could be a trap. Though, the Half-King ain't never betrayed a word with me. Ask how far the chief's waiting."

"Where is our red brother?" Washington asked. "We will follow you to spring our own trap?"

"Good!" replied the young brave. "We are two nights away. We will wait for you at the creek that runs red, the one the traders call, 'Redstone.'"

"I know where that is," said Gist. "It's about thirty-to-forty miles southeast of the Forks, along the Monongahela. The Frenchies' trap must lie near there. Still, I'd be careful."

"Tell the Half-King not to despair. We're coming. Tell him our hearts burn with affection for our forest allies. Give us three days," the Colonel motioned, holding up three fingers. "Three days!"

"Good! Three days! At Redstone we will wait. But only three days. Who knows what the Frenchmen will do? My great-father chief has many wigwams to think of."

Washington nodded his understanding. "Tell him his English brother's words are straight. That behind us, many warriors are coming. We will regain the Forks for his people and wigwams! Our English troops will bring great guns and more warriors. Already you see their coats behind us. Your interests are as dear to us as our lives. I give you my pledge of honor and we to you our own belt of wampum," he gestured for Gist to present one to them.

That night, Washington shared with Mackay the Indians' report, but the proud Scotsman seemed indifferent. "We will know what to do, when the time comes," was all he said.

Early the next morning, Gist led the combined parties cautiously down a rocky ridge, thick with glossy laurel, to emerge on the banks of the Youghiogheny. Roiling gray water swept over hidden boulders and lapped menacingly at the wild banks. The men, horses and oxen, even Mackay's cattle, sought shelter under the wet hemlocks and white syca-mores and waited for the water to abate. At last, they crossed the river. "This way!" Washington called, as he marched his troops, with Mackay's following, in the direction of the Great Meadows. There, at last, they made camp.

Darkness crept silently over the field. The rain ceased. A wispy streak of purple clouds glowed with effulgence, as the sun's soft disc sank into the ridgelines of distant black trees. "Keep your fires low," Gist ordered Washington's men. "We are not that far from the Redstone. Be alert! Sleep with your flintlock at the ready."

Washington's men lay down, some in their muddy tents, most on the soggy ground. Rain began to fall again. Miserable, wet, and cold, the men curled under their dank blankets and prayed for dawn. On the edge of the clearing, Mackay's white tents glinted in the downpour. A lone whippoorwill's monotonous cry punctuated the patter of the heavy rain. Wolves howled in the inky distance. Heavier and heavier the rain fell. Suddenly, shots rang out! Men sprang to their feet, their arms in hand. Someone was approaching the camp. It was Torn Ear's grandson. Water glistened on his naked torso; feathers in his shock of upright hair loomed white in the falling rain. He held his right hand erect for attention. Washington saw him and motioned for him to come to his side. "Gist, get here! Find out what's happened. Torn Ear must be near!"

"Yes," said the youth in a sudden deep voice. "Come. The French are here. My grandfather calls you. He knows the way. We must be there by morning. Many men. Fifty soldiers. They are hiding in ravines. Come!"

"Burke, Tillson, select your best company and follow me into the woods," Washington ordered. "Go!" he said to the young brave. "Stay before us, just within sight."

Silently, Langdon and Tillson assembled four squads and sent them after the Colonel. "Captain White!" Tillson called to Washington's youngest officer. "You are in command until we return."

Langdon nodded for Tillson to move forward. "I'll bring up the rear," he whispered.

For thirty minutes or more, the shadows of Washington's squads moved through the black forest. Thunder rumbled. Crackling shafts of lightning illuminated the rocky shelves and ridges around them. They crossed a creek, descended a ravine, and followed the young brave into a copse of tall beech trees. There, under the bark of a leaking lean-to sat Torn Ear. A score of braves surrounded him.

The chief rose to greet Washington. "It is good you come. Three miles in darkness, fifty Frenchmen lie in wait. They crouch in forest like panthers, stalking prey. We have found their footprints in the grass. Their trail is fresh. Follow us. By morning, we shall strike. Is my young English brother with me?"

"Yes. Lead us there that I might see. Then we can hold council."

The Half-King's warriors slipped into the darkness with him. His grandson beckoned for Washington's forces to follow. Rain soaked and cold, Washington waved for each squad to move forward. Just as dawn began to fill the sky with a thin slit of yellow, Torn Ear signaled for all to stop. He waved for Washington to join him. Langdon and Tillson crouched in wait. The chief pointed toward a hollow depression in the forest, encircled by rocks and ferns. The smell of wood smoke drifted in the morning air. An owl hooted somewhere in the deep woods. Langdon could hear its wingbeats as it took to flight. "There! There they hide to strike. My braves are ready. Many scalps ache in their hearts. The time for blood has come."

Washington glanced uneasily toward Langdon. His orders were not to attack but to fight defensively only. Yet, if the French were hiding in ambush, was he not justified in striking first? He looked toward Tillson. Tillson understood his dilemma. He too understood the diplomacy of the wilderness. A plan had to be offered. "Colonel, why not divide our forces into two units. We can come in from both sides. Torn Ear can close the gap at the rear. As we sweep in, they will fall back toward him. If they don't fire at us, we can take them captive."

Langdon could tell that the Colonel liked the idea. "Explain it to the chief," Washington instructed him.

Langdon knelt on the forest floor, swept aside soggy debris, and drew a sketch for Torn Ear. "*Ici.* Here is where your braves will stand. *Compris?* When you hear us fire, block their escape."

The Half-King nodded with sufficient comprehension. His jaw stiffened. He raised his arm and snuck with his braves into the trees beyond the depression. Washington divided his men, two squads to encircle the camp to the east, two to the south. Torn Ear's braves would come in from the north. The forest grew lighter; the citron hue of dawn spread across the rocky glen before them. Patches of mist rose as the sun's first rays struck the wet foliage. The fresh air of the morning wafted gently. The odor of forest humus drifted up. Washington waited and looked toward the sky. "Up!" he ordered the men beside him. "Up, surround the sides of their encampment! Now!" he shouted. Up they rose, running through the rocks and ferns. Over the leaf-covered ground they sprang toward the encampment below. A crackling volley of musketry belched from the Frenchmen's guns. Tillson's men fired in return. Clouds of smoke engulfed the combatants. Cries of the wounded rose above the clamor. Torn Ear's Indians' shrieks mingled with the clatter of arms. The Half-King's warriors were taking scalps. Crumpled before Washington in the wooded depression lay a half-dozen dying or dead Frenchmen. As the smoke cleared, a panic seized the remaining liegemen. They threw down their arms and ran toward their captors: some toward Tillson, visible and tall in his scarlet coat; others toward Gist and the Colonel. Torn Ear's Delaware's descended on the wounded, clubbing and ripping off scalps and filling the air with hideous whoops. "Stop, stop!" Washington waved his arms. But the frenzy of killing went on. "Quickly, get behind us!" Washington ordered the captives. "What a senseless slaughter!" he groaned, fearful now that his Delaware allies could not be stayed until the fallen were mutilated. With revulsion, he watched as Torn Ear hacked a Frenchman's skull open and bathed his hands in its victim's brains.

123

By midmorning, the skirmish was over. As the smoke and fog cleared, Langdon looked down to behold the bloodied head of François, who knelt mortified beside the corpse of the officer Torn Ear had killed. Beside him crouched Yellow Hawk, nursing a wound to his left arm. He cupped his right hand over the gash. The savage glared at Langdon! With contempt, he spat at Tillson. The Half-King approached, but when he recognized him, he turned away.

"*Vous idiots!*" François exclaimed with venom in his eyes. "You have killed our envoy, Ensign Coulon. He was bringing you *rien* but news of our capture of the Forks." Suddenly, François recognized the woodsman before him. "Langdon, is that you? Tell your Monsieur Washington that he has *assassiné* le Sieur de Jumonville, the Marquis du Quesne's ambassador to his own Governor!"

Langdon did not know what to say.

"You have violated the rules of diplomacy," Philippe continued. "Not since the Treaty of Aix-la-Chapelle, has anyone fired on an envoy! I am sorry it is you, Langdon. How are you part of this? It is bitter to meet like this."

Langdon knelt beside him. In shock and with sorrow, he sought to console François, but the latter would not be comforted. It was not an *assassination*, Langdon told himself. How could he think that? "François! It is I who am sorry! Here, let me bind your wound."

"No! I will wrap it myself."

"Captain, please! It is I, Langdon. Have you forgotten so readily? Please! What will Louise think? Or Hélène?"

"Louise? She left us for you! Have you forgotten? It is different, now. Go! Please! That is all I ask."

Langdon struggled to his feet. He placed his hand beside his mouth and whispered in Washington's ear. "We should let him go, along with his Indian. The gesture may well save our lives."

The Colonel stared down at the Captain and recognized him. In truth, he was dazed himself. What should he say? "Please stand, sir, and listen to me. I'm going to release you and your savage! Take your ensign's body back to the Forks. We didn't want this encounter, either. I too am under orders. Surely you can appreciate our claim to the Ohio." He stared again at the Frenchman briefly; then walked away with a heavy slump of his shoulders. He knew the French would counterattack. He had to think clearly. He had to let this pass and find a location to fortify. Should he proceed to the Redstone or fall back to the Great Meadows? Mackay would have to rally to his side, British pride, notwithstanding!

Chapter Fourteen

THE REPORT OF WASHINGTON'S "victory" both pleased and annoyed the Governor. As he paced his office, he stopped momentarily to focus on the map Washington had sketched earlier. He ran his fingers across the brown parchment, pausing to press down on the inked-in letters "Forks of the Ohio," "Turtle Creek," "Allegheny River," and "Ft. Le Boeuf." All so distant, yet so close! So many dreams of expansion and wealth hanging in the balance. What annoyed him, however, was the loss of the Forks and the garrison Tillson was to have built. That was their gateway to the Ohio. Now the Company would have to forfeit its claims, if not reimburse angry investors. Already they owed three thousand pounds sterling to creditors in England. Moreover, he'd have to requisition additional supplies for his Colonel, and somehow rush them off before the French realized how vulnerable he was. It galled him, too, that Mackay had allowed his Scottish pride to imperil the situation. But the Colonel's insistence on being the warrior's equal was idiocy. The Regular Army fought Britain's battles; the militia's role was purely one of exigency. Nothing more! He took a deep breath, called for his servant to bring him more wine, and sat somberly at his desk.

"Your wine, sir," the black man bowed. He placed the decanter of claret in front of the unshaven Governor, poured him a glass, and backed slowly away.

Dinwiddie raised the top to his walnut desk and procured a piece of paper. He laid it on the desk's surface and smoothed it out. He dipped his quill in ink, and began to write:

My dear Colonel Washington! You have launched us into a war. The French captives you delivered to Winchester insist you fired first. My orders were to take the Forks and construct a garrison. Still, I understand your decision to defend yourself against ambush. The Crown cannot fault that. Now, however, I am obliged to explain your behavior, or lack of experience, to the foreign ministry's office. This, I do not relish. Nor do I wish to receive further complaints of disparity between Captain Mackay's Regulars and your "brave, deserving" militiamen. An army proves its valor by overcoming obstacles and hardships, not by whining about salaries and supplies. You have lead and iron bars in your supply wagons. You left with a sufficient quantity. Do what armies do in campaigns far from home. Forge your own weapons. Repair your own carts. Live off the land. Take full command of responsibilities. Come back victorious. Do not lose another "fort." Everything depends on you. I am confident you will prevail. Now enough of this matter! We are all servants of the King.
Yours sincerely, the Honorable Robert Dinwiddie, Lieutenant Governor of the Colony of Virginia, this day of our Lord, May 12th, 1754.

The Governor placed the quill back in its stand, folded the letter, and sealed it with a drop of hot wax and the press of his stamp. "There!" he muttered. Now it was time for him to shave and prepare for the ride to Lady Ashby's!

The fragrance of magnolia and honeysuckle sweetened the air with a pungency that only spring afforded. Ducks settled on the river. A pair of tame geese strutted on the lawn of Anna's great yard. A young doe and her fawn bounded off as carriages arrived for the occasion. Two riders emerged on the edge of the estate. They paused to rest their steeds before trotting up the oyster-shell drive. A footman greeted them with a smile and helped the lady dismount. "Welcome, Miz Burke. Miz Anna says you was comin'. I knowed it was you from her description. She's waiting inside."

Tall amber tappers burned brightly in Anna's hall and dining room. A young black boy waved a peacock fan over the silver bowl of strawberry punch to shoo flies away. The Governor and members of the Assembly, along with investors of the Ohio Company, ambled about the table.

"The news is not good," shared the Governor. "It fills me with both despair and elation."

"True!" replied Carter Wright, "but the Colonel did hold his own against the attackers. He's a tough entity, I tell you."

"That's the problem. Just who was attacking whom?"

Anna fanned herself nervously while waiting in the hallway. She had invited Sarah, too, but felt an air of relief when only Louise and Langdon's brother entered. "I am so pleased you could come. I have reserved a room for you upstairs." She stepped toward Louise and kissed her cheek. Jonathan cleared his throat and bowed slightly. "And how is your sister?" she addressed him with a look of uncertainty.

"She remained at home, with baby Helen. It is kind of you to ask."

"Goodness! I trust they'll be fine. I can only imagine life on the frontier, with all its isolation and hardships! But I wanted you to come. The Governor says Colonel Washington's letter mentions your husband," she smiled at Louise, "and even the gallant Sir William! He received it a week ago, and I wanted you to know. They are both well. Isn't that wonderful in so desperate a time!"

Louise brushed back a strand of her long brown hair and feigned a smile in return. Her large oval eyes concealed her concern both for Langdon and for Sarah. "Yes! We too have worried and were horrified when we learned of the prisoners taken to Winchester. I have a cousin whose husband we fear is with them. He's a French officer, and we care for him as much as for our militia."

"Well, the Governor's right here, and it won't hurt to ask him, provided we can tear him away from his pastime," she smiled. "Young Sir, would you mind asking his Honor to favor us with his presence?"

Jonathan nodded and approached the Governor. He felt unequal to the task, though he was dressed in his best backcountry brown jacket, white shirt, dark breeches, black hose and black shoes. On the other hand, the Governor sported a silky cream frock, ruffled cravat and silky cream hose. Even his high red heels intimidated Jonathan. Still, Jonathan felt of sufficient gentry to approach any British dignitary. Was he not Virginia born and Virginia reared? Once established on their estate, he and Langdon would both be eligible to stand for office.

Anna watched him as he stepped up to whisper in the Governor's ear. The paunchy man raised his head and stared strangely at both her and Louise. Immediately, a thin smile broke across his lips. He excused himself from his group and came toward them.

"I do not believe I have had the honor of an introduction," he stated, eyeing Louise. "You are as fair as the fairest," he bowed. "How may I help you?"

"Your Honor, my husband, Langdon Burke, is with your forces on the Ohio. We know he's safe, under the Colonel's vigilance. But I have a French cousin whose husband is an officer in the region, and I fear to know if he's among the prisoners at Winchester."

"Do you know his name, my charming dear? I should certainly want to relieve your anxiety."

"A Lieutenant de Robert, François-Philippe Gabelle. He may be a Captain by now."

"Ah! You know the man! Yes? Or no! He's not among the prisoners. How quaint that you ask! The Colonel actually mentions him. He was captured but released. It was his sad duty to return a fallen comrade to their Fort. A miserable mishap! A terrible debacle for us! You can rest assure the man's all right! But who knows where it will lead."

"And Captain Tillson, how is he?"

"Ho! I wish I knew! But from Washington's report, he's a valuable asset to the Colonel. Along with your Langdon! Really, my dear, I wouldn't worry. They are seasoned soldiers and quite capable of caring for themselves. Now, if you will excuse me," he glanced back restlessly toward Carter and other members of the Company. "My Lady," he addressed Anna, "it is always a pleasure to attend your functions. I do wish Lord Dunswell were still with us." He bowed courteously and returned to his knot of planter friends.

Langdon did not appreciate Torn Ear's attitude toward the Colonel, but Washington appeared to be letting the insults slide, or perhaps was too preoccupied with the potential of a counterattack to take offense. After all, he needed the chief and every Indian ally Half-King could muster.

"Why did my English brother scold his Delaware chief?" Torn Ear demanded. "Did I not lead you to their lair? Our hatchets cried for their scalps. Do you not know the French will now come for me? My life will mean nothing to Joncaire. My advice to you is to send for soldiers, many, many more. The French are too numerous. Their boats clog the Forks like maggots on a corpse. But what does my English brother care! Do you care for my people? Your red brother thinks 'No!' You are too young to listen to my voice. For Torn Ear to lose one brave is to lose too many! Who will feed my family? Must I crawl like a dog before the French fathers with belts in my hand? Young brother, the River is theirs! Do not be so arrogant! They have taken it from you. Shelter yourself and your warriors before the thunder of their guns breaks you like reeds. Better that we had killed them all. Yellow Hawk will tell where we are. Does my English brother now understand what this old chief knows?"

Langdon glanced toward Tillson, Gist and the Colonel. Washington stood up and stared into the council fire: "I have heard my brother's words. Their anguish falls heavily on my heart. Your wisdom is hard and ways different. There is truth in your words. We shall retire to the Meadows and prepare for attack. Tell your people to follow us. Our rations are few, but we can hunt and eat together."

"I must gather my people! Then, Torn Ear will come. We will fight together, but Half-King his way, and you, yours!"

Everyone rose to break up. Suddenly, George Croghan and Thomas Montour emerged from the forest. Langdon had not seen them since the 1751 excursion with Gist. Montour had painted his face like an Indian's. Large gold earrings swung from his pierced ear lobes. Seven Mingo warriors stepped into the clearing behind them. They had guided the two agents to Washington's camp. More shocked than Gist was Torn Ear, whose countenance fell at their appearance.

"Well, if it ain't the devil's angels themselves," Gist greeted them. "What brings you here?"

"Contrecoeur sent us. As soon as de Robert returned, we were ordered to find you. These Mingo braves have been following you for a week. They've acted as Contrecoeur's eyes since you descended the Laurel Ridge. Contrecoeur wants you to retreat; otherwise, you'll never make it. The French have a force of over fifteen hundred men at Duquesne, not including their Huron, Algonquin, Delaware and Shawnee allies. You will be annihilated if you stay."

"That is what Torn Ear has advised!" the Half-King interrupted. "We must disperse like leaves in the forest. When the wind blows from the north, it is not good!"

"Whatever you do," Croghan suggested, "this is no place to remain. I can buy you a few days. I can lie about your numbers, but the Mingo braves will have to be bribed. Can you give them a gun, or a keg of rum, or one of your horses? They serve the French only for what's in it for them. They are not like the Algonquin or Huron. But close to it!"

"What do you think, Mr. Gist?" Washington asked. "How many guns did we capture from the French? Can we spare any?"

"Most are not worth keeping, but three or four are expendable. Torn Ear's braves seized the best. But our powder is low and lead close to diminished."

"We will give them three guns and two horns of powder. Will that do?" he asked Croghan.

"No! Better make it seven. They can swap or barter the better among themselves. They'll keep quiet long enough for you to withdraw. Contrecoeur is adamant about your leaving. Especially now that Ensign Coulon is dead."

Washington looked about. His face filled with disappointment. "We'll fall back to the Meadows. I can't forfeit the field. The Governor expects us to build a fort. Retreat is out of the question. I am resolved to accept the inevitable."

"You won't have much time. That's all! We'll delay our own return. We will leave by dawn."

By mid-June, Langdon stood upon the completed parapet with Tillson. The two overlooked the rough fortification that Washington had dubbed "Fort Necessity." For six weeks, they had labored side-by-side with the militia, cutting, stripping, and dragging oak logs for the fort. Washington himself had measured it off with his theodolite. The structure lay on the south side of the Meadow, yet within gun range of a line of trees on the upper edge of the large clearing. Both he and Tillson had agreed to its design: a distended quadrilateral cage of upright logs, sunk two feet into the soil, but rising eight feet above ground. The longest side of the fort measured one-hundred-sixty-feet in length. A storehouse squatted in the center, covered with hides to protect gunpowder and food provisions. The most galling obstacle for the Colonel, however, had come from Mackay's Regulars, who refused to lift a finger, as well as Torn Ear himself, who mocked the entire ordeal.

"Half-King not your slave," he railed at Washington. "You want your red brothers to dig like women and sleep like pigs. You send us out every morning to spy, to lurk in the forest. Do you care if we are ambushed or butchered like cattle? No! Their odor is in our nostrils everyday! You think yonder stumps will stop bullets? That your Indian allies will hide there, while you cower behind logs? Do not take us for fools! That is not how we avenge ourselves."

All this Half-King repeated while daily his squaws and children devoured the militia's dwindling supply of corn, bacon, and rum. Each day the men's morale sank. Only a small number of the able rose each new morning to work on the fort. Half of the militia was ill with sores, fever and dysentery. Mackay's soldiers watched from afar. At night they butchered a beef and drank rum. Half-King's families danced about their fires and repaired holes in their wigwams. Langdon shook his head with disgust. He marveled that the Colonel bore their reproach with equanimity beyond his years.

As June's muggy days unleashed nightly rains, the hides over the powder began to leak. Corn in the food bins rotted. Supplies disappeared unaccounted for. Less than six days of provisions remained. Even Mackay's steers bellowed from hunger; only one-fifth of their number was left to slake the troops' appetite for beef.

On the evening of July 2, a surly Torn Ear appeared in front of the fort. He was stripped naked to the waist. His leggings sagged loosely about his hips. He cradled his vintage gun in the crook of his left arm. "Where is this brother of mine called Washington? I go to paint my face for war. I am sick of this place. I am not a woman. I will fight alone. You will see! Tomorrow the enemy will come. My English brother, listen! I, Half-King, have spoken."

Tillson nudged Langdon, where the two rested against a gun slot on the parapet. Cautiously, he pointed toward the wigwams. Squaws were disassembling Torn Ear's hut. Smoke obscured the others. A silence hovered about the Delaware camp. No drum sounds reverberated from the forest. Only a few children played in the open.

"I don't see the first brave," said Tillson. "Do you?"

"No," replied Langdon. "Not a one!"

"We'd better double our guard tonight and send out our own scouting parties."

"I'll lead one myself," said Langdon. "Wait till he leaves the clearing. I'll take Gist and one of his men with me."

"I'll warn the Colonel. Be careful! It looks like we're in for more rain."

As darkness settled over the tiny fort, Langdon, Gist and one other crept from its palisades and ran, crouched, toward the western edge of the Meadow. Mackay's Regulars were to the north, against the back wall of the fort. They had pitched their own camp just beyond a wide ditch that the Colonel's men had dug the day before. In the front, new palisades enwalled a trickling creek in case the French sought to lay siege.

As black rain clouds formed over the clearing, the three entered the woods, each fanning out in a different direction. Thunder rumbled in the distance. A cool drizzle began to fall. Slipping from tree to tree, Langdon watched, waited, and listened, ever attune to the night for movement. The drizzle became a steady rain. It was difficult to make out objects, let alone distinguish sounds and motion. As dawn approached, he caught sight of figures stealing through the underbrush, creeping silently across the saturated leaves and wet forest litter. It was Joncaire, Handsome Dog and a line of naked savages, skulking their way toward the Meadows. They moved like shadows, suspended in wisps of white fog. Langdon hugged the ground and waited for the party to pass. They were headed toward Torn Ear's end of the clearing. Quietly, he turned and stole back toward the east and Mackay's side of the fort. Gist was already in the clearing. Langdon raced to the old guide's side. "They're coming!" he whispered. "Where's your partner? We haven't much time."

"Killed!" replied Gist. "They got him with an arrow. While they were scalping him, I fled."

"Look!" pointed Langdon, as he nodded in the direction of Torn Ear's camp. "Deserted! Gone!"

"I'm not surprised," said Gist. "And just when I was beginnin' to trust the bastard! Him and his damn speeches! We'd best get in. The French don't like to strike 'til dawn. Nor the Huron or Algonquin. Too many spirits in the forest. Better warn the Colonel."

Early morning came and passed. Sweat dripped from the foreheads of Washington's militia. The few who were well enough to fight waited and swung their hands at the flies. Mackay's Regulars stood at the ready, facing the long clearing in front of the fort. All the men, both Washington and Mackay's, stood outside the parapet. Their plan: fire, then leap behind the parapet, reload, and fire again.

A noisy flock of crows appeared and winged its way across the field. Their cawing signaled a great commotion in the forest. Without warning, a wall of liegemen and yelping Indians burst from the tree line. The wave of warriors seemed to double in size. White puffs of gunpowder appeared, then the roar of rifles. Across the field the screaming regiments of men and savages charged. Washington gave the order to fire. The volley rattled the air with its torrent of bullets. The militia fell back and scrambled over the wall. Mackay's column of red jackets raised their muskets. Down came the Captain's sword; out belched a roar of flame and lead. The French troops, led by Captain Louis Coulon de Villiers, wavered, broke, but still rushed forward. Washington's men reloaded. As the enemy grew closer, they stood, aimed, and repulsed them with a thunderous volley. The wave of French and Indian attackers lurched, men fell amid the stumps; standing soldiers turned, and stumbled back toward the forest. Washington smiled. "We've stung them!" he yelled to Tillson. "Look, they're running." As the last man disappeared, a strange silence ensued. The men behind the fort peered over the palisades. The welcomed lull, however, did nothing to obviate their fear. Then, without warning, from every side of the Meadows, lead zipped into the logs, ripped through the hides covering the powder, and struck militia and Regulars alike. Scores fell before they could clamber over the logs. From every angle, hot lead thudded into the fortress. Washington called retreat, and as many as could, crowded within the palisade of inner walls. Wounded men lay outside in the ditch. Those who were able crawled toward the creek for water. Mackay's Regulars fared no better. They listened and watched as their depleted stock were shot or collapsed and their mounts succumbed to the hail of fire. Twelve of Washington's men lay dead. Mackay's Regulars suffered an even higher loss, no less than nineteen. More than seventy of their combined force was wounded. Through the long afternoon and into the evening, arrows and lead poured into the enclosure. The night grew dark. A stinging rain drenched the wounded and dying. The hides collapsed, and its treasure of gunpowder dissolved into a black mush that floated away in the runoff. As morning dawned, the Colonel and Mackay crawled toward each other. They peered over the walls. In the distance, a squad of liegemen approached under a white flag. De Robert, Joncaire and Handsome Dog led them.

"*Voulez vous parler?*" shouted François. "We are willing to accept your surrender. What is your wish? Have you not lost enough brave soldiers? Our only thought is for you to leave. If you are there, Langdon, come out and speak with us. Or send your interpreter, van Braam. Le Sieur de Villiers wants only what is best for all. *Ça va?* If you don't come, you will all die today."

"Where is van Braam?" asked the Colonel. "Ah, there you are! Sir, take Mr. Burke and plead for the best terms possible."

"Yes, sir!" replied the muddy, husky, but frightened Dutchman. "What is the one essential you want?"

"To bury our dead and protect the wounded. And keep our arms, if possible."

"Yes, sir!"

Slowly the two went out to meet de Robert's delegation. De Robert kissed Langdon's cheek; then escorted the men across the clearing. Two hours later they returned. Van Braam delivered the announcement. "First, their soldiers captured and taken to Winchester must be returned. Second, the dead, their guns and backpacks are spoils for the Indians.

No exceptions. The wounded we may carry at our own risk. Third, you, Colonel, are to acknowledge that you *killed* their envoy and started all this. Fourth, we may leave with our colors and rifles, and provisions for five days. Nothing more."

"I don't like it," said Washington. "They're trying to transfer the blame on us. Ask them to remove it. Plus, grant us safe passage. We can't make it back to Willis Creek without their promise. Will they keep their savages off us?"

"We will return and see."

Once more Langdon and van Braam slipped out to parley. This time they were kept until late in the afternoon. The bodies of the fallen had begun to stink. Those farthest from the walls had been stripped and scalped. As Langdon entered the French encampment, he noticed Joncaire, leering at the end of a double line of painted Huron. Suddenly, someone shoved him. It was Handsome Dog. A hail of clubs and sticks came crashing down on Langdon's neck. He held his arms aloft, dodged the next blow, and lunged into the nearest savage. Back and forth he twisted as he ran with his arms upraised. A fist struck him in the face. He reeled and stumbled. Joncaire's image wavered drunkenly before him. The Frenchman reached out and seized him. With bloody arms and bruises on his face, Langdon staggered past the last warrior. They had had their sport. Handsome Dog smirked and pushed him toward Villiers' tent. "You make good savage!" the Indian shoved him along. Langdon entered the Captain's tent and sat benumbed beside van Braam. While he rubbed his face and hands, he listened to the final terms. He felt too dazed to comprehend the subtle nuances that the French seemed to demand. At their return, van Braam divulged the verdict. "Lives, colors, rifles, and provisions, yes. The guilt clause remains. Safe passage for only three days! A Company of Captain de Robert's liegemen will escort us to the Youghiogheny. That's the best they will do. I have the papers, sir, for you to sign," he handed them to Washington.

Suddenly, the Colonel's eyes betrayed the reality of the defeat. His long face grew pale. He stared at the black muck under his fingernails. "Captain Mackay, do you wish to sign first?"

Mackay glanced at the young Colonel with absolute horror, and yet strangely with respect. He signed his name. "Here!" he said. "You sign, too."

The next morning the sky cleared. As they marched out, Tillson steadied Langdon past the mutilated bodies. Drummers tapped in cadence as Mackay's Regulars passed with their colors furled. Bagpipes squealed to the glory of Scotland. Mackay held his head and sword erect. He alone was mounted. Only three other horses had survived. Colonel Washington walked, while the wounded rode. Langdon glanced about and nodded toward the clearing for Tillson to observe. Hundreds of Frenchmen stood in formation in the clearing, while their half-naked, copper skinned allies lined the upper Meadows and filled the air with shrieks of triumph. Through the Indians' midst ran Yellow Hawk. He raised his hatchet and waved it for Tillson to see. A bright scarlet open jacket flopped on his chest as he raced along. Others were visible, too.

"We shall come back," Sir William said to Langdon. "I can't believe we lost."

From his own vantage, François watched the procession stagger across the Meadows, while he waited for Montour's Mingo to join him. He spurred his horse and gestured for his liegemen to flank the wounded stragglers. His side had won! Their fort a reality! The region entirely their own! No Frenchman should have felt prouder. Yet, a dull hollowness ebbed in his chest. He inhaled deeply. The pungent odor of gore burned the back of his throat. The rank putrefaction of the battlefield forced him to cover his mouth and nose with a soiled handkerchief. The reek of gunpowder still clung to his clothes. Already vultures, hunched in black silhouettes, perched in the treetops, while others circled high overhead in the hot drafts of the July sun. Their shadows glided across the field, as one by one the birds dropped down to feed. From somewhere out of his childhood schooling, the words of the Vulgate stole from his soul:

Venite, videte opera Domini ...
Come behold the works of the Lord,
The desolations he has wrought on the earth!
He breaks the bow and shatters the spear
And burns the chariots of fire!
Desistite et agnoscite ego sum Deus!

Chapter Fifteen

ANGDON CROSSED THE LAST GAP through the humid Blue Ridge range and paused to admire the valley below. The gap lay midway between the Big Lick to the south and Winchester to the north. Bees hummed in the hazy air of late afternoon. Old Humpback Mountain cast its enormous evening shadow across the ridges he would need to descend. Langdon dismounted and rubbed his horse's ears. Poor Pellas had fallen at Ft. Necessity. Langdon had marched on foot to Willis Creek. Once across the river, he purchased a new horse with "script" that Washington had provided. The money was more of a promissory note than anything, but the Winchester livery owner accepted it just the same. "Old Arduous!" he smiled, as he patted the sturdy, gray-and-brown quarter horse's mane. He would probably want to rename it, but at the time, "Arduous" best captured his mood.

Overhead, the hickories, white oaks, and pine formed a welcome canopy after the long trek down the Warriors' Trail. The hot sun would soon sink beyond the dark mountains behind him. If he rode all night he could reach his cabin. But the slow climb up the coves to reach the gap had exacted its toll on Arduous. The sweet odor of ripe black berries drifted in the air. It was time to make camp, to find a pleasant place to hobble the horse and rest before the morning summoned them to a new day.

Still a strange uneasiness gnawed at the back of his mind. Off and on all day he had felt it. It was the unusual degree of the forest's silence that troubled him. From time to time, he had glanced back, feeling as if someone were following him. He and Arduous had spooked two deer near the top of the gap. The animals seemed especially jittery, as if they sensed something too. Langdon had watched them bound off, with their large white tails hiked high. Perhaps a bear had startled them, or his and Arduous' scent. He remounted and guided Arduous toward a rocky cleft that loomed half-concealed behind a growth of small pines. He nudged the animal past the cleft's lichen-encrusted fissures and quietly reined up. "Whoa!" he whispered. A green vireo cocked its tiny head to one side and peered at him. He could see its black beady eyes. It flitted its wings and fluttered away. Just then, a figure on foot appeared on the mountain path, stopped, and studied the ground. It was the Half-King's grandson, the youth who had warned them about the French. The boy wore only a loincloth, ankle high moccasins, a mixture of feathers in his hair, and a necklace of bear claws. He was armed with a bow, a quiver of arrows, and a blue hatchet tucked inside his waistband. A purple gash oozed with dark blood along his left ear. He glanced in Langdon's direction, froze, then released his breath when he recognized the frontiersman.

"Ho! Half-King is dead! Ambushed! All my family – all are butchered!"

Langdon dismounted and led his horse from the thicket. "I'm not surprised. Torn Ear predicted it would happen."

"Yellow Hawk, Ottawa and others came to kill us! We could not go back to Logstown. We hid at Gist's cabin, but they found us." He held out a hand toward Langdon. It contained the shredded remnants of a wampum belt. "It's all I have. 'Go to Burke!' were Torn Ear's last words."

"When did this occur?"

"A half moon since the battle in Great Meadows. I escaped."

"Where was Gist? Had he not gotten back?"

"No! Gist is still at Willis Creek. He sent me here. 'Go to the long low gap in the mountains,' he said."

Langdon could not help but feel empathy for the boy. "How are you called? You know my name's Langdon?"

"Yes! Blue Hatchet is mine!" he touched the tomahawk in his waistband. "A gift from Joncaire, when he first came down the river. He is a different man, now. Coup de Sang is different, too. Since the Onondaga made Torn Ear King of the Delaware, the French have not been happy. 'A bad road,' as grandfather called it."

"I'm honored that Half-King favored me. Tomorrow we will be at my cabin!" he smiled. "It's different from your Ohio." He placed his left hand on the young brave's shoulder. "If I may, Blue Hatchet, I'd like to adopt you as my brother. If you will accept?" Langdon raised his right hand as a signal of sincerity.

The young brave gripped Langdon's upright hand with his own. "My white brother, you are more like a father. We all have one Father. He sees from above. But I see my white father eye-to-eye. I think that is best."

"Yes," said Langdon. "I agree. Now let me take a look at that gash. If you're going to be part of our family, you'll have to work. And keep clean. Wait till you meet my sister, Sarah."

"Work for women? No! I will hunt. Maybe I will fight with the tall Colonel again and the tall English warrior. I will scout and hunt for my white father and trap for him in the forest."

"Very well!" One thing at a time thought Langdon. Now that the Ohio disaster was behind them, Blue Hatchet couldn't have come at a more opportune time. If Sarah would agree, he and the brave could go on to the Holston and begin the task of surveying the grant for settlement.

"I look forward to all that," said Langdon. "For now, let's make camp, and see what's left in my saddle bags."

Captain Tillson had scarcely arrived in Williamsburg, when Dinwiddie's formal servant knocked at his quarter's door with a note from the Governor. Like Dinwiddie's other servants, the man was clad in a white shirt, purple vest, purple jacket and breeches, and white hose. His black shoes and brass buckles sparkled in the late summer sun. *Come to my mansion at your earliest disposal. The Honorable Robt. Dinwiddie*, was all the note read.

"Tell him I'll be there this evening, just as soon as opportunity permits."

"Yes, suh!" the black man replied. "He's most troubled. Lord, if he ain't fit to be tied. I'll fill his wine cup several over 'fore you arrive. That'll calm him, if I may be so bold."

"You know him to his bones, don't you?"

"Yes-suh! Though when he's mad, he calls me his 'house nigger.' He's got two sides to him! One as the Governor; the other as master. He'd whip me if he knowed I'd told."

"In England, we don't approve of slavery, yet we tolerate it wherever we go. I'll not divulge a word. Thank you for the warning. What's your name? I'd like to know."

"Clarence. Don't ask me why. But that's my name. I've got no other."

"Mr. Clarence! I'll be there."

William hated that he'd not slipped into town earlier. He had so wanted to visit Anna first. He could only imagine what awaited him with Dinwiddie. Whatever it was, he was first and foremost a Captain in the service of his Majesty's special envoys. Dinwiddie knew that. As Tillson bathed, he mulled the thought. He would suggest they return to the River, this time with a larger force and attack Fort Duquesne from north of the Monongahela. If he could post a letter to the foreign ministry's office without Dinwiddie's knowledge, perhaps the Duke of Newcastle, or his brother, would support the idea. He dressed, put on his finest scarlet jacket, fluffed jabot, black boots, white wig, and polished sword, and rode the several blocks to the Governor's Palace.

As he arrived, the Captain was surprised to encounter a quay of carriages, wrapped about the Mansion's circular drive. He dismounted and hitched his horse to a long brass post. Many planters and their wives, delegates of the House of Burgesses, and respected small landholders crowded the entrance and waited to enter. The Captain took a place in line and, once inside, sought out the elegant dining room and its sideboards of meats and brandies. Dinwiddie was stationed in his usual position – near the fireplace and favorite armchair. He hailed Tillson with an upraised glass.

"Gentlemen! Please greet one of our bravest, straight from the battlefield! *Major* William Tillson! Yes, Major!" he smiled.

Heads turned and a score of planters nodded with approval.

"Tell us, Major," began Mr. Custiss, "just what happened? We've heard untold rumors. Everything from extreme incompetence to exaggerated valor!"

"Yes! From disgust to defeat!" alleged another. "Sir, is the Ohio lost?"

"Only for the moment!" Tillson replied. "I've yet to submit my report to the Governor," he gestured toward the transparently uncomfortable Dinwiddie. The Governor's miffed countenance could not be concealed.

"Indeed! Only for the moment!" the Governor repeated. "I'll know more, once Colonel Washington reports."

"Major, is it true that a French ambassador was *assassinated*? That would be most grievous, if so," a Tidewater planter asked.

"No one was *assassinated*! But nine or ten Frenchmen were killed in a skirmish. It was most unfortunate, but the encounter was unavoidable. If we had not defended ourselves, we would have been recipients of their attack! Of that, I am confident."

"I am pleased you were there to corroborate the facts," mumbled Dinwiddie. "I am eager to know the details myself. But for now, lets enjoy the evening." He glanced away momentarily, then continued. "Congratulations, Major! The promotion was overdue. Now, gentlemen, if you'll excuse me, a delightful lady has just graced us with her presence," he nodded toward Tillson. "You might know her, Major."

William almost lost his balance as he turned toward the foyer. There stood Anna, Lady Ashby, in a lemon cream gown of layered silk and linen, with silver slippers and a double strand of pearls resting on her long neck and graceful chest. Silver earrings and silver sparkles in her hair gave her a regal appearance that aroused William to his depths. He immediately shouldered his way through the crowd to greet her.

"Anna!" he said, as he took her gloved hand and kissed it. "It is truly you!"

"Where's your Mr. Burke?" she asked.

"I didn't come that way," he replied, sensing her suspicion. "I left him at Willis Creek. The Colonel and I rode together to Alexandria before breaking off. Please don't think the less of me. My only thoughts have been of you."

Anna's face brightened. She leaned in toward him. "Can you escort my carriage back tonight?" she whispered. "My heart's longed for you since the hour you left."

"Yes!" he whispered in turn. As he stepped back, he studied her blonde curls, her majestic poise and stunning beauty. "Anna, whatever my faults, know that I love you."

Her lips parted as if to reply. She swallowed the lump in her throat, coughed into a handkerchief, and turned to greet the Governor. "Your Honor!" she curtseyed. "You are always so kind to include me," she kissed him on his pudgy cheek. "You are truly a Lady's dear!" she flattered him.

The Governor drew in his stomach, readjusted his wig, and kissed her hand. "Sir William, I envy you, down to your boots!" he halfway sneered with a lewd glance at the Major. "Incidentally, Mr. Tillson, we need to chat before you leave. I'll be in my office after the second minuet. Please be prompt!" He smiled at Lady Ashby and returned to the tippling crowd by the tables.

With an elegance only Anna could display, she and William stepped gracefully to the strings of the Governor's in-house quintet of violins and woodwinds. With hands held in seductive touch, they smiled and traded secret kisses, as they bowed and turned in the minuet.

"Will you wait in the parlor for me, while I endure the Governor?" he asked her.

"Of course!" she replied. "You won't be long, I trust."

"Hopefully not. He's generally gruff, but brief."

They exchanged smiles and lovers' glances and completed the second dance. He bowed and slipped through the guests toward Dinwiddie's office. The bulging, squat figure was seated at his desk. A wisp of tobacco smoke drifted overhead. He looked up, lay down his clay pipe, and nodded for William to be seated.

"Now, just between us, what the hell happened? I've received letters from the governors of Maryland and Pennsylvania decrying their situations. Indians are conducting raiding parties all along the frontier. Just how bad was the defeat?"

"Thorough! Sir! We were overwhelmed. Our fort was pitifully inadequate, but the best we could construct at the time. Your Colonel evinced heroic resolve. His men never quavered, nor did Mackay's. But, sir, the French outnumbered us. Their Indian allies were eager to kill. And the weather was the damnedest I've ever witnessed during a battle."

The Governor wet his lips with his sensuous tongue. "I have no stomach for defeat. Once his Majesty's council hears of it, I'll be the butt of his lackeys' disdain. We must retake the area! Our claims are as legitimate as the French. Plus, we can't hold back the tide of settlers moving through the colonies. They are hell bent on forcing the issue. Removing squatters requires energy and resources. The House of Burgesses could care less. Plus, evicting settlers generates decades of resentment. I can feel it building in the streets and taverns here, let alone imagine what it's like west of Culpepper and down toward the Big Lick. And that's where Mr. Burke comes in. He knows that region. Don't lose contact with him. I want a fort built, just west of his place, across the mountains. And I want it named for *me*! Any savages coming across the Alleghenies will most likely enter there. Or so I've been told."

"I'll make the journey, sir, and assess the area. Thank you, also, for securing the promotion. I am truly grateful."

"Nothing at all! Just this warning! Be prepared to go back to the Ohio. Once I receive Washington's report, I will plan another invasion well into the interior. The region will be ours! Lead plates and all! Plus I have other schemes up my sleeve!" he smiled. "Now let's enjoy the remainder of the evening."

For William, galloping behind Anna's carriage passed as in a dream. The summer's night sky scintillated with a million stars. Riding past the live oaks, festooned in glooming beards of Spanish moss, added to the pang d'amour that throbbed in his heart. As they clattered up the drive to her estate, her footman greeted her with a sleepy yawn. "My, my, past midnight!" he intoned in his mellow voice. "Does the Lady care for a glass of sherry, or anything?" The tall servant recognized Tillson as William held his hand up to assist Anna from her coach. "Captain! A pleasant surprise!" he exclaimed in droll fashion. "Reginald!" he called loudly. "See that the Captain's horse is fed and quartered. Do come in, Lady Ashby, before you catch a cold. Missum, shall I prepare a room for the Captain?" he eyed the tall Major before glancing uncertainly at Anna.

"Yes," she replied. "He'll need to stay."

"Yes, 'um!" he bowed, as they passed him and withdrew to the living room.

"Please do bring the claret!" she called. They sat together under the glass pendants of a sparkling chandelier, aglow only in starlight from outside. "Shhhh!" she whispered, as she tilted her head back, turned her lips toward William, and kissed him. "I have waited for this moment so long! You mustn't disappoint me, you know!"

He held her fingertips to his lips and kissed them. He removed his wig and caressed her in his arms. His nose rubbed against her chin as he kissed her again. "Why ever would I do that?" he teased in a low voice. "After the claret, I want only you."

She laid her head against his shoulder, but sat up abruptly as the doorman brought in the wine.

"The Captain's room is prepared," he stated. "May I bring anything else?"

"*Major!* Major Tillson!" she corrected him. "He's a major now! Imagine that! He'll be a general by his next visit, I fear."

"Yes, 'am!" he smiled, sensing it was his cue to leave. "Good night, ma'am! And Major Tillson! I've never served a general, sir!"

William shook his head good-naturedly. "No need to, yet!" he smiled. "Thank you, sir!"

They drained their glasses amid tender kisses, quietly rose, and tiptoed up the spiral staircase. Anna beckoned for him to follow. They entered her dark bedroom, illuminated only by the night's stars, undressed, and climbed onto the high bed of downy quilts and linen sheets and, rolling in each other's arms, slipped into the throes of love.

"Anna, when I return, will you marry me?"

"Yes!" she whispered with tears in her eyes. "But why and where must you go?"

"To the frontier and Ohio again. Perhaps next spring, the Governor's offensive will be over. Whom shall I ask for your hand?"

"The Governor, perhaps. My husband had no siblings. If he says 'No,' I'll marry you anyway," she kissed his lips. "Now hush all this. Just your touch fills me with joy. Hold me," she trembled, "and love me! Please, don't leave until you have to! The servants understand."

Chapter Sixteen

RAVELING UPRIVER BY CANOE and feeling the spray in his face, François felt a rush of vitality. Yellow Hawk paddled in the stern while he and a young Algonquin took turns at the bow. He raised his paddle as sparkling drops rushed past, then bent forward anew. They would arrive in Venango by evening and forge on to Le Boeuf in two more days if fortune provided good weather.

He had not shaved since escorting Washington's party across the Youghiogheny and his suntanned face now bristled with a coarse black beard. The white cuffs of his topcoat were damp and soiled, adding to his unkempt appearance. Beads of water dripped off his hands in the bright sunlight. On they paddled. His thoughts wandered. Hélène would be five months pregnant now. That Louise-Marie and Langdon were already parents stung. Pride weighed against sadness, an uncomfortable pairing that oscillated in his mind. Pride, because they had defeated the Colonel's militia and British Regulars, but at what cost? So many had died on both sides.

Reviens, Éternel! Délivre mon âme;
Sauve-moi, à cause de ta miséricorde,
Car celui qui meurt n'a plus ton souvenir;
Qui te luera dans le séjour des morts?

As the sun set in a violet blaze behind the oak and birch forest,

Frazier's garrisoned cabin came into view. A flotilla of canoes and log barges cluttered the gravelly beach, but the Indians brought the craft to shore in a quiet scraping of its bottom on the river's sands. As François disembarked, the flamboyant figure of Joncaire appeared in the clearing. He had fastened an eagle feather to his black hat and had painted his exposed torso like an Indian's. His blue coat hung open, and its gold cuffs appeared stained with dark blood. His leggings and moccasins were new, almost milk-white, and a British bayonet swung on a leather strap from his waist. To his rear stood Handsome Dog, silent but alert to their arrival.

"You are too slow!" the Frenchman said testily to François. "We beat you here two days ago. Come in and I'll apprise you of my new assignment. Come! Coup de Sang will take care of the braves. *Viens, mon chèr! La guerre contre le vain Dinwiddie a sûrement commencée!*"

As the two men sat in the main room of the cabin and sipped hot rum, Joncaire slipped into conversation. "We are in for a grand time! English settlers are falling back all across the mountains. My orders are to harass them at every opportunity – to stalk, threaten, burn and drive them back, deep into Pennsylvania and New York. Any killings, of course, will be left to the savages. They are best at that. We are to foster an air of neutrality. How civil and genteel!" he boasted with a grizzly huff. "Such are the orders from no one less than the minister of war himself – Le grand Sieur Antoine-René de Voyer d'Argenson! Quite remarkable! *Non?*"

"The Court must be elated!" Philippe replied. "I fear I'll be reassigned to Duquesne. Boredom has set in now that Washington's feint was rebuffed! How deluded! They actually thought we'd withdraw."

"I know! *C'est incredible!* They did fight, though, especially your Burke! I wish we had him on our side! Such a wrenching swill they left behind! Even I grew sick."

"I too! I fear one day I will have to kill him, if he doesn't kill me first!"

"Ah, François-Philippe! Do not think like that! It is we who must kill him, if it is necessary. Perhaps we can leave that to Coup de Sang or Yellow Hawk. Then our consciences will be free. Isn't that so? But if I must kill him, I will. Rest assure, I will! Destiny is on our side. We could not live in a nobler time! *Je suis très content*! Try to be happy yourself. It is unbecoming to wallow in remorse for one's enemy. *Non?"*

"*Vous avez raison!"*

"Of course! You studied too long under priests, immersed in their Latin and love of *philosophie*. Who is your hero, now? Pascal? Descartes? Montaigne? Or this nouveau chap, Voltaire?"

"Neither! Rousseau! And his '*man adorned only by the hand of nature!*' as he puts it. He is so close to the truth! *Vraiment*, he is!"

"*L'homme de nature*! Yes! In all his savagery! *C'est moi*, I must confess!" The long-haired mustached Frenchman grimaced. "I did not know what life was until I took it from a brave *homme* who was determined to take it from me! I have never forgotten the moment. *Jamais*! When do you leave for Le Boeuf?"

"In the morning! I can hardly wait to see Hélène! She wanted to come with us, but Coulon refused."

"Yes! You are lucky! It is just as well she didn't. Duquesne's no place for a woman, even if her mother were Ojibwa. I knew her mother's father. He was killed near Fort Niagara in a raid by Seneca. They cut off his hands and feet, slit his chest open, and ate his heart and entrails in her mother's presence. I was just a boy of ten. My own father died the next day from a neck wound he'd received in the skirmish. I was fascinated by all the gore, traumatized I suppose! I was too terrified to wonder what would happen to me. I wanted to be a savage, to skulk through the woods, to whoop and shriek like an Indian. I wanted revenge for my father. That night a relief party from Niagara surprised the Seneca. I hid in a blanket but watched the attack. It was magnificent and horrifying! Later, a captured Iroquois said that the English on the Mohawk River had encouraged the raid. The Huron, Ojibwa and other Indians with the party forced him to run a gauntlet. They slashed, cut, clubbed and beat him senseless. Then they tied him to a post on a scaffold. For three days they continued to beat, cut and singe his body. An old woman ate off his privates and gnawed his fingers to nubs. At night they left him to recover, only at dawn to urge the children to torment him in every imaginable way. They poked hot sticks in his groin, ribs, buttocks, ears, and eyes. Finally, the man broke in a scream of despair. He defied the Spirit of Evil to mock his death. He called on the Spirit of Good, on the *bon Dieu* of the Six Nations, to come and take him away. To bear him off to the land of the sleeping spirits! This only inspired his captors all the more, who heaped brush and armloads of dry branches under the scaffold to burn him alive. I can still hear his face and hair crackling in the blaze! It will take years to civilize the savages, but this land is ours François and worth fighting for. Every English who dies under the blade, or falls from the thump of a lead ball, brings but a tiny moment of solace to a child's memory. That is the truth, *mon chèr*. The bloody, hellish truth I doubt your Rousseau will ever know."

François stared at the hardened Joncaire. Why were the English so damn persistent? Life for them meant only expansion, the destruction of fur-bearing lands and forest, and the annihilation of tribes and culture he had come to admire, if not love.

Upon his arrival at Le Boeuf, François quickly swept his eyes across the beach in search of Hélène. He was distraught not to find her among the well-wishers. With a noisy grinding sound, his canoe scraped onto the sand. A muddle of natives, squaws and several liegemen watched him step ashore.

"We received word of your coming," an ensign stated. A deerskin belt was cinched about his white waistcoat. His leggings and moccasins appeared new. "One of Joncaire's runners brought the news. Colonel Du Gardinay, our new commandant, will see you in his quarters. He said to tell you that your wife, Hélène, has gone to Presque Isle to have her baby. Du Gardinay is waiting for you now."

"Thank you! Do you have any idea why I was recalled from Duquesne?"

"None, sir! I'm sure the Colonel knows."

"Very well! What's been going on here?"

"*Rien de tous*! Nothing at all! Other than to supply you at Duquesne!"

"Odd! They've pulled Joncaire off the river, too."

The Ensign glanced away, as if he knew something he wasn't to divulge.

The commandant scarcely looked up as Philippe entered the room. "Captain de Robert, sir!" François reported.

"Sit down, Captain, and forego the formalities," the Colonel waved his right hand with a flip and a twist of his wrist. François could smell whiskey on the commandant's breath. "No offense, but the officials at Montreal have schemed up a devil of a project for you. Yes, I'm sorry, but for you!" He scraped his chair back and stood erect, all five-feet-two-inches of his lean, diminutive self, slightly disheveled in a bright blue jacket and adorned with topaz earrings. He looked up at François. "I know, don't say it! But welcome to Le Boeuf!" He extended his hand to Gabelle in a friendly manner. "They're sending you off to Chouaguen. That's the fort the English call 'Oswego.' Yes! The Fort there! From Presque Isle, you will go overland to the fort. Shouldn't take more than a week, if that long. Don't ask me anymore. They'll tell you the rest at Presque Isle. They don't trust me either." He smiled again.

"What happened to Hélène? My wife?" he asked with urgency. "I was expecting her here."

"*Oui*! I know. But fall is coming soon. Our surgeon mends bones. Dresses wounds! The best midwives reside at Niagara. From Presque Isle, she'll need to go there. You will see her soon, I am sure. *Non*? I think so. For now, we have a more delicate matter to consider. Like a scout to guide you! Your Yellow Hawk is Algonquin. The Iroquois despise them. You will need a Seneca, or Onondaga, or Cayuga. Someone like Joncaire's Handsome Dog! Do you trust him?"

"Yes and no! He follows his own path. He will come back with scalps. But he's fearless. That I know. Unfortunately, he and Joncaire are already engaged in their own pursuits east of the mountains. I'm afraid we're too late."

"Perhaps and perhaps not. *Alors*! These matters are never simple, are they? Maybe they'll send you alone! *Ah, bon*! It's not in our hands. Come, refresh yourself! Let's have some wine and meat! Tomorrow will come soon enough!"

The overnight canoe and portage trek to Presque Isle left François exhausted. The boggy, dammed-up waters by what few beaver remained did not facilitate easy passage. Yet, this marshy network of paths and canoe slips provided the major supply line for Le Boeuf, Venango, and smaller outposts downstream. François was both disappointed and concerned that Hélène was not at Presque Isle either. The fort's captain told him that she had fallen ill with a fever and vomiting, but was quick to say she recovered but asked to go to Ft. Niagara where she could be cared for by midwives. He was less sanguine about the fortification of Oswego. "My message for you is urgent. There are rumors that the English have installed guns at Chouaguen, large enough to keep a fleet from approaching. Montreal wants to know if that's true. Also, if so, their size and location and how many troops are garrisoned there."

"Aren't there enough trappers and traders with access to the fort to know that?" he asked. "Why must a Frenchman go in?"

"Because, since Contrecoeur's victory against the Virginians, the commander at Chouaguen has kept all non-Englishmen out. Including Algonquin and French Indian allies. You know enough English to pass for one. Or so they say in Montreal."

François sought out a chair and sat with his face in his hands. He brushed back the salty hair in his eyes and ran his hands across his beard. "Ah! *Moi*? An Englishman! I don't believe it! There must be more to it than that! *Que pensez vous*?"

"I don't know, sir! But they've picked you. Joncaire's Handsome Dog will meet you on the Genesee River three days from now. One of our Cayuga scouts will guide you to the rendezvous site. No one else knows of your mission. That is all I know, sir."

Trekking through the bogs of northern Seneca and Iroquoian lands thoroughly depleted François. Only the lay of the land and its rich vegetation of swampy grasses, cane fields, berms of spruce, alders, aspen and birch broke the monotony of the slogging ordeal. Reaching the Genesee River, however, brought no reprive.

"Look!" pointed his guide. "Tracks! Not Indian. White men have come this way. See. Many tracks, boot prints. Deep in mud." He bent down and ran his finger inside one. "Maybe a day old. Two at most! They came by canoe. See where they disembarked."

"Yes," said Philippe. "It's very clear."

"Ho! Then canoes returned," the tracker said, pointing up river toward the steep sandstone hills to the south.

"Where does this river empty?" asked Philippe.

"Into Lake Ontario between Niagara and Oswego. This is place where Coup de Sang is to come. Trail to Chouaguen cut across here," he pointed into the alders and brush along the right bank. "Long march, one day long and you will be there! Handsome Dog is probably watching now. It is best I go. He is no friend of Cayuga. I think it best I keep away."

François glanced about. So did his guide. His long knot of black hair shook with hawk feathers. His naked torso flinched in the September sunlight. His copper skin glistened with bear grease. He pointed up river. François turned, but saw nothing. When he glanced back, the guide was gone. Moments later Coup de Sang emerged out of the forest. He said nothing, nor did he gesture. He waded out into the cold green water, waved for François to join him, and the two swam across the river.

"I have been to this place," Handsome Dog said, as they waded ashore. "Many Cayuga killed British here years ago. Now they have made a treaty, but it is not good. Every year more English break the treaty. They settle on the edge of the forest. They seize native cornfields that once were Iroquoian. Very bad! The chiefs send delegates to Albany. Many speeches are made. Pipes are smoked. Wampum exchanged. But the white man keeps coming. I do not think Joncaire can stop him. But I fight to kill. It is all I have left. Let us rest here and tomorrow we will sleep in Oswego. So say Joncaire and the Frenchman from Montreal. He says to Joncaire 'Go!' and Joncaire goes. After Chouaguen, I leave and return to '*le Noir*,' as we call him. Yes! 'The dark one.' You did not know? We are all dark inside. Even you, Monsieur. All along the wilderness, the hatchet is raised. It has been that way since Champlain. I have said too much."

"No! Not at all. I fear you are right."

Dawn came in a mist of cold rain. Wet and muddy, François rolled over, then quickly got up, soon striding at a half-run behind Handsome Dog. Steadily and tirelessly, the big Indian strode through the wet sedges and ferns, his eyes on the path before him. They had eaten only a palmful of corn. Philippe's body ached for more. Thirst nagged his throat, but

Tekacayah plunged on. Toward noon he stopped to kneel at a brook. "Rest!" he ordered. "By dark, we will be there. Eat no more. You will get cramps." He cupped his hand and drank from the clear cold stream. François paused and slaked his thirst as well.

Wet ground and trickling creeks checked their progress, but on raced Handsome Dog. François loped just to stay within sight. A dull sun broke through the overcast sky, illuminating the changing foliage in the brushy forest. The yellow leaves of the aspen and the red hues of maples quavered in the fall breeze. Clusters of wild grapes baubled within his reach. Wilted blueberries served as a welcome snack. On they loped. Toward late afternoon, broken clouds drifted east in a massive shelf of slate sky. The sun bristled low and crimson. Night would soon descend. Suddenly, Handsome Dog stopped and pointed northeast. A dim glow of crocus light – pale silver against the black receding clouds, indicated a town, or a village, "There!" Tekacayah pointed. "Chouaguen."

"How do we approach?" François asked.

"Tonight, no! Tomorrow, we will walk in from where the sun comes up. English like show of bluster. I will lead you. You will see. Tonight we will sleep here," he gestured toward a small clearing beside a creek.

Tekacayah built a small fire while François gathered spruce boughs for a shelter from the cold. A clear sky opened above, punctuated with myriad white and faint blue stars. A loon's call honked in the darkness. A lone wolf's howl drifted across the night. Soon others joined in. The eerie sound of their yelps and howls throbbed with the heat of a chase, then slowly abated, and faded into silence.

As François lay down to sleep, he wondered if Rousseau had ever heard a wolf howl. He doubted as much. At least he agreed with the Genevan's ideas of savages more so than Locke's. Neither possessed the faintest knowledge of *vrai homme de nature* — the true Indian in all his state of nature. Rousseau, at least, admired the savage's cleverness, strength, and lust for freedom; whereas Locke had imagined him to be uneducated, uncivilized on the level of a pagan heretic, and unworthy of the lands he called home, thereby making him expendable and exploitable. Sadly, Locke refused to believe society and the savage as compatible entities.

He glanced toward the sleeping Tekacayah, driven from his own land. Far off in the distance, the wolves began to howl again. For all his love of nature, he longed from time to time to be reminded of his past, when with his parents he attended operas and concerts. A Quebec rendition of Jean-Baptiste Lully music, or a performance of a Jean-Philippe Rameau opera, or even one of Monteverdi's would mellow his soul. His mother had desired he learn the violin and flute, but he had spurned both in favor of his father's epee. Now, in New France, it was a Tulle musket at his side and a steel knife in his belt that defined him as a noble. He pulled the edges of his blanket about his collar and slowly fell asleep.

"Wake, now Frenchman." Handsome Dog ordered. "Up! Wash your face in the creek. Brush your clothes off. We go to fort now, from where the sun rises. Hurry, while dawn is still white."

Whatever François had anticipated was contradicted by his first sight of the fort. He had expected a log blockhouse, a little less sophisticated than Ft. Le Boeuf. But to the contrary, Chouaguen's blockhouse was built of stone with a four-to-six-foot stonewall around it. Galleries and bastions for guns wrapped about the seaward's northern wall. A narrow neck of land and small offshore island protected the fort from a frontal barrage. Additional blockhouses served as anchor posts at the ends of the long wall. A dirt street between a row of stone houses, storage sheds, and wharfs along the Chouaguen River formed the approach to the fort. Dogs barked in the street. Smoke drifted from the chimneys. Crowds of townsmen milled about. A wagon with a load of wood trundled past. They nodded to the driver. Handsome Dog strode head erect to François' left, his eyes focused on the fort's stone steps. In the morning breeze, the British Union Jack fluttered atop the stone blockhouse. Warm sun bathed the fort. Not until they reached the first step did anyone notice or seem to care.

"Not so fast!" a British soldier protested. He held his musket perpendicular in his hands. Suddenly, he was joined by other scarlet-clad troops: a squad of seven or more.

"Let them pass!" ordered a voice midway up the stairs. An officer in a blue jacket, black boots and black hat stared down at them. His slender face and pale skin immediately caught François' eye. It was Ensign Ward, the man who had surrendered the Virginia fort the morning the fleet arrived at the Forks of the Ohio. "Captain de Robert, I see!" he greeted him. "You're a captain now. Do come up. We've been expecting you. But your savage stays behind. You understand?"

"If you insist."

"I do. He can stay there," he pointed to a huge elm, just outside the fort. "He will be safe with the others, until we are through."

Others? François turned toward the elm. In a cordoned ring, sat half a dozen men, guarded by six or more British Regulars and two Iroquois. He recognized the captives as his own liegemen, members of his company from their ill-fated encounter with Washington. Philippe looked up toward Ensign Ward. So this is what his mission was about, along with his superiors' wishes to know how well-manned Oswego was!

"You are not surprised, I trust?" Ward commented. "Governor Dinwiddie wants to negotiate one last time, an exchange, if possible."

"How on earth did you get here?"

"From the Susquehanna and over the mountains to the Genesee. Three weeks, all told! Your Frenchmen moved well."

François followed the ensign up the remaining stairs to the entrance of the massive blockhouse. As he hurried along, he noted as many gun emplacements as he could, size of cannons, and number. He had to assume the total number should be doubled. Perhaps twenty eight-ponders and six swivel guns in all. In the distance below, he could see log abatises being constructed. It would take a long siege to bring the fort to its knees. But if one climbed the heights behind it, one could easily subdue the fort from the rear. Companies of troops were stirring from their tents for the morning drill. How many, he could not estimate. But he had seen enough.

François was shocked to meet the fort's commander. Short, bald and without a wig, he looked like a caricature of the typical British officer.

"My name is Captain James Mercer. We are of French descent but have been English for years. And your name, Monsieur? May I have the honor?"

"Captain François-Philippe de Robert, sir! May I know the meaning of this 'exchange'? I know Ensign Ward. I recognized my own men. Where are the others, if I may ask?"

"Let us be seated," said Mercer. "We have much to discuss." He walked toward a wide window that looked out across the Lake. "Please," he gestured toward a bear-skinned covered chair. "First, let's have some port? Then let's discuss."

Ensign Ward poured each of them, including himself, a glass of dark purple wine.

"It has come to this," Mercer began. "The Governor of Virginia wishes to exchange all of your men, that is, provided Du Quesne abandons Ohio and Frazier's post at Venango. Furthermore, raids along the Alleghenies must cease. Le Boeuf is another matter for Pennsylvania to negotiate. I must say the colonies' governors are still at odds over whose claims prevail and who's responsible for what. That's to our pity," he coughed, "and your gain. But, it's the Ohio Dinwiddie wants. Virginia's rights go back to 1607. He demands access to it, free of interference or any French claims to ownership. He is adamant! Do you understand?"

"Yes. But such a demand is not in my hands to address. Only the Marquis du Quesne and his advisers in Montreal can make that decision. I'm sure, Monsieur, you understand."

"I do. For that reason, we are willing to release seven of your men as a token of our earnest desire to return all of them. But that will occur only when your presence no longer dominates the river. The Governor wishes to pursue his legal interests at once."

"Legal or not, I cannot say. But I am grateful for the exchange. When may we proceed?"

"The Governor has prepared a document for you to present to your superiors. Once they have signed it – in our interests we hope – the remaining French soldiers will be released at Winchester and escorted to the Ohio." Mercer paused, handed the document to François, and lifted his glass to his lips. "This is your last opportunity to withdraw with honor. There will be no further offers. War seems imminent, Monsieur. I fear it as much as anyone. The Colonies will not be constrained. Is that clear?"

"Yes. But we French have been there since the time of La Salle. Nonetheless, I am pleased to escort the men home. Most are from Ft. Niagara. I must ask one favor, however."

"What is it?"

"May we have three canoes to make the journey? Otherwise it will take longer through the bogs and sandy hills. Plus, we have no food, nor guns for protection. The entire way lies within range of Iroquoian attacks."

Mercer turned toward Ensign Ward and nodded approval. "You may leave whenever you wish."

François craned his neck to scan Fort Niagara's walls. He could see its *fleur de lis* flapping in the late September breeze. The men with him lifted their paddles and cheered. "*Voilà! Nous sommes chez nous!* We are home!"

The canoes skidded onto the bay's sands. François stepped out and strode swiftly toward the towering walls. Townsmen and soldiers waved to the liegemen below. A cannon thundered their arrival. A second followed, white plumes of smoke dissolving in the wind. Up, up the steep flight of stone steps bounded François. Women and children ran along the gleaming parapet. Alone in the brisk gusts off the bay, stood Hélène. A white apron covered her cotton blouse and deerskin skirt. Her single black braid flopped in the wind. As he approached, he stared at her body. Her firm but slightly rotund *ventre* filled him with joy and relief. "Hélène!" he seized her in his arms.

"You are back! Make them let you stay." She put her hands to his face and kissed his lips. She clutched his white jacket and pressed her face against his sleeve.

"You will make it! I know you will."

"Ever the optimist," she said, smiling. "I have always been brave. Isn't that so?"

François embraced her against his chest. "You are more than that," he said. "Vastly more! You are all that any Frenchman could ever want!"

Chapter Seventeen

THE HAZY LIGHT OF THE SETTING SUN bathed Tillson in its amber glow as he halted on Tree Notch Road. Should he take the lane that led to Langdon's farm, or journey toward the distant gap of the Blue Ridge? If the former, he would surely see Sarah. Could he trust himself not to fall in love with her, again? With Langdon, Louise and Jonathan present, little time would remain for amorous glances, chatter, or contact. Besides, Dinwiddie's order included fostering rapport with Langdon and reliance on his knowledge of the Great Warriors' Road. Without that knowledge, Tillson knew he'd be at a tremendous disadvantage, especially with respect to the most favorable location for a fort. Plus, there was the pending offensive that Governor Sharpe of Maryland had been commissioned to lead. Much to Washington's disappointment, the decision had utterly devastated the Colonel, but Langdon needed to know about it. He turned south onto the lane, glancing back to make certain that his packhorse was in tow.

Twilight descended before he arrived, but he found the cabin, nonetheless. He could see its spire of thin smoke gray against the silver screen of dusk. It was not until he dismounted that he noticed the young Indian by the log barn. Startled, he reached for his pistol, until he recognized the brave as Torn-Ear's grandson.

"Ho!" the young man hailed. "I remember you with Washington at Fort Necessity! I am Burke's son now. All my family are wiped out. Gone!"

Tillson stood awkwardly in the pink glow of the October dusk, not certain what to say. Just then, the orange light of the cabin's interior illuminated the darkened yard. Langdon had come to the door.

"William!" he called in surprise. "It's William!" he repeated, as he turned his face back toward the room. "It's Sir William Tillson!" he called with a welcoming smile. "What brings you here? Surely, good news, I trust."

"Yes!" the Major replied. "A new assignment, which requires you!"

"Blue Hatchet! Take his horses to the barn. Then come on in. Both of you."

"Gladly!" Tillson answered. With an uneasy roll of his eyes, he watched the feminine figure who approached the door. It was Sarah.

"William! I so hoped you'd come again! What a wonderful surprise. Do come in! Louise, hurry! It's William! Jonathan, help Blue Hatchet with his horses." An expansive smile filled her face. She reached out to embrace him as he stepped inside. She placed her arms around his neck and shoulders and kissed him on the lips. The ends of her red hair tickled his right ear. Her slender nose, rouge lips and freckles about her eyes captivated him anew. His spirit tried to resist, but his arms enfolded her firm body against his own. A helpless feeling sank within. He kissed her on each cheek in return. "It is good to be back," he whispered. "You are as lovely as ever."

"Hush!" she laughed in a lusty, teasing tone. "We were just sitting down to eat. You must tell us the news. We haven't heard anything in weeks. I have never felt so isolated."

"Plus, we have news for you," added Langdon. "Louise, show him your belly."

Louise hurried to Langdon's side, her hands placed over her upper abdomen. "Sometime in late November," she exclaimed. "Our second child." Behind her toddled Helen Marie, with her tiny hands tugging on her mama's dress.

Tillson could not help but blush. He leaned forward and kissed Louise on her cheek, then swooped up the child in his arms. In all his life, he had never felt so much wanted or at home.

After enjoying a repast of braised rabbits rubbed with home-grown sage, corncakes, greens, and ripe apples, which they washed down with cider and apple brandy, Langdon and Sarah, along with Jonathan and Blue Hatchet, gathered about the low flames of the fireplace. While nestled against bear rugs and mink-lined pillows, they engaged in the latest news with William.

"Tell us what's going on in Williamsburg," said Sarah, gently squeezing his hand. "We've been out of touch with everyone since Langdon came home."

"The Governor is resolute about regaining the Ohio. It's all he talks about, sends dispatches about, and insists we all assist him with. He has secured a colonel's commission in the Regular Army for Horatio Sharpe, the Governor of Maryland, whom the King has authorized to invade the Ohio again. Or so claims Dinwiddie. It is difficult to assess who is commanding whom. The Governor plans to convene the Assembly to requisition the required funds.

"But that's not all of it. Poor George begged him for a commensurate commission as Colonel in the Regular Army, but Dinwiddie turned him down. He's still furious over the debacle at Fort Necessity. Governor Sharpe sent a dispatch that he'd be willing to sign on the Colonel as a subordinate, but his militia would be relegated to different units within the Regular Army. Of course, the good Colonel balked. It was too high a price for his pride to pay. Thus, he's resigned as Colonel of Virginia's western militia and has returned to overseeing his mother's plantation at Mt. Vernon."

"I admire him," said Sarah. "Why he's never married I'll never know."

"He's still young," spoke up Langdon. "He's still in his early twenties, you know."

"And ambitious," added Tillson. "And in love! He's been courting a Miss Sally Fairfax since his return."

"From what I hear, she'll want a wealthier pursuer, someone more akin to her English ancestry," said Sarah. "Not that I can blame her, if I were she." She busied herself by picking up a darning needle and frayed stocking and working on it.

William sat in silence, embarrassed and yet drawn to Sarah's radiance and unashamed candor. He cleared his throat and glanced toward Langdon. "What about yourself?" he asked. "And Blue Hatchet here?" he leaned toward the young brave. "There must be a story somewhere."

"Yes," stated the young Indian. "Torn Ear's last words were to find leathered-guide." he gestured toward Langdon. "I am his new son now. The rabbits we ate, I killed. In back of the barn are bearskins, too. I want to fight with this Sharpe you name, to avenge my fathers. Will you take me when you go? I am strong and will not run."

"I'm confident you'll make a great warrior, but who's fighting under whom and when has yet to be determined. Besides, winter's coming on. If I've learned anything at all, the inclement elements of winter are too daunting to wage war at this time. At least, in this country. In England, it is cold but different. And the same is true of Europe. There you have roads, harbors and means to haul cannon and move troops. Here, you have none of that. Plus steep mountains and rivers, tracts of impenetrable forests, deep ravines and blinding blizzards, scarcely any roads, and paths that mire men and animals in ice and mud. Simple logistics are sufficient to defeat the ablest forces."

"*Bon Dieu!*" declared Louise. "François and his cohorts thrive in such conditions. Have you any idea how cold it is in Canada? At Ft. Niagara or Montreal? Let alone Le Boeuf, Frontenac or Quebec? I shiver to think of it," she laughed. "I know you are braver than that! Our scariest seasons were always the winter, when the Mohawks crept through the snows to ambush our hamlets. Never, *jamais*, could we let our guard down! Nor are they doing it now, I suspect. At this very moment, I wager François, Joncaire, the Marquis of Duquesne and the entire French force are preparing for your Governor Dinwiddie's *invasion*, or this Monsieur Sharpe's threatened onslaught. Colonel Washington should count it a blessing to be spared. Nor do I want you, Langdon, Jonathan or Blue Hatchet exposed to such folly." Suddenly she stopped, pressed her hands against her lower abdomen, and cried with glee. "He's moved. The baby's moving! I've just felt another kick! Forgive me! But I am filled with joy!"

Langdon leaned sideways and kissed her. Everyone laughed. Jonathan refilled their mugs with cider and brandy. Blue Hatchet held up his cup. "A mixture," he boasted. "I am learning to drink like a white man and not get drunk," he said to Tillson. "Very hard lesson," he smiled. "But necessary."

"Langdon, you haven't told me about yourself, or what you've done," William inquired. "I'd love to know. I can't imagine you've been idle since your return."

"Oh, this and that! Actually, Blue Hatchet and I made it to the Holston, to the land grant accorded us."

"What's it like? Will it do? I can't honestly see you as a planter. You have to be destined for greater challenges. No?"

"You sound like a Frenchman. The truth is it was quite an adventure. The Great Warriors' Road cuts through some of the richest land in Virginia. I can see why the Crown wants it colonized. The area's still wild. It's forested with oaks and pine, tall poplars and hickories. In the mountains, swaths of laurel, locust, walnut, persimmon, and berries grow in profusion. Numerous caves and salt licks dot the land. Cool springs gush everywhere. We were able to survey the acres allotted to us. Clear creeks and deep woods form the boundaries. The land runs along a ridge of red clay, perfect for tobacco and raising cattle. I can see myself happy as long as I can still be a woodsman. Perhaps one day I might aspire to be a delegate to the House of Burgesses. You would find it appealing."

Tillson smiled and, without thinking, reached for Sarah's hand. She clasped it before setting her darning aside. He was shocked at what he had done, but he couldn't let go of her hand. It was like a magnet. "At this rate," he coughed with awkwardness, "I'll never see England again. Incidentally, tomorrow I'm bound for the Blue Ridge, to seek out a fort for Dinwiddie. Can you go with me, Langdon? I'll stay no longer than a week. Then return."

Langdon glanced first at Louise, then at Sarah and Jonathan. "I suppose so. But you're looking at a three-to-four-week journey at best. Would you be willing to take Blue Hatchet? Near the headwaters of the James, there are ideal sites. I passed many on my way back from my trek with Gist. I'm certain Blue Hatchet can guide you. Do you know the region?" he asked the brave. "It's high in the mountains. Deposits of iron ore have turned the rocks brown."

"Yes," replied Blue Hatchet. "I remember such rocks and river. Half-

King took us there to hunt elk in the snow. Many gorges and steep cliffs make the way narrow. It is a good place to defend. Plenty of water, too."

"Then it's settled," said Tillson, releasing Sarah's hand, but not before caressing it one last time.

The journey across the Blue Ridge, down to the James, and up into the mountains took two weeks. Blue Hatchet walked beside Tillson's horses, only occasionally running ahead. Langdon had offered Arduous for him to ride, but the Delaware preferred to travel on foot. "Much faster!" he said. "Too many rocks and fallen trees to ride horses. White man is spoiled. The French move much better in the woods."

Toward the end of October, near a pool of hot springs, Tillson spotted a clearing near a wooded hill. A landscape of sugar maples and yellow hickories stretched off to the east. All about, the mountains were aflame in red, russet, and yellow-brown hues. A gurgling spring bubbled out of the meadow's lower end, and a rocky promontory on the ridge above formed an ideal defense line. Above all, the mountains' forested slopes would provide ample timber for a large blockhouse. Its numerous rocks could be hauled in for bastions and fortifications. "This is it!" William declared. "We will spend the night here and reconnoiter tomorrow. What do you say?"

Blue Hatchet nodded approval but pointed to the sky. Dark clouds loomed to the west. They had materialized as if out of nowhere. The air turned heavy and damp. A blustering wind began to moan. The sky grew darker. A snowfall appeared imminent. "No place to stop!" said the brave. "Come, let's find a cave."

Just as the snow began to fall, Blue Hatchet spotted a ledge of rocks, protruding over a shallow cave that looked out across the valley below. They scarcely had time to hobble the horses before the wind, whistling about the rocks, sent huge wet flakes flying into the cave. The two huddled beneath the rocky shelf, built a low fire, and dined on jerky and apples. Louder and louder howled the storm. Wind whipped cold snow into the cave and all but extinguished their fire. Together, William and Blue Hatchet sought shelter behind the horses and shivered as the gale piled increasingly deeper drifts at the cave's entrance. Toward morning the storm abated, and a bright clear sky opened blue above them. By noon, the glare on the ice was blinding. Nevertheless, the two struggled up to the rocky ledge above the clearing to look west. As far as they could see, ranges of white-dusted mountains undulated across the horizon.

"Look!" grunted Blue Hatchet. "Foot prints! Shawnee. See! They were here last night. The spirit of the mountains was with us. A war party! Hunters would have stayed to stalk elk and bear."

Tillson studied the purple imprints in the snow. "Dinwiddie claimed this would be the place that Indians would most likely cross. I wonder if Gist advised him. Or maybe Burke or Washington." Sir William wrapped his cloak about his chest and shoulders. "I've found what I was sent for." He glanced about at the mountains, taking in the snow, ice and the forest. Only the wind broke the silence. A cold shiver seized his sides and spine. "We'd best go."

Chapter Eighteen

THE HONORABLE ROBERT DINWIDDIE glanced out of his office at the falling December snow. The soft white flakes created a somnolent wonderland, but the letters he held in hand brought no peace. One was Colonel Washington's resignation. The other bore the seal of His Majesty's Court. He had opened it second. Its terse yet lofty rebuff piqued his self-esteem while soothing his ambivalence toward Washington.

To His Majesty's Lieutenant Governor of the Colony of Virginia, may God's blessings and goodwill bring courage and hope. We are alarmed with news of Colonel Washington's failure to hold the forks of the Ohio and the loss of His Majesty's Regulars in an ill-suited defense for engagement. Moreover, the Court was shocked to learn of the "assassination" clause in the surrender document. We view all this with grave disappointment. Thereby, the Duke of Newcastle, burdened as he is with State affairs since his brother's death, has assigned defense of the western colonies to Major General Edward Braddock. You shall proceed to provide housing and comforts for the General, preferably near Alexandria, where sufficient troops and war materiel may be stocked until an invasion of the Ohio can commence. By order of His Majesty, King George II, this 13th day of November, in the year of our Lord, 1754.

On that same snowy December day, Major William Graham Tillson, with an eight-member squad of British Regulars and a crew of back-woodsmen, labored midway through the completion of an oak block-house. It stood surrounded by a high wall of oak and hickory logs, with raised platforms for swivel guns and loopholes for flintlock and musket fire. A path protected by rock walls provided access to a nearby spring. Tillson paused to admire the work amid the swirling flakes. Far downslope, a team of horses struggled to drag logs up the hill. Woodcutters in woolen shirts swung their axes in syncopation to fell more trees. The sound of their axe-blades ascended rhythmically upslope. Through the cascade of falling snow, Tillson watched as Blue Hatchet descended the ridge above in something of a jogging run. The brave pointed up the hill. There on the crest of the mountain ridge appeared a dozen or so red-skins. Others crouched behind a line of dark cedars and thick chinquapin groves. A hail of arrows arched upward into the downy sky before falling like sticks around the log fort. A Shawnee, chasing Blue Hatchet, raced through the snow, only yards behind the youth. Tillson opened his mouth in horror, when a woodsman standing beside him raised and fired his rifle. The lead ball caught the Indian in his chest. The red man gripped his throat before collapsing and sliding downhill. Blue Hatchet reached the outer wall, climbed it, and leaped to the ground. Tillson ordered the squad of Regulars to commence an orderly sortie: four men firing, while four men reloaded. Their orders were to descend to the woodcutters and escort them back. The woodsmen took cover behind the fortifications and began firing at the Indians. Suddenly, shrieks from below revealed a horde of savages knifing the woodcutters to death. "Back!" Sir William ordered. "Back! Kneel! Fire and reload!" Slowly his squad returned to the fort, as arrows continued to fall about them and lead thumped into the logs behind them. Two men were struck. A third lay dying inside the log barrier. "Stay low and fire only when certain," William called above the musket roar. "Don't waste your shots. If wounded, crawl into the blockhouse."

Snow began falling faster and harder. The flurry diminished visibility. An Indian would appear, stand up, fire at close range, then disappear in the snow. "Steady! Steady! Keep your order. Wait for targets!" Tillson's warm, calm voice created a measured hopefulness that brought order and strength to the men. Twice Blue Hatchet stood, attracting a Shawnee's attention making him a mark to be shot by one of Tillson's men.

Toward late afternoon, the storm drifted east. The snow changed into a cold drizzle, then ceased. As it did, a red sunset exposed the Shawnee on the slope. Tillson commanded a full volley from every man. The Indians rose from behind the stumps and mounds of snow and scurried over the ridge and out of sight. They left no wounded behind, but trails of blood were visible in the glowing slush.

"How many have we lost?" Tillson asked.

"Two dead, five wounded. Plus the men downslope!" a corporal reported.

"Retrieve their bodies," said Tillson with sadness in his voice. "We'll resume work on the fort tomorrow."

One hundred miles southeast of Tillson's Fort Dinwiddie, Langdon and Jonathan paced in the dirt yard, between the barn and spring, and back into the cabin. Langdon carried Helen Marie in his arms, bounced her about, and kissed her red cheeks. "It won't be much longer," he whispered in her cold ear. Icy patches of mud and snow littered the yard. A raw wind foretold of freezing temperatures. Sullen clouds masked the fuchsia sunset that struggled to cast shadows across the fodder and corn stobs in the field behind the house. Mrs. Weir, her daughter, and Sarah bustled about inside, heating water and greasing hands to assist Louise in her travail. She had been in labor six hours.

Langdon entered the cabin. "Little Helen can't take much more. We're all three freezing."

"Just keep her occupied. Fix her supper and keep the fire going," replied Sarah, who sat beside Louise.

Langdon approached his wife and glanced down where she lay on a mound of quilts between the kitchen table and fireplace. Sweat trickled off her brow, brown hair and pale cheeks. A cold fear crept across his heart. His face felt tight and hot.

Louise stirred, looked up at him and tried to smile. Her complexion had changed from pale to ivory. She raised her hand to clasp his. He had to bend down to grasp it. He set his little daughter in a chair by

167

the table and caressed Louise's clammy hand. Her fingers were swollen, wet, and lifeless.

"Louise! It can't be much longer," he said, clenching his teeth. With his fingers he pressed her hot hand.

She smiled and winced with a sudden sharp pain. "Oh!" she cried. "Oh, *bon Dieu!* Tears streamed down her face, about her neck and chin.

"Good! Good!" praised Mrs. Weir. Her white bonnet slipped forward, blocking her vision, before it caught on her thin nose and withered cheeks. "I can feel the baby coming. The baby's coming! Don't stop!" she pulled the bonnet loose. Louise shook off her exhaustion and bore down, her eyes squeezed tight. Langdon corralled Helen and left his wife to the care of the women. Finally, in a final heave, Louise delivered her baby into the hands of Mrs. Weir. "Look!" Mrs. Weir exclaimed, holding up the baby, with its bloody umbilical cord and grayish-blue placenta half intact. "A boy!" she laughed contagiously. "A big whopping boy!" She held it up for Langdon to see. Tears filled his eyes and Sarah's.

"Louise," he whispered, as he kissed her lips.

She motioned for Mrs. Weir to place the baby in her arms, across her breasts.

"Do you have a name?" asked Mrs. Weir. "You gotta have a name, you know."

"I know," laughed Sarah. "Robert Langdon Philip Burke. Named for his daddy and François. God rest his soul, wherever he is!"

"*Oui! En quelque lieu que ce soit!*" uttered Louise in a tiny voice.

Chapel bells summoned the fort's officers, townsmen and the poor to the holy midnight mass at Fort Niagara. Torches of wind-blown flame bordered the snowy pathway. Cannon fire celebrated the sacred hour. Votive candles flickered softly beneath wooden crucifixes beside nightstands in many homes where tiny whalebone statues of the Blessed Mother were venerated. It was the night of the dear Savior's birth.

O peuple fidèle, Jésus vous appelle.

Venez, triomphants, joyeux!

François knelt before a silver crucifix in his own quarters and rubbed prayerfully through the beads of his mother's rosary. "Holy Mary, forget us not in this barren place! Mother of Christ, have pity on us! O Savior God, just this once, grant my love a child's cry! A baby who might live! I pledge my life in exchange." He paused and listened to the bells. Solemn yet majestic, they tolled in cadence across the citadel's plain. He rose from where he knelt, glanced into the room where Hélène lay in childbirth pain, stared at the old Indian midwife swaying before her. He stepped out into the night. Heaven's dome twinkled with a million glowing stars. "Even the darkness is not dark to thee," he recalled the lines of Psalm 139. *Ipsae tenebrae non erunt obscurae tibi.* The thought filled him with humility and a burning hope. Yes! It was possible! It was possible, yes! He turned and hurried back to his quarters, to the room where Hélène lay. The old midwife was bent over Hélène's legs. The odor of blood caught his nostrils. He put his hands to his mouth. "O God!" he uttered, as he lurched into the room. He stared down past the old woman, past her gray hair and deerskin dress. "What in the hell are you doing?" Then to his shock she turned and presented him with a baby girl, wrapped in a white deerskin shawl, redolent of cedar, sage, and spices, with a knot on her tummy, where her umbilical cord had been tied.

"You happy? *Non?*" the woman smiled. "French woman sleep now. I care for baby till she wakes."

François knelt, clasped Hélène's hands in his own, kissed and caressed them. He brushed her hair back gently with his hands and kissed her lips, her nose and eyes. "We never selected a name, did we?" he whispered. "We were afraid to, for *mauvaise fortune*! Bad Luck!" He stroked her brow. "Anna-Marie Noël? It is Christmas Eve. Will that do? O my God, my dear, you did it! You gave birth to a child! A beautiful child! May all the saints that venerate the Holy Mother cradle you in their arms! Now sleep, as the old woman said. Sleep! Sleep, my dear! Sleep!" He kissed her lips again, and turned to take the child in his arms. "Anna-Marie Noël!" Tears formed in his eyes. He fought to retain his composure. Am I not a man, he thought. A Frenchman, at that? A Major in His Majesty's Marines? But when he stared down at his child, his own child, his and Hélène's firstborn, he couldn't restrain them any longer. Down they slipped across his cheeks and dripped onto his sleeves. My God! My God! I am such a lucky man! *Mon Dieu!*

PART THREE

Charlemagne's Roland on the Monongahela

1755

Chapter Nineteen

FRANÇOIS WAITED RESPECTFULLY in front of the blue satin draped windows and black fur-caped armchairs of Du Quesne's small hallway, outside the Marquis' office.

"You may come in now," directed a crisp voice.

François glanced up. It was the Marquis himself. The Governor stared at him with an aloof, but penetrating eye. His finely powered white wig framed his pale oval face. Steel cold eyes studied Philippe. Their lids appeared scarcely open, revealing as much as they concealed of the man's aristocratic bearing. His blue coat, beige vest, and white cravat created a perfect balance. His thin lips gave way to a gracious smile. "Ah, *bon!* You are here." He held a crumpled document in both hands. François recognized it as the letter from the commandant of Fort Oswego. "They must take us for fools," he slapped the document against the back of a chair. "Come into my office and let's talk."

Inside Du Quesne's office, the latter slumped into a leatherback chair and rested his boots on a bearskin-covered stool. "You see we can't do this," he motioned toward the letter. "Do you know what his Majesty's orders were when he sent me here in '52? Major, they were terse but clear. First, defend the Ohio valley and drive out its British land-grabbers. Second, reinforce the Ohio with forts and establish alliances with the native tribes—all the way down to New Orleans. Third, capture their Oswego. It's a thorn in our side. And fourth, eliminate as much waste and expense to the crown as possible. Sir, this place is rife with corrupt officials and ill-disciplined militias. That is why I prize men like you. I have been criticized and will no doubt be replaced. But I shall not fail the King. So! The answer to our sirs in Oswego is a blunt, *Non! Compris?*"

"Yes, sir!"

"Listen, and keep this to yourself. It's still winter. No? Yes! And we have spies in London. Do you know what they say? What they hear? As early as last fall, the British are planning a three-pronged attack on New France. Yes! The first along the Hudson Valley; a second in the north to our east; and the third against Fort Du Quesne. It's almost March. But we are prepared. The British have assigned a General Braddock and some two thousand troops to capture the fort. I have ordered Joncaire's friend and new commander, Sieur De Beaujeu, to replace Contrecoeur and prepare for an imminent assault. And you, sir, Major de Robert, will accompany the vanguard to arrive, hopefully, before April, and to assist Joncaire and his savages to spy out the adversary. You will also act as an adviser to Contrecoeur until Beaujeu arrives. This is a great honor, you understand, and you will need to depart soon."

François attempted his best to appear elated. "Yes, your excellence!" But his heart sank in his chest. He would have to leave Hélène and tiny Anna-Marie Noël. It was still winter, with streams and lakes frozen, and what few paths in existence, impassable. Plus, food and game scarce! Native allies would balk at leaving their camps yet again for another skirmish with the British. Young braves, Yes! But the wiser warriors, No! "When will the vanguard be ready to leave?" he asked.

"Once the snows begin to melt. You'll join them at Ft. Niagara and lead them down the confluences as conditions permit. You'll be well supplied and armed. Then I must have you back here. We will need you at Crown Point, if they attack there."

"As you command, sir!" François rose to his feet and bowed politely to the Marquis.

For whatever reason, the drop in the spring temperature made the young Colonel incredibly restless. Although almost April, March evenings at Mount Vernon were nonetheless cold. His manservant, Cicero, had provided him with a mug of hot rum; still, Washington felt the night's icy fingers slip down the back of his shirt to pimple the flesh on his ribs. The commission he had sought was now his. Braddock himself had signed the document. He would assist the General, as well as be in command of his own Virginia Regulars. Tillson and Burke would be at his side. Sir Halket and Colonel Dunbar's 44th and 48th regiments would be under his advisement as well, "since your vigilance and woodsman's experience is so coveted by us," Braddock's letter conceded.

But such an acknowledgement had not come without Dinwiddie's aid, nor without the support of Braddock's aide-de-camp, Captain Orme, nor without his personal humiliation. The obsequiousness of his own draft to the General tormented his pride, but what other choice did he have? As he had written to Orme on March 15:

I have ever cherished an inclination to serve in your General's ensuing campaign as a volunteer. That your letter of 2 March, 1755 informs me of his desire to welcome me into his family has greatly inflamed my earnest wish to be a laudable servant to my King and Country and fulill the highest trust of our General's command. How I long to attain even a small degree of knowledge of the Military Arts. With joy I await further dispatch of our General's orders as soon as he arrives in Alexandria.

Now he held in his left hand Orme's greatly anticipated reply:

The General wishes to inform you of his pleasure for you and your Regulars to join him at Wills Creek, as soon as his forces have ascended the Potomac or made their way through Maryland, as appears to be the advice of his engineer, St.Clair. Your Governor has been alerted and has agreed to provide munitions and necessary war materiel for the campaign. We shall see you there. I think that I shall be very happy to form an acquaintance with a person of your esteemed character. I also long to meet your famous guide, Mr. Burke, and your Governor Dinwiddie's trusted and honorable liaison, Major Tillson, of whom I have heard so much. It is our pleasure to serve with such courageous and brave men.

Washington set his mug down and directed his steps immediately to his office. Quickly, he drafted his orders to Burke, with a copy to Tillson. His message was terse:

> *Meet me at Willis Creek, as soon as your situations permit, with supplies and as many of our Militia as can be assembled. The Governor has promised provisions and powder, tents and other ordnance, but apprise each man to care for himself. Attempt your best to be at the site by mid-April. George Washington.*

That same evening, Sir William lay with his arms about Anna. Her white, delicate flesh scented the room with the fragrant eau de cologne, with which she had bathed her body only minutes earlier. Tenderly, William kissed each breast while running his fingertips between her cleavage, around her navel, and about her tiny, hazel, bristly pubic hairs.

"You know I am pregnant," she whispered. "You are going to marry me? You promised! Remember?" her soft words betrayed her desperation.

William froze in mid-motion, before releasing his breath. "Of course, we will," he fondled her hands in his own, as his lips searched for hers and his mouth covered her warm lips. "But I can't see how until this Braddock campaign's over. Can you disguise any bulge until I return? Then we can properly marry."

"Yes. But couldn't you announce our engagement before you depart? Before this battle, or whatever it's going to be called? I would feel so relieved if you would." She kissed his chest and sweaty palms; then looked him straight in the eye. "William, I love you. Please, I can't be shamed."

"It is I who feel shame!" he kissed her. "Tonight. This very night! It is still early, I shall dress and ride to the Governor's masion and announce my intention. And I shall ask the Governor for your hand, for the hand of the lovely Lady Anna Ashby. And the week I return, we shall marry — however pregnant you are. I pledge my honor and all the nobleness I have ever possessed. Will you go with me? The Governor likes a bit of theatre, a bit of the gallant and a rogue's surprise. He's no saint himself."

"William! You have to go alone. He'll see in my eyes that I am harboring a child. For all his tippling self-righteousness, he's no fool. The last thing I need is for the Ladies of the Tidewater to roll their eyes and gossip. 'O, there goes Lady Ashby! Have you heard?'"

"You're right. I'll go first thing in the morning," he kissed her lips. "Whatever my faults, I love you. And I will never dishonor you. I promise you that with all my heart."

"And this Sarah? I know you're fond of her. Do you really mean what you say?"

"She's only a friend! Believe me! Langdon's sister, that's all. The frontier is so different. I have to rely on them," he paused, as he searched his heart in a loss of words. He hated to tell a lie, or deny his fondness for Sarah. He struggled for the right words. "I will never betray you! Whatever happens, Anna, I will always come back. That is my solemn vow. I promise with all my heart."

Tears welled into huge sparkles in Anna's eyes. She placed her hands over her face and cried. "O William! I love you, as I have loved no other. Please, please be true to me. For I shall ever be true to you."

He placed his arms about her shoulders, her naked breasts, and clasped her in his arms. Tears rolled from his eyes, too, and trickled slowly down his cheeks. "I will be true, Anna. On my honor and devotion to the Crown, I swear, I shall be true. There will never be another but you. Never another, save thee."

Langdon read Washington's dispatch with anguish. He so wanted to return to the Holston and begin construction on a cabin. Even more, he wanted Tillson to design a real house, with stone foundations and layered granite slabs, tall chimneys and porches that looked out over the land, and tool sheds and outbuildings to shelter livestock, grain, and smoked hams. He expelled a quiet breath, as he glanced through the haze of the red-tipped buds on the mountains' oaks and hickories and wished he were turkey hunting instead of turning over sod. Somewhere up on the Blue Ridge slopes, Blue Hatchet was lying in wait for the black-feathered birds, but here he was, engaged in the thankless tasks of farming, How his heart ached to return to the wilderness! But without slaves, such as Dinwiddie and Lady Ashby owed, he was condemned to the chains of toil. But the tempting idea of owning human beings filled him with revulsion. Indentured servants? Yes! But slaves, No. Landless Scots, Irish, and English wretches were pouring into the Colonies. Dinwiddie could surely arrange a family or two to assist him with his dreams! And maybe Tillson would come as well. Maybe his romantic fling with Lady Ashby would sputter and his obvious passion for Sarah take wing!

But this Braddock thing! This British insistence on seizing the Ohio for Virginia's glory and the good of the Company's profit! It all seemed so convoluted, greedy and unworthy! Yet hadn't his own grant been seized from others? No one seemed to care. Not even the Assembly. He thought of Louise, her cousin Hélène, François, Joncaire and even Handsome Dog. There would be conflict again. Bloodshed. The forest and rivers would swell with the vessels and arms of French Marines and the cackling howls of their Indian allies. None of it bode well. He was becoming too philosophical, he mused

As they sat at table that evening, Louise fought to restrain her tears. The children, Jonathan, and Blue Hatchet hunched near the hearth. Sarah reached across the table and pressed Louise's hand. "Hopefully, all this fighting will end soon. Maybe the two sides will recognize some common ground. They're good at drafting treaties, exchanging prisoners and flags, and all that falderal! But what a waste of lives!" She turned away from Louise and Langdon. Tears moistened her eyes. "Alas, Sweet William! How I want that brash, stubborn, fool! I guess it will never be!" she smiled, as she turned back toward Langdon.

"Don't despair! Whatever his faults, he's never lost his lust or passion for you." He glanced toward the children, Jonathan and the almond-skinned Delaware, Blue Hatchet. "Who knows what this Braddock expedition will bring! Fame, no doubt, for Braddock. New lands across the mountains! New tribes with hearts to win! And of the French, who knows what? Certainly, Fort Duquesne will not melt away, or its guns fall silent simply at the approach of His Majesty's army."

"That's my worry, too," stated Louise. "I don't want anyone butchered or killed! Especially, not you or François! You must find each other. We must send Blue Hatchet to protect you. You must promise to come back, alive!"

Chapter Twenty

THE SMALL INDIAN PARTY OF JONCAIRE, Handsome Dog, and their handful of seasoned warriors watched the distended column of Sir Halket's 44th Regiment slog its way slowly through the mist on the road below. Around them rose the green slopes of Maryland's spring forests. Wisps of light rain and gray fog concealed their location.

Joncaire grunted with pleasure. At the rate the enemy was traveling, it would take the Regiment another month to reach the foothills, let alone the forks of the Ohio. He nudged Coup de Sang: "Ripe for the plucking, *non*?" he smiled. "We should slit a throat or two."

Handsome Dog wiped a trace of red war paint off his lips. His high cheekbones glistened with drizzle. "It can be done!" he pointed to a straggler who had paused to rest beside a log. "Look!" he nodded, as the soldier struggled to his feet and glanced about for bushes, behind which to relieve himself.

"Not yet! Darkness will soon descend. In the wet and cold, they will huddle to keep warm. Then we can slip in and knife a few. Maybe take a prisoner."

"I want this one," said Handsome Dog. "They will not see me in the mist. I will bring back his hot scalp. You will see."

"Don't be foolish! *Attendez*! There will be time for scalps, later."

"Tekacayah tired of waiting! This one is mine!" Slowly he rose in a crouched position, adjusted the war club in his right hand, and slipped down the hillside through the fog. Just then, a break in the column occurred, leaving the straggler entirely alone. Moments later, the figure of Handsome Dog appeared. Down fell his club. His knife flashed in the rain. No one on the road detected the slightest movement, or rustle of death in the leaves. Minutes later, the Iroquois returned, hunched like a goolish specter in a dream. The black paint under his right eye revealed the dying straggler's fingerprints. In his left hand dangled the soldier's dripping scalp.

"*Alors*! Time to leave," whispered Joncaire. "We will come back to their camp tonight."

The three other braves stretched out their hands to stroke the fresh scalp. Pleased smiles broke the surfaces of their painted faces.

"Shhh! Till later," Joncaire advised. "Let's sortie."

Slowly the day passed. Finally, evening evolved.

Fine drizzle continued to mingle with the fog. Imperceptively, a wispy darkness stole across the narrow road and engulfed the forest on both sides. Campfires glowed in the damp dusk. Exhausted men huddled in wet gear, or sat hunched forward, clasping their knees in front of smoky embers. White tents protected most, but not all. Firearms angled stacked and covered with black tarps. Lone sentinels leaned against wet tree trunks. The smell of beef, beans, and biscuits permeated the air. Pockets of laughter, cursing, and weary grunts contributed to the muffled bivouac of the encamped Regiment.

Joncaire sought to count the tents. They were too numerous and too far apart for an exact tally. He exhaled a long breath. He and his party had been following Halket's troops for three days. The muscled Frenchman calculated the Regiment to number at least 700. He knew a second column of equal strength lay encamped two days behind. His Ottawa braves were watching him. They wanted scalps. Only Handsome Dog had obtained his. They would not cease to pester him until they had their own pelts. Joncaire peered through the mist. Coup de Sang crouched beside him. Two sentinels had strayed just beyond contact of their unit. They had laid their muskets against a tree. One had removed his pipe; the other was in the process of opening his tobacco pouch. The Ottawas pointed and nodded toward Joncaire. "I remain with you," Handsome Dog said. "Let them go." Joncaire gave a signal with his right hand and braced himself for the emotional strike. Silently, the braves rose. In an instant, they caught the sentinels from behind. Long knives flashed in the mist. No sounds of struggle slipped thought the forest. When the braves returned, two held up trophies of bloody hair. The other, the victims' guns, pouches, tobacco, and shiny buttons! *"Bon!"* whispered Joncaire. "We've lingered long enough. Contrecoeur must be informed." Handsome Dog nodded his approval. The dusk had turned to darkness, but Joncaire and his party had already disappeared.

When Langdon arrived at the Potomac, he marveled at the contingent of British troops that swelled the area and the hills beyond. Companies of Red Coats stretched as far as a mile from the newly erected fort, named for Lord Cumberland. The Provincial units Langdon had assembled curled in a wobbly bow-shape as they negotiated the swift crossing. They reminded him of wooly worms struggling to stay afloat. Langdon nudged Arduous into the rapids and crossed with the men in front of him. Blue Hatchet rode on a large white mare to his left.

Once ashore, Langdon spotted Washington among a cluster of aides-de-camp. Slowly, he guided his horse toward them. Blue Hatchet followed at a short distance.

"Well, Mr. Burke!" the tall Virginian hailed him. "I see you've brought your Regulars in stalwart style," he smiled toward a pleasant Captain on his right. "We finally got ours from Alexandria here a week ago. Mr. Burke, it is my pleasure to introduce you to the General's aide-de-camp, the honorable Captain Robert Orme. Captain, one of our most valuable guides and frontier scouts, Mr. Langdon Burke!"

Langdon dismounted and shook the Captain's hand.

"We've heard much of you, sir, and your knowledge of the Ohio beyond the mountains," said Orme. "I had no perception that the distance from here is still miles and days away."

"Yes, sir! Close to a hundred! It'll be no easy campaign," Langdon replied, as he studied the officer. The man was moderately tall, incredibly groomed, with long reddish hair streaming out beneath his black, gold-bordered, tricorn hat. His nose, eyes, and brow formed a gracious T-shaped visage, on which the rest of his fair face hung. A thin dark moustache, thin red lips, and slightly dimpled chin added to his over-all aristocratic countenance. His long crimson coat and tan trousers set him apart from the others. Far from a dandy, he nonetheless projected a debonair air. Sarah would have fallen in love with him in an instant, Langdon mused. Yet, she would have judged him to be too effete com-pared to her more robust Sir William. Which made Langdon wonder where Tillson was.

Washington noted Langdon's glance past the other officers. "Major Tillson's with the General, along with His Majesty's regimental com-manders," he stated, in something of an embarrassed drawl. "They're having high tea and no doubt discussing arrangements amongst them-selves."

Langdon realized that the lanky Washington had been excluded. "We'll show them what to do when the time comes, Major," he replied. "Sides, our own men are waiting on your orders, sir!"

"Of course! Excuse me, gentlemen," Washington tipped his cap to-ward the group of aides-de-camp. "Mr. Burke's a taskmaster, as you can see. I've my own duties to perform!"

Orme saluted the Major in a friendly gesture. "We've ours as well. Braddock will soon be summoning me to record his thoughts of the day. As you know, tomorrow he's expecting delegations from various tribes. Several are already here," he pointed toward the fort. "But they don't seem happy or well disposed to help."

"I'm not surprised," noted Washington. "They're as tired of all this as we are. Most favor the French, but once they see our number, they'll change their mind."

"Guns, gifts, and rum always help," added Burke, "plus keeping our treaties. The chiefs I've known are wary of all of us — French and British alike. Our traders and survey parties aren't welcome, anymore. They won't be pushed."

"Sir, you'd better relay the General's orders to your Mr. Burke, here," Orme interjected. "From what I see," he observed, as he glanced toward the river's beach, "his Milita won't like it anymore that yours did, or our troops!" he added.

Langdon looked into Washington's face. The latter had drawn his lips into a thin line of silence. A pale blush broke momentarily through the gray pallor of the young Major's face.

"Mr. Burke, the General's ordered that any deserters 'shall be hanged from the neck until dead.' Any one refusing an order shall be 'whipped.' Waggoners too. I've already lost three men, and Colonel Halket and Captain Dunbar's regiments have lost four. Two slipped away last night, one during the march across Maryland and a fourth since departing Alexandria."

"St. Clair hasn't made it any easier," said Orme, politely.

"Who's St. Clair?" Langdon asked, embarrassed not to know.

"The Quartermaster and engineer in command of wagons, food, guns, roads — all our supplies."

"What did he do to make himself so favorable?"

"He's ordered any farmer, household, or able-bodied man or woman who refuses forage or supplies to be whipped as an example. Plus, their lodgements are to be used for quartering troops. He's stirred up a hornet's nest since his arrival in February. *Favorable* is not quite the word."

"We all have to deal with him," Washington consoled Burke. "You'll manage. We'll pass it on to the men." He hesitated and looked past Langdon toward Blue Hatchet. "Isn't that Torn Ear's grandson? He's grown, hasn't he?"

"Yes, sir! The boy's sixteen or so. I've inherited him so to speak. He's been with us since the old chief was murdered."

"Murdered? We've heard he's been invited to attend tomorrow's council."

"That I don't know, but Blue Hatchet claims he died. Was killed after we left Necessity. He won't be here. The boy watched him go down."

Washington stared at the stout youth on his horse. "He'll make a valuable guide. I want you to select a group of experienced men to patrol our perimeter. To watch our flanks in the coming days! We'll need to take every precaution. I'm sure some of your French in-laws are out there right now, watching us. Wouldn't you suspect the same?"

"I would! Joncaire in particular! And maybe even François. You do remember him?"

"That I do! And to my regret! I never thought the Jumonville incident would have such deleterious consequences." The tall Major tried to smile. He offered his hand to Langdon and gestured with his left hand to Blue Hatchet. "I fear the hard part's just begun."

Langdon cast a glance about to determine where he should bivouac. The bulk of the Virginia Regulars had encamped above the river and west of Willis Creek. Perhaps Washington had requested the area in the hope that his unit would lead the vanguard once Braddock's forces decamped. Braddock's headquarters appeared to be just south of the fort, but parallel with it. Black loam and red muck still clung to the dark logs, which St. Clair's men had flung up. To his surprise, Langdon recognized the Pennsylvania trader, George Croghan, descending a slope near the large Indian camp east of the fort.

Croghan recognized Blue Hatchet first, then Langdon. The burly trader made straight for the two.

"I heard about Torn Ear," he said to the youth. "You are a warrior, I see. Your people are gone, though. Wiped out by Delaware and Ottawas committed to the French."

Blue Hatchet studied the man's eyes but said nothing. His grandfather had traded with Croghan. Sometimes Croghan had cheated them, trading worn out blankets and weak powder for their best pelts. Sometimes he had befriended them, especially if Hurons were present and wanted to trade captives for guns. Croghan would settle such affairs so as not to implicate his grandfather's people.

"Very well," chortled Croghan. "Perhaps some of your Delaware, Lenape, or Seneca kismen are with the group I've brought in," he nodded over his shoulder toward the Indian camp.

"I will go and see," Blue Hatchet replied, as he led his mare away from the river, mounted and rode upslope.

"Can we talk?" Croghan asked Langdon. "Walk with me," he pointed along the water's edge. "There is much to be said."

Burke paused and stared at the wary trader. A lone eagle feather poked from the side of the man's fur cap. His powder horn hung loosely about his left shoulder. He was using his rifle barrel to support his stance, having placed its butt in the sandy soil at his feet. "What is it?" he asked. "Is it about François?"

"Yes, and no! Montour will be here soon. You remember him? Yes? He came to your camp with me after the Jumonville *massacre*. Captain Montour is more French than anything else. He's been at Ft. Dusquesne with Contrecoeur and de Robert. They are sending him here as a translator, more for themselves than for us. But I need him. He's in the woods now, with a party of Algonquins and Hurons, sent to spy. I met with them last night. Your François is all right. He sends his greetings. He and his French woman have borne a child. All are well. He warns you to stay away from the fort. If Braddock's forces attempt a frontal attack, he fears you'll be killed. I told Montour I'd pass on his message. He hopes to see you at the Council. That's all."

"Thank you. I'm not sure what role I'll be assigned. Just a guide right now."

"Well, watch it! Joncaire knows François favors you, but his braves are another matter. Be on your guard. Whatever your post, be alert. Don't tell what you know about Montour. He's caught in the middle, you know, just as I am," the trader smiled. "It's been a great life till now. The Valley's been everyone's, open to anyone. That will change, I fear, whichever side wins. I hate to see us held back. The land's so fair and the game so bountiful! As for the French, they've stabilized some of the tribes, but they've turned others against us. I don't know what to believe. Your General, though, is sure one hell of a rouser for a fight. God only knows where it will end. I've said enough. Take care, Mr. Burke."

"I am grieved, too. Much obliged!"

It was not until late evening that Langdon finally discovered Tillson's whereabouts. His tent was near Washington's and within earshot of Dunbar's Regiment. To something of Langdon's surprise, Tillson appeared unkempt, seated on a collapsible stool in front of a low fire. A goblet of claret tilted at an angle along the fingertips of his right hand. His crimson jacket lay open; wine spots stained his white shirt, so also grease droplets and flecks of crumbs. Langdon approached in full view, but if the Major saw him, he neglected to look up.

"Hello! It's me, Burke! Why so glum! Isn't this what you've wanted, the chance to advance in a major engagement?"

Sir William scarcely seemed to notice. Where was his mind? Langdon wondered.

"Sir! It's me! Burke! Are you all right?"

Tillson looked up. A vacant stare filled his face. His eyes focused on Langdon, but his mind seemed elsewhere. "Sit down if you will," he motioned. "Sorry I don't have another stool. The ground's wet. Try that log over there!" he pointed with his left hand. "Would you care for a drink? The claret's gone, but there's brandy inside. A gift of his Excellence, the Governor! And rum from Anna's cellar," he said with a twinge of insolence.

Langdon sat on the edge of a stump and laid his rifle across his lap. The air felt muggy, the May night damp and redolent of campsmoke. "Something's wrong. Should I come back tomorrow?"

"No! The General's denied me a command. Says I've become Dinwiddie's 'lap dog.' He never said it in as many words, but the officers around him got the point. I'll be attached to George's units. He's going to be elevated, made part of the General's inner 'family.' I felt I deserved more," he glanced up. "Pardon me, Langdon, but my dear Mr Burke, the General's one royal coil of British offal, if you don't mind my saying so. I wanted to be included! That's all."

Langdon shifted uncomfortably where he sat. No words of consolation flooded his mind just then. "O hell!" he finally managed to utter. "Wait till the fighting starts! That's when our knowledge of the woods will pay off. They'll see!"

"Yes! I suppose."

"Incidentally, Sarah sends you her love. You realize she treasures you. She speaks of you all the time. I understand your love for Anna, for Lady Ashby. We all do. It's just a fact that Sarah's in love with you, too."

"I know. And I her," Tillson confessed with a pained smile. "Can I trust you?" he suddenly asked. "I mean confide in a way we've never talked?"

"Of course! I've never cared for duplicity anyway."

"I've never thought you did. But listen, Anna's pregnant. Really!

Several months by now! And I haven't even proposed. She wanted me to, but it didn't work out. The evening I promised I would, Dinwiddie wasn't at home. I was supposed to announce it there. I've really messed it up! I never meant to hurt her, to . . . to leave her like that! And the truth, as you know, is that I love Sarah, too! Both of them! Truly, Langdon! If God exists, I need to be killed out here somewhere. Die in front of the fort! Fodder for the brass French guns! I was so sure and vain!"

"You'll feel better in the morning, once the powwow with the chiefs begins. Besides, both Louise and Sarah placed me under a vow. They made me promise I'd return you safe and sound. They made Blue Hatchet promise the same. They've done their best to domesticate him. The poor brave hasn't let me out of his sight, till now."

"Where is he?"

"Somewhere in the Indian camp. Hopefully he'll discover some kinsmen among the Seneca and Lenape."

"You make me feel better," Tillson stated. "Why don't you bivouac near me. I certainly don't belong among my own, at least not at the present. That way we can watch each other's back."

"I've already set up for the night, but I'll see. Tomorrow promises to be the real start. I hope to interject myself into the Council through Croghan, or his French friend, Montour. Remember him? The handsome half-breed with rings in his nose and ears, painted like a savage, with his French musket gripped and primed for action?"

"Yes! I do. I hope to get in on that, myself." Sir William rose and sloshed out what drops of wine remained in his goblet. "Tomorrow!" he mumbled. "Till then."

"*Salut*! As our Frenchies would say! Good night!"

As evening mists rose above the forks of the river, François and Contrecoeur walked about the walls of Fort Duquesne, pausing periodically to inspect a log, or rifle slot. Torches on the bastions lit the night with red sputtering sparks. The confluence of the Allegheny and Monongahela murmured steadily, where the two rivers converged to form the Ohio.

"What do you think?" the commandant asked François. "Do you think the fort will hold? Joncaire claims we're up against the best the British can send. Close to two thousand men. With cannon and howitzers, guides and militia. Plus that youthful oaf we defeated—Washington! He's determined, isn't he? O to be so naïve!" he stopped to pat a log.

"Sir, that oaf's one proud man. He'll bear more watching than Braddock's troops. But Braddock's no fool. They say he's quite a disciplinarian, with dedicated and loyal officers. His troops are professional and battle tested. He's banked and supplied by England's top minister of war. I think we'll need to prepare for a long siege. Perhaps blockade the river with logs and barges. Cetrainly, clear more forest and mount abatises in a defensive perimeter."

"What do you know of Beaujeu? By the end of the month, he'll be in command here, and I'll be heading to Montreal."

"Only what I've heard. Brave, intelligent, experienced, a favorite among Indians! He's lived with them most of his life, like Montour. He won't give in. Nor will I, sir. We beat their Virginians at Ft. Necessity. I personally escorted them out of the area. Their arms were inferior to ours, except for the long rifles. Their fighting skills crude; their men discouraged, ill-trained, ill-supplied, and ill-fed. I think we can hold them off."

In the darkness, under the glow of the torches, where its wavering light undulated softly on the water's edge, François looked up into the rising mist. "This is our land, Sieur! It belongs to us. English spoil it. Wherever they press, they exhaust the soil, fell the forests, and defile the tribes with disease and squalor. I will fight beside Beaujeu to the last breath, if I have to," he struggled to smile.

"Major! Please! Don't be so gullible. Who'll care when we're dead! Will the forests? The rivers? Or the savages?" He smiled, while placing his left hand on François' right shoulder. "If only the court had recognized our need for resources long ago! More Marines! Arms! Vessels! Even decent couples to populate the woods! We're just pawns, Monsieur. Just pawns! We've much to do. Let's have some rum and look at the charts again."

Chapter Twenty-One

DAWN BROKE COOL AND MISTY over the sprawling British encampment. The lowing of the large herd of livestock, the smoke of morning fires, the sounds of men rising to the regimental calls to muster—all filled the air with the day's summons to duty. Langdon stretched his arms full length, dusted off his leather shirt, waistband, and leggings, and slipped into his moccasins. Still wiping sleep from his eyes, he walked downslope to a spring near the creek. Blue Hatchet had already preceded him and was kneeling cautiously by the water.

"French beads!" the young brave pointed to a string of circular, blue glass baubles shining in the mud. "Algonquins are here," he nodded toward the Indian lodges across the creek.

"I'm not surprised. The Council meets today, but who knows when."

"I spoke with Seneca people last night. They come, only because of Croghan and their old friend, Montour. They are uncertain of this Great White Warrior, this Braddock. They fear he's ignorant of Indian customs. His braves took women at the evening dance, slept with many, but left no gifts. Very stingy! The old chiefs and sachems are unhappy. I'm not looking forward to Council. You will see."

"I've suspected as much. They say the General's arrogant, too sure of himself. Rude, not only to subordinates, but to his officers! I can't imagine he understands warfare with the French, or how their allies fight. Wait till one takes an arrow in the chest, or watches his comrade's hair ripped off with a single blow!"

"Yes! Remember what your women said. I know what to do."

As noon drew near, Captain Orme approached Langdon and Blue Hatchet. "Good morning, Mr. Burke!" he addressed them. "The General requests your presence during the Council. Your young brave may come, too. The Frenchman Montour has reported that you know sufficient French to parley with him and the Seneca, should that be necessary. Only a few chiefs have come, and they seem very dispirited. Braddock's discouraged, to say the least. Perhaps they'll warm up to you in a way they haven't to us. Please, this way," he indicated with his left hand.

Langdon and Blue Hatchet followed the Captain toward a makeshift log bridge. Once across, they climbed a shallow slope to a large white tent. Regimental guards stood at ease in front of the tent, but to show good faith, had stacked their arms to one side. A crowd of curious natives had gathered outside. Langdon estimated that the total number of Indians could not have exceeded ninety-to-a-hundred. Camp gossip had boasted that up to four hundred fighting braves were to join them. That was not the case. Near the tent, a supply of goods lay stacked in two ox-drawn wagons. A squad of scarlet-glad soldiers stood guard beside them. "I will remain here," said Blue Hatchet. "You go inside."

As Langdon entered, he recognized Croghan and Montour, along with Torn Ear's old friend, Shinglis. Two other chiefs sat in silence beside him. He noted Washington's presence, along with Tillson's, plus several somber appearing figures, native and British. Seated in a canvas chair, behind a wooden table, sat Braddock. He was dumpier than Langdon expected, far ruddier too, but donned in a handsome scarlet jacket that any officer would have envied. His white cravat swallowed his fleshy neck, but his eyes twinkled and sparkled with a sense of the magnitude of the moment. Wampum belts, stretched out on the table, formed an appropriate setting for the chiefs to admire. A cask of rum was visible to the left of the table. Cups bulged from a leather pouch.

"So, Mr. Burke! I've been told. Welcome! Please sit next to your countryman, Major Washington. Mr. Montour, please translate my every word. I want these people to understand how badly I need them." Slowly the General stood erect and lifted one of the peace belts.

Montour rose and stood beside the General.

"My children of Pennsylvania and Virginia and all its lands to the Ohio, peace and welcome! Our great King and kind Father of the British, George II, is pleased to greet you. Only the distance that separates him from you prevents his being here today. Your knowledge of the forests, their paths, rivers, and streams, is coveted by us. Without you, we would be blind in our journeys across the land. Our treaties with you stand inviolable. Our commitment to peace is preserved in these fine belts." He leaned forward and lifted the longest and heaviest of the shell strands for all to see. "Mr. Montour, please translate and extend to each chief a belt of friendship and peace," he nodded.

Montour bent sideways and gathered the smaller belts in his hands. He translated Braddock's words, then with silent dignity, gave each chief a wampum strand. "To you, venerable father," he said to each in turn as he handed them out.

Slowly, an elderly sachem rose to express his gratitude. In his own hands, he presented a fine white belt to Montour to give in turn to the General. "We are pleased to meet our Father's great warrior, who has come across the vast sea. But we are old and fewer in number. Disease and hunger, poverty and treaties have left us homeless. The White man's greed has been our food. What is our Father's wish, now? We want only to live in peace and die near the graves of our fathers and children. I, Scaroyady, have spoken. Now I will weigh your words." He looked about the seated delegation; then he sat down.

Montour translated the chief's words and stood quietly aside.

Braddock appeared unruffled, but Langdon could see that the old sachem's straight talk had unsettled the General's buoyant mood. Braddock took a deep breath and resumed. "The French bottle our progress to the west. They enflame your own native enemies with talk of guns and violence. They spill blood wherever they lurk. They take your women and children as captives and sell them as slaves. Mr. Washington tells me they steal your wives and hunt down your warriors to torture at will. Not until the French are gone can there be peace across the mountains. Be brothers with us. Help us fight the French and your old enemies. I have brought you goods, draughts of rum, knives and guns. Your courage and wisdom are needed. Our army is vast and strong. You too can be part of this great campaign. We welcome you with open arms. What is your wish? To join with us, or let this opportunity pass?"

Before Montour could translate, the frail Scaroyady rose to his feet a second time. He glanced toward Montour, then began in English: "When I was young, I walked where I chose. I hunted where I wanted. I camped with my wives and children under the stars," he pointed to heaven. "Game was bountiful! Geese and fowl abundant! Fish filled our streams. Our corn grew tall and yellow. Our lodges hung filled with deer and bear meat. Our enemies were few. We lived in peace. Then you came. You forced us from our homes. You left us with fevers, sores, and killing disease. Our camps echoed with our death songs. We moved. We moved again. Still, we are forced to move even more. What is our life to you? What do you give us in return? Now you want us to raise our war cry, so that we may die and be no more. I, Scaroyady, have spoken. I accept your wampum and give you mine in trust. I am not a fool! Give us time to think about your wish. Our great English Father has given us many goods, many kettles and pots, blankets and guns and strong knives. We have become dependent on you. Let us talk about this alone. We will come again in the evening. Is that not so?" he directed his question to Shinglis and the others. They sat without nodding, acquiescing in silence. "So. We will return in the evening."

The General had been standing all this time. The huge wampum belt sagged in his hands. He scrunched his mouth but held his peace. "We shall await your decision," he directed his reply toward Montour. "Tonight, we shall have a great feast, with rum and gifts for you and your children." He turned toward an enlisted soldier just inside the tent. "See that each delegate receives a cup and a full draught," he smiled awkwardly toward his guests. He released a disappointed moan before reseating himself at the table.

Langdon glanced at Washington, Tillson, and Orme. All were silent, each keeping his thoughts to himself. Langdon pulled himself up and slipped outside to rejoin Blue Hatchet. He wasn't needed, he knew. Councils with the Indians all seemed alike. A true sadness sank in his heart.

As evening drew nigh, the great blue sky filled with dark shadows to the west. Streaks of purple, pink, and orange concealed the setting sun's soft disc. Tom-tom sounds reverberated throughout the forest. A blazing fire silhouetted Shinglis and Scaroyady's half-clad natives, as they danced about communal fires. British cooks, cloaked in canvas aprons, turned a slaughtered beef over glowing coals. The hiss of its broiling fat filled the air with the aroma of grease and glaze-blackened meat. Barrels of rum had been opened, and Indians whooped half-drunk, half-dazed as they danced at their host's gala.

Langdon strode toward the General's tent to take his place at the Council. Montour held the flap for him as he entered. "Do not fear!" the Frenchman whispered. "Enjoy this night. Joncaire's purse has bought them off. They will be gone by morning. He sends his farewell: *'Salut! N'approche pas le fort.' Vous-savez, oui?"*

"*Oui! Je comprens. Dite lui d'accepter mes sentiments, le meilleure! Mais je dois faire ce que mon commandant demand. Tant pis, tant mieux!"*

Montour stared hard at him. Langdon understood what his glare meant. He would have to take his chances at the fort. He had been forewarned.

Langdon sat through the Council, half-listening, half self-absorbed. He wondered how Louise, Sarah, and the children were doing. If they failed to capture Duquesne, what would their fate be? Indians would pour across the Alleghenies and raid every town and cabin within reach of their tomahawks. They must not fail! Scaroyady's eloquent voice awakened his ears again. The chief spoke in his own tongue.

"We have reached our decision. We have come to tell our White Father Braddock that we will fight with him, perhaps. We understand Gist's son is rasing arms to the South. Our old enemies, the Cherokee, are being courted. We fear their presence among you. They will want the spoils. They are still smarting from their many defeats with our cousins, the Iroquois. They treat us all alike—as cowards before our Father's people. We will watch and see if they come. If not, we will join you. We give you our solemn vow. We are not like their women. We pledge our knives to you. We will be your scouts. We prize your wampum pelts. May the Great Spirit hear our voice and decide who among us lies. If the Cherokee come, we must go. Is it true? We must know. That is all I, Scaroyady, have to say."

He seated himself to the pleased grunts of the other chiefs and Indians. Montour stood quietly beside the General and translated the old chief's words.

Now Shinglis rose. His right shoulder lay bare; an ermine pelt covered his chest and left shoulder. A hat of pheasant feathers with blue and red ribbons decorated his cap. His white leggings boasted a fringe of black scalp hairs. White beads glistened on his tan moccasins. He cleared his voice. Then spoke, this time in his own tongue:

"Ho, ho! Great War Chief Braddock. Have you come to mock us with this word about Fort Duquesne? I have seen it myself. I have parleyed with the wise Gist and the French Fathers at their fort. They are strong. With many guns, many ships, and many tribes on their side. They will not surrender to you. They own the Ohio. Since the time of their Father, La Salle, they have filled the rivers with their boats and canoes. They have traded with us for years. Their guns are not as reliable as yours. Their blankets coarse and rum sour. But they keep their word. They do not fill the woods with stinking villages of squatters. They trade with us. They provide us goods. They warn us to fear the English. If we fight with you, their Ottawa and Mingo allies will attack our villages and take our women and children. Our blood will be on their knives. With broken bones, we will fall in their gauntlets. What promises do you have to offset these bitter woes? Will you give us lands? Will you leave us in peace? Speak, for summer is coming, and we must return to our lodges, lest they attack while we linger here."

Montour translated word-for-word what Shinglis had spoken. Braddock listened with astonished indifference. His self-pride glowed on his face. He rose and addressed the sachems: "I am shocked at your womanish words. Where are the brave warriors that fought us once in the woods of Maryland and Virginia? Our Great White King of England has sent me with two thousand troops to level Duquesne. If we falter or fail, yes, the allies of the French will stream across the mountains to take your scalps and ours. As for lands, we cannot promise you more. Where is your courage? Your commitment to your lodges and people? We have the great thunder guns, numerous resources, muskets for you, and trained soldiers to protect you. What will your enemies say when they learn of your temerity today? As for the Cherokee, we have requested their assistance. But now that I have heard your voices, I will ask them to halt short of the River, only to block what enemy may escape their way. Is that not reasonable? We have meat to eat now and drink and gifts. I await with humble heart your reply." With great ceremony he reseated himself, but not without glancing uncertainly toward Washington, Montour, and his staff. Once again, Montour translated the General's speech.

Scaroyady rose to his feet and looked about the Council. "If the Cherokee come, we leave. If they remain south of the great River, we will join you. Let us smoke the pipe and enjoy the feast you have prepared. If my brothers wish to say more, let them stand. No one here is a coward. Your reference to our 'womanish words' bites into our souls. You have much to learn. Even your own missionaries have taught us your Golden Rule, but we have not heard it from your lips. Still, we have come in peace. Let us mingle now with your people. I have no more to say. Nor can my ears hear more." He reseated himself and awaited the pipe that was passed about the men. He puffed on it gently. Finally he stood with his head erect and moved toward the table and a mug. The other sachems joined him. No smiles broke the solemnity of their glares about the tent. Montour offered each a cup of rum. One by one they stared at the General. They drank their rum in silence, before leaving the Council.

"Damn, damn, and thunder!" Braddock muttered under his breath.

By early morning, the Indians were gone.

"A message for you," a Virginia Regular, dressed in buckskin, addressed Langdon. He was short in stature, with a thin growth of blond beard and the countenance of a woodsman. The morning sky glistened silvery-blue in the East. Quietness hovered over the camp and forests above the fort. He and Blue Hatchet had been up since dawn. Still, it seemed early for "messages" of any kind to be delivered to anyone. Langdon accepted the sheet of folded paper. "Thanks," he said to the frontiersman. "Is the sender waiting for a reply?"

"Yep!" answered the woodsman. "It's from the Major himself."

Langdon glanced through the note. *You and your brave take horses and scout the area to the north and west. Hunt along the way. Look for signs of an ambush or potential sites for one. Return in a week. Major George Washington, Commander of His Majesty's Virginia Forces.*

"By all means," replied Langdon. "Tell the Major we're on our way."

The spring sunshine filled the forests northwest of the Creek with glimmering shimmers of light. For two hours, Langdon and Blue Hatchet rode slowly up through the wooded slopes. Pollen speckled the underbrush with yellow-green dust. Dog hobble, Mayapples, trillium, and dogwoods greeted the riders with displays of white and pink blossoms. Mushrooms grew in abundance in the dark patches of damp shade. Oak and maple leaves, hickory and poplar trees created a soft patena of new growth along the higher ridges. Spring had launched itself into its vernal world again. The prolific annual wonder flooded Langdon's soul with thoughts of home, crops, Louise and Sarah, Jonathan and children. There was much for them to do. Fear, too, that Cherokee and Shawnee war parties might launch raids while they were gone.

The two rode on. Toward late afternoon Blue Hatchet raised his arm and pointed toward a flock of turkeys creeping through the undergrowth. Their pink combs and yellowish beaks could be seen, bobbing above and through the tangles of ferns and small plants. Langdon gave the nod and, just as a bird started to lift into flight, Blue Hatchet shot it with an arrow. The others flapped away in a thunderous burst of feathers. The young warrior retrieved the bird and flung it up, spurs high, behind his saddle.

Since early morning, they had been following several sets of moccasin tracks. Langdon noted that the fresh prints descended out of the mountains and ran parallel to the main path that led from Willis Creek toward the Youghiogheny. It was the trail that he, Washington, and Gist had taken when ascending the route to reinforce the Virginia Volunteers. In no way could the narrow path support Braddocks's army or accommodate the huge wagons and heavy guns that St. Clair had in tow. The bold moccasin tracks crisscrossed it at will.

"That has to be Joncaire's party, or Montour's. What do you think?" Langdon asked Blue Hatchet.

"Probably came together. Prints are very fresh!" the youth pointed. "Seepage has not filled in! Maybe two, three hours old at most! Braddock should be careful."

"Agreed!" Langdon relaxed in the saddle and glanced about. "There's not a site on these slopes that wouldn't make a perfect ambush."

"Yes! But Torn Ear liked steep areas or wooded vales. They make escape faster. Too many gentle rises here! Not enough undergrowth. No deep downfall for sudden attack! Should we look for shelter, or try sneaking closer?"

"Let's ride on. They don't seem worried about anyone following them. Perhaps by dark we'll detect their camp."

Just then a gun roared softly in the distance. Its muffled cough left no doubt. Langdon nodded toward the young brave. The two dismounted and guided their horses slowly along the trail. They stopped and cocked their heads to listen. To the southwest the sun was already sinking behind the wooded hills. Its rays of yellow and gold sent limpid sheens of light high into the faint blue sky. A cool breeze forewarned of a still cooler night. The dankness of the woods, steeped in rotting leaves, piqued Langdon's nostrils. Slowly, they advanced up the trail, then guided their horses into the woods. A squirrel clattered up a tree. Birdcalls ceased. Langdon could feel his own heartbeat.

Blue Hatchet nodded toward faint sounds just beyond a ridge of pines. A low fire had been lit. Four to five figures appeared, then disappeared. Voices rose then fell to a hush. The woods suddenly grew silent. "We've been spotted," whispered the youth. "We must mount and ride. Quick!"

Blue Hatchet's warning scarcely escaped his lips when an arrow thudded into a pine trunk, just missing the boy's right ear. The two swung into their saddles and galloped out of the woods. A gun roared, and lead whizzed by Langdon's horse's neck. A second roar shook the silence. The ball caught Blue Hatchet's horse's tissue in its left flank and exited with black gore out the other side. The horse stumbled headlong, hurling the youth into the underbrush. An Ottawa appeared, raised his arm, and hurled his steel axe toward the boy. It struck a stump between the youth's legs. Quickly, Langdon turned in the saddle, raised his flintlock, and fired. The Indian screamed and brought his hands up to his face. Blood spurted red over the native's hands and down his chest. A second savage raced toward them. Langdon turned his horse about, as Blue Hatchet held up his arm, caught Langdon's, and hopped behind his saddle. Down the path the two rode, the frightened Arduous galloping as fast as its legs could carry it. Once out of range, they dismounted and led the horse up a rocky stream and into a glen of vines. Langdon held to the horse's reins, as he and the boy lay down. No one appeared to be chasing them. Quietly, Langdon reloaded his gun. The enemy's party had lost one dead and had killed Blue Hatchet's horse. They would likely be content for the night, or move on, fearing that Braddock's British might be close behind. Langdon doubted that Joncaire would take the chance. Only after a long silence, however, and night began to settle in, did Langdon signal for Blue Hatchet to rise and follow him.

They returned up the trail. In the fading dusk they found Blue Hatchet's white mare. Her eyes loomed wide; blood glistened slick on her upper side. The boy bent down and patted her damp neck. He ran his fingers along her mane. With silence he turned and looked up toward Langdon. His blanket and jerky bag were still tied to the horse's saddle. The turkey was gone. His bow lay broken, though his quiver dangled across his back. "My gun!" he suddenly blurted. "There!" he pointed under a mat of crumpled brush and trampled ferns. Quickly, he scrambled toward it and picked it up. It was still loaded and uncocked. Both men expelled sighs of relief. They hastened toward the ridge, where they had seen the fire. Its ashes lay scattered, though its pink embers glowed faintly in the dark. A deer's intestines and head had been discarded, but its heart and kidneys were missing. A quick energy for the fleeting party, no doubt! "We'd best camp upridge," said Langdon. "Tomorrow we'll trail them more."

Blue Hatchet rubbed his shoulder. "I feel like true warrior now! *Non*?" he said in French.

"Yes or no, that was a close one! Let's look for a spring and place to camp. We'll hunt tomorrow."

Morning broke in a soft clap of thunder. Cold rain began to fall and dampen their blankets. Hurriedly Langdon and Blue Hatchet rose, chewed a string of jerky each, and fetched Arduous. Carefully they made their way back to the trail. Langdon mounted while Blue Hatchet jogged ahead. Soon the rain turned into an icy deluge as they reached the muddy path. Black puddles formed between the layers of woodsy debris. Langdon had to dismount. Harder fell the rain and sleet. Down and down it poured. They found shelter under an overhanging ledge of rock, covered by laurel, vines, and galax. The rain continued steadily until streams of runoff sloshed across their moccasins and footgear. Slowly, the storm abated; the thunder rumbled farther and father away. The rain ceased and warm beams of golden light burst through the forest in steamy haze.

For another hour they followed the soggy path. Any remnant of footprints, however, had been washed away. While in the process of resting, Blue Hatchet raised his head and nodded for Langdon to remain still. Something or someone was descending the trail. Sounds of animals slipping in the path filtered through the misty light. Just then, a bearded woodsman mounted on a bony horse and leading two mules half-slid, half-splashed into view. Bundles of pelts straddled the struggling mules. "A morning!" called the startled man. "One hell of a fine day!" the grizzly figure hailed. "Well, don't look so blamed scared! Names Joseph Banner. Trapper, trader, woodsmen, esquire! If you two ain't a sloppin' mess! What's brings ye this way?"

"I guess you've been out a long time. We're headed toward Duquesne. What do you know of the French ahead?"

"Armed and waitin'. Indians pilin' in from all around. Never seen so many savages in one place. Drinkin' and firin' guns day and night. Commander there was beside hisself. I was lucky to make it through."

"Did you by chance pass a party of Indians last night or this morning? They shot one of our horses. A Frenchman might have been with them."

"You bet your skinny asses! Who's that savage with you, anyway? Friend or enemy?"

"Friend! What happened, if I may ask?"

"Caught me off guard. Four of 'em! They was hidin' on a rock. This big ass brave wanted to hatchet me, but the Frenchy wouldn't let him. They throwed me down and would of taken my pelts, save for this wampum I carry." The stranger dismounted and produced a quilted strand of mother-of-pearl shiny beads. "Come from the Iroquois themselves. Bartered for it one winter, years ago. It's saved my ass many times! Sides, I didn't trap these furs but traded for 'em. The big Indian plum fell all over hisself once he seen the belt. Strange power these things have. He wanted it. Offered me his gun for it. I refused. The Frenchy spurred them on. They was carryin' a dead one on a pallet. Face was blown to hell! Well! I'm fixin' to reach the Creek by night. Be careful. Lots of ambush ahead! Them rascals could be lurkin' anywhere. *Salut!*" he chucked in French. He remounted and pushed past them. "Don't take to lingerin' long," he called back over his shoulder. He began to whistle as he dropped out of sight.

"I guess we'd better check some of the sites," Langdon said.

"Do all white men hate us?" asked the youth. "Perhaps I should go back to my people?"

"Aren't Louise and I your people?" asked Langdon. "Sarah and I would be lost without you. You are my son, no? My brother! I wouldn't have it any other way."

The brave looked intently at Langdon. A glimmer of pride sparkled in his eyes, as the two remounted Langdon's horse.

Chapter Twenty-Two

ANNA REELED WITH NAUSEA as she struggled out of bed. The May sunlight dazzled bright in the lacy curtains where Daphne, her chambermaid, had drawn the drapes aside. Muggy air poured into the room through the open windows. Flies buzzed in the curtains; dead mosquitoes hung trapped in the cheesecloth netting that surrounded her bed.

After rushing to her toilette, she reached for a damp cloth and wiped her splotchy face. "O God!" she muttered. She pulled on the cord by her nightstand and waited for Daphne to come up the stairs.

In her hands she held the only letter William had managed to post. The Governor had delivered it the preceding week. He had driven over in the early afternoon with Clarence. Oddly, the two men—master and servant—behaved as if old friends. Clarence, ever polite, ever well-mannered, ever obsequious but bold to chide in his disarming way, and Dinwiddie, sweating lightly in his green satin jacket and white shirt, stuffed into white breeches, set off by his silk stockings and clumsy shoes.

"Anna! Dreadful news!" he addressed her, as he sat in the parlor sipping tea. "They're under march, but only ten miles past Cumberland! Washington's men are taking the brunt, scouting the woods and fending off savages," he chuckled with a sneer. "But our illustrious General, Mr. Braddocks, is already weary, fuming from delays; miserable from the heat. Ah, mountain spring! Humid and wretched! But he wouldn't listen to me. Let him pay for it with the sweat of his brow. Yes! But here, dear, a post for you from your handsome Major," he smiled. "You do look uncomfortable, Anna. Is the heat bothering you?"

"Yes! Terribly!" she feigned as she fanned herself by the cool drafty fireplace. "I trust Sir William is well," she attempted to smile, as she accepted his letter from the Governor.

"Braddock's made him Washington's aide-de-camp, so to speak. Imagine? Part of his staff, but not really. The General's no fool! He knows William's attached to me. As for George, he's gained quite a foothold with the Regulars and the old chief. But I don't like the rate they're traveling. The French must surely know of their whereabouts. Taking the Fort won't be as easy as White Hall thought." He glanced toward Anna. He could see that his banter wasn't having the slightest effect on the dejected lady. "Well, Lady Ashby," he sputtered, as he rose to his feet, "Williamsburg's calling! And the Assembly hasn't voted funds yet for the Provincials or their aid." He bowed slightly as he set his cup of tea on a nearby stand.

Clarence, who had been sitting in the hallway, suddenly entered the room. Dressed in purple attire, save for his white shirt and stockings, he made a handsome figure, one surely the fairer members of his race must admire, Anna thought, as she watched him step in. "Governor, Sir!" the man addressed Dinwiddie with feigned timidity. "Haven't you forgotten something? What yous and I was talkin' about on the road."

"O great thunder!" Dinwiddie exclaimed. His face turned crimson around his jowls, his cheeks white about his mouth and eyes. "Lady Ashby! My sincerest apologies! May I be the first to congratulate you? Major Tillson has asked me for your hand in marriage. Imagine? Me, of all persons! He wishes to wed you immediately upon his return! Do you accept?" he asked with envious embarrassment.

"Do I accept?" she laughed, with a rush of hot tears to her eyes. "Yes, your Honor. But, of course! How your news delights me! O goodness, how soon might that be?"

"No one knows, my dear! We must settle this Duquesne thing first. Let's hope he returns a fit man," he dragged out his last words with an uxorious smile. "We must simply wait and see."

Anna released a deep sigh. Daphne had yet to arrive. She re-dampened her cloth with more water and wiped it gently across her face, mouth, and lips. A smile formed on her lips as she thought of William. She ran her hands down her flanks and ribs. She had to be at least four months pregnant. Her dresses and slips felt snug, but signs of her fecund condition hadn't caught any eyes yet. Yet! She thought. "O William!" she whispered to herself. Her hands felt weak, sweaty, and clammy. Her stomach convulsed. With tears in her eyes she rushed to her toilette again. Nothing but the heaves! Her sides ached.

She collapsed in her largest armchair and glanced through William's letter again. With joy and excitement she relished each word:

Dearest Anna,

How art thou, precious love? Is the wisteria in bloom, with all its laven-der clusters? Has it climbed to your windowsill? Have your gorgeous magnolia blossoms opened to perfume Ashby Hall? Do you still love me? Do you still want me? I left you in such a cowardly fashion! Shame is my companion by day, remorse by night. But I am sweeping all that aside. Just moments ago, I penned a letter to our honorable Governor. I have asked him for your hand in marriage. It is official, my dear. I am yours forever, if you wish it. Somehow you will let me know.

As for this campaign, it has become a nightmare. The going is slower than anyone imagined. The road west is narrow, entangled with roots and foliage, far too tight for our guns and wagons. Even the troops have to march in single file. Perfect for ambush! Burke is ever vigilant, along with his savage, Blue Hatchet. Washington rides proudly among his men. He has the General's ear, even over his regimental commanders. A terrible event occurred last night. Two of Dunbar's men deserted. Burke's party of himself, Blue Hatchet, and one other were sent to trail them. They found the men scalped, mutilated, and roasting on spits. Some of their back meat had been eaten. A horrid lesson for all the rest! One of Washington's regulars slipped away, too. Morale is low. I had so prayed this expedition would take less than a week. With all our guns, ordinance, firepower, and disciplined men, the Fort should fall shortly upon our arrival. If so, I may be ordered north, with new regiments to invade the French forts along the Lakes, especially north of Crown Point and along Lake Champlain. While at Boston, I traveled to the Lake. It is so beautiful, the mountains so green and forests pristine. Whole hillsides swell with blue berries in the late summer. We could have a cottage there, until time to return to Virginia and your Tidewater estate. I long for your arms. Try to write me. I love no other save you. Forgive my ramblings and manly heart.

Ever your lover! Your husband to be!
Sir William Graham Tillson,
Major in His Majesty's Service and liaison
to the honorable Lieutenant Governor of Virginia,
Robert Dinwiddie. Somewhere in the forest,
west of Willis Creek.

Anna stared past the window, its sill scented by the clinging wisteria and the melancholic humming of dying flies. She looked up. Daphne had just entered. The black girl had curled her black hair in ringlets, similar to Anna's blonde coiffeur.

"Miss Anna!" the girl blurted. "You've been cryin' again. And sick! And you was so happy knowin' your man's comin' back! Don't you know what it is?" she glanced toward her cloth and pale mouth. "You is pregnant, Miss Anna! You with child! And it's gonna show soon! Ain't that so? But don't fret! I know what to do. And I ain't tellin' no one, cause you like my sister! It ain't fittin' that your man left you like this! Handsome or not! Here, Miss Anna, let's wash up and get you dressed."

Darkness had crept across the cornfield, the latters' green shoots only inches tall above the split-rail fence. Shadows smothered the livestock stall; the strong aroma of collected manure and urine drifted in the night air. A milk-white moon gleamed off the outer walls of Langdon's cabin. Inside, Sarah, Louise, and Jonathan watched in silence through the loopholes in the rear of the house. One, two, three copper figures appeared, then disappeared along the border of the woods. In the moonlight, even the oak leaves glowed lambent. Soon, the figures reappeared. Racing silently, they approached the edge of the split-rail fence. Sarah's heart thumped in her chest. Louise's hands trembled. Jonathan aimed his rifle through the closest loophole, held his breath, and fired. The spark in his flintlock flashed yellow; the roar awakened the children, who commenced to cry from the corner where they were sleeping. A puff of white smoke veiled Jonathan's face, then dissipated. Quickly, Sarah handed him a second rifle. He aimed, fired, and reached for Louise's gun. She had spilled the powder on the floor; the ramrod still poked from the barrel. A loud shriek pierced the night. A lone Indian raised his arm in defiance and fired at the loophole. The warrior was naked, save for the skimpiest loincloth. The thunk of the bullet sent chips into Jonathan's face. The Indian ran toward the stall and disappeared. Two wounded savages followed. They stumbled off into the darkness without a sound. Jonathan took a deep breath and wiped the smoke and gun powder from his brow. His brown cropped hair hung limp in his face. "I don't think they'll come back," he volunteered with uncertainty.

"Louise, see about the children," Sarah tried to comfort her. "I'll reload the guns and check the pin with Jonathan."

Outside, the two stole quietly toward the animal enclosure. Blood glimmered in the moonlight's path about the barnyard. The cow lay dead. Chickens clucked and flapped their wings in the shed's rafters. Brown and red feathers floated in the air. The intruders had attempted to steal one of the horses, as its reins were cut, but its hoof thumps brought relief to Jonathan's ears.

"Thank God we still have mounts," Sarah stated with relief.

Inside, Louise sought to regain her calm as she huddled near the fireplace with her youngest child. The fire's warm embers glowed pink under a film of fine white ash. "Where do you suppose they are now?" she asked the two. "We haven't heard a word since late March. I so worry for Langdon. How many chances can he take? The good Major is too found of him."

"I know," said Sarah. "I can't help but wonder about William. The whole frontier lies wide open."

"My fear's for the folks in the valley," mumbled Jonathan. "Maybe we'll hear something soon."

"Let's pray so," Louise whispered. "The days and nights are so long now that spring has come. And so lonely! We fear for ourselves, but what about François and Hélène? I worry about them everyday."

"They say deserters are leaving the camp. Only last week one showed up across the gap. He was returning to South Carolina. They say he was 'fearin' for his life,' at least that's the word the traders are passing."

A glum silence descended upon the group. Gradually, the women fell asleep. Jonathan propped himself sideways against his loophole, and peered out into the moonlit field. Nothing stirred in the wooded land-scape. His rifle lay limp across his lap. Slowly his eyelids closed, and he too joined the women in sleep.

The May sky pulsed with shafts of bronze light, as the morning sun broke free over the woodlands at Fort Le Boeuf. Hélène scanned the French Creek for signs of northbound canoes, but none was in sight. The commandant had promised her safe passage to Fr. Machault, and then to Fort Duquesne, as soon as the last detachment of French troops had disembarked. Now two weeks had past since the Marines had left. And another week since the ragbag force of grumbling Canadian militiamen had followed. The latter had been called to arms only the month before. They pushed off in a flotilla of fifty or more canoes. Hélène had watched them embark, each man encumbered with his backpack of clothing, knives, Tulle musket, hatchet, and other necessities. An entire morning was required for their launch.

Slowly, she turned away. Did François even know she was coming, or attempting to come? On her back, little Anna-Marie Noël slept in a wicker papoose. Hélène scrunched her lips and watched for just any boat to ripple the water. She turned to look north. *Bon Dieu!* Yes! There, in the shadows, one was coming! No, two, at least, three canoes rounded the bend. A *fleur de lis* flapped docilely in the morning breeze. Seated behind the canoe's Algonquin rower was none other than de Beaujeu. She had met the Captain at Ft. Niagara less than a month ago. He had made it his headquarters until the militia had arrived and sailed for Le Boeuf. Per-haps he would take her with him to Fort Duquesne? He was handsome, refined, and modestly tall. If there were any features that defined him they had to be his pale complexion, long nose, wide brow, and shoulder-length blond hair, tied with a silk ribbon, behind his neck. Of noble birth, would he condescend to accept her company? Would he escort her to

Fort Duquesne? She ran her hands through her dark hair and descended the bastion steps. He might remember her. After all, she had been introduced to him as Monsieur Major de Robert's "*belle femme.*"

"*Mais oui!*" he had said. "I've heard of him. One of our finest officers, yes! Travel's with Joncaire, I believe? Very knowledgeable and effective negotiator! Yes! Knows the Ohio well, *Non?*"

"Yes, my Lord," she had replied politely.

Now he was here. Canada's greatest Indian fighter, or so Montreal claimed. She rather thought the honor belonged to Joncaire, or Coup de Sang, or even Yellow Hawk. But he was Montreal's man. Chosen by Duquesne himself! Appointed to succeed Contrecoeur and hold the forks of the Ohio. His Majesty's Kingman of the vast domain from the Mississippi to the Great Lakes!

As his canoe scudded ashore, several young officers hurried to assist him. He would have none of it, however. He waved them aside, stretched his legs, and strode toward the gates. Hélène anticipated his approach and timed her casual "bump" into him perfectly. "Ah, Monseiur! I do beg your pardon," she groaned, as she adjusted Anna-Marie's papoose on her back. "You're Captain de Beaujeu, isn't that so?" A curtsy was in order, but she was too proud and too fully half Indian to acknowledge the respectful custom.

The Frenchman studied her, smiled, and began to press on when suddenly he wheeled about and bowed stiffly. "De Robert's wife? No? I believe so," he smiled admiringly. "Yes! You are a brave one, indeed."

"Forgive my affrontery, Captain, but I was promised an escort to see my husband. He's at the Forks, and I have a right to see him." Her dark eyes focused on the agate blue of de Beaujeu's.

He stared into hers without flinching. "So, what sort of 'right' is this? I've not heard of it before. Though it is not uncommon."

"I want to see him. That's all. May I go with you when you leave?"

The Captain rubbed his pale chin. "*On verra!*" he replied. "*Peut-être!* We will see. Yes. If it works out! *Bonjour,* Madame," he bowed; then entered the fort.

Hélène stared hard after him. She knew to keep her distance. It was said that in war he dressed like an Indian and fought like one, with musket in one hand and tomahawk in the other. She would wait for a later opportunity.

As she savored that possibility, she revisited a tucked away moments of her own childhood. One afternoon in her mother's Ojibwa village, she had followed a French trapper walking into the woods. He turned around to meet her and in his hand he held up a strand of pearls.

"*C'est à toi!*" he said, jiggling them to her delight. "You can have them. "Come, see. Just for you." Drawn in by the bearded man's melodic French voice, she reached for the offered jewels. She had never touched beads so perfectly round and smooth. With eyes bright and happy, she looked up into the trapper's face. But what she saw made her breath catch with horror in her throat. In one quick motion, the trapper jerked the pearls from her hands and grabbed her wrists.

"Ma-ma!" she yelled, trying to pull away from him, but his grasp was too strong. Instively, she stopped pulling and lunged at him, her teeth bared. When she clamped down hard on the trapper's hand, he let out a howl and slapped her to the ground. Quick and lithe, she rolled away from him, leaped to her feet and took off at a run toward her people's lodge. The trapper cursed and went for his knife, quickly catching up with her. She could see his knife, its blade gleaming in the wooded light. Suddenly, the trapper was no longer running, he was falling. "Ah!" he cursed, his foot caught under a root. He lost his grip on the knife, which sailed out of his hand, coming to rest in front of her. Reaching on instinct, she picked up the knife, blade tip pointed downward. Before the trapper could struggle to his feet, she trust the blade into the soft flesh of his neck the way she had seen her uncle kill a fallen deer.

She ran without looking back.

The next day, an old sachem approached and sat with her outside the lodge. "*É-len!*" he called her." My little one. You are part French. *Non?* As your father would say."

She nodded.

"Yes child, but remember you are also Ojibwa. And our ways are as holy to us as the French man's." The chief pointed to the sky, blue and smoky from the day's silent Ojibwa fires. "The Great Spirit watched over you, Manitou above. He has many spirits who hide in the forest to help us. It was his spirit in the root that tripped the man. You were right to kill him with his own knife. Manitou held your little hand as he has held so many in times of war and danger. Now we must say a prayer for the root—for the spirit who saved you. Let us return to the forest and sprinkle it with sage and cleanse the root with cedar berries. You may carry these." He handed her a bundle of dried sage leaves, blue and aromatic, and poured a palm-full of berries into her hands. "Smell," he instructed. "Remember, Manitou hides his spirit even in something as small as a berry."

As they walked, the sachem continued his instruction: "Then, we must sing a song, a death song, for the man who wanted to harm you. His spirit is evil, but we must sing for his spirit and its place in the after-life, that it never escapes. Come now! Take my hand." He smiled as she rested her hand inside his, holding the cedar berries in her other hand and cradling the sage in the crook of her arm.

Slowly the day drifted by. An overcast sky blocked the warmth of the sun. A chill seized the air. As evening drew closer, Hélène climbed the steps to the quarters assigned to her by the new commandant. Fortunately, it included a window that afforded a view of the creek. Darkness filled the small room with dank and musky odors. She cracked the window and peered out. Small glowing fires pulsated deep red along the creek's bank. A chair, washstand, small table and straw mattress comprised the room's only furnishings. A feather pillow and faded blue blanket lay folded on the mattress. She lit two soapy brown candles, changed Anna-Marie's mossy diaper, and rewrapped the child to keep the baby warm. She arranged the chair by the window, opened her blouse, and let the infant nurse. She was in the process of burping the baby, when a lone canoe slid silently ashore. The slight sound of its bottom rubbing at the water's edge caught her attention. She turned, looked out, and clutched Anna-Marie against her chest. It was François! He and Yellow Hawk had beached the canoe and were walking toward the fort. Before Hélène could wave, however, two Algonquins met them and pointed to the barracks outside the fort's walls. Within moments, all four walked out of sight. Hélène collapsed in her chair and hugged her baby. At least, François was safe! But did he even know she was there?

Inside the barrack's largest room, de Beaujeu rose to meet de Robert. "Major, I'm honored to meet you. I've heard nothing but favorable reports of your handling of affairs at Fort Necessity. Please, be seated. Have some wine and something to eat." The Captain gestured toward a table of venison and wine, bread and rum. "Please! Help yourself."

"I am astonished, Sir, for your kind deference," François replied. "We know you've been assigned to the Fort. Monsieur Contrecoeur stands ready to transfer his command. We're prepared, if I may say so. But I gather this meeting is for something more. *N'est-ce pas?*"

"Of course, but please refresh yourself. The evening is long and I have much to ask. But most can wait till tomorrow," he smiled. "You have a visitor who desires your company, I believe. But first my major concern. We can polish the details tomorrow. We've no more than four-to-five hundred troops. Rumors have it that Braddock has thousands. Far more than we! Plus mortars and howitzers, guns and six-pounders! Two miles of wagons and endless supplies! Can we count on the Indians? We need a thousand warriors if possible. Every tribe west of the mountains, up and down the river and across the Ohio! Can you inspire five or six hundred to join us? Without them, we'll have to burn the fort and retreat. Those are my orders, as despicable as they sound. Can you?"

François had scarcely lifted the glass of wine to his lips. So this was why not even the fort's commandant had been enlisted. He sipped a few swallows and set the glass down. "I can't promise you a thousand! But all across the mountains, even along the Ohio and into Michigan, the chiefs are frightened. They know their lands are in danger. They fear the British even more than they detest us. They'll join with reluctance. I'll see what I can do."

"I need to know names of the chiefs. How many might join us. I have medals and wampum for all who do. Guns, tobacco, powder — all they'll need to repulse the enemy. But we need them. Tomorrow, we'll talk more. I intend to stay here a while and send out runners to as many chiefs as possible. The Caughnawagas, Abenakis, and Hurons are already assembling. Langlade's bringing down the Ojibwas from the Lakes, along with the Pottawattames. Canoes have been sent to contact the Miamies, Shaw-

nees, and Mingoes. On your way back, I need you to enlist the Wyandot."
He stood up behind the small oaken table where they had been seated.
He appeared relaxed and highly confident. "Please continue. And take
what you want, Captain, or François, if I may call you that. Your guest
awaits you—a beautiful woman at that, with a baby in her arms! You will
find her in the guest room, overlooking the creek."

"Hélène! *Oui?*"

"Yes! Incidentally," he suddenly broke off, "the Marquis has sent you
a gift. A book. Here!" he handed François a flat package wrapped in a
soiled silk cloth. "He said you'd like it. I've one of my own my great-
uncle gave me. I've carried it since childhood. *Le Chanson de Roland*! It
made me want to be a man! *N'est-ce pas*? I think so," he nodded toward
a diminutive tome beside his glass of wine. "I was reading it when you
came in."

François accepted the package and unwrapped the thin enclosure. It
was Rousseau's first chapter of *Discourse on the Inequality Among Men*.
"I've heard of this!" François acknowledged. "They say he's making
quite an impact."

"*Mais, oui*! But a free man's ideas of justice eventually clash with a
King's. *Non*? He's lucky he's Swiss and can hide behind magistrates. Still,
enjoy it. And do take some meat and drink to your charming *femme*."

François tucked the tiny tome in his pocket, gathered up the table's
cloth, together with some hard bread, a hunk of venison, corn, and a half-
bottle of *vin rouge de St. Loire*. "Thank you," he uttered with appreciation.
"I had a feeling she'd be here. If you don't mind, I'll look forward to the
morning."

"*Bien, sûr!*" de Beaujeu replied. "*À demain!*"

François excused himself, hurried to the fort, and mounted the stairs
to Hélène's room. She had watched him from the window. She opened
the tiny room's door. He set the cloth and all its contents on the narrow
table, and together the two embraced. Slowly they backed up toward the
bed, such as it was. Never had she felt so warm, so natural and hungry,
submissive and passionate as they slipped into each other's arms.

Chapter Twenty-Three

THE LONG LINE OF BRITISH TROOPS appeared strangely vulnerable, in spite of its vast string of uniformed soldiers that stretched out of sight along the mountain's slope. Ahead and to the rear, the endless scarlet cord crept upgrade through the lush green bushes, churning up the black leaves in its path. Langdon watched the procession, nudged his horse forward, and peered through the trees for Blue Hatchet. Behind him rode Tillson, and farther downslope Major Washington. For the past two weeks, he and Tillson, and sometimes members of the Major's staff, rode flank as scouts for Braddock's lumbering army. At least he had come to meet the principal commanders among the Provincials.

For reasons to which Langdon had never been privy, the various units of the Virginia Provincial Rangers had been divided between Sir Halket and Colonel Dunbar's Brigades. Dispersed among Halket's command were Captain Polson and Captain Wagner's Rangers. He knew both men, especially Wagner from Fort Necessity days. Scattered among Dunbar's Brigade were six companies of Rangers, two from the Carolinas and four from Virginia. He favored Captain Steven and Cox's forces best, since they accepted the harshest conditions without whimpering or expecting special treatment. Only two of the six captains actually possessed uniforms. The rest dressed no differently from their frontier soldiers, save Polson and Wagner who somehow obtained coveted, blue knee-length coats, similar to Washington's. Only the ribbons and fringe on the officers' hats set them apart from the soldiers they commanded.

As for the British, Langdon avoided as many of their officers as he could. His orders were to report to Washington alone. If there were any man he feared, it was Sir John St. Clair, the Quartermaster General. Insistent, intent, and impossible to avoid, St. Clair expected his orders to be executed with precision *and on time*. Without hesitation, he had stragglers whipped and axemen flogged, if they dallied along the way. Still, the going was slow, the road too narrow and entangled with laurel and brush to widen to his specified twelve-foot swath for the cannons and fifty some wagons to follow.

Two weeks had passed since the army had pulled out of Fort Cumberland, yet Langdon reckoned they had covered less than 20 miles. At that rate, it would be fall before they reached the Ohio. As he sat astride his horse, he watched as Braddock himself pressed his horse through the long line of halted forces and rode on over the crest of the forest's shoulder. Washington galloped to catch up along with the General's small band of aides-de-camp.

Langdon spotted Blue Hatchet, on foot about forty yards ahead.

"We're being watched," said the brave. "See?" he pointed to a broken laurel bough beside a trickling spring. The print of a moccasin heel glistened in the soft mud beside the brook. "How can such a horde be hid?" he stated with dismay, as he stared through the trees toward the road. "The forest has many eyes. As many as the French wish! Look! Another. See?"

Langdon glanced at the footprints. It was as if the stalkers wanted their enemies to discover such evidence. He nudged his horse forward and motioned for Blue Hatchet to slip up hill. As the youth disappeared in the undergrowth, Langdon deliberately guided Arduous at an angle upslope. He slid out of his saddle, tied the mount to a bough, and crept quietly toward an overhanging rock. His nose balked at the odor of something sickening just beyond. His flesh began to crawl; the hair on his foreams tingled. He crouched as he crept closer to the rock. Flies buzzed in a menacing swirl just beyond him. He placed his thumb on his flintlock's hammer and peered around the rock. Impaled on a broken spear point leaned the fire-blackened head of a Virginia deserter, missing since their arrival at Willis Creek. It had been severed with a stone knife, still embedded in the neck. Maggots crawled out of the skull's eye sockets. The face had been charred to a black crisp. Langdon pressed his hand over his mouth. How long had they played with it before breaking camp to steal back into the woods? He stood erect and waved for Blue Hatchet to come and see the remains. Below in the woods, Tillson guided his mount to join them.

"Vigilant! We just have to be vigilant!" reiterated Washington, when Langdon reported the news. "With any luck, we should make the Youghiogheny in another week. But, by the mercy of Job, we may lose another twenty by then."

That evening, Langdon sought out Tillson's tent. It was a small officer's version, more like a lean-to with a flap. The Major had set up camp closer to fires of the British than to the Provincials.' He found Sir William in the process of polishing his boots and knocking cakes of mud from his gaiters. "Good evening, sir," he addressed him. "Mind if I drop in?"

William glanced up, somewhat startled that Langdon greeted him with a hint of formality. "Of course not! Sit down! That was one grizzly sight, wasn't it?" he remarked. "Can you imagine how long the man must have suffered before he expired? Beasts! Just bloody beasts! That's all they are!" Suddenly he stopped. "Your Blue Hatchet isn't with you, is he?"

"No. He watches over the camp in the woods some nights, all by himself. He prefers the quiet of the forest to the smoke and laughter about the fires. Plus, the women! He finds most of the men's wives coarse and rowdy, compared to the women of his grandfather's tribe."

"Can't say that I blame him. I'm sure there must be a lady or two, but the ones I've observed fit his description." He paused and looked out into the night. Smoke drifted in stifling screens to stagnate in the forest's canopy overhead. The smell of beef and beans, grease and coffee mingled in the drafts of warm air. "Did I tell you that I wrote Anna and promised to marry her the week we return? I sent the post through Dinwiddie, but haven't heard back. Have you heard anything?"

"No. Only the usual rumors that suppliers feed the camp."

"Oh! I haven't heard," he stated inquisitively.

"Shawnee and Cherokee bands are probing the border. Small raiding parties are attacking all along the Wilderness Road, from Winchester down to the Holston Valley. Who knows how Louise and Sarah are doing? Luckily, Sarah's tough. She has to be. And Jonathan's strong enough to help!" He dropped his voice and looked away. "It isn't good."

"Good are bad, does it matter now? I've been in this country long enough to feel alienated from my own family. Do you know that on the Tillson side we go back to the era of Henry V? My noble ancestors, if I may defer to them, were granted titles only because of the scurrilous schemes they were willing to perpetuate to save their skin? Under Elizabeth, they engaged in despicable acts of duplicity to avoid the same axe that severed Mary's head. Nothing to be proud of, I assure you. The Grahams were nobler. They fought against the Scots and later Cromwell's crowd of king haters. My mother was a servant girl; my father, Lord Tillson, forced his wife to claim me as her own. My birth mother nursed me until I was two; then they sent her off. God only knows where. I joined his Majesty's regiments at the age of nineteen. I was present at the Battle of Cherbourg when our forces defeated a battalion of French near the town of St. Marie-Herbourgh. I sometimes wonder why I'm here. Not in any religious sense, of course. I'm a Deist if anything. A despiser of pious Orthodoxy! But, I wonder. Do I have a purpose? And if so, who's the purpose giver? Myself, I suppose. And as much as I love Anna, I don't know anymore. Just a bad night, you could say. Too many days in the woods! Too close to death and its odor. This whole thing of empire—so senseless, Langdon! What do I really want? Is it the glory of war? The fear and courage that overwhelm you in battle, like we experienced at Necessity?" He took a deep breath. "Didn't mean to make you my confessor," he smiled, as he glanced toward Langdon. "Maybe all of us wonder if we'll come back, and if we do, what difference it'll make. No doubt we'll destroy the French and capture the fort."

"Listen, William! Anna loves you. She's carrying your child. Her life would never be the same if you don't come back. Sarah loves you, too. She'd bear you a child right now, married or not. Washington needs you. Maybe Braddock and the British figure they've got enough officers without you. I want you to come to the Holston with me. To oversee the land and salt mines I know are there. To create our own little empire and explore the meadows and hills beyond the Alleghenies! How I want to go back and hunt and ride through that land they call 'Kintuckie!' Give yourself time. You'll probably be the hero in this war. Then I want to go home."

"Ever an optimist!" William sighed. "Good night, Langdon! You need to rest yourself." William glanced out into the night. The multiple fires had begun to fade. The silhouettes of stacked guns cast long shadows through the trees. An owl hooted deep in the forest. Moments later it hooted, but farther up the mountain.

Langdon raised his head. Somewhere Blue Hatchet was out there. He would need to steal away and reply. "Good night, Sir. Sleep with your firearm beside you. You'll sleep better if you do."

"I will," said Tillson, as he waved good night.

Langdon slipped quietly through the woods in the direction of the last call. Slowly he climbed through the dark. Below he could see the smoldering fires and the gray bands of smoke that the pink flames emitted. The smoke rose high into the tress, shrouding them in a ghostly fog. Men were bedding down, retiring for the night. Langdon stopped to look and listen. He cupped his hands to his mouth and answered the darkness with a whipperwill's cry. He waited and crouched beside a tall white oak. Even in the moonlight, he could see its bark's grooves and the tiny green leaves of a vine that summer had awakened on the oak's trunk. He could feel his heart beat. A rustling sound in the forest drew closer. It was Blue Hatchet. A pensive sorrow seemed to have come over the youth. Langdon raised his arm to signal recognition. "What is it?"

"White wolf!" he responded with a vacuous puzzlement in his eyes. "I found a lair, but no wolves. Then, I saw a fire! The wolf's eyes! Large, like gleaming shells! Green and wild! It loomed like a spirit in the woods. My heart stopped. Then the white wolf slunk away, but with its head turned, waiting to see if I'd follow. I did. It led me in the dark to an Indian burial scaffold; then it sat under a wrapped skeleton with a torn scalp. It is grandfather's grave, I think! Hard to know! I recognized the ripped cartilage on the left ear. The wolf rose and led me to a small meadow, white and yellow in the moon's glow. Far off I saw Laurel Mountain, gateway to the Youghiogheny. Torn-Ear's mother's clan was kin to the wolf. It's an omen, Burke. My people want me to come home. I was afraid and hooted like an owl. What do you think?"

"*Stunned!*" Langdon wanted to whisper. It probably had no meaning. Just an eerie encounter in the night! A strange animal and a frightened youth! "I think it's a good omen. The white wolf's a good sign. *Non?* Perhaps it was transferring its cunning and ferocity to you, its strength and vital spirit. Good to have where we're going, *Oui?*"

"I think my white father drinks too much rum. Let's return to camp," the brave smiled.

For a long while after the fires had died, Langdon pondered the meaning of Blue Hatchet's wolf. The wolf sees in the dark, always a fitting symbol for warriors. And for the Algonquins, was it not the emblem of the North Star, the Great Spirit's eye to guide them home? Perhaps the wolf—if real—were only a dog, and the corpse's ravaged ear a victim of time? In truth, it was a perplexing omen. No doubt it would haunt Blue Hatchet until his mind cleared. Langdon lay on his back and stared up through the thin smoke at the silhouettes of the trees. Hickory and pine, oak and poplar were each distinguishable. Even in the darkness, he could tell them apart. The night sky blazed ambient with stars. He pulled his blanket across his shoulders and adjusted his body on his bed of laurel leaves. Overhead, the twinkling glory throbbed with infinite majesty. He hated to close his eyes. But fatigue and worry had exacted their due. Almost immediately he fell asleep.

Chapter Twenty-Four

O N A MILKY CLAY BANK, two hours past Fort Machaud, Yellow Hawk brought Philippe's canoe ashore. Hélène needed moss. François wished to search for guns that he and Joncaire had cached two years earlier. The lily ensigna, carved into a towering oak, marked the general location. The cache itself had been hidden two hundred steps past the tree but perpendicular to the river. While Hélène gathered patches of dry moss for Anna-Marie, François directed Yellow Hawk toward a prickly pile of deadfall near a copse of alders and buckeyes. Within thirty minutes, the two found the armload of Tulle muskets and powder horns that lay wrapped in a tarp of canvas and bear oil. A separate tarp contained a pouch of wampum belts. "*Bon!*" exclaimed François, "these should do."

Aboard again, they followed the river downstream until a gurgling tributary of swift water intermingled with the roiling swells of the grainy Allegheny. "We'll camp here," said François. "In the morning we'll head upstream for Wyandot villages."

"There are too many," advised Yellow Hawk. "Chief Black Hat's lodge is many creeks inland. Best to send runners to ask chief to come. Send him powder horn and tobacco with promise of gun. He will come. He has hated the English for a long time. The Iroquois drove him from his old hunting grounds east of the river. They carried English guns. You will see."

"Will he understand the urgency? That we don't have time for long councils and rum?"

"Yellow Hawk doesn't know. Why not wait in first village, and I will search for him myself."

François liked Yellow Hawk's idea, though he disliked the thought of being alone with savages he didn't know. Still, he would have his "squaw" and child. That could be both good and bad. *"D'accord,"* he muttered with cautious misgiving.

At early sunrise, Yellow Hawk awakened a sleeping François. Hélène sat nearby, beside a small fire, nursing Noël. "Up!" nudged the big Indian. "Long way to first village. Come. We must go soon."

Once more they launched their birch canoe. François stared down into the clear stream as the sunlight reflected the canoe's white-and-black patchwork. He deliberately dipped his right fingers into the cool water as he brought his paddle around. The muscles in his arms and back stretched with each stroke. Bending birch branches and vine-entangled oaks created a misty tunnel of olive shadows as they paddled upstream. Sunlight filtered through the glowing canopy in yellow rays. Woodpeckers drilled in the forest, their staccato pecking echoing through the trees like drumbeats. For two hours, Yellow Hawk and François paddled. Suddenly, the forest grew silent.

"Listen!" said Hélène! "Drums."

"They know we're coming," said Yellow Hawk.

François steadied his paddle as the two rowers let the canoe drift ashore. Within moments of its touching the bank, a tall, red-scared, broad-shouldered native, dressed in deer leggings with a hawk-and-turkey feather cape about his shoulders appeared in the green brush. A black stovepipe beaver hat adorned his head. A plume of scarlet and yellow feathers dangled from its crown. A droll yet somber smile played about the corners of his mouth. Nicotine stains coated his teeth.

"I am Black Hat, sachem of Wyandot villages in East. For three days we know you are coming. Word of Great White Father's war rings through the forest. Huron and Ojibwa passing through bring the story. 'Come. Gather at French Fort! Great English army approaching! Many scalps for lodges! Are you brave or tied to your womens' aprons? We see you there.' *Non? C'est la vérité. Oui?*"

"Yes! It's true!" affirmed François. "I have guns and tobacco, powder and wampum belts for Chief Black Hat. May we sit in council before we leave? Your presence brings us great joy."

"Council lodge prepared! First, you eat; then we smoke! Black Hat savor great taste for spirits. Long winter. Great thirst. Where is rum? We dance and drink. Tomorrow we gather for council. Come now!"

François disliked the chief's agenda. But protocol came first. "*C'est bon!*" he sighed with resignation. "Let's smoke and parley in peace. Our Father in Montreal cares for his Wyandot children. He sends many gifts by canoe. They will await you at Fort Duquesne."

A glint of disappointment filled the chief's face. He had not expected a delay. Nevertheless, he replied, "Your coming fills my heart with joy. Long have I wished to avenge our sorrow on the gut-less British! Let us smoke, eat, and dance."

François smiled at the old chief. What choice did he have? "Your words are well spoken," he said. Afterwards, as he lay with Hélène by the fireside and watched the young braves cavort in front of the Council House, he found his thoughts taking him back to an evening years ago, when his father had left him in the street near his archbishop uncle's home. A gang of ruffians was rounding a corner and saw him standing alone by the cottage gate. They began to mock his dress of lacy blouse, frizzy cravat, knee-length blue trousers, red garters and blue stockings, and yellow vest, and soon descended upon him amid cruel curses and doubled-up fists. Stunned and frightened, he fled. Midway down the alley, his father appeared, feet spread wide, blocking the narrow path. His heart thumped with fear, then, seeing his father emotionless and still, he stopped, caught his breath, and looked up at *son père*. The tall de Robert said nothing, but simply handed François his sword. Though only a boy of eight, François accepted his father's epee with confidence, turned, and whipped it through the air, as he had been taught. "*Avance ton pied!*" his father whispered. "*Courage! Mon petit! Toi seul dois ce faire. C'est maintenant ou jamais.*" He took a deep breath, stepped forward, then broke into a run back toward the ruffians. Taken aback by his sudden menacing presence, the ruffians fled. As arrogant as Coup de Sang and Yellow Hawk could be, the *gift* his father had given him that evening had taught him never to flinch when opposed.

Early the next morning, while the village and its elders slept, François, Yellow Hawk, Hélène and her baby slipped into the canoe, pushed off, and paddled downstream for the Allegheny again. François expelled a pensive breath as he bent over his paddle. He had left three guns, sufficient powder, tobacco, lead, a hatchet, and fine wampum belt for the unflappable, rum-thirsty Chief. Surely, the old man would want more and show up at the fort.

Washington sat relaxed in his chestnut brown saddle as the noonday sun baked the Great Meadows in waves of sweltering heat. At last Braddock's army had arrived at the site of the ruins of Fort Necessity. In spite of the oppressive heat, the Major felt invigorated to glance across the brushy field where he had dared to stall the French. The log palisade had been dismantled by hand, but the dirt redoubt was visible. Prickly thistles and broom sedge, wild blue and yellow flowers, and tendrils of green vine covered the trenches of the dirt enclosure. "The wilderness doesn't wait long, does it?" he commented to Tillson, mounted beside him.

"No, sir! It doesn't. Now that I see it from this advantage, we were lucky to survive. I guess we owe that to Villiers and his officer, de Robert."

"Major, it was our stubbornness," the tall Virginian smiled. "I don't think they'll be as kindly this time. Not with this force breathing down their necks," he nodded toward the horde of redcoats emptying into the sprawling meadow. "Damn, but they'd make a great ambush," he suddenly uttered. "I've been trying to enlighten the General for the past two weeks, but he won't listen. He can't conceive of an Indian attack turning back his army. Look how they bunch up. Even in columns. They laugh at our 'mishy.' They've no concept of Indian *devilry* or French connivance. They'll be the death of us if we aren't careful." He pointed to a deerskin dressed figure on the ridge overlooking the breeze-swept meadows. "Burke's up there, too, somewhere, scouting as far out as the Youghiogheny. He's to report the moment he encounters French parties. I can't imagine they haven't informed Contrecoeur of our presence already."

"That's a fact! But Braddock's regiments pose a formidable wall. Have you ever witnessed one line after another advance, fire, fall back, reload, as their sister company steps forward, fires; then everyone repeats the movement again? The volley is deafening. Lead bullets glow in the air. Clouds of smoke blind the enemy's view. The commander shouts and the regiment lunges forward, firing and falling on the foe with bayonet. Men literally drop their muskets and run. It's a terrible sight. Men scream when their arms are blown off. It was bad enough at Necessity and the Glen and the surprise attack at Dinwiddie's fort. If we could just lure them onto the field, where they've no place to run or hide, we'd obliterate them!"

"Yes! Like in this meadow," Washington gestured. "But it won't be that way till we reach the fort. Once there, we should level the place. I doubt if the battle rages more than a day. Our cannons will force them to flee."

"Let's hope the Fates favor the same."

With the coming of early evening, the Great Meadows began to cool. Tired but restless, Braddock ordered his brigade commanders to form up the troops and pass them in review. He wanted the Provincials in particular to observe the army in its marching array and note the firepower the units represented. The howitzers and cannons were still two days back, but all of Halket and Dunbar's 44th and 48th Foot were present. "Orme, we need a morale boost" Braddock barked. "Duquesne's less than 35 miles northwest. Pass the order!" With that, the General mounted his finest stallion and, flanked by his aides-de-camp, nodded for the parade to commence. Up went the skirling of the bagpipes to the flurry of the Union Jacks and the rattle and staccato of the thigh-swinging drums. A series of regimental marches, "Scotland, I Leave Thee," "The Glen is Mine," and other tunes squeaked from the pipes. The British fifes squealed their inspirational tunes. Braddock smiled with pride. The commanders' swords glinted in the sunlight as they saluted the General. The rhythmic cadence of the drums created a hypnotic spell.

From where Washington sat astride his mount, the spectacle alarmed and awed him. How he wished he were commanding a unit! Leading his own brigade, attired in His Majesty's reddest coat, with all its gold embroidery and brass buttons, boasting a black hat capped with its white cockade! Yet, as he glanced about, he felt perfectly at home with his rag-tag Provincials, dressed in deerskin leather, homespun clothing, weathered coonskin caps or faded felt tricorns. They stood at parade rest, behind the 44th and the 48,[th] opposite the General's reviewing party. "Damn," he thought. "How delusional war is!"

As night's shadows blessed the weary with welcome rest, Braddock ordered beef to be slaughtered and kegs to be opened to the delight of all. "They need the respite," was all he uttered to St. Clair.

"It's a wanton waste of prized supplies, if you ask me, Sir!" the officer objected. "You'll regret it, I wager," he bowed with an obsequious smirk.

Braddock sneered at his Quartermaster General; then waved him away.

Once more, the pipers struck up a medley of tunes and jigs, ballads and love songs. The men whose wives and lovers had followed them danced late into the evening. The night sky throbbed with the orange aura of the fire's glare. The aroma of meat and ale mingled with the sounds of the boisterous men and their merry partners. Couples slipped off into the darkness. Burke, who had just returned, watched with envy and sadness. Tomorrow the trek would resume, and the path as narrow as ever. Fording the river would be no easy task. "Enjoy it," he said to Blue Hatchet. "For me, it's meat and bed."

With the coming of dawn, Braddock assembled all the women — matrons, maids, maidens, and children — and a handful of staff. Seated on his horse with Halket and Washington by his side, he cleared his throat: "We're here to engage a mighty enemy, an eager core of Frenchmen and their ruthless savages. It is best for all present that you ladies depart. Embrace now and gather your things to leave! Major Washington, if you please. I need your aide's help and Mr. Burke's to escort the women across the Meadows and past the cannon — if the damn things ever come into view! Are you in accord?" he asked.

Washington wiggled in his saddle. His long face and pale countenance masked whatever objections he reserved. "Yes, sir!" He turned to Tillson and Burke. "Gentlemen, you have your orders. Return as soon as you can."

Tillson saluted Braddock, then the Major. Burke stared at the disheveled cluster of frightened women and young girls. Husbands stepped forward and kissed their wives. Lovers fondled in the morning heat, palms and lips pressed together. Six wagons were cut out of line and prepared to ferry what women and children they could. At that, many would still have to walk. Tillson rode up alongside Burke. The cumbersome wagons dipped and lurched as the older women and those nursing children boarded. Finally, the desultory vessels bore their bonneted cargo across the Meadows and up through the trees. Tillson rode hurriedly to the head of the column, Burke to the rear. Langdon turned in his saddle to find Blue Hatchet jogging behind him. At this rate, they would miss the battle. "Take your time," he offered. "We'll save our energy for the race back."

Two days passed, as the wagons lumbered over the slopes and down the trail. On June the 29th, Blue Hatchet raised his hand for the convoy to halt and listen. The wagons had pulled over into a clearing, scented with noonday violets and bright drafts of sunlight. Someone was singing in the forest. His booming voice rose up from the path below and echoed off the rocky ledges to the north. Indistinct yet voluable, his words mocked any tune the signer had in mind; nonetheless, they bellowed up with enthusiastic force and joy.

"There's a bit of Irish in all that roar," the lead wagoner smiled. "I'd wager it's the devil himself, if not the Preacher Renwick Martin. He couldn't sing his way out o' Hell, if he had to."

Langdon rose in his saddle to stare down the trail. The rocky swath of hacked roots and felled logs filled the woods with a redolence of resin and sap, pine gum and dark soil, pungent and pleasing at the same time. A lustrous canopy of green pine and leafy oak limbs obscured a clear view. Yet, the singing was unmistakable. The words of Isaac Watts's "Before Jehovah's Awful Throne" became distinguishable. Women in the wagons picked up the tune and sang in reply:

Wide as the world is His command,
Vast as eternity His love;
Firm as a rock His truth shall stand,
When rolling years shall cease to move,
When rolling years shall cease to move.

Blue Hatchet's mouth dropped open in dismay. Langdon had to smile. What a hell of a hymn to be singing! "When rolling years shall cease to move?" Precious God! Yes, there he was! The Scots-Irish Presbyterian Parson Renwick Martin, in the flesh, nonetheless! Langdon nudged his horse forward to meet the hardy itinerant cleric.

"Aye, Mr. Burke!" he smiled, as he reined up his mount in the road. His black attire and black boots bore smears of mud flecks and dried red clay. He was mounted on a misty gray mare. "The cannoneers said I'd find the likes o' you soon. They did! And the Mrs? I hear ye added a wee one to the fold! Aye, tis a pleasing thing to be fruitful and multiply!"

"Reverend, of all people! I never expected you!"

"Aye, ye didn't. But as our Lord Jesus as a wee one said: 'Dinna you know I 'ave to be about me Father's business'? He was half Irish, ya know! With a tad of Scottish in his brogue, they say."

"Well! The army's two days travel ahead. Braddock's ordered us to escort the women back to the cannon squads and their waggoners. After that, they're on their own."

"I dinna like the sound o' that, laddie. Not at all! The Cherokee are a runnin' free along the Big Road, since they've heard of the Duquesne thing. I've got dispatches for the General, from the Governor himself. I'll take the women and their lassies back, if you'll deliver this for me," he handed Langdon a saddlebag of letters. "But first I'll have a rest. I've a thirst an Irishman would, lo, be ashamed to confess," he smiled. "But," as he surveyed the line of wagons and their guests, he continued, "I doubt ye've got a drop."

Just then Tillson rode forward. "Reverend, I'm Major William Tillson, the Governor's liaison to his Majesty's troops. There wouldn't be a letter in there for me, would there?" William removed his hat and smiled. Dust and sweat freckled his brow and face. He waited for the minister's reply.

"So ye are, are ya? I've met your lovely bride-to-be," he bit out the words "*to-be*." "Aye, there's a sweet-smelling letter, just for you," he replied. "You'll not get home too soon, ya know, if ya know what I'm thinkin'? She's a needin' you, lad. God bless ye both," he nodded toward Langdon and Tillson. "Tis transformin' grace we need, not my tongue," he smiled. "Kin I rest now, before I guide these ladies home?"

"Yes!" said William. "I've a pint of brandy just for you," he glanced back toward his saddlebags. "I don't envy you the long road home."

"Nor I your road ahead. Now let's dismount and offer prayers, before I take that draught."

The reverend slid out of his saddle and motioned for the men to dismount. All along the wagon line, the women and children — save for the drivers and nursing mothers — climbed out and knelt in the clearing.

"Aye, God above and seer of all, ya know we're here. What kin our tongues say that ye, Lord, dinna already know? The way is narrow and the forest dark. Ye red children are everywhere. Ye cursed French goad them on. Their King's to blame, and ours no doubt. Danger's everywhere. We ask yer blessing God Most Fair. For safety through the woods, that hearts be spared and children grow to praise your providence and holy love. In our Lord's name, we beseech Ye. Now hear us as we pray together, 'Our Father, which art in Heaven, …'"

Slowly, everyone joined in. Tillson felt awkward and miserable where he knelt on the soggy ground. Slop from the road seeped through his trousers, just above his boots. "God," he whispered. "Be with Anna, whatever my fate befalls."

After prayer, Tillson remounted and glanced up to see the first team of oxen struggling in the road below. The snap of whips, the slapping of leather harnesses, the clack of wooden yokes, and the shouting of exhausted men filtered through the sunny canopy. The echo of axes widening the road reverberated through the gleaming rays in the trees. Slowly, the heavy line of cannon and carts, six-pounders and howitzers, trailed by wagons of munitions, cast-iron cannon balls, and powder, creaked into view. A young officer with blazing blonde hair led the procession. He had tied his hair in a single braid, which bounced from shoulder to shoulder on his red coat. He paused in the road and waved with his hat to the waggoners and the women in their white bonnets. Then he saw Tillson and urged his horse forward to rendezvous with Burke and the Major.

"I suspected as much," he said with fatigue. "Braddock's done this before at home," he nodded toward the cramped vessels of women and children. "How far ahead is he, if I might ask? Lieutenant Silverston here, Sir," he saluted William.

"Major Tillson and Mr. Burke," he replied. "Two days at best."

"What's the road like ahead?"

"The path's a little wider past the next few ridges. There's some rock you'll have to blast out of the way. But the General can't attack till you arrive. The Monongahela's not that far, now. How's the going been?"

"One miserable trek of hell, sir, if I may speak. We've lost eight mules and two oxen so far. Plus three men are nursing bruised bones, one at the thigh when he slipped under a cart. God, he screamed! Forgive me, Sir, if I'm out of line."

"Not at all. The Parson here's going to escort the women home as far as Willis Creek. Mr Burke here," he deferred toward Langdon, "his guide, and I will be returning to the regiments as soon as we leave. Do you have any special messages for his Excellency?"

"None! No, Sir! Just that we'll get there as best we can, as soon as we can." The young man tipped his hat and returned to his unit below.

"Well, Reverend!" said Burke. "This is where we leave you. Godspeed and give our regards to the Governor, if you see him. And if you chance by my place, give my love to Louise and Sarah, Jonathan and the children. That's all I ask. Hopefully, by the fall we'll be home."

"Reverend!" Tillson interrupted. "Will you stay a minute while I hasten a letter for Anna. Just in case you see her. You will, won't you?"

"Aye, Sir, ya know I will. I'll be returnin' by Winchester and maybe by Burke's, if the valley's clear. And a week later I'll be clatterin' into Williamsburg, where I'm about as wanted by your Episcopal lords as flies at the King's table. Here's some parchment of me own. Scribble what ya can with this quill while I relieve my thirst with that pint ye promised."

"Fair enough," replied William, as he exchanged his pint for a sheath of rag paper and the minister's inky quill. While still seated on horseback he wrote hastily:

Beloved Anna.

We're still on the road to Duquesne. The Reverend Martin hopes to carry this to you. Am plump, healthy, in sound spirit, and mentally well. Have received your letter at this incredible instant, but haven't opened it yet. Pray that our infinite Father might grant success. God bless the King and you most precious love. Time prevents me from writing more, as the call to war is near at hand.

Yours faithfully, William Graham Tillson. The 28ᵗʰ of June, 1755.

He folded the letter and gave it to Martin.

"An' here's your pint to ya!" smiled the Preacher. "Empty a tad, but not too dry. May the Lord bless you all the way!"

William and Burke bade farewell, and with Blue Hatchet by their side, turned in the clearing, and goaded their horses back onto the trail. "Here!" said Burke, as he bent down and extended his arm, caught Blue Hatchet's, and swung him up behind the saddle.

As dusk settled about them, Landgon led the threesome toward a copse of gnarled hackberry and dark green holly. "Lets camp here," he said.

Blue Hatchet glanced about the solemn woods. "I like it too," he added. "We are not far from the white wolf's lair. Perhaps it will call tonight. It has no home, like my people. I must listen for its voice. I know it will speak the truth."

"I certainly hope it isn't out there," objected Tillson. "I'm sorry, but their howls unnerve me to the bone."

After a supper of beef and corn, they bedded down. The night air turned chilly. A cold breeze fanned the embers of their tiny fire, creating an eerie specter of white coals. Black clouds formed to the west and obscured the stars. A sudden rush of wind brought in a loud torrent of rain. They crawled beneath their tarps and listened as the heavy drops splattered onto the fire, dowsing its flames.

Tillson lay curled in his blanket under the tarp. He so wanted to re-read Anna's letter, but he could remember its every word:

William,

I can feel our child moving in my womb. It is the most wonderful and terrifying feeling I have know. I vacilate between exuberant joy and paralyzing fear. I must be farther along that I thought. Daphne worries about me everyday. She has let out the waist band of all my gowns and housedresses. I don't dare venture out in public. But, two weeks ago,

I did attend a ball at the Governor's masion. My hoop skirt concealed my bulge, though it is still slight, but my breasts have enlarged. Our Honorable Governor Dinwiddie was quite taken by their pleasant size. He remarked that perhaps "my dear, you are indulging in too rich a fare of pork and duck, or port and sweets." I rolled my eyes and kept quiet. I worry about you from morning to night and wake up crying. You must come home to me safe and sound. Stay close to the Major and Mr. Burke. I trust them and their knowledge of Indians and the frontier. Everywhere here one speaks highly of General Braddock and his well-trained army. A portrait of his Excellence hangs in the House of Burgesses to instill pride and support in all Virginians. The cannon is fired every morning and evening with prayers united in the Bruton Parish Church on behalf of the General's expedition. I pray for you constantly, inspite of my unworthiness. But Mr. Martin, who saw me just before he left, and who suspects my condition, as I could see it in his eyes, kissed me on the cheek and said: "Remember, Lassie, Paul assures us that love covers a multitude of anxieties. In His arms he will bear thee up." How I hope that is true! I know the passage the Reverend was quoting. The word is "sin," not "anxieties," but the good parson was being circumspect.

O William, what a dreadful yet thrilling time!
Your happy and tearful Anna. June 12, 1755.

For a long while after the rain had subsided, Blue Hatchet listened to the sounds of the forest. Water dripping from the holly leaves created a hollow feeling in his breast. Were any members of his mother's family alive? Would he ever meet them again? Would they recognize him or he them? Foxes barked somewhere in the night. The deep cough of a horned owl drifted through the treetops. Moments later, the screech of its cry signaled a fresh meal or near miss. The dripping rain grew fainter. The silence of the great woods closed about. His eyelids fell heavy again, and he dropped into slumber once more.

Chapter Twenty-Five

THE QUIET FOREST SHIELDED the four figures that looked out over the narrow trail below. The swirling reddish-muddy waters of the Youghiogheny warned of massive activity upriver. Even François noted the sloshing swells before Joncaire could speak. "They're coming," was all he muttered.

Yellow Hawk had warned of the approach of the British three days earlier. Handsome Dog doubted they had traveled as far, but any uncertainty vanished now. Broken dogwood twigs and clumps of flowering laurel floated swiftly by. A soldier's backpack and, what appeared to be a boot's sole, bobbed in the foam near the river's north bank. Handsome Dog stepped out of the foliage and retrieved the bag. Water spilled out as he lifted it up. The tall Indian peered inside. "Shhhhuh!" he winced, as he flung it back into the stream. A large black watersnake slithered out of the pack as it floated to the surface again. "*Mauvais! Mauvais signe!*" he uttered, before crossing himself in Catholic style. "Bad! Very Bad!"

"Perhaps it's a trick?" ventured Yellow Hawk. "Their evil spirits go before them to frighten our braves."

"Trick or not, they're damn well coming and they don't mean to stop until they destroy us and the fort," said Joncaire. "By now Beaujeu should be near. He won't arrive any too soon."

"Many red brothers are coming, too," said Yellow Hawk.

"Yes! We will do what skinny Liegemen have no stomach for," Handsome Dog grinned, as he motioned toward his knife. "This river and the great one ahead shall run red with English blood. Tekacayah not lie this day. My heart feels good! *Très fort! N'est-ce pas?*" he stared at François. "It is time you wipe blood off your knife, too, Frenchman. *Non?* I shall watch to see."

"I will take my share, but it will be with a gun, and bayonet, if necessary. I suppose it's all the same. Rifle or tomahawk! *Non?*"

"No! Gun too easy. Brave Indian fears no death. White men fear except Joncaire and Beaujeu. You will see. My waist will hang with scalps. Our Great French Fathers will be pleased."

As they returned to Fort Duquesne, François observed a large party of Indians bunched about its entrance. For the past three weeks, bands of warriors had been trickling in from across the Ohio and the Great Lakes. But the band crowded about the narrow log entrance struck François as more menacing than usual. Most were young, painted for war, naked except for loincloths. They were openly unruly. A few yelps and high-pitched tongue-wallowing cries erupted amongst the group as they spotted de Robert and the others. Suddenly, all fell silent. A tall Frenchman in a lacy white blouse pointed in their direction.

"Look!" said Joncaire. "Beaujeu! It's the Captain and his savages from the Lakes. *Alors! C'est bon! C'est magnifique! Oui?*"

"I'll not contest that!" François acceded.

Beaujeu recognized Joncaire and then François. He waved for them to join him. "My brave children!" he addressed his Indians. "Here are our Fathers and brothers who will lead us when the time comes. Welcome!" he called to the four. "We could not be in better hands. Come, the Commandant wishes a council. Many chiefs are already assembled."

Beaujeu motioned for his braves to permit François and the others to pass through the gate. "My children," he addressed them anew, "find shelter now for the night. See what lies along the river. Be wise as the owl and innocent as chickadees. Tomorrow, we will rejoin each other, if not tonight."

Disgruntled, his followers melted away. "Well, it's good to meet again," the sinewy Beaujeu extended his hand to François-Philippe. "And you, too, you grizzly assassins," he smiled as he exchanged glances with Joncaire and Handsome Dog. "I am ready for this fight," he said without bravado or humility. "It's time we repulsed the English for good. Montcalm is coming in the north. They are counting on us here. What news do you have to cheer us?"

"Cheer?" retorted Joncaire. "Rather, *courage, Mon chèr*! *Courage! Avez bon espoir!* The old *chien* Braddock has brought his entire army. They low and slosh like cattle in a forest. If we stand our ground we can take them."

"*D'accord!*" affirmed Tekacayah. "But braves fight best in the woods."

"*C'est vrai!*" added Yellow Hawk. "Better for Frenchmen to hide behind walls!"

"Mind your tongue," smarted Beaujeu. "I will lead my brothers myself. I too fight best on the run in the forest, gun in one hand, tomahawk in the other. Enough! Let's go inside."

"If I may, I'd rather pass this one up," François objected respectfully. "I've seen enough councils to know what happens."

"*Eh! Mon vieux!* It's your dear one, isn't it? *Votre chérie! Non?* I can't blame you. We'll chat tomorrow. Joncaire can bring me up to date. Besides, I loathe upstaging Monsieur Contrecoeur until he departs next week. I understand. She is beautiful. *Non?* I know so," he smiled. "*À demain!*"

François bowed with gratitude and hurried toward the quarters reserved for officers with wives. Hélène awaited him outside the door of the ground level log apartment. She was seated in a wicker chair, nursing Noël. She had braided her sleek black hair into a single shining cord down the middle of her back. Her white blouse hung open, exposing a comely brown breast. The tiny child's lips curled about her mother's nipple. With eyes closed, her little cheeks puffed as she suckled the breast. François knelt and kissed the baby's cheek, then Hélène's warm lips. She rolled her dark eyes up and smiled. "*Je suis content*," she said. "You should join your men. Tonight, let's father another child. The French girl wants your love, your body and passion, but the Ojibwa in me wants your son." He took her hand and pressed it and kissed her mouth again. He opened his lips, but his mouth kept silent. Nor did her eyes require a verbal response. Their glance transferred what their hearts kept sacred.

Fires burned long into the night. Contrecoeur and Beaujeu listened patiently to the Indians. Sachem after sachem rose to speak. "We risk our lives for you, and for what?" a proud Mingo asked. "Yes," affirmed another. "We Ottawa have come long journey. Long have we traded with you. Long have we exchanged wampum and gifts, furs for guns, powder, paint, tobacco and beads. We are brothers. You call us your children and we call you our fathers, but we are all one. We are many and you few in number. If we die, who will sing our song? Will the English buy our furs? No. I think they will kill us too. What do my brothers say?" he directed his words toward the other chiefs.

Slowly, one clad in a mink mantle and French trousers stood. "I, White Eyes, of the Potawatamies and Miamies am old man now. I remember the time before La Salle, when the forest and rivers were ours alone. Now we share them with you. Our lives are different. We wear your shirts, your hats, your belts, your knives. We carry your guns and powder. But you carry our hearts, our souls. We are slaves to your drink. Where can we go now and flee your presence? Our old women squabble for your trinkets and blankets. The old ways are gone. We will perish if you treat us so. What promises can you make to return the forest to your people, the Red Man? I, White Eyes, want to know."

"I too," spoke another chief, as he struggled to his feet. "I am half Shawnee and half Delaware. But I may as well be half French and half English. My young braves crave your fire. Rum has robbed them of their guts, their fighting spirit. We are all women now. My heart is too sad to say more. But my arm is strong. I choose to die with this arm raised," he shook it, "than sulk in disease and vermin. I will cower no more."

"Hear! Hear!" many concurred.

Silently, a tall, copper skinned, handsome Indian rose. His broad shoulders were draped with a French officer's blue coat. His blouse was of French silk. A blue sash crowned his long black hair. His trousers of white deerskin gleamed in the fire's light. "I am Pontiac," he announced with solemnity. "I fear no one! I choose my enemies as well as my friends.

Listen, old men. Listen, revered fathers. I am your son. The forest is changing. The White man is here to stay. Sadly or not, that is true. Our French
Fathers have brought us wonders we never imagined. Since the days of
Champlain, my people have welcomed our Great Father and his Sons
from across the great waters. If we do not fight with them, with whom
shall we fight? Each other? What do the English care for us? Land! That is
all they want. Land and forest, our game and corn! Do not be deceived. I
will not waver. Will you?" He glared about the assembly of Indians seated
in front of the fire and to the left and right of Contrecoeur, where Beaujeu
and Joncaire sat cross-legged on bearskin rugs. "I have heard of these
men," he gestured toward them. "They bring great medicine and promise.
Courage and spirit! I stand with them. Pontiac is not a fool! Life is too dear
to sell out to the English cowards. I speak in peace. I speak with truth."

As the fires burned lower, the chiefs became restless. Captain Beaujeu motioned for François to come to his side. "What do you think?" he
asked with surprising respect for François. "Did the ships arrive from
New Orleans? The ones with presents and rum? Montreal promised they
would."

"Yes. They arrived with Captain Coulon de Villiers a week ago."

"Villiers! Jumonville's older brother! *Non*?"

"*Oui*. His eldest! Both he and François have vowed revenge for their
brother's death."

"Good! Such anger serves incentive well when seasoned with discipline. Perhaps we should break out a keg with tobacco for the sachems.
What do think? Do we have at least another week before Braddock's
forces stumble upon us?"

"Maybe less, five or six days at most. At least, the rum will keep them
here, and their braves. Personally, sir, our best ally's still in route."

"Oh? And who's that?" he asked stunned. "Of course! *Mais oui! Langlade, non?*"

"Langlade and his Michilimackinac braves. Word is they're less than
two days up river. Scalps hang from his belt, I'm told. Some are Cree to
the far north; most are British!"

"I know. I fought beside him on Lake Huron. Let's proceed with the
rum."

Joncaire, Coup de Sang, and Yellow Hawk led the procession to the storage rooms. Together with help from members of the *Compagnie de la Marine*, the Indians rolled out an oaken barrel of sweet rum from Jamaica. At the same time, Joncaire snatched up a leather bag of mild Carolina tobacco, shipped with the rum from New Orleans.

Drums began to sound throughout the sprawling encampment. Eager hands dragged dry timber from the edge of the clearing and set it ablaze in front of the fort. Tom-tom beats reverberated under the protruding bastions and along the border of the forest above the river. François turned toward Beaujeu and the Commandant. "Good night, Messieurs! If I may! I believe we have at least five days. Then, who knows what will happen."

"Never doubt our resolve," smiled Contrecoeur. "We will fight with victory in mind. I expect the same from all."

"No one will fail you, Sir! Nor our allies! If we can keep them occupied, I believe we'll win the field."

"*Oui!*" concurred Contrecoeur. "*If* we can keep them inspired! *Voilà le tour!*"

"*Jamais doute cela! Mon Sieur!*" Beaujeu chuckled. "My hero has always been Roland, the bravest of the brave who served Charlemagne. I'll be your Roland. We'll slaughter them at the pass, *mon très distingué Père.*"

"Yes!" Philippe whispered. But it was Hélène his heart desired, his sole desideratum. As he walked toward his quarters, he wondered if Rousseau had any true notion of what real savages were like. Still, he loved the Genevan's musings about *l'état naturel de l'homme*. Man's natural state! And just what was that? Indeed, what was man's true *histoire, dans la nature qui ne ment jamais*? Nature never lies, to be true. François inhaled the warm July night's air. How strange, he thought. How strange he felt. Half savage and half civilized, thousands of miles and leagues from his beloved France. But this was France now. This was his home. And he would defend it with all his might. Let the British come!

Two nights later, Braddock assembled his war cabinet to determine their final approach. They were less than fifteen miles away. His large canvas tent glowed yellow with flickering candlelight. The silhouettes of his staff members could be seen from outside. Langdon watched as the officers and others moved about, their long shadows creating distorted patterns inside the tent's walls. He could make out Wahington, St. Clair, Dunbar, Halket, Gage, Stewart and others as they shifted positions. Tillson's tall lean frame caught his attention the most. Braddock had signaled for him to come to his side. The large man was thumping his fingers on a deerskin map that Gist had made some years earlier. Langdon stepped closer toward the tent, stopped, stood still, and listened. The voices inside were voluble enough to be heard. The sentinels at the flap noticed Burke but simply tipped their hats, since they knew him to be one of Washington's guides.

Langdon could hear the General release a tense breath. "Very well. We'll cross twice. Once here," he thumped the map, "and then again just west of Turtle Creek. Burke's Indian boy reports that both fords are passable. Agreed?" he stood erect and glanced about the staff.

Murmurs of quasi-concurrence confirmed the General's wish. A few mumblings of uncertainty caused some nervous laughter, then silence.

"Tillson," the General raised his voice again. "Why don't you accompany Captain Stewart's Provincials as part of the advance guard, and, you, Colonel Gage, take several companies of your regiment and follow Stewart's people as closely as possible. St. Clair, your workmen will need to be next. Hopefully, you can muscle the six-pounders and at least one mortar forward to use immediately, if necessary. Halket, I want you personally to bring up the rest of the 44th. Major Washington, his Provincials, I, and Dunbar's 48th will come with the main body. The waggoners and carts will form the rear guard. Once we make the second crossing and find a suitable clearing, we'll regroup for the final push. I want this whole campaign to achieve its objective by July 15th. By then, our supplies shall have dwindled drastically and lead and munitions spent."

"Yes, sir!" a thin chorus of voices confirmed the General's wishes.

"Let's drink some wine," he said. "To his majesty and our success!" he raised a goblet.

"Hear! Hear!" the men replied, searching the tent for goblets and wine for themselves.

Langdon shifted his weight from his right to his left foot and walked silently away. Near the Youghiogheny, he found Blue Hatchet. The young brave had remained by its banks where he had discovered a canoe hidden in a band of dog-hobble. Stems of the plant's sweeping boughs still contained clusters of white blossoms. "I think this is one of ours," said Blue Hatchet. "For miles up this river and on the Mononga-hela, Torn-Ear led us on many hunts. Sometimes we fought Shawnee. Sometimes Lenape people and Delaware. Always, we were hiding ca-noes. The moon will be dark tonight. It is hard to see rowers in water. Do you want to go spy on Duquesne? We can be back by morning. Is my White father game?"

"Game? Yes! But tired. We don't want to risk being seen. Or still worse, captured."

"That won't happen. I give my word."

Langdon looked at the youth. He was almost his own height. His handsome face glowed in the dim starlight. He knew the boy wanted to prove himself, needed to seek revenge for his grandfather's death. The paddle down river and back would be arduous at best. They would have less than nine hours of darkness to cover the distance and return. "All right!" Langdon replied, almost shocking himself with his decision. "*Allez-y! Oui?*" he added in French.

Quickly, the two slipped into the water and climbed into the craft. Within moments, they were paddling silently downstream toward the confluence of the Youghiogheny with the wider Monongahela. Within an hour, they glided past Turtle Creek. Soon, the bulky shadows of the fort appeared. The campfires of its allies created an ocre dome of velvet light in the distance. The forest on the north bank loomed impenetrable. Pirogues, canoes, and barges jammed the river. Scores of wigwams crowded the spaces about the fort and up the bank into the trees.

"There are thousands of them!" exaggerated Blue Hatchet. "Even more across the Ohio. See! Way low, like a snake along the river. See? Not good."

"No more than I expected, nor less," intoned Langdon. "Washington will need to know, even if we don't say anything to the General. We'll have to warn Sir William. He's been assigned to lead the advance guard. I'm not sure where the Major will want us."

Chapter Twenty-Five

"I will be with you. We will fight together."

"We'll see. Crossing the Monongahela twice I don't like."

"Then we will fight in the woods. Much better to kill there," he said in a sad voice.

Langdon turned and looked back at the youth, where Torn-Ear's grandson sat in the stern. "I wish it were otherwise," he replied softly. "Best to turn about and paddle home."

As the night deepened, an edge of the moon struggled past clouds to illumine their path upriver. A warm mist settled upon the cool current. The dip of their paddles formed tight swirling circles. "Listen!" Blue Hatchet said. "Wolves! Far to the north! No?"

Langdon extended his paddle forward and pulled it back along the port side of the canoe. Water sparkled in the moonlight as droplets dripped from the oar's milky blade. "Active, aren't they?" he replied. "Strange how we hear them and then not again for several nights."

"They are spirits! The spirits of my people. There is great medicine in their cry."

Langdon continued to pull on his paddle. A young doe and her fawn splashed into the river near them. He watched as the deer drifted out into the current and swam toward the south bank. A raccoon's eyes glowed in the dark, as it too watched the deer bound off once ashore. Starlight bobbled in the water. Langdon could feel the river's tug as it vibrated against the canoe. He thought of Louise, Sarah, his children and Jonathan. He thought of François and Joncaire. Would they meet in battle? Would he even know where they were? Just stay away from the fort, he remembered Montour's warning. The howling of the wolves commenced anew. One after the other, the members of the pack filled the night with their eerie cries. Langdon rested the paddle on his lap and listened as the canoe slipped through the water. Quickly he began paddling again. Just ahead, the dark glow of the army's encampment hovered orange through the forest. Where had the time gone? What day was it, anyway?

Chapter Twenty-Six

THE FOREST ABOUT FORT DUQUESNE resonated with drumbeats. From everywhere, Indians spilled into the camp. François' own heart raced to the sound of the drums. Yellow Hawk had just returned from Turtle Creek. He had gone at Langlade's insistence. Contrecoeur had urged caution. He feared lest the British capture a French or Indian spy. If Braddock knew how few French troops they had, it would only embolden the General's resolve. "That we cannot allow!" Now, the restive camp awaited Yellow Hawk's report. All eyes watched the jogging figure as he slowed his pace and came into full view. Indians yelped as he passed them. At last he stopped before the Commandant, François, Villiers, Joncaire, Langlade, and Beaujeu.

The Algonquin raised his right arm and howled with pride. "They are coming! They are crossing the Monongahela now. They march to music. *C'est la vérité*! To fife and drum and Irish bagpipes! Men in women's skirts! Many red coats!" he spread his arms apart from fingertip to fingertip. "Many, Many! Glorious sight for Frenchmen's braves."

"Did you see any cannon? Big guns! How many and how far are they away?" asked Contrecoeur.

"Yes! Two cannons heavy in the river. Brass guns and horses! The red coats stretch for miles. Maybe by tomorrow, by mid-day they'll be near. But," he paused, as he studied the Commandant's face, "first, they must cross the river again."

"Good! We can meet them at the river, form a defense line at the ford," suggested Beaujeu.

"Will your allies join us?" Contrecoeur asked the Captain. "We haven't enough Marines."

"Of course!"

"It'll soon be dark," observed Langlade. "My Michilmackinacs will fight, but only if the other chiefs agree."

"Well! Call them in to parley. *Mon Dieu,* we can't afford their footdragging or speeches to save face! Joncaire, for Heaven's sake, assemble the sachems as quickly as possible. Monsieur Villiers, plan a defense of the fort. Call every Marine to his post and send out guards tonight. Quickly, let's meet inside! Invite all the main chiefs. The others will follow if Pontiac, White Eyes, and Black Hat agree. Damn! If we lose this fort, I shall have to hang myself. *Bigre!* By the cross of St. Pierre, may *God* spare us!"

François clasped arms with Yellow Hawk. "I will take blood tomorrow!" he assured the Algonquin. "Villier's death will be avenged."

"Good! We will fight together. Red brother and white brother. Now you speak the truth. I see it in your eyes."

As the chiefs began to assemble, Philippe hurried to Hélène's quarters. "Tomorrow we'll clash with the British. I know Burke will be there. We've known this all along." He paused and knelt beside his wife. "God help me not to find him! I don't want to kill him. I shall come back to thee! I'm unclean now. The chiefs are gathering. If they agree to help, they'll paint themselves for war. They'll dance all night. I'll need to stay with the leaders."

"*Mon* de Robert!" she smiled, "always *mon* chevalier!" She pressed François to her bossom. Tears moistened her eyes. She ran her limber fingers through his coarse black hair. Bending forward, she smothered his lips with her own. "Whatever happens, will happen. Just come back alive. If the fort falls, I'll wait for you at Le Boeuf. Louise is strong. Our fathers were brothers. Only our mothers were different. As for Langdon, he's on his own. But kill the British! We owe them nothing! Nothing but our knives and lead! May Mary keep you in her arms! Kill them, François; just kill them. Then let's go home!" Suddenly, she laid her face against his hot cheeks and kissed his mouth and eyes. "Get your things! I'll not sleep till you come back with scalps."

On his return to the pow-wow, François noted that the older sachems had gathered in front of the fort with their backs to its walls. The younger and more eager chiefs sat opposite them, awaiting Beaujeu and the Commandant's appearance. With quick steps the two entered the circle and stood before the grim chiefs.

"My brothers and faithful children," Contrecoeur began. "The British are less than three hours away. Your French fathers are few. Our soldiers are young and inexperienced. We number less than four hundred. You, my children, are many. Your fathers need you. Do you want us to fight the red coats alone, or will you join us now, as tomorrow is near? Speak and do not be afraid of what your words may say. Whether you depart or remain, many will die either way. We your fathers must stay. We have loved and befriended you. We will not abandon you. Come now, each in turn, rise and speak. Your fathers listen."

Pontiac rose and struck his breast with his fist. "You have heard my voice from the other day. I am not like a bird that flees in the wind. My braves and I raise our arms with the French. To do otherwise would be cowardly. We do not wear skirts like these women with squealing pipes. We are not fools. This is our home, the great Ohio and all its Lakes! We have no other place to which to go. We have not crossed the mountains to torment the English. Yet, they cross our rivers and lands to ravage and steal what is ours. Who among you cannot see that? I am not blind. I will join with father Beaujeu to fight to the end! I have spoken! Let others speak as well." He looked fiercely at those about him before taking his seat.

Langlade rose next. "I chief Michilimackinac, French and Indian, born to this land, side with Pontiac. Since Father Champlain, we have hunted, traded, lived, and married among your people," he addressed the silent chiefs. "We are one. We have always been one. Our wars between us have divided us too long. Better to fight a common foe than shed our own braves' blood. If our French fathers are defeated here, then we have everything to lose. Do you think the English will love and protect you as our French fathers have? No! They will burn our cornfields, drive us from our homes, and set fire to our hiding places in the canes. Our bear, deer, buffalo, and elk will disappear forever. Their rafts will despoil our rivers. Their filthy log huts will spread across the forest like plagues. We will die of their diseases and hatred of us. No! I will not flee like the frightened bird. No! I will stay and fight. What, my brave brothers, will you do?"

Chief Black Hat of the Wyandot, who had yet to speak, stood next. "My braves are few, our lodges thin across the forest. We have heard of these British. Their traders have found us in the wilderness. There is good and bad in them. We are tempted to wait and see, but we are not cowards. Will the English stay in the East? We ask ourselves that time and again. We do not cherish war. We do not want a false peace. But we are not like the raccoon that hide in the high trees only to fall at the marksmen's arrow when he sticks his head out again. Better we think to fight. My French fathers, we are all unsettled by this. Never have I seen so many warriors." He glanced toward François, the Commandant, Beaujeu and the others. He looked to his left and right toward Pontiac and Langlade. He seemed totally dispirited, if not overwhelmed by the crisis at hand. "I have said too much! My arrows are straight! My hatchet is ready." He turned slowly and reseated himself. His painful ambivalence was apparent to all.

An old sachem by the gate motioned with his hand for someone to assist him. François rose and helped the old chief to his feet. "Speak, my father. We are sons and brothers here."

The wrinkled, redfox-robed figure steadied his lean frame on a silver sword-encased cane. His matted braids hung limp about his shoulders. A brown-and-gray-feather-tattered headpiece set low over his ears; his eyes glowed white with a thin web of cataracts. He cleared his voice. "Great fathers," he addressed the Frenchmen, "we know whose sons and brothers you are. You have called us your children and we understand why. You think we are too primitive to be like you. Yet we are people. Our forefathers taught us how to hunt and live and to care for ourselves. We wish you had never come to our homeland. But, too many seasons have passed to quarrel now. Snow and sunshine, rain and drought are our brothers, too. I am of the Lenape nation that once roamed the woods of Pennsylvania free. Now, who am I? Where am I? Where are my children? My fathers' graves? Those of my mother's people? We are not even permitted to hunt on old lands or gather acorns, berries, and wild grapes, or fish in our ancient streams. The white man's ways are a curse. Our Great Spirit has turned his face against us. We never dishonored his spirits in the forest or mocked his shame of us when cold and alone. Yet, look at us now. Who is this Spirit of the white man? Why does he hate us so? Even your black robes," he turned toward the Commandant, "with their crosses and holy water look down on us. I could go on. But why? This is a good place to die. I ask only that you bring back many pale captives to our scaffolds that I might sink my knife into their eyes and brains."

Many heads nodded. Even Pontiac's. "It will be a good day," he mumbled.

"Have we decided?" asked Beaujeu, as he sprang to his feet. "Must I fight the English alone? You have spoken at length. Pontiac is with me. So is Langlade and all the brave warriors of the Lakes. But we need more! The British are many! Their red coats stain the forest with their hauter and pride, their arrogance and mockery. My children, your father Beaujeu and his brother, Dumas, cannot do this without you. Surely, you will not let your own father perish for fear of the English gun! I know you better than that. Midnight is falling. Dawn will rush in all too soon. The proud Braddock sneers at us even now. 'I will march them into the mud!' he is thinking. Brothers, fathers, children, noblest of braves, valiant warriors! I call you my own. Listen to this story. Many many years ago the great warrior Charlemagne defeated his enemy, the Moors, only to be betrayed as his braves returned north and home. They came to a pass in the mountains of the steep Pyrenees. Charlemagne had to go on. His enemy had accepted defeat. But, no! Their leader conspired to trap the great king and bring him low. He turned to his noble knights, his great warriors like you, and asked for his bravest of braves to protect his rearguard and defend the pass. Among them a hero named Roland volunteered. With his mighty arms, bright sword, and sharp lance, he rallied his children to fill the pass. The enemy stole forward. They lured him into battle. His braves fought nobly. Many scalps fell to his knife. Many he hoised on his shining blade. Down fell his enemy in piles of gore at his feet. But he was too few. His enemy too numerous. His fathers sounded the horn for Charlemagne's help, but Charlemagne's braves were too far away. Under many blows and mortal wounds the great knight stumbled. Treachery! Treachery! There was none to save him. He knelt before the earth; his enemy sprang over him; out thrust their knives; away slipped his spirit. The great Roland praised his God Most High, rolled to his side and died. Is that what you want of your father, Beaujeu, and his Captain Dumas? Is it? The assassins draw near. Our fort is their goal. The forest our pass! Must I sing my song alone? The song of Roland! The song of Beaujeu? Come, my brothers! Let us go to this place, meet them, and severe their heads with our hatchets. Then the Great Father and his sons in Montreal and here, you and your sons, too, gathered together, shall stop the English that threaten our lands. *Alors, mes enfants*! Will you come? Or will you hide here?"

From across the encampment, an up-roar of anger and pride filled the woods with savage energy. "No! We will not betray our father! Yes! We will go!" shouted the young braves. "We will not let our father die in the woods by the river. No! No! Now we shall sing our songs and paint for war!"

Chapter Twenty-Seven

AHEAD, THE TALL PINES ROSE resplendent in the late-morning sunlight. Washington glanced up through their graceful boughs and past the hickory leaves, where the sun blazed in fierce yellow fury. Already, sweat coursed down his face, neck, chest, and back. He wanted to remove his long coat and stove it behind his saddle, but the British about him seemed quite comfortable in their white blouses, lacy scarves, and garnet jackets. Their boots glittered black and silvery in the warm rays. On the other hand, the General appeared clammy, overcome by the heat. Not even the fife and faintly audible bagpipes seemed to soothe his irritable mood.

"Miserable damned insects!" he swatted at the gnats that swarmed about him. "Where are we anyway?" he demanded of Captain Orme.

"About to make our second crossing, Sir! Gage's men are already across. Frightfully great music, wouldn't you say so, Sir?"

"Hell! As long as it boosts morale I can take the pipes What are we, about five miles away?"

"Yes, Sir!" Washington answered. "We should sight the fort in about two hours. We should hear from Burke soon. He's up ahead with Stewart's rangers and Blue Hatchet."

"Good! I've sent Tillson upfront, too. I want his Majesty's spoiled-ass Governor," he smiled at the Major, "to receive the best firsthand report we can send back. St. Clair claims that half the beef and crackers he provided are crawling with weevils. The cheapskate! Your colonial Lords have become quite a nuisance, sir," he frowned at the young Virginian. "But, we're here, and I dare say the French damn well know they can't hold their fort. By next year, we should be in Canada, at the gates of Montreal or Quebec. Don't you think so?"

"Sir, I wish I knew. I serve at the Governor's command. And at the mercy of our Burgesses, when they're in the mood to fund!" he attempted to smile. "The Ohio would be nice to claim — as provincial as that may sound."

"Well, we'll not worry about that. Look! We're at the river ourselves. I shant get my boots too wet, I hope. I prefer to stay dry on the outside," he smiled, "and wet within."

"Here comes Langdon," Washington pointed to the buckskin-clad rider fording midstream.

Hastily, yet with caution, Burke negotiated his horse toward the General and Washington's mount. The sunlight dazzled in the water as the horse's hooves splashed over the bottom's slick rocks. "Sir!" he paused parallel with the Major. "Indians appear to be in the woods on a hill. Can't tell how many. We've only six riders upfront, plus the axemen and six-pounders. Should we wait for the main body or push on?"

"Tell Stewart to press forward! We'll be on his heels in minutes," Braddock replied as he bent down to wipe shining droplets off his spurs. "By now the French know we're here anyway. But, just in case, we'll move on the double."

Langdon stared at the General, then the Major. "All right, Sir! We've hit a lot of entanglement. Brush everywhere! I'll warn the militia to increase their watch. Some of Polsen's men are with us. Good day, Gentlemen!" he tipped his hat out of courtesy. He looked back at Washington, dropped his eyes slightly, along with his chin. Surely, the young George recognized how close to danger they were!

Washington raised his right forefinger with a quick acknowledgment of Langdon's glance.

Langdon smiled to himself, as he recrossed the ford. Scores of enlisted men looked up with envy. Their scarlet jackets bulged opaque with water. Their gun pouches and powder horns dripped with gleams of spray from the river's current. They crossed with their muskets overhead. In their tipsy tin helmets, they looked like toy soldiers struggling to remain afloat. Langdon goaded his horse forward and, after climbing the ford's gravelly slope, galloped up the fresh trail toward the vanguard.

As the canopy emitted less and less sunlight, Langdon's ears caught the rhythmic sound of the axemen's blades. He slowed his horse to listen again. Strange! That wasn't an axeman's blow; it was more like the crackling pop-pop racket of musketry. Langdon picked up the horse's pace. Ahead, the teams drawing the six-pounders had come to rest. The men beside them appeared confused.

"What's that, young fellow?" An older man asked him. "That ain't injuns, is it? I thought them Frenchies was still a couple o' hours away."

"Might be! Might not! Whatever, be on your guard. Be sure your rifles are primed," he ordered, as he rode past them. He nodded casually at their blond-braided ensign as he passed.

The clap of musket fire and muffled rumble of discoordinated vollies increased. There weren't that many in Stewart's group or Gage's vanguard, Langdon knew. They must be firing at will.

He galloped past more troops of the 44th and their stunned leaders. "It's an ambush!" Langdon tried to explain. "Seek cover and come quickly!"

Tillson was up there, somewhere. And Blue Hatchet! The stifling odor of black powder drifted down trail. Mists of smoke mingled with it. Gray wisps dissipated in the underbrush. The firing grew more intense.

Up ahead, on foot, Tillson watched in horror. Hundreds, if not a thousand, Indians were streaming unabated through the forest. He recognized Joncaire, then Handsome Dog. They were forty to fifty yards uphill. A Frenchman, dressed in Indian leggings but painted like a savage, raced ahead of them. Bands of young braves howled beside, behind, and in front of him. Black paint adorned his right cheek and red his left. His naked chest also bore paint: yellow, blue, and white. He carried a Tulle musket in one hand and a steel tomahawk in the other. Tillson ducked quickly and covered himself with leaves at the base of a basswood. Within seconds, a score or more of savages passed him. They were firing into the axemen and first squads of Stewart's troops. Elements of Colonel Gage's 48th began to bunch up awkwardly. Before they could raise their muskets to fire, a sizzling wave of lead and arrows zinged into the faltering group. The lead balls made a "zunk-zunk" sound as they struck bone and flesh, splattering blood on the sleeves and coats of comrades. Someone was trying to rally the shocked troops. His voice called out commands, but the hissing lead balls and shrill yelps of the attackers drowned it out. Tillson knew he had to do something, that he couldn't' simply lie there in a terror induced paralysis. He took a deep breath and sat up. He was armed only with a sword and bulky pistolet. When he felt for the latter about his waist, he realized it was gone, missing no doubt somewhere in the leaves. A burning sensation seized the back of his throat. He stood, with his back to the tree to survey the skirmish. A running Indian lunged at his chest. He raised his sword and rammed it into the red man's torso. The weight of the warrior caused both of them to topple. Purple blood oozed out and trickled along William's blade and onto his hand. He kicked the Indian aside and pulled out the sword.

Sixty yards uphill Blue Hatchet dodged a war club swung wildly by a stocky Shawnee. The brave couldn't have been much older than he, just heavier he thought, as he struggled with the longhaired youth. "Damn Delaware!" the brave hissed as he gasped for breath. He brought his knee up and caught Blue Hatchet in the groin. Blue Hatchet dropped his war axe. As he doubled over, however, he seized the man's braids and dragged him to the earth. The two rolled against the sharp branches of oak deadfall. The limbs were sharp and stiff. Blue Hatchet leapt up and shoved the man's face into the branches. The Indian groaned, then slipped over, face up. An iron sharp twig had penetrated his left eye and sunk into his brain. The distorted face stared at Blue Hatchet. Mucus dripped from the Indian's nose and mouth. Blue Hatchet searched frantically for his weapon, found it, and slammed its sharp edge into the Shawnee's skull. As if acting from some ancient instinct, he unsheathed his knife to take the scalp when a Frenchman raced up. It was Joncaire! Beside him stood Coup de Sang. Tekacayah seized Blue Hatchet by the throat and plunged his knife into the youth's ribs. Blue Hatchet's body rose with the knife. As he glanced down, he could see a rib protruding from his sliced flank. Out popped the knife, covered slick with blood. "I shall die," mumbled the youth, as he collapsed in a faint.

"Let him die!" said Joncaire. "We'll return for his scalp. *Bon Dieu*! Look! The British are falling like red leaves. Come!"

Blue Hatchet's senses revived in a reeling tide of pain as he watched the two steal toward a disorganized line of frightened soldiers. They crouched, raised their muskets, fired, and raced into the moil of death. Joncaire looked like a goose gliding into a misty pond. Clouds of gunpowder choked the air. Blue Hatchet crawled into the deadfall and lay beside the dead Shawnee. Groups of racing Indians leaped over the branches in pursuit of scalps. He thought of Torn Ear, Burke, Tillson. He pressed his fingers against his rib cage. To his relief, the sliced bone slid back in place. All grew dizzy. He tried to rise but fell back unconscious.

Two hundred yards down trail Langdon's progress slowed to a halt in a scarlet sea of fleeing soldiers. Many had thrown their muskets away. Others were running into the woods, anywhere to find safety. Hordes of Indians yelped and fell upon them, shooting point blank, clubbing, ripping off scalps, maiming the wounded, cornering others to take as captives. Langdon spurred Arduous forward. Units of soldiers were still standing, their officers, too, desperately attempting to maintain order. In the midst of the chaos the men stood firm, only to fall in groups of two and three after exchanging vollies. Suddenly, Langdon's horse reared, neighed violently, and collapsed in the road. Blood spurted from its neck. Langdon rolled off and picked up his rifle, his eyes searching for William and Blue Hatchet. Cautiously, he ran forward. Bodies lay in the soft muck; the moans of the wounded rose in mournful mutters. Langdon slowed his pace. Bullets thunked about him. Men slumped and sank to their knees before dropping face down into the slosh. Sporadic vollies of musketry echoed about him. He coughed, stopped, and realized he couldn't see a thing. Hot lead zipped past his ears. The stench of human feces and vomit, intestines and blood hovered in the air. Suddenly, a wall of fleeing men knocked him down. On hands and knees he groped toward the side of the road to escape their boots. Their hard leather heels made sucking sounds in the mud as they fled past. He reached a ditch, scrambled to his feet, only to be knocked down again.

Still farther down the road, a Highlander Regiment of kilted Scots marched on the double past Washington's horse. Led by a wail of inchoate bagpipes, they disappeared into the thickets beside the path. Their commander held his sword aloft and saluted Braddock as they passed. Members of Dunbar's 48th Foot jogged in unison behind them along the road. Struggling teamsters jammed the route with their frightened horses and heavy carts. Washington could hear them as their panicky efforts bottled up the narrow lane. With painful insight, he realized the General had no grasp of the calamitous condition of the situation. "Sir!" he called above the frantic commotion. "With your permission, I'm taking leave to command the Militia!" He waved his hat and rode after the 48th.

With fortune on his side, Washington began to spot members of the Provincials. A bold figure clad in buckskin, a blue coat, and black hat called to him from the fringe of the road. "Here! Sir! Over here!" It was Captain Steven.

"Fan out!" the Major shouted. "Stay behind the trees. Where's Cox's unit?"

"To your right, sir! They're holdin' off a bunch on a hill," he pointed north. "Crawlin' with savages."

"Continue, then! Have you seen Colonel Gage or Major Tillson?"

"Not since this hell broke loose! They're upfront," the Captain nodded into the shadows of the forest.

Washington turned in the saddle. Suddenly his horse bolted and crumpled under him. The big animal snorted and stretched out its neck. Its flesh quivered and eyes looked up in shock. It died as the Major pulled himself out from under the saddle. The bullet that felled the horse had just missed his right leg. The young Major bent down and patted the horse's neck. Quickly, he rose to his feet to search for a new mount.

Half a mile away, François waited by a spring for word of Beaujeu. Ensign Langlade had just passed him. The young French-Indian chief was racing toward a hill that provided higher ground. Several dozen Hurons loped behind him.

"Where's Beaujeu?" shouted François. Fear gnawed at the corners of his mouth. He could taste it in the back of his throat. Beaujeu had bolted ahead before he could join him. Captain Dumas, Beaujeu's second in command, had urged him to wait for Villier's reserves. But they had yet to show.

Langlade glanced back, but his forward momentum prevented him from comprehending de Robert's concern. "Come with us!" he shouted. "Beaujeu's Indians have stopped them. Hurry! *Venez avec nous! Vite! Monsieur!*

François relaxed his thumb on his musket's hammer and hurried after Michilmackinac's party. Sounds of the battle rattled through the pines and oaks. Occasional glimpses of red coats wavered into view; then disappeared behind floating clouds of thick gunsmoke. He could see Black Hat. The latter had found an excellent blind beside a mound of fallen logs. He and his Wyandots were meticulously firing, yelping, and reloading, as they crept closer to the British line.

As Langlade's Hurons swept on through the ferns and ground cover, François caught the figure of a grieving Abenaki, weaving to and fro over a fallen comrade. In the forest's sunlight, the man's hair was blondish-red. Rays of steaming air stole solemnly through the trees. François quickly approached the pair. The Abenaki looked up. Blood glistened on his hands. In his lap lay the silent figure of Beaujeu. A musket ball had pierced his throat, another his heart and lungs. His breathing was heavy, barely audible. The war paint he had daubed earlier on his face and chest shimmered in seeping red, yellow, and black smears. The hero of Nova Scotia was dying! "Help me," François said to the Indian. "Let's prop his body against a tree. We can't let him die in vain." The Indian nodded approval and helped François carry his "father's" body to a large, shade-dappled beech tree. There they laid him against its white trunk, his face turned toward the battle. François could not dismiss the Captain's eyes, wide brow, and fair face as he pitched headlong toward his own uncertain destiny. "*Mon Dieu!*" he muttered. "*Gardez Hélène et ma petite, je vous prie, Seigneur, mon Dieu!*"

On a small hill just north of the main body of Braddock's troops, Langlade's warriors crouched behind fallen timbers and waited for their chief's command. The young French-Indian sachem looked out across his painted line of braves. Naked, save for loincloths, leggings and moccasins, they lay calm amidst the dense brush. His pride for them was evident in his gray eyes as well as in their relaxed and self-confident readiness. He waited as a company of Dunbar's footmen came up and, standing at attention, stared helplessly into the thick woods. The officer on horseback seemed seasoned enough to command the men's respect, but Langlade could see they were appallingly exposed, making perfect targets for his braves. He raised his musket and laid its barrel on a moss-soft rotting trunk. His followers observed and pointed their guns at the nervous red coats less than forty yards downhill. "*Commencez feu!*" Langlade cried. Flames belched from the French muskets. Puffs of smoke erupted above the logs and drifted through the forest's undergrowth. Hurriedly, the savages reloaded, as groups of Dunbar's red coats dropped their weapons and crumpled in the road. A volley of fire rose from the British line, but its searing pellets clipped only leaves and twigs, plunking harmlessly into the forest ground. Langlade's guns flashed with smoke and flame again. His braves yelped, rose to their feet, and began darting from tree to tree. The British line held firm, but the officer on horseback had fallen. As musket balls and arrows pummeled the standing, men began to double up and collapse. Others stumbled over the wounded. Those able to continue battle fired aimlessly at the trunks of the towering trees. Langlade rose and ducked behind an oak and quickly reloaded his gun. He brought the musket around, held it steady against the bark, and felled another soldier. Waves of his braves were now leaping into the road, clubbing the standing and wounded. The British column wavered, its men searching for targets, as more colleagues fell. Langlade leapt into the road and, bringing his hatchet down with great force, crushed the face of the closest soldier. The man's eyes caught the brunt of the tomahawk's blow. The black blade sank through cartilage and bone and deep into his skull. Gray cranial matter oozed down the man's mouth and chin as he slumped into the road. A kneeling soldier begged for mercy, as a brave beside him slit his throat. The man's head turned sideways, his eyes rolled back, as blood spurted in a red shower down the soldier's white shirt.

Skirting the scene from side to side, the tall Pontiac picked his way among the fallen, stabbing the wounded to death before halting to rip a golden chain from an officer's vest. He dropped it in his lead pouch and raced to keep up with the battle. His own braves fanned out to his right and left and began firing at a line of Provincials just ahead. Pontiac motioned with his arm for his braves to steal to the woodmen's left. They quickly responded, darting from tree to tree. The buckskin-clad militia were difficult to see, but Pontiac knew how to trick them. He yelped and leapt out of hiding before darting behind a thick pine. A shower of lead chipped bark off its scaly trunk. As white puffs of powder drifted from the woodmen's guns, Pontiac's braves charged.

In the hot pursuit, the enemy's resolve weakened. Conducting itself remarkably well, the American force retreated while reloading. A tall British officer withdrawing with them, inadvertently exposed his position. Pontiac was struck by the man's demeanor, height, dignity, uniform, and overall bearing. He wanted him alive. The officer appeared armed only with a sword. Pontiac raced toward him, dodged the swing of his blade, and tackled him to the ground. "You are mine," he said. "I will kill you if you escape." He turned the officer face up and held his knife to his throat. "How are you called?" he asked in French.

"Sir William Graham Tillson. Aide to the General himself." William replied.

"I don't speak English. *Ne parle pas votre lanque.* I will keep you and see."

Suddenly, William slipped out of the big Indian's grip, struck him with his fist, and ran wildly into the forest.

A shocked Pontiac rose from his knees. His face beamed simultaneously with a smile and scowl. "English! Vain and stupid! We will find him. He will make a good captive for torture."

Pontiac picked up his knife and gun and pressed on after his warriors.

Farther back, François jogged along the newly cut roadway. He was shocked at the number of dead red coats. They lay crumpled in heaps. Some had already been scalped. Others' throats had been slit and gorgets taken. Brains speckled the corpses; entrails bulged beneath uniforms or lay in stringy coils on the mutilated bodies. On he loped. The sound of gunfire was sporadic; it rolled upslope in sudden roars, followed by feeble murmurs of the retreating army's effort to stave off defeat. Just then he looked up to find two figures standing in the road: Joincaire and Coup de Sang.

"Ah, you've made it!" smirked Joincaire. His belt was crimson with scalps. So was Handsome Dog's.

"Yes!" muttered Coup de Sang as he followed François' eyes to his own string of scalps that dangled from his loincloth. "Where are yours?" he asked.

"Beaujeu's dead! Killed moments ago! Have you seen Pontiac or White Eyes? Or Dumas? Is anyone in command?"

"Who knows, my friend? We have them in a rout!" gloated Joincaire. "I hate the news of Beaujeu. But the day is ours! Don't you grasp it? We've saved the fort. La Belle Rivière is ours! Come! Before the British escape!"

The two glared at him, swung about, and raced down the trail.

François followed, passed a writhing redcoat, and paused to examine the man. He was still alive, his legs shattered and left arm blown off. Should he assist or kill him? Memories of Jumonville leapt to mind. The senseless killings in the Glen near Fort Necessity! Beaujeu's bravery and all-so-mortal end! He stepped forward, bent down, and removed his knife. "My God!" he muttered to himself. With his right hand he placed the knife against the man's forehead, ran it quickly across his brow. Blood seeped out in a bright red line. His hands began to tremble. "*Have mercy on me, gentil Jesus*! But this, I must do!" With all his strength, he pulled the man's hair back with his left hand. It made a soft tearing sound as it ripped loose. He cut it clean just above the back of the man's neck. He shook it as tiny beads of blood dripped off. His mind revolted with disgust, yet a surge of primal pride accompanied the motion. It filled him with wild energy and dark joy. "Shit!" he muttered. What do I do with it now? He tucked it in his lead pouch, rose, stared at the silent forest, and ran toward the rumbling battle.

Washington's second horse fell beneath him as the Major rode up-hill. He slid off the dying mount and ran toward Cox's unit. "Here! Take mine!" an excited Provincial rider offered. "They're all around us!" he pointed with his long rifle into the woods.

"Where's the Captain? Can you hold here?"

"Capt'n's wounded, sir. Don't know about holdin'. But we ain't run-nin', if that's what you're askin'."

The young Major accepted his horse and mounted. As he swung the animal about, he saluted the woodsman. "Fall back! Braddock's whole line is failing. Bring the wounded with you!"

"Yes, sir! We'll flank them all the way."

Washington stared thankfully at the man, spurred the horse, and nudged it downhill through the wild vines. In a clearing just ahead, he could see the General. To his relief, Braddock seemed in full command. Aides-de-camp were crowding around him, receiving orders and ferry-ing dispatches to the rear. His horse lunged past the thick laurel, bringing him face-to-face with the General.

"Major! Thank God you're back! Have we a chance? What's going on?" Braddock had lost his hat. His scarlet coat flopped open at the chest, its buttons bright in the sunlight. His gloved hands steadied his horse. Nervously, he turned in the saddle. "It's bad, isn't it?"

"Yes, sir! My advice? Fall back to the river, before the French get there! Once across we can hold them off. For now, though, there's a group of Indians on a hill, sir," he pointed north. "They're the ones firing into us. If we could storm it, Indian style, we might take it."

"Good! Colonel Burton!" he shouted to a distinguished rider close by. "Can you get the 48th up that prominence?"

"Yes, sir! We'll try," he replied, as he turned in his saddle to lead the charge.

Orme and St. Clair cheered their own men forward. "Rally, for God's sake, rally!" barked St. Clair. "Cut the teams loose and follow us!"

To the Quartermaster's surprise, several displaced companies joined ranks and pushed through the dry underbrush. Suddenly, St. Clair winced and slumped in his saddle. With his right arm he struggled to re-main upright. He glanced at his left arm; it hung limp from his shoulder down. A bullet had lodged high in his shoulder. "On! Dammit! On!" he urged as he fell behind.

Just then, Captain Orme tumbled from his horse with a wound to his thigh. He clutched his leg and limped toward a tree. He leaned against it and fell in the leaves. Colonel Burton ordered the pipers and drummers to play. Up went the shrilling squeaks of the pipes to the quick cadence of the drums. A hail of lead cut down the first to advance. Intermittent showers of arrows zipped overhead, wounding ranks of the second and third waves.

Washington glanced at his watch. Darkness would be falling soon. Already the tall pines' shadows filled the woods with solemn shade. If their attempt failed, they would scarley make it back to the river. It was 4:30. He swung about to locate Braddock. The General was still in the road. His horse, however, had been hit. The General seemed unusually agitated, confused, if not dismayed. He clutched his chest and looked up through the trees toward the Major. Washington realized the General had been hit. He yanked his reins to the right and galloped back to the General's side. Aides had rallied, and with upheld hands, caught the General as he fell into their arms. The counterattack up the hill stalled. Colonel Gage trotted by on his limping horse; he was holding his left arm against his chest. The remaining troops looked over their shoulders. Men began to shout. Panic overtook them. They flung aside all impediments and fled. The road became clogged. Most of the waggoners had cut their teams loose and were riding the unsaddled mounts as fast as they could speed away. The road became impassible. Washington spotted Captain Stevens. "For God's sake, hold the flanks! We'll rendezvous at the river." He swung back, dismounted and hurried toward the General.

"Sir! We're retreating now. We'll rest at the ford. They'll stop there," his eyes glanced toward the enemy. "You'll be fine," he sought to assure him.

The General's wan face turned uphill. His eyes emanated the pain he struggled to disguise. Any vanity he had ever displayed was gone. He reached out and patted the young Major's hand. "Thank you," he whispered in a broken voice. "Take command, if you will!"

"Yes, sir!" replied Washington. He stood and glanced about at all within earshot. "Man-by-man, one-by-one, protect each other. Stay together. Fire only at clear targets. Keep low. Come, now. Keep it orderly. Carry the wounded if you can. We'll not stop till the river. Hurry. Bring that cart over here for the General. Clear the path. Quick now!"

Colonel Gage looked down from his mount at the wounded General. His own arm ached from his elbow to his ribs. Like Braddock, he gasped for breath and fought off the panic that nipped at his senses. "We'll see you clear, sir," he promised. "The Provincials are damn good."

"And our lads, too," mumbled the pale Braddock. "See that the wounded are cared for. I hear the savages do terrible things."

"Yes, sir!" he replied, as a cluster of aides lifted the General into the cart. "Here, there!" called the Colonel to two soldiers rushing by. "Halt! That's right! Halt and pull this cart."

The two stared inside at the General, removed their hats, and laid their guns beside him in the cart. Without further delay, they lifted the tongue and rigging and pulled it slowly down the road. Washington, Orme, Burton, and St. Clair followed. Each rode momentarily beside the cart, taking turns, while conducting the retreat as best they could. Washington's men kept up a steady fire as yelping Indians flickered from tree to tree. British troops and Provincials alike fell under the hail of fire. The units kept together and proceeded as orderly as they could toward the river.

It was obvious to all that the General's wound was mortal. It was only a matter of time. Slowly, the disjoined elements of the army fell back through the forest. Orme hated to see the six-pounders and howitzers left mired in the mud. Overturned wagons of munitions with kegs of gunpowder cluttered the way. Supplies of all sorts had been trampled into the earth. Damn! He shook his head, as he nursed his leg.

The main body of attacking Indians had long passed Langdon. Only remnants firing from a hill broke the stillness near the road where he crouched in the laurel. Where was Blue Hatchet? Where was William? He had seen neither since reporting to the Major at the ford. Hours had past now. The lull in the battle created a vacant pit in his stomach. Fear and adrenline churned inside. Many scalped red coats cluttered the road. He stood erect and jogged toward the sound of the retreat. Dark shadows played on the edge of the hill. The sun would soon sink behind the sur-rounding wall of forest and rocks. Pleased warriors, drunk with scalps, would be returning his way. Time was running out. Night was creeping in. All the faster he ran, dipping to the left and then to the right, keeping the laurel and underbrush between himself and the trail's banks. An Indian, bending over a body, raised his head. Langdon knocked him down and kept running. The sounds of the skirmish grew louder. A musket ball whizzed by his head. He waved to the woodsman who had fired the shot. The man squinted and knelt to reload. Langdon burst upon him in a fit of euphoria. "Damn! I'm one of yours!"

"I reckon so!" replied the startled militiaman. "Ain't nobody takin' chances," he gasped. "You and me's the onliest ones here. Let's get on!" he rose, cradling his gun to lead the way. "They's gone off down here!" he panted. "We're the lucky ones," he spat, as they passed a bloated corpse in the path.

"Shhhh!" said the woodsman. "Someone's ahead."

The two stopped and peered through the growing darkness. It was Captain Cox. "This way!" the Captain beckoned. "We're a ravine from the shoals."

Langdon stood erect and stretched himself as tall as he could. It was the first time he had relaxed all day. He shouldered his long rifle and ran toward the ravine. The three half-slid, half-rolled down the embankment. The three crossed the ford in a trembling current of rippling starlight. Once ashore, Langdon collapsed on the banks and caught his breath. Slowly he stood up, inhaled a long breath, and wandered toward the distant campfires in the darkness. Behind him, the muffled screams of the wounded echoed through the forest. The victors were taking scalps and prisoners.

Chapter Twenty-Eight

NIGHT SMOTHERED out the last glimmer of day. Overhead, the dark canopy of the forest obscured the twinkling stars. William groped in the darkness, stealing from bush to bush. He had hoped to slip downhill toward the river, but bands of Indians were returning on both sides of the trail. Their boisterous voices filtered through the woods. He caught a glimpse of two captives: an axeman and a sergeant. He hugged the earth and kept silent. His throat felt seared, his lungs burned from exhaustion! Flecks of earth covered his hands and face. Gnats and mosquitoes buzzed about his ears. His left sleeve dangled from his coat's shoulder, where briars had unstitched the threads.

As he lay down to rest, he could hear voices on a knoll above. They resonated with French and Indian sounds. Three figures loomed into view, silhouetted against the glow of the few stars he could see. Pulsating white through gaps in the treetops, the starlight suddenly illuminated William's face. The three stopped.

"*Ecoutez! Là! Là-bas! C'est un homme! Non? Je peu sentir son mauvais corps,*" a Frenchman stated.

"*Moi aussi,*" said another. "*Voilà! Aux tenerbres. Quelque agit. Non?*"

"*Mais, oui! C'est un angleterre! Quelle bonne chance!*"

"Geet up!" the first kicked him. "You will make a great prize. Come, now!" he pointed his musket at William. "Noooo, nooo, nooo! No wiggly, Monsieur. You are ours *maintenant*. Geeet up. *Vite!*"

Just then, Yellow Hawk and two braves came through the forest. "Ah! The Englishman! I know him!" the Algonquin smiled. "I have wanted his coat for years. Look at it now! His scalp will have to do," he bent down and unsheathed his knife. "Or is the scaffold a better fate?" he threatened, as he placed the knife point against William's throat. "I think so!" he swept his hand in mock fashion across William's Adam's apple. With that he leaped up and struck William with the back of his warclub.

William fell backwards. The big Indian's figure wavered, then faded, as unconsciousness bore William down. A wolf howled somewhere! Was he dreaming? Dying? Or Dead?

Nearby, Blue Hatchet stirred beside the Shawnee's corpse. He too heard the wolf's cry. He crawled out from under the deadfall and crept across the forest's floor; the odor of rotting flesh singed his nostrils. He glanced back. Ants covered the dead brave. Their translucent glow twinkled greenish in the dark. His right side had grown stiff; his flesh ached. Ants were nibbling at the dried blood caked about his ribs. He rolled to his left and struggled to get up. In the starlight, he watched as six or seven forms appeared ghostlike on the path below. They were coming his way. He recognized the bowed head of the battered officer. They had tied leather thongs to his wrists. "Tillson," he all but whispered aloud.

"What is that?" asked one of the braves. "I see someone in the dark."

William raised his bloodied face and stared. It was Blue Hatchet. "Run!" he attempted to yell, but the words struggled to form on his swollen lips.

A brave reached out to seize the young Delaware when suddenly a white form lunged from the shadows and knocked the Indian down. It was a huge wolf. It snarled and leapt for Yellow Hawk's throat. The Frenchmen clubbed at it with their muskets, but the enraged beast tore at their hands and flesh with its ivory fangs. It crouched to spring again. The six flinched and covered their faces. Terror seized Yellow Hawk. It was not good! It was a *chose* of dark magic. A demon spirit, he knew. He raised his arms to protect himself. But in that instant, the wolf withdrew. Yellow Hawk grunted. The wolf disappeared.

So had Blue Hatchet. He had fled the moment the wolf attacked, his heart thundering in his chest as he ran.

"Cursed timberwolf!" One of the Frenchmen swore. "Have you ever?" He turned toward William. "Get along! *Bon Dieu*, what will be next?"

Sir William choked and gasped for breath. Naked and burning with fever, he stumbled over the sharp rocks and crooked roots as the six shoved him along. He could scarcely see his way in the darkness. The forest's foliage cut his feet. Underbrush whipped at his privates. As daylight broke through the trees, Sir William looked up to see the fort, strong and impregnable in the morning light. Mist drifted from the two rivers to shroud it in a mirage of flags and bastions. Tom-tom beats announced their approach. The tongue clacking sound of delirious savages rose in volume as the captors hauled him into view. Indians spilled out from the woods to gawk. Eagerly, they formed two parallel lines. The tom-toms beat faster. The Indians grew closer. They smacked their clubs and gnarled sticks against the palms of their hands. William's heart sank. His bleeding feet throbbed with cuts and sores. The raw arches of his feet ached. Could he make it? Is this where he would die?

Yellow Hawk yanked on the cord about his neck. To his right, William could see a scaffold of timbers, hastily throw up. Tied to stakes, five captives slumped limp in twisted vines. Their torsos had been beaten bloody, their faces scorched with smoke, their testicles severed. He wondered which one was the sergeant and which the axeman. A sixth victim's visera bulged disemboweled. Coils of gore hung in lilac drapes about his legs. Black sockets replaced his eyes. Mercifully, he was dead. The living watched as Tillson's party shoved him toward the howling savages, gathering to form a gauntlet. Someone cut his wrists free.

"Anna!" he whispered to himself. "Anna! Anna!" he suddenly called aloud. "God I shall do this!" he shouted above the savage roar. "Damn you, Frenchmen! Damn you, savages!" With that, William clenched his teeth, set his mind on Anna alone, transcended all thought of his fear and pain, and ran headlong at the mob. He butted the first Indian in the groin, smacked the second with his fist, wrested the third's club from his hands, and swung it wildly at the fourth. Trunchants pummeled his back, face, head, and neck. He bit his lips. Its salty blood ran down his chin. "Damn you!" he shouted with each blow. With shoulders and elbows, he rammed his tormentors, clubbing as many as he could. Blood blinded his eyes. On he ran, stumbled, regained his balance, and swung his club again. A large Indian stepped in his path, whirled his stick at his throat, and sent William reeling backwards. Dozens of Indians fell upon him with their clubs. Suddenly, they stopped. William rolled on his back and looked up. It was the large Indian who had wrestled him to the ground in the forest. It was Pontiac. "Enough!" the red man said. "*C'est bien assez.* He is too brave to kill." With that, he reached down and clasped William's wrist and pulled him up. "Now, you belong to me!" he stared with black eyes. "Come!" he ordered, as he led him away.

From the closest bastion, François watched as Pontiac conducted Sir William past the fort. Earlier, he and Contrecoeur had pleaded with the chiefs to spare the captives.

"No!" White Eyes had expostulated. With anger he swept his hands across his chest.

"This thing you suggest is repugnant," Black Hat added.

A crippled sachem had shaken his cane at them. "French fathers, this is not for you to decide. It brings us pleasure and cleanses us. It is the way we let them die."

Ensign Langlade had remained silent. His Michilimackinac braves had returned with ten hostages. Just an hour earlier, they had hatched them to death in the field in front of the fort and had impaled their decapitated heads on posts as one entered their camp.

"Forget it," Joncaire smirked. "Why do you think they came so far? For trinkets and beads?"

"Still, I hate it!" Contrecoeur confessed. "They have made us accomplices of their own *sauvage état*! Isn't that so, François-Philippe?"

"Yes, I fear!" he answered sadly. He realized the scalp he had taken was still in his pouch. François turned from his protected vantage and descended the log steps to the parade grounds below. He was in no position to intervene. Was he not one of them now? He was next in command after Captain Dumas. But any moral authority he possessed was stained. Still, should he not try to do something to save William? Afterall, the two had faced the Iroquois together. They were civilized. They were not savages. *"Alors!"* There were no easy answers. Besides, the man was his enemy. Fraternity with such had to cease! Great God! If it had not been for their Indian allies, the British would have captured the fort? It was a miracle that they had won. Perhaps in time, Pontiac would release him. Was it not wiser for him to wait? So he argued with himself as he crossed the commons.

Many officers had gathered in the center. Dumas looked up and beckoned for him to join them. "It's for Beaujeu!" he said. "See! Captain Villiers has placed him on a bier. *Non*? It is so sad! He loved war. Was without fear; indeed, peers! How dearly France has been diminished. They say he loved Roland's *chanson*. I remember so little of it.

Pour son seigneur doit homme suffrir
Pour notre roi bien mourir.

Or something like that. He was valiant. Now he's dead!"

François stood at attention. Contrecoeur and others joined the assembly. Beaujeu's Abenaki braves stood quietly by. A priest in a white cassock knelt beside the bier. Slowly, Philippe knelt along with the other Frenchmen. Together they prayed The Lord's Prayer. The priest raised his arms to heaven. "God, bless this victory and our King! Forgive our sins, O Holy Savior, for blood is on our hands. Receive our prayers for this fine youth, whose sacrifice we render back in sorrow and thanksgiving. May our Blessed Mother and thy dear Son enfold him in eternity." The priest rose and sprinkled the bier with holy water. Then he folded his hands and began to sing. François recognized the Latin words from the ancient hymn his own uncle had taught him to chant:

Qui diceris Paraclitus, altissimi donum Dei,
Fons vivus, ignis, caritas, et spiritalis unctio.
Hostem repellas longius, paceque dones protinus,
Ductore sic te praevio, vitemus omne noxium.

Chapter Twenty-Eight

To thee we cry, O Paraclete, gift of God Most High,
Font of life and fire and love, Thou sweetest unction from above.
Drive from us far the foe we fear, and grant us peace as we kneel here.
For if Thou art our guide and rest, thy path we never shall transgress.[1]

The priest motioned to Beaujeu's braves and stepped back. A group came forward, lifted his bier, and carried it away. They departed the post and wrapped his body in a rug of bearskin and beaver fur. Before tying it, they laid in several boughs of cedar and sprinkled handfuls of crushed cedar nuts over his corpse. Finally, they shouldered his body and carried it off into the woods.

"It is best not to follow them," said Contrecoeur. "He was more than just a Frenchman. He was a *vrai père* to them, their brother at heart."

François crossed himself and headed for his quarters. It was almost noon. Outside the fort, the yelps of Indians reached a new crescendo. He knew he must find Pontiac and bid for William's release. First, however, he wanted to bathe. Perhaps Hélène would go with him.

"You seem different," she said, as she watched him wash his face and arms, chest and body. The shallow tub in which he sat provided narrow quarters at best. Constructed from a hollow log, its rough sides scraped his hips and barely permitted space for his feet. "Here," she poured in a bucket of warmer water. "Look how the filthe floats to the surface!" She bent forward and continued to scrub his back with a wad of woolen cloth. "Your face, your eyes! I hear Langlade's braves killed many. Look! Look at me, François! What did you expect? I'm proud of you! There may be more before we drive the English home." She bent closer, studied his face, mouth, lips and throat. "Kiss me!" she placed her lips on his. "Let's go home. Ask Dumas to transfer you upriver. I want to return to Ft. Niagara. Or Frontenac! That's where we belong." She sat back. Her dark eyes sparkled in the room's dull light. Her black braids rested against her shoulders and back. Her milk-filled breasts rose round and luring with each silent breath. She smiled and kissed him again. "*Non? J'ai raison? Oui?* Of course," she smiled as she handed him their only towel.

---

[1] A freely adapted translation of Michael Martin's edited *Veni, Creator Spiritus*.

He looked up at her. Whatever darkness plagued his soul she always seemed to exorcise with candor. "You're right." He struggled to his feet and began to dry off. "I need to visit Ponitac's camp. He's captured Burke's friend, Tillson. You may remember him. I need to go alone"

She kissed his chest and dried him off some more. "It's just as well. Noël needs me here. Why not take Yellow Hawk?"

He daubed himself again, redressed, and returned her kiss. Once outside, he crossed the commons in search of the big Algonquin. The brave was nowhere inside the enclosure. He passed through the gate and stared out toward the scaffold. Many women were tormenting a new group of captives. Children were poking sticks into their ribs. The old sachem who had begged permission to torture at least one captive looked down toward François. Momentarily, he stopped whatever he was doing and descended the planks. Blood stains covered his hands. Streams of it had soiled his leggings and moccasins. "I am avenged," the old man said. "I shall go home in peace." He raised his hands. His fingers clutched two eyeballs, one in each hand.

François tried not to blink. "I am pleased old father that your soul has found comfort. We are grateful that you are here."

"Yes!" replied the old man. "I am ready for your rum." He wiped his hands against his leggings and ambled proudly toward the fort.

François' body began to tremble. A tremor passed through his hands and torso. He gripped himself about his chest with his own arms. Slowly, the convulsions ceased. He shook off the inexplicable seizure and set about to find Yellow Hawk. Halfway toward the conversion point of the two rivers he spotted the brave with a group of Seneca and Wyandots. Black Hat was gesticulating with his hands, pointing toward one of the Senecas. They were drunk. The Seneca held an English pistol in his hands. Black Hat appeared to want it. He seized it. Suddenly, the gun discharged. The bullet struck the Seneca in the right arm. He howled and collapsed to his knees in the dirt. Yellow Hawk knocked the chief to the ground and wrested the weapon from him. "Go! Go!" he shouted at the Wyandot. "You, too!" he said to the Seneca. He pointed the empty gun at both of them. "Go now! Already the sun has passed the middle sky!"

With angry glares, the two warriors rose. Slowly, they backed away.

Black Hat eyed Yellow Hawk, his temper about to erupt. From the corner of his eye he caught François. "You, you came to us for help. And we, we came and fought for you!" he pointed his finger at him. "*Non*? Now you send us away. We will meet again! I promise!"

The Seneca nodded with concurrence. Soon, they slipped into the crowd of sullen Indians who had gathered about.

"There you have it!" Yellow Hawk addressed Gabelle. "We cannot unite long enough to save ourselves. To fight for you bleeds us even more. Pontiac is right. We need you, but the cost is more than it is worth."

"Maybe so, maybe not! Do you know the whereabouts of Pontiac's lodge?"

"Yes! But it will do you no good."

"I need to see him."

"He's left. He crossed the river before noon, Pontiac and all his people. Plus your English soldier. You will not find them! They are hours gone. Come, did you take a scalp? My hands are bloody. See! We fought all day and night. Are yours? I wish to know."

You bastard! François thought. Who made you my master? Instead, however, he stepped closer to Yellow Hawk and reached into his pouch. "Here!" he showed him the British's soldier's matted hairpiece. It was still sticky with blood.

The startled Indian's face turned red, deeper than the reddish copper of his native flesh. "Yellow Hawk has no home but the ashes of your camp. The fire of your lodge! I will not speak so again. This, I vow! For you!" he handed François the English pistol, as he accepted the scalp.

De Robert's heart softened; his pent up tension abated. The air in his lungs leaked out with a sigh. A fragile instant of euphoria swept over him; then vanished. He slipped the gun in his belt. He needed Yellow Hawk, as savage and cruel, simple and arrogant as the Indian was! "Come. Like it or not, we are brothers," he stated.

"*Mais, oui!*" the Algonquin smiled. "Yellow Hawk will never offend you again!"

Chapter Twenty-Nine

THE MUGGY JULY AIR weighed mercilessly upon Washington's neck and shoulders. He had removed his hat. Beads of grit glistened on his brow. His long folded coat lay across his saddlebags. He had rolled up his white sleeves. Captain Orme stood beside him. They had both dismounted to care for the General.

"Where are we?" the wounded Braddock mumbled. An ivory cast discolored his face. His robust countenance had vanished. Oozing blood soaked his shirt. Flies hovered about its crustier edges. "Water! I'm going to vomit," he whispered. The proud man turned sideways and coughed. A string of bloody mucus dripped from his lips. His eyes rolled white.

"Sir, we're near the Great Meadows," said Orme. "You've been delirious since the battle. We're in retreat, sir."

"Yes! I know. Our losses, what are they?"

"We're not certain. Sir Halket's dead."

"Sir Peter, you mean?"

"Yes."

"And his nephew? Did he make it?"

"No, sir! Both were killed. Just after you were wounded."

"What about yourself?"

"Wounded in the thigh, sir! Not that bad."

The General stared up at Washington. A lump had formed in Braddock's throat, making it large and swollen. "I haven't seen Tillson," he said in a weak whisper. "Was he killed?"

"Here, sir. Take some water," Washington offered, as he placed his left arm around the General's neck, raising him to sip from his flask. He tilted the container to allow a few drops to moisten the man's lips. "No, sir. Burke's Indian lad says he was captured."

"I'm sorry to hear that," he said. "Major! I can't catch my breath." He reached for Washington's hand.

Washington clasped it and pressed his fingers tightly about the General's. "We're going to stop and rest. Your wound's too deep to probe."

Braddock looked up into the Major's eyes. He struggled to sit up, paused, and sank back into the straw. Whatever light his eyes had retained for the past three days ebbed away. The man's eyelids closed. Suddenly, they opened with a faint "click," only to close again.

Washington looked away, then toward Orme. "The Big Meadows are near. With your concurrence, Captain, let's bury him there. We're still a week from Willis Creek, at best!"

Orme placed his fingertips on the General's temple, then eyelids. He leaned forward to listen for the faintest sound of Braddock's breathing. "Nothing!" he said. "After all this effort! What a way to die! You poor, sir," he addressed the General. He glanced up and out across the forest. Intense heat beat down with oppressive measure. The soft mud in the road leaked with seeping springs. Orme swallowed the hard swelling in his own throat and covered the General's face with Braddock's blood-soiled jacket. Its rancid odor singed his nostrils.

Blue Hatchet and Burke came up to lean beside the cart. "Major," Burke addressed him. "There's a pleasant spot near the Meadows, looking out toward the distant glens. May I recommend we bury him there?"

"It'll soon be evening," Washington replied. "St. Clair's behind us, spiking the cannons. When he comes up, we'll inter the General in the road." He thought for a moment. "Get word to as many of the Militia as you can." He turned to Orme. "Captain, form your companies when we get there. We need to bury him with honors. Perhaps some drummers and pipers can be rounded up."

Large thunderheads rumbled over the briary Meadows as the Corps drew near. Drummers lined the road as St. Clair and Colonel Dunbar assembled the surviving units of the 44th and the 48th Foot. Lightning flashed deep yellow within the towering black clouds. Their convoluting shapes boiled higher and higher, bringing an eerie darkness to the field. Light rain began to fall. Pipers from the Highlander Brigades pumped their squealing bags and began playing a Scottish lament. Waggoners dug a deep pit in the road and filled its bottom with straw. Washington and St. Clair, along with Orme and Dunbar, lifted the General's cloak-wraped body from the cart and lowered it into the pit. Thunderclaps drowned out the pipers as a torrent of rain swept across the Meadows. An English flag and a Union Jack were furled and placed across the General's body. The four stepped back as rain pummeled the grave and streams of runoff splashed into the hole. Quickly, the waggoners covered the grave.

"Run the cart over it! Back and forth!" St. Clair ordered. "Dunbar, dismiss the brigades. All of you listen. We're less than seven hundred, out of two thousand. Stay together. Major," he addressed Washington. "Keep your Provincials on our flank! Everyone. Buck up! Assist the wounded. Look for stragglers. Damn if we haven't suffered enough. You've heard me. Now move on."

Burke looked toward Blue Hatchet, then the Major. He knew their assignment. He beckoned to the Indian and, wading through the wet broom sedge, made his way toward Cox's militia on the right flank.

When nine days later they reached Fort Cumberland, Burke approached Washington and waited as he counted the last groups of Provincials passing through. "You did a great job!" the Major congratulated Cox and Polsen. "God knows when they'll get paid. Perhaps in Winchester, or Alexandria."

"Sir, I think most of the men are happy just to be alive. They're ready to be dismissed, at your word."

Washington stared at the two, then at Burke. "We were routed, Gentlemen. Defeated! All but massacred! Great God! I can only image what Dinwiddie must think! Let alone the Crown! You have farms to go back to, shops, crops to harvest." He swung to and fro in his mount. His horse pranced and snorted lightly. Buttons were missing from his coat. Flakes of dried muck and red clay soiled his hat. "This is probably the end for us. Thank you, each. Please thank them all. I don't know what else to say. We fought well. The General, for all his valor, just didn't know what to expect." He paused. "See that each man receives what powder and lead he needs. They'll be coming across the mountains soon," he nodded toward the forest. "The French, they'll not give up. Nor their savages. Perhaps we'll meet again."

"Yes, sir!" replied Cox.

"Sir!" Polsen spoke up. "Don't feel so glum! Hell! If'n it had just been us, we could of whipped their asses good!" He removed his hat and smiled. "Look after yourself, sir! You ain't done nothin' we ain't proud of."

"Thank you, Captain. I suspect the Colony will see it otherwise. Farewell!"

"Farewell, to you!" Burke raised his voice. "Sir!" he approached him closer. "Listen, I don't know how to say this, but, please tell the Governor about Sir William. His Lady friend in Williamsburg will want to know. They were in love."

"I understand, Mr. Burke." The young Major stared at him, as if he suspected the secret that William had shared with the guide. "Perhaps you'll come to Mt. Vernon some day, or Williamsburg again. You'd make a great burgess."

"That'd be nice," he smiled. "Right now, I just need to get home and face Louise and Sarah. They weren't expecting William not to return."

"We must keep in touch," replied the Major. "See St. Clair before you leave. He's promised me horses for both of you—you and your brave." He swung his mount about and trotted along the west bank of Willis Creek. With pride, he wished his men farewell. "Till another time," he said, in a proud but soft voice.

PART FOUR

The
Plains
of
Abraham
1755-1759

Chapter Thirty

SIR WILLIAM RAN AT A FAST PACE to keep up with the forward warriors. Snow was falling heavily, obliterating the footprints of the fleeing Chippewa. They had descended across the narrows of Lake Huron, continued by canoe, and attacked Pontiac's camp that night. The chief's youngest son had died in the melee, along with one other brave.

"Hurry!" Pontiac panted. "We will do well to catch them. They aren't that far."

Snow swirled in white wisps about the two as they lengthened their strides. One of Pontiac's braves was pointing to the ground. "Blood! See?"

William slowed up, stopped, and looked down. Yes. There it was. Even in the semi-darkness of the whirling flakes he could see the blood stain. It had caught in the snow and feathered out to form a wet scarlet circular shape.

"How many?" the chief asked.

"No more than four. They are running in each other's steps. Their canoes cannot be far."

Faster, now, all three ran! From somewhere up ahead, an Indian shrieked. A musket fired. A second rumbled through the snowfall.

Pontiac slowed his pace. Two Chippewa lay dead in the snow. A third was wounded. An arrow had caught the fourth in his back. The sharp tip had ripped through the brave's lungs. When Pontiac rolled him over, blood squirted in a dark stream across the Indian's naked chest. It dripped at a steady rate on the frozen path. The big chief walked over to the wounded enemy. "Cursed dog!" he said. He raised his warclub and crashed it into the Indian's face. "May Manitou turn his face from you. May you never see your children in the spirit world!" He brought his club back past his shoulder and swung it down a second time. This time the hard stone axe cracked the Indian's skull. The hollow "thunk" reminded William of the lead balls that had pelted the logs of Ft. Necessity. "Good! He is dead!" uttered Pontiac. "Come, my brother," he addressed William. "We must sing my son's death song until my heart is avenged!"

As they made their way back through the snow, William so wanted to escape. He had attempted it twice, only to be captured and returned. The first time, Pontiac scolded him. "Have I not been like a father to you? Have you not begun to teach me your own words? Now you do this thing! You would have died on Duquesne's scaffolds! But I—I rescued you. Why is my British brother ungrateful?" The second time, Pontiac slapped him. He shoved him down in front of a council of sachems and older braves. Glancing about, he motioned for a squat eerie figure, sprinkled with white powder, to come forth. "He is yours, Altoona," he said to the half-flint, half-pink-and-rose speckled albino savage. "He has an evil spirit!"

The misshapen-faced, skin-blemished Ottawa stepped forward, gord and wooden cup in hand. He stopped and looked down on William. "Get up!" he sneered. "White demon!" he muttered, as William struggled to his feet. "Tremble, I have great power. I am sorcerer!" He looked back at Pontiac, as if to reinforce his authority. "You," he stared with tobacco-blackened teeth at William. "Out! Out white demon! You are Ottawa! Get out, devil! Now!" The sorcerer took a gulp of milky slime from his wooden cup, stepped closer, and spat it in William's face. "Demons hate sour bear's milk! Now your demon will leave." He turned aside, with his right eye focused on William. Suddenly, he sprang back toward William and rattled his gord loudly in William's face. "Away!" he shouted. He raised his arms, forming a wide circle, hugged Sir William; then, without warning, shoved him to the ground. "Demon gone now!" he assured Pontiac. "If it returns, British devil must die."

Pontiac stared down at William. "You heard the sorcerer. Next time, death!"

William rolled to his right side as he rose to his feet. "I wish to live. *Je vous assure.*"

Pontiac shook his head with doubt, yet equally with approval. "It is settled, then! Come, teach me more English words! There is great fighting going on in the east. I must know what to do when the English come. They are too many now. The French are too few. Without us, their Fort would have fallen."

In the twilight east of the Blue Ridge, a rider paused on the Tree Notch Road and glanced up at the snow-covered ridges. With momentary hesitation, he turned his horse south toward Langdon's. The black man could not keep his cold hands from trembling, though shoved deep in gloves. His black cape, purple housecoat and purple scarf provided scant protection from the numbing wind. No one had told him it would be this cold! Ice had frozen on the insteps of his boots. Shiny crystals of hail collected on his blanket, secured behind his saddle. The horse's mane had already turned white. Clarence kicked the animal's flanks and raced on. The swirling freezing pellets anesthetized his chin, nose, and cheeks. Sleet rattled in the trees.

Sent by no one less than the Governor, his message was urgent! "Tell the Burkes to come quickly. She can't last much longer. Langdon's the only soul I trust, plus that lusty wench of a sister of his," the Governor had added with a lecherous lift on his toes. "Just get 'em here! If you have to, ride night and day!"

"Yes, suh! But are these directions right?"

"I can't promise. I've never been that far west of the Blue Ridge. But that's what folk aver. Just hurry! We don't need anymore embarrassment than what's already surfaced!"

"Yes, suh! I'll find them. But don't you want a more experienced rider? I ain't never been past Williamsburg!"

"No! This carries the highest propriety," he alleged with gravity. "Now get on!"

Yes, thought Clarence, lest they think you're the father! He could see the transparent worried look in the Governor's eyes.

When an hour had passed and still no cabin came into view, Clarence became frightened. Had he taken the wrong road? Was he even on a path? Let alone a road? He slowed the horse's gait and hunched forward over the saddle. Darkness filled the woods. The icy limbs in the treetops creaked as the horse clopped by. Another twenty minutes passed. Thirty! He was freezing. He peered into the icy gloom. Something was ahead! A split-rail fence emerged in the pale light. An inch or more of ice had created a slippery crust on its top rails. "Ahhh!" he uttered with relief. In the distance he saw a yellow glow and caught the smell of smoke. His horse neighed and shook its bit. It picked up its gait on its own accord. "Thank God!" Clarence muttered as the cabin came into view.

His knock brought an instant response. "Who goes there? Identify yourself!" It was Mrs. Burke's voice.

"Clarence! The Governor's manservant, ma'am! With a message. Please let me in. I am cold to the bone. And so's the horse!"

"Manservant?" she uttered as she opened the door. "What's happened? Come in! Jonathan, take Mr. Clarence's horse to the barn."

"Yes? What is it?" asked Sarah, as she came to Louise's side. "Here, let me take your coat. Goodness! How long have you been riding?"

"Five days, ma'am, and four nights. I wasn't to lose no time," he said with exhaustion.

"Sit down. Here you must be starving," she added. "Is the Governor with you?"

"No'm! He just sent me."

The children had gathered about the door and were peering out into the night. Jonathan pushed past them and stepped into the raw cold. "Get back in there," he ordered. "Lest a wolf gets you!" he smiled.

"Shut that thing!" called Louise. "Your father won't be back till midnight! Now get back to the fire." She turned uneasily toward the Governor's servant. "What's the message?" she wrung her hands. "Are the Indians raiding again?"

"No'm. Ain't half that simple."

Sarah placed a wooden bowl of venison and onion soup before him, along with a spoon. "What is it?"

"Miss Ashby! Her baby's comin' soon and Daphne's ill. Too sick to look after Lady Anna! She's got a bad fever of some kind. One of the field hands died last week of the same. Can you come and help her? Her baby's due, any day now!"

"O God! Is there any word of William? We haven't heard a thing!"

"No ma'am. We don't know nothin' either. Some general in New York sent a letter to the Governor. He swears he's heard that an Ottawa tribe has captured a white man during Braddock's retreat. Beyond that, he knows nothing mo'e."

Louise sighed. "We know about Anna. It's William who's got us worried. Hopefully, he's still alive."

"Ma'am, Miss Anna's in worse shape right now than Mr. Tillson. Daphne tol' the Governor she's been bleedin' this whole past month. An' weak. She's real weak."

Louise sat beside him and ran her fingers through her hair. She watched as Clarence spooned down the remaining morsels in his bowl. "We've got some cider you can have," she said.

"I'm fine. Just so sleepy, ma'am! Not even tolerable. I could collapse right here."

"I can't blame you." She glanced over her shoulder toward the hearth. "Just bed down by the fire. When Langdon gets home, we'll decide what to do."

"I'll go help her," said Sarah. "Wouldn't you, if that were Langdon's baby?"

Louise raised her head, somewhat startled. She opened her mouth but didn't say anything. "I guess so," she muttered. "Now let's settle down. Langdon will be home soon."

"May I ask where he is?" inquired Clarence. "I hav' to return in the mornin'."

"He and Blue Hatchet are hunting. They heard wolves last night, chasing deer. This morning, however, the deer tracks turned out to be bear. They're hoping to bag one."

Clarence relaxed. He finished his soup and curled up on his bedroll by the fireplace. He stretched out, rolled to his side, stared at the fire for a minute, and fell asleep.

"Imagine! Riding five days and four nights, and not certain where he was going!" exclaimed Louise.

"Imagine Anna! Alone! Frightened! Miss Ashby, pregnant all these months! And no William in sight!" She expelled a long slow worried sigh. "The truth, Louise. I love him. I pray every night he'll come home! To me! I wish I were Anna! Pregnant! Even if alone!"

"O Sarah! We have to hope for the best! I wish he loved you, too."

"O he loves me, Louise. That's all over his face! I arouse him every time he comes. It's just that Anna's closer. She knew how to catch his eye."

"Yes, but with her legs," Louise replied with a slight raise of her eyebrows. "Sarah, you'd best rest. Tomorrow will be here soon enough. I'll wait up for Langdon."

The fire burned low, the candle had sputtered out. Louise awoke with a startle, her mouth dry and lips chapped. She peered out the window. Slowly, dawn was rising in the icy darkness beyond the forest to the east. Clumps of frozen snow littered the bare yard. A thin wedge of cold clear sky struggled to peek through the woods. Sarah, the children, Jonathan and Clarence were still asleep. Langdon had not come home. Nor Blue Hatchet! The cow would have to be milked, chickens shooed out of the shed to peck on their own, and hay tossed to the horses. With Clarence's mount, the barn held four. Their own, the two St. Clair gave Langdon, and the Governor's servant's horse. She dropped the cloth curtain and tidied herself in the only mirror they had. She had slept the night in a chair by the table and her eyes appeared weary and dark. Her long brown hair hung tangled from neglect. Calluses lined the upper crescent of her palms. She wondered if Lady Ashby's hands were as soft as hers had once been. She peered out the window anew. Langdon should have returned by now. His hunt was meant only to track the bear. Perhaps the ice storm had forced them to cave up. Still, she was anxious that neither had come back. Both were on foot. They should have taken horses! "Darn!" she mumbled. "*Merde! Merde alors!*" She thought of Hélène and

François. Langdon had told her what Montour had warned. Was François still there, at Ft. Duquesne? And Hélène, too? Did they know about William? Where was Langdon?

As dawn broke through the icy mist in the gap, Langdon wriggled to free himself from under the bear's weight. Blue Hatchet had found a warmer spot in the cave, but Langdon had curled up beside the bear. Its black fur had kept him warm, but his nose stung from the cold, along with his ankles and feet.

"Up!" he said. "Get up!" he repeated, waking Blue Hatchet. "We need to get home."

Blue Hatchet stirred, slipped out from under a layer of cedar boughs, and stood erect. "The bear's meat stiff already," he nudged the ursine's huge mound of fur. "Perfect for butchering." He squatted beside its carcass and reached under its fur. Producing his knife, he sliced off a thin sliver of yellow fat, placed it in his mouth, and began chewing it.

Langdon did the same. "We need to move on," he said. "Let's make a travois and drag it. We can cut it up in the shed or side yard."

Blue Hatchet snipped off another piece. The two stepped out of the shallow enclosure and set about securing vines and limbs to construct a travois. They loaded the bear and took turns dragging it down the path to the valley floor. Neither said anything as they pulled, jogged, and crunched through the icy mix of slush and snow. Twice they stopped to seek shelter from bitter gusts of wind.

When they arrived home, Blue Hatchet pointed to the frozen hoofprints in the turned-up mud of the yard. They leaned the travois against the cabin, just as Louise came to the door.

"You're too late! What took so long?" she demanded. "I know, the storm!" she answered her own question. "*Bon Dieu*, you're here! You won't believe what's happened."

Langdon looked up where she stood in the door's entrance, the warm glow of the fire silhouetting her still comely figure. A puzzled expression filled his face. "What is it?"

"Come in! I'll explain." She noted the bear's carcass. "I hope it's a fat one!"

"Well! What is it?" repeated Langdon, as he and Blue Hatchet followed her into the house.

"Lady Ashby! Her baby's due, and Anna's sick, weak, if not failing! Dinwiddie sent Clarence to fetch us. Sarah and Jonathan rode back with him this morning. It doesn't sound good. If my intuition's half right, Lady Ashby might lose her baby, or still worse, her life. I have the strangest feeling that Sarah will be bringing Anna back here. That's selfish and petty. But I can't shake it off."

Langdon knocked the ice off his black, rabbit-lined boots and sat on the bench at the table. He didn't know what to say, let alone think. No, it wasn't petty or selfish to resent caring for another soul, but the Governor must have pondered a long time before enlisting their help. "Precious!" he addressed Louise. "Come and sit with me. Here," he placed his right arm about her shoulder. "If Anna needs us, it's the least we can do to care for her, or William's baby. We'll just add another room, if we have to. Come spring, we'll sell and move to the Holston. It's time we moved on, anyway."

Louise kissed him and tossed her long hair back across her shoulders. "If I had stayed in France, I'd be a duchess by now," she smiled. "Or a paramour of his Majesty's. Imagine?" She held her hands up and looked pleasantly at her fingers. She turned them with droll delight. "Maybe even playing the clavichord! Or cards with the King in bed! What do you think of that?"

Langdon glanced up at Blue Hatchet. A wide smile creased its way amusingly across the youth's face. "But of course, Chérie! Or paddling some fur-runner's canoe along *les grands lacs du nord.*"

"You know too much! Why don't you get your butt out of here and skin the bear! Or is that asking too much?"

"Yes, ma'am! You're right," he kissed her mouth and lips. "Come on, Blue Hatchet. *On-y va!*"

Chapter Thirty-One

"**M**iss Anna! Please, Miss Anna, wake up! I ain' so well myself," moaned Daphne. Patiently, she swabbed Anna's swollen face and splotchy brow with a cloth she had dipped in perfumed water. The delicate lavender scent of the cologne drifted through the cold room and lingered about the bed's clammy air. Lady Ashby's labored breathing added to the fearfulness felt by those who attended her. "Miss Anna, Honey! You gotta wake up! You gotta help us have this baby. We can't do it for you."

"Yes-um," hummed Aunt Sally, a big black mammie at the foot of the bed. Her breasts were large and brown, curved and visible above her white blouse and gray woolen sweater. "Honey, I's done this many times. Now come to and he'p us!"

Anna moved her hips ever so painfully. Her small frame bulged with the baby's large shape inside. She opened her eyes. Red tearmarks stained her cheeks. Strands of her blonde hair clung matted about her face. She clenched a leather belt in her teeth. Big Nell, the white overseer's wife, placed Anna's hands against the headboard for the second time. "You gotta push, Miss Ashby," the stout woman coaxed. "You're small, and the baby's big."

Anna felt for the board and pressed her arms back and tightened her pelvic muscles as hard as she could. She bit into the belt and pushed and pushed and pushed. Suddenly, her arms went limp, she sobbed, and fainted again.

"It ain't workin'," lamented the white woman. "Can you feel the baby's head?" she asked Aunt Sally.

"No'm! Not yet. She's gotta spread herself more. She ain't fit to bear children like I is."

Big Nell looked up at the wall clock. "Six-thirty! The poor thing's been in labor since eight. That's ten hours and a half."

A commotion outside the house interrupted their watch. Nell went to the window and looked out. The houseboy was holding a lantern. A cold wind caused it to swing in his hands. Its somnolent glow wavered as the wind tugged at the encased candle's wick. Save for the lantern's light, the opaque darkness swallowed the riders. "It's Clarence and that white woman the Governor sent to fetch. I reckon their kin?"

"No, ma'am!" replied Daphne, who had come to the window as well. "That's Miss Sarah and Mr. Burke's brother, Jonathan. He's cute in the light."

"How can you think of a thing like that when Miss Anna's sufferin'! You oughta be ashamed of yourself!" scolded Aunt Sally. "Git back here and help. 'Cute?' 'In the light?' You'd best be careful, girl! Look at what lustin' done to Miss Anna! And where's her lover now, poor man? Ain't nobody got the slightest idea. I wish that country parson wus here! He'd know what to do, but we're the ones who's got to do it."

Moments later, Sarah entered the room. She slipped her woolen cape off and handed it to the housegirl. She eyed the women and approached the bed. "Don't be offended," she said to the glaring group. "I've not done much of this myself, save for my sister-in-law. How's Anna doing?" she asked, as she removed her scarf and allowed her red hair to fluff out.

"Terrible!" Big Nell replied. "I ain't never seen a woman take it so hard. She's too tiny of frame. Poor thing! Look at her! Ain't neither of 'em gonna make it, if she don't have this child soon!" she patted Anna's stretched tight stomach. "Look at that! God help her!"

"Anna!" Sarah whispered as she pulled up a chair by the bed. "Anna!" She reached in her purse and slipped out a tiny silk pouch of cloves, scented with crushed mint, wintergreen, and cedar resin. Carefully, she placed it under Anna's nose and pressed the tiny bag with her fingers. The redolence of the mixture tingled

Anna's nostrils. She wrinkled her nose, sneezed, and looked up.

"Anna! It's Sarah! Langdon's sister! It's all right! I'm here to help," she mopped her forehead with the cloth Daphne had been using. "You've got to help! The baby's ready. I know it hurts. But William loves you. He'd be here if he could."

Anna reached up and caught Sarah's hand. "Sarah! William's talked about you. He loves you. I know." Hot tears glittered in her puffy eyes. Her face had taken on an ivory cast. "That's all right!" she whispered. "What does it matter now?" Her voice seemed small and far away. She stared up at the bed's lacy inside canopy. She had sewn it in herself. A glint of time past, of some memory of long ago, slipped slowly across her eyes. Her breathing grew faint, the color of her skin gray. With incremental effort she spread her legs, rose slightly in the bed, gripped Sarah's hands tightly, and screamed: "O God! O God! God!" Suddenly, she fell back, her body relaxed, and out popped her wiggling baby. A boy!

"Anna! Look!" said Aunt Sally as she held the baby for his mother to see.

"Miss Anna! Look, Miss Anna! It's your fine baby!" said Daphne. "Don't you wanna see your baby?"

Anna's eyes had turned glassy. Sarah could see her own reflection in their pale shimmer. She pressed Anna's hands in her own, bent forward, and struck Anna's chest with her head. "Anna! Anna! Dammit, Anna! Don't do this!" Tears trickled down Sarah's face to hang like pearls on her lips. "Anna. O Anna!" she wiped the tears away. "O Lady Ashby, please, please! Please, please!"

Anna was dead.

In the dense forest, northwest of Pontiac's camp, William stumbled across the frozen earth. To his relief, the icy rocks over which he clambered left no sign of footprints. They were too slick with ice and rain. Plus, in his months with the Indians, he had learned how to avoid leaving trace of one's passage. He stopped to catch his breath. His exhaled air formed a white mist about his cold mouth, while the air he gulped singed his lungs with each numbing gasp. He had fled just at dawn, in a freak blizzard that struck the camp while its residents slept. He had chosen the northern path in the hope that Pontiac would have expected him to feel south, or, at least, east. But where he should go? Or what lay ahead? William had not considered. He had acted on pure impulse, out of desperate longing to make his way back to Virginia, Williamsburg, and his cherished Anna.

He carried scant provisions, other than the knife attached to his belt and the small pouch of pemmican he had stuffed under his deerskin shirt. Fortunately, he had snatched a bearskin robe before exiting the warm wigman. Time had not afforded for more adequate preparation. Searching the treeline for telltale signs of pursuers, he rose and ran on through the frosty undercover and into a spruce woods.

It began to snow. Down drifted flake after flake, concealing the slightest instep or heel mark his moccasins left. The falling snow melted as it struck the surface of his warm cheeks. He gulped the downy morsels to quench his thirst. Faster and faster it fell. Slower and slower he ran. It was all he could do to make moderate progress as the snowfall deepened. Noon came and passed. Still the snow fell. Darkness descended across the woods. A small lake, slate-colored and frozen in the distance, came into view. With labored steps, he struggled toward its dim shoreline. With any luck, he'd find shelter there, perhaps fish, fresh water, and a place to hide for the night.

With fumbling motion, he staggered into a copse of birch trees, themselves protected from the storm's wind by a wall of tall white pines. Quickly, he gathered fallen boughs, a mat of thick needles, and built a tight lean-to on the edge of the pines. Here he could see across the lake, around the edge by which he had come, and through the birch trees. All about the silent woodlands lay in a field of lazy white. William crawled into the shelter, rubbed his feet and body with his cold hands, and gulped more scoops of mushy snow. With hard-earned self-discipline, he allowed himself but a palmful of pemmican. The greasy compot of venison, corn, and bear fat provided but a meager repast as dusk arrived and the snowfall began to abate. At sunset, a pale line of cold blue sky appeared briefly in the west. Suddenly, a single ray of sunlight burst deep red across the horizon; then the winter disc set. Twilight descended, snow flakes dwindled, and finally ceased. December's long night crept through the trees. The night deepened and the vast northern sky filled with stars. A wolf howled, another, and a third. William gripped his knife and curled tighter into a fetal ball.

Anna! Anna! He wondered. If only he could be with Anna! Surely her child — his child — Yes, their child — had been born by now. Was it a boy or a girl? Stillborn or alive? Healthy or frail? O Anna! The wolf howls decreased, grew distant, and diminished. Cold, but alive and conscious, exhausted but uninjured and strong, William hugged his sides under the heavy bear cloak and fell asleep.

At sunrise, he was awakened by a sharp sound in the crunchy snow. He jumped up, with his knife in hand. It was Pontiac!

"My brother," the tall Ottawa smiled. "It is not good to hunt without a gun! Here," he stated without an eye-blink. "I Pontiac give you this musket. Come now, let us hunt together. The snow has brought new herds of deer to our lodges. You were wise to shelter here," he waved his hand toward the lake. "We can fish before we go. Isn't that so?"

"Yes. My father!"

"The English are coming closer. Soon, I will exchange you for traps and guns. I know that it is your wish. Just now I need you. Come! In these silent woods the spirits hold our fate. We must not tempt them or look away."

William adjusted the robe about his shoulders, looked deeply into Pontiac's eyes, and realized how fortunate he was! If only Anna were beside him!

Chapter Thirty-Two

RANÇOIS FOUGHT his plummeting dejection as best he could. He sat with Villiers in the old office of Fort Duquesne's moldering walls, pondering the forts's fate with as much sadness as its once-renounded commandant equally displayed. The alternatives before them appeared glum. It was September 1758. A new British force lay encamped just hours away. Only a week earlier, he and Villiers had stopped their advance party at Ligionier. But now they were poised in the Pennsylvania woods to strike again. "Ah, bon!" sighed François, as he glanced about the room at the four others who joined them: Joncaire, a newly arrived Lieutenant de Chambord, and two Canadian officers of the *troupes de terre*. "How close are they? Did you actually say 'five miles'?" asked the Lieutenant.

"Yes," one of the Canadians answered.

"Patience!" the balding Villiers advised. "They haven't arrived yet," he observed as he stared out into the cold night. "My brother and I vowed, with all our heart, to avenge Joseph's death. We are still unappeased! Nonetheless," he sighed with a grim smile, "we dealt them a punishing blow at Ligionier. Indeed! Coup de Sang's party butchered a hundred or more. *C'était incrédible*! It's just that they have so many to sacrifice and we don't."

"Unfortunately!" Joncaire mumbled. "There's no way we can stop them. To think, we once defeated their whole army! In less than a day!"

"I wish I had been here," de Chambord boasted politely. He wrapped his long thin fingers about his clay pipe and puffed on its stem thoughtfully. "But all's not lost! Montcalm's forces still hold Carillon. Morale is high! The British suffered terrible losses. I watched it with my very eyes. Hundreds of Highlanders were killed in front of the abatises! The Indians cut off their heads and impaled them on spikes, then wrapped their kilts about the poles. Grizzly! *Bon Dieu*! It was grizzly, but thank God, a victory!"

"*Mais oui!*" Joncaire riled with anger. "But have you heard what happened at Frontenac? The British destroyed it just three months ago!"

"Yes, I heard! I came by way of Oswego and down the headwaters of the Allegheny. Surely we can rebuild it once hostilities cease."

"Ah, *mon vieux*! The war has turned against us. In just three years, we've lost all that was once ours! It took years to construct Frontenac. Now it's gone." He shook his head with disbelief at the young officer.

"Enough!" snapped Villiers. "I can't speak for Ticonderoga. We've got our own Frontenac to deal with here!"

François sat forward and placed his face in his hands. Outside, the night wind blew, cold with the smell of snow. "Like it or not, the British will hit us tomorrow—all five thousand of them, if not tonight!" François stated. "*Messieurs, quelle solution présentiez-vous?* Time is on the wing, as the bards say. Everywhere we are in chains, as Rousseau puts it."

"I have but one suggestion," Villiers proffered, "whether poets or Rousseau might care or not!" He stared intensely about the small chamber, fixing his eyes on each man in turn. "Blow up the fort! Set powder kegs in the bastions, in the inner quarters, and beside the walls. Cross ourselves," he gestured with mock piety, "light the fuses, and run. And to think! I was here when we built it! De Robert, you too! *C'est une extrême chose à faire. Grossier!*" he stated with despair.

The six looked at each other, avoiding one another's eyes. In the distance, they could hear the Highlanders' pipes and steely rap of the British Grenadiers' drums.

"Listen! They're racing to beat the clock! Damn them!" Villiers cursed.

Each man rose, hesitated, and departed with reluctance to his station.

"*C'est un grave moment!*" Joncaire shouted to Handsome Dog. He waved to Yellow Hawk as well. "Set powder kegs about the fort. We must blow it before the enemy arrives!"

Coup de Sang brushed several liegemen aside as he ran with Joncaire toward the powder magazine. Yellow Hawk watched but followed François instead.

François hurried toward his own quarters. So few momentos remained. Thank *le bon Père Tous-Puissant* that Hélène and their baby had withdrawn to Ft. Le Boeuf. At least they were safe. But, for how long? He could not comprehend the renewed British assaults! Why weren't they content to occupy the colonies? The mountains still belonged to them. And why did their new foreign minister insist on blocking France wherever its troops unfurled the *fleur de lis*? From the Caribbean to India, it was total war! He glanced about! Everywhere the few remaining soldiers were breaking open powder barrels and stacking them against the palisades. On the bastions, de Chambord and a handful of Marines were desperately spiking the cannon. "Yellow Hawk!" François called. "Here," he tossed the Indian a backpack of powder, lead balls, and flints.

Villiers called across the compound to de Chambord. "Hurry now! That's enough! Get down." He turned toward Joncaire. "Wait till we're all out. Then light the barrels and run for the bateaux!" He signaled for Philippe and the Algonquin to follow him. De Robert acknowledged with a wave of his hand and ran toward the gate. Sleet was beginning to fall. Just as he and Yellow Hawk reached the canoes, the blasts commenced. Tumultuous explosions filled the night with crackling flames. Stinging showers of burning bark hurtled across the darkness to plunge hissing into the water. Billowing columns of pungent smoke disappeared into the numbing rain. A fiery glow illumined the dying fort. One by one, explosions spun sparkling debris of red and yellow into the night. The two fumbled with their canoe, took turns boarding with their guns and supplies, and pushed off into the river. Swiftly, the current bore them into the dark Ohio. It spun the canoe about. They struggled to gain control. With tremendous effort, they paddled toward the Allegheny, heads down into the stinging sleet. Momentarily, François paused, lifted his paddle out of the water, and looked back. Both wonder and horror confronted his eyes, as he stared at the numerous fires. He realized they had failed to spike all the cannon, or destroy the swivel guns, but of what value were they now? Slowly, he dipped his paddle into the river again and set his face with Yellow Hawk for Ft. Le Boeuf.

South of the Big Lick, Langdon, Louise, their children, Sarah, Anna's child, and Jonathan, reined the wagons to a halt and stared out across the north bank of the New River. It's rolling current scintillated blue and white, as the ford's rocks kicked up droplets of water in the afternoon sunlight. The soft rouge, reds, browns, and chestnut colors of mid-October stippled the forest's trees the entire length of the river. Behind Jonathan's cart bellowed the tethered cow. Chickens clucked in their homemade cages, where Sarah had tied them to the lead wagon's stays.

Langdon had sent Blue Hatchet ahead to scout for Indians, if any were about. As he stared down, Langdon could see Blue Hatchet's mount's hoofprints in the gravelly pebbles along the river. They had filled with water and turned dry around the edges. Higher back on the bank, his hoofprints had already hardened where the sun had dried them red. Blue Hatchet was to have met them here, but the twenty-year old Delaware was nowhere in sight.

"Could he be injured?" asked Sarah.

"Or lost?" stated Louise. Behind her seat, the children peered over her shoulder: Marie Louise eight and her five-year-old brother. "Mama's he's kicking me," Marie whined. "No I'm not," Robert protested. "I'm tired and wanna get out."

Anna's little boy—blond and three-years old—held to Sarah's neck. She let the reins of her wagon fall limp in her hands and reached back to hug the child.

"Daddy, where's Blue Hatchet? I wanted to ride with him. You promised I could," Robert whined.

"Thank God you didn't. Maybe tomorrow," Langdon replied. "I'm worried, son! Blue Hatchet should have been here by now." He glanced at Louise and the children. "We'd best not cross. It's not too early to camp. The sun'll be setting soon," he nodded toward the pink clouds in the dusty sky to the west. He tugged on the horse's harness to turn the wagon about. Slowly it creaked and jarred as he urged the animal upbank and into a grove of willows.

Sarah slapped her horse's reins and followed. Jonathan guided the two-wheel covered cart—cow and tether, banging milk pails and spring house crocks—behind her wagon and hopped off to help the children.

The warm air gave way to a chilly night, and fearful of Cherokee warriors or Shawnee on the prowl, Langdon kept what small fire they built concealed from the river. Night brought out all the sounds his woodsman nature loved, but he knew how terrifying they were to the children. "Shhh!" he comforted each as one by one they fell asleep in the wagon. Sarah kissed little William Ashby, as she had named him, before placing a quilt about his shoulders and feet. Louise covered her own with a blanket and joined Langdon and Jonathan by the fire.

"What do you think?" Sarah asked, as she nestled beside Louise.

"Who knows?" replied Langdon. "The wilderness keeps no schedule. Listen! Already the forest is settling down."

The four sat silently together. The tiny crackling fire illumined their hardy faces, their hands and white tanned throats.

"Soon the owls will hoot!" Langdon offered. "Then the wolves will raise their ancient cry. And the deer will bunch together, run, and scatter quietly."

"The wolves I can take," reminisced Louise. "They sang us to sleep in the northern woods night after night. It's the cougar and the panther I fear. Even Handsome Dog and Yellow Hawk were afraid of them, as if they possessed evil spirits."

"And Indians!" added Jonathan. "The Great Road is still theirs. I wonder if they realize what 'land grants' mean?"

"I've wondered the same for Blue Hatchet," said Louise. "What home does he have, other than ours? Where can he go? Do his people even exist any more?"

"Shhh! Someone's coming!" Langdon whispered as he sprinkled the fire with dust. "Hopefully, they haven't smelled our smoke."

The four hugged the weeds beside the wagons and searched for movement along the shadows across the river.

"There!" whisered Langdon. "To the left!"

A small canoe was making its way down the river. The starlight on the water trembled in a thousand tumbling ripples. Two Indians paddled ever so quietly. If they sensed the Burkes' whereabouts, they never disclosed it, but continued paddling in the dark. Moments later they passed out of sight.

"Jonathan, take the first watch. I'll take the second," Langdon said. "Louise, Sarah, watch the children and try to sleep."

"Wait!" Jonathan exclaimed, his voice barely above a whisper. "Across the river! Above the ford! By the sycamores! In the shadows! See? A man! He's standing by a horse."

"It's Blue Hatchet!" Langdon stood and waved to the youth. He motioned for him to cross. "Don't shout!" he advised the women. "We might not be alone yet."

The four watched as Blue Hatchet mounted and rode slowly into the stream. Water danced about his horse's forelegs as the rider and animal made the crossing. The horse quickened its gait as it struggled up the bank. "You are safe!" Blue Hatchet smiled. "They're gone," he added, as he dismounted. "The two you saw are the last of the people. I stumbled across them yesterday. They were breaking camp by the river."

"Who are they?"

"Small tribe from the mountains of North Carolina. Too many whites taking land. No good hunting, they said. Too many clashes; too many deaths. Their children die of disease. They hope to follow the river to the west," he pointed, "and into Kint-tucy-y. They are few and leave their fathers' graves with sorrow. They want to see no more woodsmen or trappers. They don't understand the ways of the white man. They will not survive, will they?"

"Blue Hatchet! We are no better off ourselves!" said Sarah, as she hugged his chest.

Langdon stared at the boy and turned his eyes away. He did not want the Delaware to see the hard truth in his own face.

Chapter Thirty-Three

FRANÇOIS MOUNTED THE STEPS to the old walled citadel of Ft. Niagara, pleased to be back in the city Hélène so loved. Summoned by the deputy *intendent*, Sieur Albert Soisson de Marson — second only to the new governor — François could not imagine the meeting's purpose or any post to which he might be assigned. He entered the Castle's interior and climbed the spiral staircase to the intendant's office. Awaiting him at the top of the steps stood a tall, lacy-cuffed, grim-faced Frenchman. "*Je suis Sieur de Marson,*" he introduced himself. He extended Philippe his right hand. "*Bonjour, mon bonhomme!*" he managed to grunt. "*Mais, mauvaise nouvelles! C'est dommage! Néanmonis, merci,* for journeying so far! This way!" he bowed slightly toward his richly furnished salon. "We are down to mere necessities," he waved his hands in feigned disgust. "The British have forced Montcalm from New York. All across the Lakes, they have gained footholds. But, *alors*! That is not why we're here. Please sit down," he motioned, as he seated himself between two windows that looked out upon the bay.

"You are needed in Quebec. Yes, Quebec! We are gathering our bravest forces there. But first, another task! A waste of time, I wager. But my *pensées* mean nothing to de Rigaud. Have you met him? He's Canadian, you know, through and through. No?"

"No, I haven't. But the news did reach us at Ft. Le Boeuf. What's happened to Du Quesne?"

"Recalled! Assigned to the navy. Who knows what they do in Paris?

But, your reason for being here," he glanced down at a shuffle of loose papers. "Ah! Yes! A letter from the Colonies, addressed to Marquis de Rigaud. You know," he paused, "they don't seem as ill-disposed now that Fort Duquesne is theirs. 'Fort Pitt!' Imagine? Named for a commoner at that! Still," he expelled a nervous breath, "your assignment. This letter was sent to the Governor of New York, who sent it by courier to Montcalm, who delivered it to de Rigaud. Yes," he peered over the top of the single sheet of paper toward François. "Quote: '*Most Excellent Marquis de Vaudreuil-Cavagnal! As Lieutenant Governor of Virginia, I, Francis Faquier, request the following exchange of prisoners. In our charge at Alexandria, we incarcerate ten of your former liegemen, captured at Jumonville. We wish to exchange them for a British major, whom we believe the Ottawa chief Pontiac holds somewhere near Lake Huron. Your ten for our one appeals to us as a just offering to bring this chapter of our colony's enmity with Canada to a close. Your ten shall await you at Fort Pitt upon a positive response to this request. The officer's name: Sir William Graham Tillson, a major in his Majesty's service and former liaison of Governor Dinwiddie's expedition to the Ohio. Composed this 12th day of February, 1759.'*" He let the letter slip from his fingers to settle atop a pile of other correspondence. "Can you find him? Pontiac has moved his camp, we are told. No one knows where he is. Can you do this thing by spring? Then, it's off to Quebec!"

"Sir, I know this man, this officer. I was present at Duquesne when he was brought in. I should have insisted on his release then, but we were engorged with Braddock's defeat. We were in mourning over Beaujeu's death. I was bitter. It was a time of great elation, as well as savagery. Our native allies were not to be denied their sport."

"Yes. I have witnessed those things too."

"I should have searched for him years ago. This will not be easy. My guide and I will do our best. But, by spring? That, I can't foretell. My wife is recovering from a second miscarriage. I hate to leave her at Le Boeuf."

"You can bring her here, but," he looked out across the lake to the east, "the British would love to capture this place. Forgive me, sir, but I'd encourage you to leave her at Le Boeuf. Or better still, take her to Fort Presque Isle. That's where you'll depart. Incidentally, this dispatch," he handed him a sealed cloth document, "commissions you to acquire

293

whatever 'gifts' you'll need to persuade the captors. Take it! Good luck!"

François attempted to smile. He stood awkwardly, almost unsteadily, and balanced himself against the deputy's desk. Whatever words he might have replied he suppressed. Better for de Marson not to know what he really thought, or how he truly felt.

Within three weeks, he and Yellow Hawk were ready to leave. As they stood in the snow outside the gates of Presque Isle, François clasped Hélène's hands in his own and raised them to his lips to kiss. She had entwined red threads into her black braids, along with a tassel of tiny silver beads in each. He looked into her black eyes, as they drew him into her soul, where in truth he wanted to be. He kissed her with his cold lips and nudged her nose against his chin. "I'll be back as soon as I can," he promised.

Little Noël shivered beside her. She reached up and tugged on her father's coat. François bent down, picked her up, and kissed her lips. "I'll be back, *ma petite!* And with a tall soldier, too."

He set her down, turned, and with lumbering strides set off with Yellow Hawk on snowshoes. Each dragged a narrow wicker sled, tied about the waist. The fur wrapped bundles on each sled carried blankets, guns, tobacco, and other supplies. They picked up their pace, then bent into a low pull, as they angled toward the distant open water on the edges of the frozen lake. There, a single-mast vessel sloshed in the icy waters to bear them toward Michigan.

In two days, as fog blanketed the coast, the vessel arrived at an icy inlet on Lake Erie's western shore. Forest shadows slipped by in the fog. Snowflakes whispered in the wind. Evening darkened the sky. The ship's captain's looked shoreward. A worried frown formed under his bearded lips. "Eh! You are here! We must leave before this ice," he pointed, "encases the ship. *N'est-ce pas?*"

"*Oui!*" François replied. "We understand."

The two disembarked and were rowed to shore by a stocky mate. They watched as he returned; then they waved to the ship's captain and trudged off into the snowfall. An Indian village lay just to their northwest. After crossing a narrow stream, they jogged with their sleds jerking behind them toward the central lodge. High atop the council house, the *fleur de lis* whipped in the frigid wind. A wooden cross, affixed to an abandoned chapel, indicated where once a Catholic priest had ministered the sacraments. Broken windowpanes witnessed to the harsh environment the priest no doubt endured. François wondered where the cleric was or how he died. So many died, especially the novices, sent fresh from the coastal towns of France. Their supply had never diminished until the blockade of last year. Thank God he had not followed his uncle's path!

As dogs barked, an old man and several squaws filed into the open and watched them approach. Yellow Hawk was in the lead. He stopped and greeted the old man in Algonquin. François joined in the salutation himself. "*Kwe-Kwe!*" both hailed the bundled figure. Then Yellow Hawk rested and waited for the old man to speak.

"*Bienvenu!* Frenchman!" the gray, stringy haired Huron replied. "What brings our young father to Kaagaagiw's camp? I, Black Raven, welcome you. Winter is bitter, too cold to hunt. The Ottawa have turned their faces from us. We are hungry, dying. Our newborns freeze in their mothers' laps. What have your wars brought us? Nothing but death and sorrow! Pontiac's braves alone fare well. His league with the Potawatomie, Ojibwa and Ottawa block us from moving westward. Your boatmen and trappers want only our best pelts. The guns in exchange are old and broken. The blankets reek of disease. It was not so in my great-great-grandfather's time. At Montreal he met Champlain." He stared about and eyed the sleds with envy. "Come inside. It is too cold to waste words here. Too *kisina*! Perhaps your great Father has gifts for his children." He motioned with his hand for the two to enter and waited while they removed their snowshoes and set them against the lodge.

The air inside the lodge stung François' fingertips. It was scarcely warmer than outside. A low smoky fire emitted only a faint light and minimal heat. Its coals glowed yellowish-orange in the semi-darkness of the room. Eight natives sat about; a roomful of others peered down at them from their raised sleeping frames. Two little boys cowered naked against their mother; a girl in deerskin sat behind an elderly woman closest to the fire.

"*Bonjour!*" François removed his fur cap and gloves. His heart sank as he observed their miserable condition. "*Ça va bien, j'espère!* You are kind to share your lodge with us," he motioned with his left hand to include Yellow Hawk. "We journey west." He hesitated and glanced toward Yellow Hawk a second time. They had left their sleds outside. "A few gifts," he whispered to him. He nodded for the big Algonquin to bring something in. "We have gifts for you. Food! Tobacco." He addressed himself to the chief. "May we sit and smoke. We have far to go. We are searching for a," he combed his mind for the right words, "*un très important homme*! A very good man," he sought to assure the chief. "Strong, wise! An *anglais*! Taken prisoner after the fall of Fort Duquesne."

"We have heard of this man," the chief nodded. "Sit. Let us visit. Let us smoke. We are thirsty! We can tell you what we know."

François squatted on the cold earth beside the chief and warmed his hands briefly. He didn't wish to appear cold, weak, or obsequious.

A pipe was handed to the chief. He lit it with a stick, placed against a coal. The red ember glowed brightly as the old sachem sucked loudly on the stem. A white puff of smoke drifted from his mouth. With solemn gestures, he handed the pipe to Philippe. Yellow Hawk re-entered and sat beside him. François puffed on the pipe and extended it to his guide. Yellow Hawk engaged in the ritual and returned it to the chief

"Kaagaagiw!" François greeted the chief. "Can you tell us about this man, this *anglais*? We have been sent to find him and escort him to the Ohio. His people long to see him again. He is like a son to many. His Father in England prizes him above others."

The old chief took a second puff and watched the white smoke dissipate in the lodge's cold air. "We have lost valued sons, too." He looked somberly into François' eyes. "What have we heard?" he repeated the question. "Much and nothing! That he teaches Pontiac his tongue. That Pontiac protects him from his tribe's leaders. This *anglais* is like his son, his brother. Once, they came this way. The evening sky burned my eyes with orange glare. I could not look into his face. He stood with back to sun. Tall! Quiet! They stopped for cornmeal. Shared moose with us from a fresh kill. The English repaired my gun while Pontiac spoke. Then! Phashoooush!" he whistled, as he slapped his hands together. "They were gone. No one knows where Pontiac lodges. He moves from wigwam to wigwam, camp to camp among his league of *killers*!" he suddenly emphasized. "No one dares to talk back. His way is like the storm. He comes in the wind with thunder and lightning. *Animikika! Wawasakonese!* We listen and obey!"

François sat forward, grateful, yet perplexed and silenced by disquietude. The old chief had confirmed what he most feared: that finding Pontiac, let alone Tillson, would take days, if not weeks or months, if ever at all. His shoulders drooped; his countenance sagged. Yellow Hawk nudged him. It was time to share their rum and go to bed.

Early the next morning, they departed. The last day of February passed. The icy rains of March commenced. Day by day, François consulted his compass. A week of freezing weather forced them to abandon their march. Two days and nights of a howling blizzard, mixed with skin-stinging sleet, tested their fortitude. "No good!" exclaimed the big Algonquin. "Look!" he pointed to two sets of tracks near their feet. Deep in snow, crystals of ice had all but filled them in. "We have fooled ourselves!" he grunted with dissatisfaction. "We have walked in a wide circle. In spite of your magic box," he frowned toward François. "Best to camp! No good to search now."

When finally the storm began to abate, Yellow Hawk raised his hand in a sign of caution. Something was moving in the forest. Voices broke the silence as Indian silhouettes appeared in the sifting flakes. Three figures lumbered into view, hunched forward with heavy packs of fur on their backs. Seeing the Frenchman and Algonquin before them, they stopped and stared, too startled to react.

Yellow Hawk pointed his gun, but kept silent.

"*Nous sommes ici en paix!*" François quickly stated. "We seek *Pontiac!*" he emphasized the chief's name with authority. "Can you take us to his lodge? We carry an important message."

"We are Ojibwey! Not Ottawa," the largest of the three replied. A cape of wolfpelts enwrapped his chest and upper body. A white homespun trader's shirt overlapped a pair of deerskin trousers. A mantle of deep, soft, rouge fox fur adorned his braided hair. Knee-high leather stockings and fur-lined moccasins completed his attire. "Pontiac's camp is to the north! We go there ourselves. Come, white man. Give us tobacco. We have buffalo in our packs. What are you against us? We are three; you are two."

Chapter Thirty-Three

"We come as friends! We will share."

"Tell the Algonquin," the Ojibwa pointed at Yellow Hawk, "to lower gun. Then we share and go. Manitou's spirits guard the forest, but night is coming. We do not wish for wolves to steal our meat." He approached and shook François's hand in European fashion, clasping it in a tight grip. "That is how we greet the *anglais* who travels with him. Strange man! We can be there by dark. Come!"

Yellow Hawk lowered his gun and nodded for François to accept the offer. "Tobacco in pouch," he said to the Ojibwey spokesmen. "I am Yellow Hawk. How are you called?"

"Long Scar!" the Indian replied. He turned in the dim light for the two to gawk at the raised scar behind his left ear. "Before scar, I was called Loping Moose. Your *anglais* do this! Pontiac judged the quarrel."

"Over what?" asked François.

"Squaw! Squaw want *anglais* for self. Squaw my first wife. Once young and beautiful, now fat. He say 'No.' He refuse to sleep with her. I challenged him to settle the insult. She is good woman. Have three children by her. Now she is too old to bear. *Anglais* much faster than I thought. He fought like Indian warrior. Good and bad flow from him like swollen stream in sudden storm or gentle meadow in sunny flower. You will see. I think a demon comes to him, inspite of Pontiac. All fear him but respect Pontiac. We wish him to go."

"I'm sorry to hear about this Englishman," François said. "Our message is for him and Pontiac. We will guard your words carefully." By now, François had unfastened his pouch and handed each man a knot of tobacco.

Each ran his piece under his nose, inhaled the aroma, and tore off small bites. The knots were deep black, sticky, and redolent of far away climes and warm nights. They nodded approval and, turning northeast, motioned for the two to follow.

François glanced up and adjusted the sled tied to his waist. Pale blue sky appeared through the last tiny flakes of sifting snow. A hard wind soughed in the trees, causing cascades of wet snow to pelt his coat. The Indians moved quickly, almost at a trot.

As dusk smothered out the pink line of sunlight in the dark forest, de Robert noticed warning posts as they approached the encampment. Pieces of scalp and dried flesh hung frozen from chest-high stakes. Feathers decorated low-lying limbs, bird signs and masks of painted faces. No doubt to keep the forest's spirits away. One by one, lodges and wigwams appeared in the distance. Smoke hovered over the fire pits and drying racks. A few horses neighed in a rope enclosure. A young boy looked up and scurried ahead to announce their coming. Within moments, the council grounds filled with curious Indians and silent children. A drum sounded, loud, at first, then its pitch grew higher and its cadence intense. Other drums picked up the beat. In front of the council house stood a large Indian, Pontiac. He stared at the five as they drew closer. A smile spread across his lips. François realized that Pontiac recognized him. The big Indian raised his hand in greeting. He motioned to a figure behind him. It was William. Sir William! He was naked of chest, clothed in loincloth and a long moose robe, leather leggings and wolfskin boots. William stepped out and stood beside the Ottawa. His hair was knotted in Indian style, his face painted red under his eyes. A long trapper's knife dangled in its sheath on his side. He stood in silence, as if he were as much the chief as Pontiac, but his eyes stared past the approaching party, and his face harbored a broken solemnity. Suddenly, he recognized François but suppressed his emotions. François could see a swelling in his throat.

"*Ça va*, great chief?" François hailed Pontiac. "We meet again. How our pasts have changed!"

"Yes, Frenchman! Word has reached us of Duquesne's fall. I fear the British are too near. Come in. We have much to say to each other," he eyed the sleds with envious interest. "Guns, I hope. Powder and lead! The way to Michilimackinac is closed. Frozen lake far too long." He turned toward William. "You know this man, *oui*? I call him *Aagimag*, for he has yet to learn to run in snowshoes."

François reached for William's hand.

William clutched it with powerful strength. His eyes searched François', but he said nothing. Respect for Pontiac was evident in his face.

Pontiac stared at the Frenchman with dissatisfaction. "I know why you are here. A trapper from Raven's camp told us. We beat him and sent him back. He trapped furs without our permission. Let us talk."

Inside the large long house, a row of old men and young warriors arranged themselves opposite François and Yellow Hawk. Seated behind the chief was the sorcerer. François recognized him as such, as he had seen many like him. Slowly, François rose and presented Pontiac with a broad lambent loop of white shells. "From Nova Scotia!" he bowed politely. "Please accept our gift and hear my words. Sir William's father in Virginia has asked our governor in Quebec for the *anglais'* return. We have brought you gifts across the snow to prove our words true. Our new governor, the Marquis de Rigaud, prizes your allegiance and support in war. New France could not survive without you and chief Michilimackinac. The British have bottled up our outlet to the sea. We wish to make peace with the English at Fort Pitt, where soldiers of our own are held in hostage. The Governor of Virginia — this *anglais'* father — wants him back. He will exchange our ten for this one man. We await your answer and words of truth."

Pontiac sat in silence for a long while. Many braves glanced toward each other, a few toward William, a few toward Pontiac. The misshapened face of the sorcerer twitched about his eyes and mouth. Without revealing his thoughts, he stared hard at François and Yellow Hawk. Pontiac rose from his squatting position with silent solemnity. He motioned for the sorcerer to come forth. "This house smells of rot and deceit. Why have you brought these men to our camp?"

The sorcerer stood awkwardly and rattled the gord in his right hand with sporadic motion. His jaw hung open from the unexpected rebuke. He rattled the hardened seeds in the red painted gord and swept it across William's head. He bent over his shoulder and shook it in his face. He repeated the ritual over François and Yellow Hawk's heads. With anger he looked toward Pontiac yet smiled with an ingratiating smirk. "We will never be safe until white devil is gone." He sneered at William and rolled the gord across his nose and eyes. "It is his demon that stinks. It is best to burn devil for Frenchman to see." He looked up at Pontiac, unable to repress his disgust. "My mouth has spoken. My magic is true."

Pontiac waited until the sorcerer had reseated himself. Without expressing appreciation for his sorcerer's ritual or words, he looked down at François. "It is easy for Frenchmen to play at war. They use us to stalk and take scalps. In turn, they parade in blue coats and white hose. I have long favored you French. You have brought us weapons and tools to improve our lives. You do not take our lands or even our pelts, but trade for furs and passage to the great waterways west. From the time of your black robes and *coureurs de bois*, we have welcomed you in our lodges and given you wives. But the wind blows strange, different now. The Iroquois hunt us down east of the Great Lake to the Lawrence. They carry English guns and sell our lands to secure their own. They are a warning for what is to come. The English here," he paused and looked down on William, "has taught me much about his people. They are not afraid of us. They raid the Ohio like we used to. They expel all before them. My heart is with you, Frenchman. My mind fears otherwise. I do not wish to exchange my *anglais* brother just yet. I must think about it more. If others wish to speak, no one binds their tongue. I, Pontiac, have spoken." He looked sadly toward William. "It has been a good brotherhood." He turned about and sat down.

A young brave stood and held up his knife. "I too fight for French fathers. I wish to exchange the *anglais* for new gun and powder. I have no tobacco, and I thirst for rum. It is a good offer you bring us. Our chief is wrong." With an awkward turn, he sat down.

No one stood for a while. The sorcerer rose and shook his gord. "Where is the white devil hiding? Has the great demon not accepted defeat? It is time for white devil to go."

Pontiac jumped up, seized the sorcerer's hand and struck him with his gord. "There is no demon in this camp but you! The *anglais* has been good. My brother," he looked down at William, "Aagimag, rise, you are free to speak. I know your heart. I wish to hear your words. *Speak!*" he commanded in English.

William passed his hands over a wisp of smoke that drifted in the lodge. He passed them over his face in turn, and brought them down behind his ears. He did not want to stand; he did not want to speak. He did not want to hurt this great warrior who had both tormented and now defended him. For three years he had suffered. Now he enjoyed his trust. As for Anna, perhaps she had already forgotten him, miscarried their baby, or married another? Who was this new governor anyway? And to what British regiment would he be assigned? Why should he return? Yet, what future awaited him here? Only a few wanted him. Only Pontiac prized him. The sorcerer would love to have him burned.

"*Anglais*. We await your words!" Pontiac summoned him. With his left arm, he pulled William to his feet. "Speak! It is time for my brother to speak! I, Pontiac, fear no words. Nor any shaman's gords!"

William stood on his own feet. He looked thoughtfully about the room, at its coppery, almond-cast figures, the bent and the strong, the frail and robust, the old fathers and the young. That he had survived their world was a miracle. That he had risen to become Pontiac's "son" humbled him. His heart felt obligated to stay. His mind floundered in a wash of vacillation and memories long past. Did he owe it to Anna to return? To ask the question shocked him! Or did he owe it to Pontiac to stay? Did he owe it to the ten to expend his life for theirs? Or did he owe it to the Ottawa and the Ojibwa to remain? They knew he was helpful and had much to offer. Neither choice appeared fair, or just. Neither appealed to his mind. Only one tugged at his heart, at his soul. Anna! He needed time to ponder the choice, but when he glanced toward the sorcerer his mind knew what he had to do. He would have to go. Pontiac would rise above it. Had he not served his captor well?

William cleared his throat. "Fathers and brothers, Pontiac and reverend chiefs, my heart is torn and my words come heavy. For three years you have mended and defended me. I came as one frightened and angry. You disciplined me, taught me your ways, and made me strong. Only my heart has remained unhealed and my memory captive to sorrows. Should I go back with these men or remain with you? Pontiac has made known his wish. Others I know differ. I have fared well with you. How can I leave your lodges and the fires of your homes? This long war between the great Fathers goes on. How can I ever forget you? Pontiac, my father, hear the words of my heart and know they are true. Never has there been one like you. Never have braver warriors fought and hunted like my brothers here. Like the thunderbird, my life has been driven by the wind, like a leaf it has settled wherever. In the east it blew me to you. Now the wind blows again. I know I must go. The guns and powder, tobacco and knives will remind you of our days together. I shall not forget them. Nor you. I William, son of Pontiac, have spoken. These have been good years. Many seasons and suns, snows and falling leaves! With your permission, I shall go back with the Frenchman when morning comes."

"Good!" said Pontiac. "Our French fathers have acted wisely to make peace along the Ohio. I, Pontiac, shall help them conduct war here. You, *anglais*, have strengthened my resolve to engage in their cause. I fear the English. I fear their power. The French have been our best fathers. In days to come, my heart will be sad, when I remember my English son. It is so!"

Suddenly, the sorcerer rose to his feet. With violent motions he shook his gord. "Pontiac speaks like woman. Smell of devil remains. Fire alone cleanses. Let him depart through flames. His!" he pointed to Yellow Hawk. "Algonquin will make good sacrifice as *anglais* leaves."

Many grunts and clacking of sticks approved the sorcerer's speech. An old chief rose. "It is good idea. The smell of flesh and burning fat quickens this old man's heart."

Another stood: "Yes! Let us test the Algonquin's spirit. We have not had sport since beating Huron."

Yellow Hawk glared at the sorcerer, then looked toward Pontiac. "Algonquin not afraid. I will fight for *anglais* to go."

"Good!" Pontiac smiled. "Here!" he seized the sorcerer by his shoulder. "Fight him. Whoever loses burns in fire. Take this!" he said to the sorcerer, as he handed him his own war club.

Many Ottawa appeared shocked. "Sorcerer gift of Manitou," the standing old chief objected. "Better someone younger."

"No!" replied Pontiac. "If sorcerer is true gift of Manitou, sorcerer will win. His magic will stun the Algonquin with the swing of his club. Take them outside."

Uproar filled the camp as Yellow Hawk was dragged into the commons and shoved into the snow. Torches were lit and placed upright in the snow. François pushed through the mob and stood beside the Algonquin. "No!" he raised his hands. "I will fight your sorcerer myself."

The sorcerer smiled, circled his French prey, rattled the gord in his left hand, and rushed toward François. With Pontiac's raised club, he swung as François ducked. He swung again but missed. Philippe crouched, circled the sorcerer in turn, caught him by the leg, and sent him sprawling into the trampled snow.

"Where is Manitou now?" Pontiac mocked the sorcerer. "You fight like an old woman."

The sorcerer quickly recovered and sprang toward François again. He nipped his ear with Pontiac's heavy club but stumbled as he brought the weapon up to strike with even greater force. François kicked him in the ribs, but lost his balance in the process. Slipping on the ice, he crashed near Pontiac's feet. The sorcerer smiled, deliberately discarded his gord, and raised his club head high with both hands. Hissing with a deep breath, he expanded his lungs with the night's freezing air to crush the Frenchman for good.

Suddenly, Yellow Hawk stepped forward, caught the sorcerer's left arm with his right hand and flung the Ottawa to the ground. Blood oozed out of the man's nose in a trickle then sank into the white snow. It crinkled in the torchlight, as it turned the ice red.

"Manitou has spoken!" Pontiac pronounced. "Let the loser burn! We have suffered his mischief far too long."

"Listen!" said François. "He is one of your own. Let him live. Take our gifts and let us go."

"No!" replied Pontiac. "My heart burns with fire. Fire the sorcerer wanted. Fire he shall receive. Take your lives and go! Go now, if you wish. Manitou has spoken," he repeated. "We have our work to do."

Hands seized the sorcerer and bound him to a post. Drums sounds began to reverberate throughout the camp. Their monotonous cadence sickened François' soul. Howls of excitement rose with fervor. Dancing feet pummeled what snow remained on the frozen ground.

"Quickly!" said William. "We must go!"

François pushed Yellow Hawk toward their sleds. "Get our guns and packs. Let them have the rest. Hurry! Hurry *anglais*. Grab what you can. Look! They've already set their twigs to flame!"

William glanced back over his shoulder as he plunged through the snow behind Yellow Hawk and François. Red embers sparkled about the terrified sorcerer. A flickering sheet of fire shot skyward and covered the poor man's face. He clutched a gord in each hand, raising them helplessly.

William watched as the gords exploded in a yellow shower of smoke and dust. As the three ran, the painful cry of the pitiful sorcerer rose to a high pitch. It haunted the night for horrible seconds before dying in silence! "Run! Run!" consumed William's thoughts. "This way!" he shouted, as he led François and Yellow Hawk toward an icy stream. Quickly, they turned over a large canoe, grabbed three paddles, floundered through the icy water into the open stream, and let the current bear them where it would.

When twelve days later they arrived on the southern shore of Lake Erie, François could hardly fathom the distance they had journeyed. They had followed the vast central and southeast river system of Michigan's lakes and streams, down to the narrow Tiffin, into the white waters of the Maumee, and finally to the banks of Lake Erie. It had to be late March, if not early April, he reckoned. "Time to camp and recover!" he ordered, as Yellow Hawk guided the canoe ashore. "*Là-bas*! Just up from that protected ledge," he pointed. "That should do."

For three days they rested and dried out their clothing. They hunted and fished, patched the canoe, and prepared to launch. "At least in five days, if not six!" François exhorted. "Then we should see the hamlets of Fort Presque Isle."

Once more they packed the canoe, pushed out into the water, and set their faces for the east. As William paddled in silence, images of Anna surfaced in his heart. Her hair, her petite stature, her lively and coquettish smile ascended to comfort his mind. After so long an exile, would she know him? Would she recognize his face behind the leathery tanned lines and multiple cuts and scares on his chin, neck, and arms? He had to think so! Why else had he lived, or endured the unforgivably harsh days and interminably lonely nights? Harder and harder he pulled, dipping his paddle deeper and deeper into the silty waters of the vast Lake. The wind picked up, slipped through his hair, and burned his nostrils, but it made his labor all the more refreshing.

Chapter Thirty-Four

THE CHAPEL OF FORT PRESQUE ISLE caught François' eye just as the choppy bay opened into the harbor. Its tall graceful spire reflected the late afternoon's burnished sunlight. A ragged *fleur de lis* flapped nosily above the fort. A handful of pirogues and a single sailing vessel sloshed against the oak-plank docks. As they paddled closer, a strong breeze created tiny whitecaps in the cobalt waters that lapped about the canoe. A child waved from the fort's walls as church bells welcomed their approach. It was Noël. Standing beside here was Hélène. More faces appeared along the wall. A cannon fired to signal recognition. Progress was slow in the rolling swells, but Yellow Hawk guided the canoe steadily toward the nearest wharf.

"Look at everyone!" François exclaimed. "If we're their heroes, God pity them!"

As the canoe bumped hard against a pier, William clambered forward to drag the bark onto the landing. Yellow Hawk and François joined Sir William, relieved to have arrived. All three stretched their muscles and glanced about.

Noël ran toward her father. Hélène had donned her in Indian style. Her little black pigtails flopped as she ran. Her white deerskin dress of many beads and dyed porcupine quills brought joy to François' eyes. He bent down, awaited her arms, and lifted her to his chest.

As Hélène approached, William recognized her. "*Kwe-Kwe!*" he greeted her in Algonquin. "*La belle Hélène,*" he smiled. "*Boozhoo!*" he added in the Ottawa tongue.

With a startled blush she gathered Noël into her arms before setting her down. "*Aanii!*" she replied. "I see the *anglais* has become a savage," she gestured toward his hair and deerskin shirt and leggings. The blue and yellow beads in his knife's sheath caught her eyes as well. "You are different, *non?*"

"I hope not! Yet, *vous-avez raison,* I fear."

Yellow Hawk sniffed the air. "Good smoke! Smell of beef, cooking!" he uttered.

Thoughtfully, the party walked up the cobblestone rue that led to the fort's entrance. Its wide gates hung partially open. Bright golden buttercups and tall bluets poked through the cracks between the stones on the path. Milk carts rested beside doorsteps. Clotheslines cluttered the narrow street. A broken chair and table appeared to have fallen off a cart and been discarded where they fell. Masons on a ladder worked to repair loose stones on the fort's interior wall. The sour smells and odors of the fort struck François as a sordid anomaly to the pine and spruce scents of the forest he had grown to love. Was this what he wanted? Still, open shutters on a bakery's oven spilled the welcome redolence of fresh bread into the rue. Near the stonewalls of the fort's central quarters, stood Moro Gaspaille, the fort's deputy commandant. His hands rested on his hips as he studied the three men. Worried lines crinkled in his face. His unkempt blue coat, white waistcoat, crumpled chemise, and soiled breeches conveyed a state of slovenness, if not careless command. Or was it something else? François pondered.

"*Eh bien!*" Gaspaille greeted him with an air of Gallic indifference. "So this is the English you brought back!" he bowed with a smile toward Sir William. "I am Captain Moro Gaspaille and you, sir, must be Major Tillson? *Non?*"

"Yes! I'am Tillson," he saluted the Frenchman politely.

"*Ah bon!* We are in something of an emergency here," Gaspaille apologized for his dress and the clutter about the fort. He held up a placard for the men to see.

Philippe stepped closer and stared at its faded words: *We have with-*

drawn to Ft. Niagara. Iroquois on the move. Low supplies. Low munitions. "What's this about?" he asked Gaspaille.

"We found it two weeks ago, on the gates of one of our outposts. We became worried when the men didn't come in for supplies. Evidently, they were surprised. They headed for the coast, or no doubt northeast."

"Why didn't they try to make it here, or head for Le Boeuf?"

"Iroquois would have cut off their path!" Yellow Hawk muttered.

William wanted to speak but kept silent. While in Pontiac's camp, he heard frequent rumors of British parties probing the area. Names like Amherst and William Johnson circulated from tribe to tribe. He recognized them, though Pontiac did not. The chief simply feared their presence or intentions.

"What does this mean for us?" François asked.

"That you'll not be descending the creeks to Le Boeuf, or going down the Allegheny to Fort Duquesne, or 'Pitt,' as the English call it."

"I need to move on," François protested. "I'm under orders from de Rigaud."

"All that has changed. You will proceed to Ft. Niagara and thence to Quebec. You are to take the English with you. Those are my orders from de Marson."

"Sir, I can make it on my own!" William interrupted. "Once at Le Boeuf, I know the way down the Allegheny. The Major will have fulfilled his orders and I shall be free to go home."

"No!" rejoined Gaspaille. "These men risked too much for you. You'll not be going there."

"Good!" stated Yellow Hawk. "You look too much like an Ottawa. The Cayuga will take you for a Frenchman."

"You'll have to stay. We need you now as much as you need us," François said. "We'll have to go together."

"The Englishman is trapped!" Yellow Hawk smiled at William. He placed his hand on the head of his steel hatchet. "Now we will see what will happen."

William inhaled a long breath, eyed the big savage and the others without flinching, and turned his face away. What did these probes by the Iroquois mean? Was Amherst or Johnson behind them? Why had the hand of fate turned against him again? He tried to smile as he glanced into François' eyes. François' face seemed as puzzled as his. Hopefully, there would be time to escape. He had tried it before. He had not become Pontiac's "son" for nothing.

As June melded into the humid days of July, Langdon paused to look across the creek bank at his and Louise's *Pavillon Chandelle*. Quite a title for so humble a two-story log cabin, but Louise wanted it named for her father's *grand masion* on the Seine et Loire near Paris. He swept the sleeve of his homespun shirt across his clammy brow and stared into the nearby woods. The pine and chestnut trees, dogwood and laurel called to his restlessness and stirred his passion to be a woodsman again. How he aspired for the shade of the rhododendron and the shadows of the forest! He glanced over his shoulder toward Jonathan and Sarah who labored beside him, both hoeing the red earth between the rows of ripening corn. He wondered what Colonel Washington was doing. If Sir William were still alive! Or where he was! As for himself, he guessed this is where he needed to be, at least until the fall. Then he would join Blue Hatchet in the woods and high mountains to the west. In fact, Blue Hatchet was hunting there now, scouting the terrain for a passage through the thickets along the sparkling creeks and rocky ravines. He sighed quietly to himself and retuned to the task of splitting rails to mark the boundary of his grandfather's grant. To the south lay an absentee neighbor's property, mangled in brush and dense briars, bent with blackberries ripe for the picking! He hoped its owner would remain in London and that one day he'd be able to claim the land as his own. As for now, it would soon be suppertime.

After dinner, Langdon walked to the cabin's back window to watch the sun's vermilion disc sink into the pink clouds beyond the mountains. Outside, on the porch, he could hear the children playing with Sarah. Jonathan was somewhere in the barn, currying a new colt. Langdon smiled and walked back to Louise. She was cleaning the iron kettle that hung on its blackened hinge beside the fireplace. "Ummmh!" he kissed her lips.

She smoothed her apron and looked up into his gray eyes. Her own shimmered, black as pearls in the hearth's embers. "You're thinking what I'm thinking, aren't you?" she queried.

"Possibly!" he replied. "Hélène and François! I wonder where they are! If he's alive, along with William! When Gist came through here, he said they'd burned the fort before retreating north. We hear so little."

Louise pressed her apron to her face to dab at the perspiration that glistened on her cheeks.

Langdon could see that her mind struggled with preoccupations, much as his own.

"Yes," she whispered, her voice soft with thoughts far away. "I don't know how Sarah bears it! She mothers little Ashby as if he were her own. I wonder if William knows that Anna's dead, or bore him a son?" She raised her head and arched her neck as sweat trickled down her bossom. "Do you think we'll ever see him again, or Hélène and François? They can't all be dead. Poor Sarah! And little Ashby! Someday he'll want to know. And she'll have to tell him." She pressed Langdon's hand and sat at the table.

Langdon kissed her cheek and wandered out onto the porch.

"There's a rider coming," said Sarah. "I can see his dust across the field!"

"Perhaps it's Blue Hatchet! It's time he returned."

"No! Look! You can see the man's hat. It's black. And his horse isn't loping. He's probably come a long way."

Langdon strained to make out the figure in the fading russet haze. The sinking sun caught the rider's image and bathed him in glowing shades of burgundy, purple, and pink. "What color is his coat?" he asked.

"Black!" replied Sarah. "It's black. He's trailing a packhorse."

Just then Jonathan came around from the barn. The children had run to tug on his hands and sleeves. He brushed them off playfully and gazed across the cornfield, too. "It's the parson!" he chirped. "Reverent Martin. See! I'd know his silhouette anywhere."

"Ohhhh!!" Sarah moaned. "I wanted him to be William." She ran her hands down her apron and fidgeted with the tangle in her red hair. "I guess a man's man," she sighed with a disappointed smile. "I wonder what he's doing here?"

They watched him cross the creek. His horse picked up its gait as he trotted his mare into view. "Well, well! A sight ye are! Fair and fancy the lot of ya! And a wee one to bless to boot! Yur a veritable Garden of Eden, ya are! Fertile and bounding with plenty! Kin ya offer this servant of God's a rug to bed down and a wee pint of rum for the night? Me thirst is like Methuselah's age—long, dry, and achin' of soul." His robust manner and engaging spirit emanated with irrepressible joy.

Sarah stepped forward to touch his boot and steady his horse as he dismounted. "Why God ever singled you out, I'll never know," she smiled. "You're the happiest rogue we've seen in months. You know you're always welcome here."

"Indeed!" Langdon shook his hand. "Guests are rare and neighbors far and few."

"Aye and no, dear lad!" replied the parson. "I passed a dozen wagons no less, with family and plow, bound for this land. They're comin' across the gap along the James an' down from the Big Lick, determined to flee landlords an' the practice of hellish rents. The Great Road's a crawlin' with 'em. There'll be towns and churches soon. Blacksmiths and tailors! And they're all Scots and Irish! Disgruntled English, Germans, criminals and hags," he smiled. "An' they're comin' this way! God help us! I must say!"

Langdon could not prevent from smiling nor Jonathan from laughing aloud.

Louise had come to the door. Ashby clung to Sarah's skirt. The children clattered up the wooden steps and awaited the parson's move. "Well, I'm not an ogre!" he growled lightheartedly, as he tousled their hair with his hands. "Why don't I just sit out here? I've a message for ya, Sarah!" he said with a bit of hesitancy. "And one from the Colonel, too," he nodded toward Langdon.

"Fine!" Louise muttered as she stared apprehensively toward Sarah. "But first some soup and *water*," she emphasized, "then you can tell us the news! Jonathan, do get the Parson a cup of brandy. We might all need one before the night's over."

"Well! Here's the news!" he sat back against the cabin's wall as he took Sarah's hand. "Sir William's somewhere in Canada, but no one knows where. 'Tis the word of the Governor himself, received a month ago from an Indian agent in New York an' his Iroquois on the Niagara. He was supposed to show up at Fort Pitt, but the whole area's amuck in trouble. Indian raids an' fightin'! 'Tis all I know. I hate to bear thee such tidings."

"I want to think he's alive!" Sarah stated. "That he's coming back! That he'll find his way home, behold his dear son, and clasp him in his arms!" she reached for Ashby, as she drew him to her breast. "I live to think that will happen!" she said with glistening eyes.

"Ah, but what if it doesn't, dear Sarah? You canna no' live your days a grievin' for a lover who mayn't come home! The boy needs a father and you a faithful man! Ya know it's so! Think on it lassie! I know a good man who'd take ya for his own at the bat of your eyelash. I do!"

Sarah stroked Ashby's golden hair and kissed his red cheeks. She looked into the parsons's eyes. She knew the "good man" of whom he spoke, to whom he alluded as she studied his eyes, his nose, his lips and felt his hand on her arm. "You're kind to say that. I'm not a saint, you know!"

"Saint or no saint, the man I know would take ya in a heartbeat!" he smiled. "I was a drunken brawler in North Ireland before God snatched me from the cesspool. I lost me own first love an' a child who died of starvation in rags, I did. God help my soul! I cried like an infant myself. 'Tis so! I'm not yur judgin' type. Think about it, Lassie. I'll be back this way again. 'Tis a savage land with a fertile soil an' rivers to make it green. I'd give my life to make it home, to have a mate like thee."

Sarah brushed her hair to one side. She pressed Renwick's hand in her own. Her mind reeled with his unabashed candor and simple offer. Still, her heart lay somewhere else. She'd have to think a long time. She glanced again into his eyes. She had never noticed their deep blue hue, nor the rugged and manly lines of his face. The small dimple in his chin caught her eye as well. God! Whatever she thought, he was one, rugged, handsome man! She coughed. Tears flooded her eyes. She rose quickly and rushed into the cabin with Ashby in her arms.

"I dinna mean to hurt her!" Martin said to Langdon. "Ya never know how your words are taken!" he paused. "The Colonel sends his own regards. He's hopin' to purchase lands in your region and wants ya to survey 'em for him."

"That I can do! It'll be a welcome change from farming, but it will have to wait to the fall."

"I dinna think he's in a hurry, but your whole Tidewater race of Lords an' Ladies is into grants now and who kin grab which parsels here and sell which lands there! Which reminds me, and is sad to report, Lady Ashby's estate is no longer her own or the lad's to have, if ever it was. Her late husband, the Lord Ashby, owed tithes and fees to several companies in London, which he never paid, and the Crown's invoked its rights and privileges to seize his place to settle the debts. The lad'll not see a thing, even if Sir William should return or prove his intention to marry the late widow. It's gone, lad, all of it's gone!"

"I never assumed otherwise," Langdon answered. "I learned long ago how political the grant system is and how nefarious waiting for titles can be. I'm fortunate that Dinwiddie pursued it for me. It's a shame he's gone."

"Aye! For all his greed and whimperin', the way to Ohio was opened, thanks to him."

"Yes! But at what price! We have relatives on the other side, you know. Louise's cousin and her Frenchman lover, her husband I suppose! They were never married, just bound together by Indian custom. We fear their whereabouts since the fall of Duquesne. The King of France never had better. It's their savage allies that trump their road to power, their empire of lakes and furs. I could be one of them, Renwick, if I might call you that?"

"Please do! I'm a man of the wilderness myself, Langdon. There's a call to it! A somethin' I canna put my hand to. Wild as the day of creation! When the mists watered the earth an' God pronounced it good! Except for wolves," he whispered, as he turned to listen to the distant cry of a far-off wolf. Its unsettling howl slipped across the hills—opaque in the dusk—and died in the field. "You'd think I'd be used to them by now," he said, as goosepimples quivered under the thick hair on his arms.

"We've got our packs—just east of here," said Langdon. "They inhabit a series of caves on a hill. A trail out of the Carolinas crosses it.

Hunters have tried to kill them, but they attack their horses and mules. Two riders from the Yadkin passed through last week. Their axe handles reeked of blood. They barely escaped. 'We're huntin' bar,' the younger said, 'and bound fer Kane-tucky! Dad-burn wolves was as thick as fleas!' he allowed. You would have liked him."

"A fine comfort ye are with such a tale!" he winked. "I've winged a many myself when I've had to. But for now, lad, I'm curlin' up for bed. May the providence of God favor us, and all yer lovely family. Good night, dear man! I'll be bound for the Big Lick again, come morning,"

Chapter Thirty-Five

THE RATTLING OF MUSKETFIRE echoed in the woods. What had begun as a muffled explosion had intensified into a cacophanous roar. Startled, François jogged to catch up with William. In front of the *anglais*, Yellow Hawk raced with his musket in one hand and hatchet in the other. A mixed brigade of Canadians, French officers, bushrangers, trappers, and Ottawa ran forward as well. Fort Niagara lay less than a mile to their north. They had marshaled in response to Captain Pouchot's urgent request for help. The British siege had come as a shocking surprise, the ambush even more so. Puffs of white smoke drifted from the forest. Lead zipped through the leaves and thumped into the runners as they sought cover. Their old commandant Villiers was in command. Joncaire and Handsome Dog crouched to the commander's left. Past the trees in front of them rushed the churning current of the Niagara. Joncaire caught sight of François and motioned for him to run for the river. Yellow Hawk caught the signal, turned, and shoved William into the brush. "Run!" he pointed toward the river. "Ambush!"

William's heart raced with hope. Now was his opportunity to escape! But in which direction? A French officer, only yards away, suddenly bolted past him, his face streaming with blood. He collapsed in a patch of ferns, blocking William's path. William stumbled over him, tripped, and crashed into the reeds.

"Get up!" Yellow Hawk ordered. "Get up!"

A hail of musket balls sang through the grass and felled another Frenchman.

Yellow Hawk lunged into the brush and disappeared down the river's bank. François plunged into the broken stubble behind him. A numbing blow stung William between his shoulder blades, just left of his spine. His deerskin cap tumbled across his eyes. It was covered with blood. He rolled to one side, fearing the shot had struck his back. Instead, he stared eye-level into the face of a dying Ottawa. A purplish hole gaped in the Indian's chest. The bullet had struck the native, exited through his back, before walloping William. He kept his head low and crawled into the woods. Yellow smoke sifted in stifling patches everywhere. Moans of the wounded filtered through the trees. William could see fallen bodies, some in plies of two and three. Men were coughing and crying. The hiss of lead and rattle of muskets continued. Figures began to emerge from the forest. Painted and savage they grew closer, whooping and clubbing the wounded. Just yards ahead, kneeling liegemen responded with sporadic volleys. A wave of arrows whined through the air. Excited shrieks exploded all along the path. Raised hatchets joined in the melee. Suddenly, a white flag appeared. Villiers was waving it from the end of a musket. He reeled from a wound and collapsed to his knees. On the Indians came, clubbing and firing into the shattered column of the stunned relief force. An Englishman's voice rose above the clatter. The Indians stopped. William sat up. Into the putrid fumes of dissipating smoke stepped a British officer, surrounded by Iroquois and English officers. "Enough!" the officer commanded. "We accept your defeat!" he addressed Villiers. "Niagara has fallen. It is over for you. It is over, my friend. Thank God, it is over!"

William struggled to rise. He couldn't lift his right arm. Nor his left! His back ached. Only then did he realize he'd been hit. The ball that passed through the Indian had lodged in the upper middle of his back. His arms felt numb. Rolling his hips to one side he managed to sit up before slumping into the grass. Something sharp nipped his throat. The burning sensation would not abate. He looked up. A British soldier's bayonet was poking his throat. The grenadier looked as horrified as William. "Don't!" stammered William. "I'm a British officer!" he muttered hoarsely. The soldier's resolve wavered, his bayonet slid off William's neck. As it did, it opened a stinging wound that set his throat on fire. The man's image doubled in size, grew grotesque, and faded into a red blur. William could feel hands under his armpits and his feet being dragged. Through the haze of numbness loomed the face of the British officer. In his right hand he held Villiers' flag. "Let him live!" mumbled the man. "Damn, what kind of savage is he? Dump him with the rest of the wounded." William opened his mouth to speak, but blood had collected in his throat. He coughed, felt a weight on his chest, tried to focus his eyes to determine what it was, threw up in the ferns, and lost consciousness.

Swept downstream, François fought to keep his head above water. The swift current propelled him faster than he could swim. He could see Yellow Hawk struggling to reach the left bank. The big Algonquin bumped ashore and clung for all his life to a low-lying beech limb. The Indian pulled himself to safety and glanced out toward François. Without hesitation, he snapped off the teetering end of the limb and hurled it toward Philippe. De Robert groped for the limb as it splashed in front of him. Pulling himself into its leaves, he rested chest-high on the branch and paddled toward a sandbar on the river's bank. Yellow Hawk raced ahead to catch him. With thrashing kicks he guided his float toward the sandbar and the big Indian's out-stretched arm. "We lost the *anglais!*" he grunted.

"Yes, but we're alive!" François replied. "Thanks to *le bon Dieu!*"

Yellow Hawk gazed unmoved at de Robert's sentiment but said nothing. He hauled him ashore and faded into the forest. François regained his composure, squeezed water out of his shirt, and followed the Algonquin.

"Listen!" said Yellow Hawk. "Guns! Big cannon! *Non?* See? Smoke rises from river's mouth! This way!" he pointed west into the forest.

Without guns or weapons, François realized the precariousness of their situation! The way back to Fort Presque Isle would take days! Iroquois would cross the river and hunt them down. "No! We must go to the Point, where they're bombarding the fort," he panted for breath.

"There we can look for canoes. Come. Perhaps we can surprise them as they surprised us!"

"*Bon!* The French major finally has good idea." The big brave's eyes twinkled, as plans of his own seemed to take root. "No! River too swift for canoe. The falls too close and way too narrow. Follow. I will take us to the lake." He motioned with his arm and set off at a jog through the forest. François cleared his lungs, took a deep breath, and ran behind him.

Two days and nights later, they arrived south of the great river's passage below the falls. Yellow Hawk found a cache of hidden canoes near an abandoned Indian village. Together they patched the worthiest bark from sections of others, coated its seams with resin and black pitch, and set off for Presque Isle.

By afternoon, a July storm materialized far out in the water. Soon, its gale-driven winds forced them to seek shelter in the chalky cliffs above the lake. Sheets of cold rain fell in torrents. It drenched the scrubby foliage and streamed off the cliffs in unbroken flows. A second day passed with no let up. With reluctance they returned to the village and salvaged a wigwam from remaining hovels. With luck, they found an iron pot coated with rancid pemmican and, picking through the maggots, ate what morsels they could. With resignation, they awaited the storm's demise.

When two weeks later they arrived at Fort Presque Ilse, no *fleur de lis* fluttered from the fort. A ragged fleet of diverse vessels rocked in the harbor. Crates and ornate trunks, wooden casks and piles of clothing cluttered decks. Armed companies of French Marines carried goods to the boats. Numerous dugouts and Indian canoes lined the wharfs. A mixture of Indians mingled with the crowds. They appeared to be sorting through castoff goods. Soldiers on the fort's northern wall fired shots as they approached. A cannon boomed. Its spherical cloud of white smoke drifted across the bay and disappeared into the trees. Gaspaille appeared beside the men, fixed his eyepiece on their canoe, and waved his hat. He pointed with his right arm to the narrow inlet where a row of canoes was banked. From there they would have to cross a wooden gangplank to the fort. One of the vessels was undertow. A large pirogue guided it slowly out to the lake. Women and children crowded its decks. "Hélène!" Yellow Hawk noted. "*C'est votre femme! Là-bas!* There! See? By the rail!"

"*Alors! C'est vrai!* Hélène!" he called. "Yellow Hawk, quickly!" he ordered, as he turned the canoe about and dipped his paddle in the direction of the lumbering bateau. It was the same ship that had borne him and Yellow Hawk across the lake in search of Pontiac's camp. It began to gain speed. "Hurry!" François urged. Cool spray sloshed in his face as the big Alogonquin steered toward the boat.

With transparent sadness, Hélène stared down from the vessel's rail. As was her custom, an irenic dignity embraced her. François could see the Stoic lines of her handsome face, her angular nose, gentle cheekbones, subtle eyes, and oval lips, heightened by her French beauty. The fullness of her breasts filled her white blouse. A headband of blue beads held her braids tightly against her head. She clutched Noël's hand. François could barely see the top of the child's black braids. "What's happened? What's going on?" he asked, not wishing to exacerbate the mounting pandemonium that burned in his chest.

"We're being deported," she answered. "Marchault's been abandoned, Le Boeuf torched. Pouchot's ordered Gaspaille to close Presque Isle. You and the French troops are summoned to Quebec. It's under siege. Montcalm can't get supplies, we've been told."

"Where are they taking you? Where will I find you?"

"At Frontenac. From there we're to go to Montreal. Where else I don't know."

"Hélène, I love you. You are all I have. I will look for you in Montreal. After Quebec, I will come for you."

"No. Come to Frontenac. Noël and I will wait for you. Trappers still pass that way, along with the Chippewa and their squaws. We'll be safe in its ruins. Come for us there."

He wanted to stand in the canoe to touch her hand, to clutch her breasts, to kiss her lips, her mouth before she was gone. But the ship's sails had fluffed out with the full summer's breeze. The vessel's sides bulged too steep to scale. Within moments the ship slipped beyond reach. Its wake rocked the canoe violently. Yellow Hawk pulled François into paddling position. The vessel turned. The ship's *fleur de lis* popped blue and gold in the breeze. Its passengers paled from sight. The boat's stern swayed from side to side as the vessel listed into the deeper water and pulled into the lake's wind.

The crashing sounds of hatchets, splitting furniture, jarred William into full consciousness. His mind struggled to regain clarity; his vision wavered between periods of bright images and dull blurs. A sharp pain pulsated between his shoulder blades. Hands set down the gurney in which he writhed; the nauseous feeling in his stomach intensified. He fought to take a deep breath; then looked up into the bearded face of a surgeon. The harried man stared down at him. He held a twisted cloth in his hands.

"Bite on this!" the sweating figure mumbled. "I'm rolling you over to remove the ball."

Hands flipped him onto his queasy stomach; the cloth was forced in his mouth, the sickness returned. Someone began cutting through his deerskin shirt. He could hear them ripping it off. Out of the corner of his eye he watched as an Indian rifled through an overturned desk. The Iroquous grunted in disgust as he pulled out handfuls of paper and ink quills.

"Where are we?" William asked.

"In the citadel. Stop moving," the surgeon snapped.

An orderly standing beside him sloshed a mixture of wine and brandy on his wound. He sprinkled a few drops on William's lips.

"You're lucky the ball's not deep."

He could feel the surgeon's scalpel as it probed into his back. "God!" he repressed the thought in a gush of saliva as he clenched his teeth on the knotted cloth. The knife seemed to go deeper. "Oh, God!" he tightened his fists as muscle and tissue quivered under the surgeon's knife. He could feel it scraping bone. He gulped snatches of air between sickening crunches on the foul rag in his mouth. Someone wiped the feverous beads of perspiration from his face. The rag equally smelled sour.

"Steady! Don't move! Damnit! Don't. Don't. Ah!" the surgeon uttered with relief. He followed his exclamation with a pleased grunt. "Here! Look at it!" he turned it over and around before William's eyes.

Suddenly, William bolted, as someone poured saltwater into the gash. He sucked in rapid gulps of air but refused to pass out.

The surgeon drew in a deep breath. "Get him a clean shirt," he said. "Damn but my hands stink." He backed away toward another man. "This one won't live," he said. "Get him off the table."

William fought to sit up, managed to roll to one side, and stood up with help.

"Don't leave yet. The squaw in the mending room will sew up the hole. You'll be fine in day or so."

William stared at the gray face of the bearded doctor. The blood-shot vessels in the man's eyes caused William to blink his own. He staggered, caught his balance, and moved slowly into the mending room. He expelled a long breath and sat exhausted on a low stool by an elderly Huron woman. She smiled at him, rubbed his hair knot with her dark hands and picked up her needle and thread. "You English! We hear of you," she said, as she squeezed the skin about his wound between her thumb and forefingers before poking her needle into his flesh. "Trappers coming here call you '*L'homme de fer!*' They say Pontiac asks of you. Such a great warrior!" she whispered in a glum voice. "Pontiac needed here!"

"Yes!" he replied, as he gazed out through a musket slit of Niagara's western bastion. The fort's walls seemed fairly intact! He felt sorry for its defenders and wondered where they were. "How long have I been here?" he asked.

"Two days you lie here. For two days! Our French fathers left before English Captain arrived."

"Who's that?"

"Ah! The father of the stinking Iroquois!" she spat.

"Sir Johnson?"

The woman scrunched up her nose and turned to assist another. "*Bon débarras!*" she muttered. "They say he departs tomorrow."

"I hope to go with him, if that's the case."

"Ah, I grieve for you. He goes to New York, his soldiers to Quebec! There, our father Montcalm will crush them! And you, too, I fear." She rethreaded her needle with a stout strand of fine gut. Her only expression was a blank stare. "Go on! *Vite! Anglais! Vite!*" she repeated.

The harsh sunlight blinded William as he made his way down the bastion's steps to the fort's stone parapet. He glanced out across the wall toward the west. A battery of French guns remained within sight across the bay. They too had been abandoned. He turned and faced the east. Already ships flying the Union Jack lined the beach. They were anchored just beyond the lapping waves. Men and supplies crowded a dozen or so johnboats, which had been commandeered to ferry them back and forth to the vessels. In one of the boats sat the British officer who had sprung the ambush. So that was Sir William Johnson! Warily, William negotiated the narrow walkway to the beach and sat exhausted on an overturned canoe.

When a half-hour later a johnboat returned bearing Sir Johnson, William stood. He steadied himself against the canoe and awaited the commander's approach.

"Sir William, I hear!" the tall, distinguished, thin-lipped agent extended his hand to Tillson. His high white brow dominated his face. A starched collar held his neck stiff and erect. Sloping shoulders minimized his otherwise courtly bearing. His attire consisted of a pale red silk coat, cream rich vest, and white trousers and hose. "I apologize for your wound. One of the Frenchmen identified you. We let them pass with honors. The prize now of Niagara is ours!" he gestured toward the stone fort. "We're sorry to have inconvenienced you. What is your wish, sir?"

"Whatever his Majesty's deems!" he replied, masking his desire to return home, to Anna and the Colony of Virginia.

"Your nobility precedes you, sir. We've heard countless stories already. We can use your gifts at Quebec. General Wolfe has requested every able-bodied loyal servant who speaks Algonquin or French to assist in the capture of the city. Would you mind accompanying us? May I hear a 'Yes'?" he eyed William with a circumspect glare.

"Yes! My privilege, sir! Will you be leading us?"

"No! My duties confine me to Fort Stanwix, and," he turned cautiously about to observe passers-by, "our reluctant allies, the Iroquois. This time they favored us. Next time, who knows? They fear the French and despise their allies. We can't always trust them, though many are as loyal as our own."

William glanced out at the ships, listing to and fro in the lake.

"They'll be departing tomorrow, if you'd care to go. Within a week they hope to approach the Lachine Rapids. From there, parties will proceed overland and pass Montreal in the dark. Wolfe plans to attack as soon as forces are assembled. By mid-September, he hopes to scale the heights and besiege the city. You'd make a good spy. *Isn't that so?* If I may mock our effete French brothers!" he half-smiled.

"Yes! I will go. But . . ." he spread his arms in deference to his weathered leggings and Indian moccasins.

"Have no concern of that! Wolfe's commanders will determine your placement and wear. His Majesty's ship *Good Gloucestershire* departs at midnight. You're welcome to board anytime. It's the larger of the two vessel's," he nodded toward the anchored ships offshore.

"Yes, thank you!"

When two hours later, along with others, sailors rowed him to the ship, the uneasy feeling that he had made an irreversible miscalculation nibbled at the core of his soul. It throbbed in unmitigated contrast to his true yearning. William glanced up at the ship; then carefully climbed its boarding ropes to the deck, dutifully following the disciplined soldiers in front of him.

"Sir!" a lieutenant saluted him as he dropped over the rail. "The officers' quarters are this way," he pointed. "You will share the Captain's cabin at his own request. We're proud you are with us, sir!"

William tipped his new cap, smiled, and made his way across the creaking planks. "*Mon ami!*" he blurted in French as the Captain appeared in the doorway. It was one of his old friends, Anselm Whithers, from his earlier years in the King's Regiment that fought at Cherbourg.

"Ah, Yes!" the fine-tailored captain beamed. "I requested your company the moment Sir Johnson reported your presence. Let us enjoy these days! If Wolfe is victorious, my God, think what that will mean!"

Tillson's face glowed with momentary pleasure. What a beau geste! What an exultant surprise. As he ducked his head to enter the cramped cabin, he looked up to behold a portrait of General Wolfe, or so the brass plate identified him. His youthful countenance shocked William. Waves of blond hair graced the man's head. Thick eyebrows protected a set of piercing eyes. His velvet coat of garnet-red and shining brass buttons bespoke of an innocence—untested. It was all there to be seen! "Damn!" he muttered. "So that's the General! I expected someone older, more rugged. More like Braddock! And hopefully, more experienced!"

"Fear not! Old Chap! Beneath that veneer of boyish grandeur is one determined adversary! God help us, to be sure!"

William repressed his true thoughts and placed his cloth valise on the cabin's couch.

"Here!" the Captain poured him a glass of wine. "Let's drink to each other and to the King!"

They clinked their glasses to the slow rocking of the ship.

"I think I'd best lie down," said William, as the pain in his upper back throbbed anew between his shoulder blades.

"Please do! We'll soon be under sail. Make yourself comfortable. God only knows what lies ahead! Here! Have another glass! See! It's the best French wine we found in their cellars. From the Loire at that! Their loss, but our gain!"

Chapter Thirty-Six

THE WARM SEPTEMBER SUN bathed the Plains of Abraham with crystalline cerulean light. As far as François could see, the river tumbled blue and white as it sparkled past his position and swept majestically downstream toward the quays of Quebec. Everywhere, the colors of autumn graced the view—magnificent yellows, brilliant reds, and dust muted hues. Across the river, elements of Wolfe's army displayed themselves openly all along the cliffs. They had deliberately stationed a regiment opposite the entire length of the city's ramparts. Scores of British frigates hugged the far banks of the St. Lawrence. Chains blocked their further passage, but smaller vessels had managed to slip through. A tiny fleet of the same bobbed in the water just upstream. Occasional guns boomed from the distant frigates to hurl eight and twelve pounders into the citadel at its bulky stone walls. Shops along the lower city had been shattered. High barricades bristled with sharpened stakes and piles of broken stone.

Along with Yellow Hawk, Joncaire and Tekacayah, their force from Fort Presque Isle had arrived only two nights earlier from Ontario. They had disembarked near the river's mouth east of the great lake; then proceeded by canoe down the river to the rapids, hastily by way of portage around Montreal, and finally, slipping past a British outpost, to the narrow landing at the base of the cliffs below. A Colonel Gaspard de Félroneige had been dispatched to meet them. They had been delayed upstream until past dusk.

The stolid man, of short stature and rotund girth, ordered them ashore with quiet grunts. "Listen up! This is Foulon's Cove! No one must see you. The enemy remains clueless about this passage. The path leads straight up to the heights. Follow it carefully. Keep out of sight. Keep your whispers low. Put out any pipes. This is the essence of secrecy," he placed a finger to his lips. "Once atop, all officers report to Monsieur, le Capitaine Julien. He will escort you to Montcalm's headquarters. Remember, not a sound! *Allez, maintenant!* Pass on!"

Philippe shifted his weight and walked inquisitively about. His impression of Montcalm still disturbed him as he scanned the enemy's position. The great general's appearance had not matched his expectations, though it fascinated him at the same time. Dressed in a modest blue velvet coat, white ruffled tie and shirt, ecru trousers and white hose, the man grimaced uncomfortably as he glanced about the assembled commanders. "Messieurs! Our reinforcements have arrived from the west, but hardly sufficient to mount an attack on Wolfe's flank." He stared momentarily at Villiers, Marin, Pouchot, Joncaire, and de Marson. "I have posted our finest troops east of the city, where the English are most likely to land. Ten thousand of France's finest are entrenched there. They form *notre défense véritable!*" He glanced in François' direction. Beside him squatted Tekacayah and Yellow Hawk. "I do not mean to belittle our native allies, but our strength lies in our own fighting force. It cannot be otherwise. His Majesty has entrusted us to achieve victory! In our arms alone! I have abandoned the west and all our forts there, but only momentarily. Why? Because we have depended on *nos enfants sauvages trop beaucoup!* Now we are confronted with a grand battle to retain New France, our *vraie racine ici!*" He moved about uneasily and gazed at the officers gathered in his white tent. Consternation dominated his face. He paused by a map on the tent's wall and thumped the heights that François and the others had ascended. "We have many vulnerable points! This is one of them. Fortunately, the cliffs are steep and inaccessible to *nos ennemis*. It must remain that way. Captain Félroneige understands, and anyone else whom he may choose to guard it. That, Monsieur de Robert, implies you, and you, as well, Pouchot. You have served our nation well, but where is Fort Niagara now? *Oui?* Where? No disrespect, but in

English hands! Under their Union Jack! *Non?* It is so. To you, de Robert, along with Félroneige belongs the defense of that route! Defend it with your honor! Am I clear?"

"*Oui!*" Félroneige replied. "On my life, I vow this day to my death, if it must be."

"No, no, no! Not your death, my friend," the General partly smiled, "but your life. When the victory's ours and the British depart, we shall then congratulate ourselves and regain our forts in the forests. Let us drink to the night and to His Majesty, *Louis Quinze, roi de la France!*" he said with a lift in his voice. "Then return to your posts. Remain there until relieved or ordered otherwise."

Glasses were filled with wine, lifted with solemn faces, and a sudden outburst of cheer: "*Vive le Roi! Vive la France! Vive Quebec et Montcalm!* Long live Quebec!"

Quietly, the words re-echoed in François' soul. He walked to the edge of the cliffs and stared down the steep path. Briars, dwarf cedars, birch, dense berry bushes — sharp with thorns and tall grass — all entangled in vine — beautifully hid the narrow trail. Its marl path of yellow clay and gray pebbles could scarcely be seen. Still, François-Philippe wished it were better hidden, if not blocked with iron grates and large stone! He should call that to Félroneige's attention, if not Julien's. It was still unclear to him which of the two was in charge. For the present, however, he was. He paced quietly back in order to appear unobtrusive to any enemy eyes. Lest the British should discover them, he had ordered his command of thirty français-canadiens to disperse and to lie prone in clusters of two and three in the dry grass. Nearby sat Yellow Hawk, alert as always. François sought a place to rest and found it in the shade of a lone blue spruce. He closed his eyes; then opened them to listen to the chatter of a tiny gray squirrel, nibbling scales off a green spruce nut, just above his head. "Shhhhh!" he whispered to the squirrel. "Can't you see I'm as weary as thou? And very preoccupied, *mon petit!*" He rolled to one side and waited for Julien, whose watch was scheduled at dusk.

On the opposite bank, a half-mile upriver from François' outpost, William awaited word of his own assignment. Wolfe had assured him his role would be vital. "Top secret!" the sweating general had advised him. "My Brigadiers and I will be meeting tonight. I'll let you know."

William scanned the northern bank for any unusual activity. "Sir," a corporal approached him, "do ya see that cove to your right. Yes. That one! The men and I 'ave noticed strange reflections comin' from it, sir. Like the sun's shinin' on something that moves."

"Please point again! Exactly where?"

"There, sir! See it? It's glitterin' now!"

"Indeed. It's one of their outposts. They're probably watching us, too."

"Ah, ya think so? Well, the Devil with them! If we was closer, I'd fire this musket square in their face!"

William smiled. "Corporal! Save it. I'm expecting word from the General himself as to when we move." He stepped to the right of the corporal to study the outline of the cliffs near the outpost, one more time.

As evening's shadows fell across the south bank, the corporal returned. "Sir, the General's comin' an' his favorite Brigadier with him."

William turned. Accompanying the General was a tall commander with long gray locks tucked under his hat. An old scar glistened white on his smooth face. The commander's eyes stared quizzically into William's.

"Sir William! Robert Monckton!" said Wolfe in a quick introductory manner. "He'll explain what we need."

"My father knew your father," he began. "The pleasure of your acquaintance is mine," he extended William his hand. "It will soon be dark. Where you've been staring is a cove: Anse au Coulon. Rumor has it that a path leads up from its shoals to the heights. Tonight's a moonless night. They say you speak French and several Indian languages. We want you to pass over in the dark and confirm or dispel the truth of such a trail. We've already made plans for a landing, but need to rid that sight of any outposts. You can take the corporal here with you. Just the two of you, plus a guide! We'll be in the General's tent when you return," he nodded toward Wolfe. "If I'm not, he'll summons me. Once back, report immediately — however late."

The General took William aside, to be alone. "If it's there, we'll be going back. Our plans are for tomorrow. But, as dark as it is, who knows?" he gestured with an upraised hand. "Vigilant's the word! Be as thorough as possible. My generals think I plan to attack farther west. But, no! If you can make it up that path, that's where I'll go."

William nodded, understandingly. Soon he and the corporal were escorted to the banks of the river and provided with a canoe and an Iroquois paddler. The Indian's scalp lock glistened with strands of gray hair, a black feather, and gold beads. His blood-red complexion reminded William of Tekacayah. His painted face glowed eerily in the dark. The brave stared at them, shifted his paddle, and pushed off as they crawled aboard and fell in their places.

Overhead, the stars twinkled with minimal light. Even the largest stars blinked dimly and pale. The Indian headed the craft upstream, then out into the swift current and paddled hard for the distant shore.

"The General's takin' a likin' to ya, sir," the corporal stated. "He's a weird one, ya know?"

"I didn't know," replied William. "How's that?"

"His other generals don't care for him. They look down their noses at him. He ain't no earl, or duke, ya know. Plus, he's sick all the time, dippin' into opium and having hisself bled! The cropper came the other night, though," he paused. "Strange man he is!"

"Oh!" William listened, as the river's spray sloshed across his legs and lap.

"I ain't no poet, myself, sir. But I was outside his tent, I was. An' he had his generals inside, lecturin' 'em on all his plans upriver. Then he stood amongst them, pulled his frail frame as tall as he could stretch it, and started into recitin' some poem writ in a graveyard. Somethin' about 'the pomp of power' an' some 'inevitable hour.' It plum frightened his generals sick, cause he seemed so moved by his own 'elocution,' if that's a word, an' bleary eyed when he finished."

Twenty minutes later the silent bark slid into the pebbles along a quiet shoals. The three quickly got out. The corporal groped his way toward the brush while the Indian studied the marly sand. He raised his head and pointed toward the briars. Traces of a pebbly path were clearly visible. It disappeared into overgrown vines and clumps of blackberries.

William motioned for the corporal to remain by the canoe. *"Viens avec moi,"* he whispered to the brave.

Quietly, step-by-step, they groped their way up the trail. The thorns bit into William's hands and snagged his leggings. Ever so gingerly he picked his way through the marl cut up the cliff. Finally, at the top, he stared down at the Indian behind him and then at the grassy knoll just above his head. William fought for a better foothold as he clasped the tall clumps of grass in his hands. Slowly, he inched forward and over the lip of the knoll. Just then the Indian grasped his ankle and tugged him back. A shadow passed nearby. The odor of tobacco drifted in the air. Yes. It could be done! But only one at a time would be able to climb it. The Indian crept past William and lay body down in the grass. He edged forward and slipped away. Moments later, he crawled back. He stared at William and held up his hands. He closed and opened them three times. Thirty men! Thirty guards. The Indian nodded, perfectly reading William's thoughts.

The way down proved more precarious than the climb up; however, soon they were scooting on the pebbles below and brushing off the clay on their pants.

"My God! What luck! I knew it! I knew it!" Wolfe exclaimed as he listened to their report. "Well done, Major! By God, well done! You've just saved us months of a costly siege!" He turned to his closest aide-de-camp. "Get me Monckton and the others. We've got work to do." He smiled toward Sir William. "Only one at a time, you say? Only one?"

"Only one, but with ropes, maybe two in tandem. The path is steep, however. And at least one guard was awake."

"True! But thirty! Only thirty! We can have two thousand men up there, if not three or four, within an hour. We can hit Montcalm before he knows it! I'll create a diversion downstream. Damn, but you've brought good news!" his mouth widened with energetic appreciation. "One moment!" he suddenly blurted. "You did say thirty, only thirty?" he seized William's arm.

"Yes! Thirty. Maybe there's another one the Indian missed. Or even more. But thirty's the number he counted."

The General rubbed his hands together. "To hell with tomorrow night! Corporal, return to your men! Lieutenant!" he addressed his aide. "Find

Monckton and Murray, Townshend and Colonel Howe. Bring them here. Damn! Perhaps we can cross tonight and attack the city by morning!" He embraced William with unabashed enthusiasm! "Thank God this moment has come! My critics have nagged me for weeks! But not anymore!" He paused, as if struggling to remember something. "Major! Sir Tillson!" he exclaimed. "Forgive me. My senses are blurred by all these details. There's a post for you. A letter from the honorable Governor of Virginia, Francis Facquier! It arrived only yesterday on a frigate from Boston. It's addressed to you." He turned and sorted through a package of papers on his field desk. "Here! I trust it brings good news! As soon as you can, meet me at the river." He slipped on his coat, snatched his sword and scabbard, looped it about his waist, and pressed on his hat. "Till later!" he smiled, departing with a quick jerk of the tent's flap.

William fumbled with the folded sheet, all but dropping the letter before finally cracking the Governor's seal. His heart thumped with muscular quivers as he steadied himself and sat in the General's chair.

My dear Sir Tillson.

We have no idea of your present whereabouts or if you will receive this epistle at all. I regret to inform you of a certain young widow's death, of which you might have interest. The late Honorable Governor Robert Dinwiddie, my predecessor, left a drawer of correspondence and private diaries in which he records your intention to betroth the late Lady Anna Ashby. His file indicates that she died giving birth to a child. Please forbear what you may consider my inappropriate reflections, however, the Governor insinuates that you might be the father. The lad, as the child is a boy, is being safely cared for by a diligent and mannerly family, which resides in the southwestern corner of the Colony. Colonel Washington tells us that he knows the family and assures you of the child's utmost wellbeing. He speaks highly of you and the family's leader, a Mr. Burke. Written this 15h day of July in the year of our Lord, 1759.

> *With profound respect, submitted by his Majesty's Lieutenant Governor of Virginia, I, Francis Facquier.*

William released a long breath. Too numb to cry, to distraught to think, he stared at the words "a certain young widow's death," then, emitting a low wail, pressed the letter tenderly to his face and kissed the words "Anna Ashby." "Anna, Anna," he whispered. "O my God, Anna!" He burst into a sob. His body shook and shoulders sagged. He wagged his head from side to side. My God, I must get hold of myself, he realized. Yet he continued to cry. He looked about to see who might be watching, who might be listening. His world had crumpled. After all these months! After all the nights and all the days of the past three years! Yet, the child was alive! A son! A little boy! In Langdon and, no doubt, Sarah's keeping. Tears collected about his lips and trickled down his chin. He wiped them off and blew his nose. He stuffed the letter in his loincloth, stood, wiped his face with the back of his sleeve, and rushed from the tent. He had a rendezvous to keep, a duty to serve his King. He would not keep Wolfe waiting at the assembling grounds by the river!

All seemed calm along the walls of the city and the cliff's ramparts. He should be sleeping, or at least resting, Philippe told himself, but the night breeze, the faint stars, the whiffs of the leaves and fragrance of the Plains of Abraham's mown hay had drawn him into the night, outside the city's walls. He ambled casually toward the meadow's vast northern fields, where the higher topography provided a clearer vista of the city's shops and stucco buildings, aglow dimly in the night.

Montcalm's attitude toward the whole siege still puzzled François. What was he thinking? How long did he think they could detain Wolfe's brigades, or endure the daily pounding from the frigates' guns? "Phefff-fah!" the distant hissing sound of a shell echoed from the river's basin. François stopped and watched its bright arc sputter across the night and drop somewhere short of the city. Whatever, Montcalm had made it perfectly clear.

"Ah, Monsieur de Robert! Why do you keep insisting I employ your savages? Do you not know what pain they caused me at Fort Henry? Or how helpless I was to prevent the massacre afterwards? Or how barbaric they behaved at Crown Point? No! You weren't there."

"Sir! With all due respect, we defeated Braddock only because of our *sauvages*," he emphasized. "Without Pontiac, Black Hat, Michilimackinac's Ottawas, the Shawnee, Delaware and Wyandots, and Beaujeu's Abenaki, we would never have turned him back! *Jamais*! They won the battle. Not we!"

"Ah, so you say! But where were they last fall when Duquesne fell? Huh! Where where they then? Gone! Fled, Monsieur! Melted back into their forests! That is why we, yes we, and we alone must win this battle! We have the finest troops from Europe just ten leagues from here. Yes, where I expect the blundering British to attack. But let me ask! Why are you so enamored of these savages? These half-human creatures of the wild? We are civilized here, *mon bon homme*! So must New France! Even the British colonies fare better than we. Besides, listen! Winter is coming. The Great River will freeze. It will lock their boats in the ice. Here, we are well supplied. We can eat moose and bear if it comes to that! What do they have? Only the forest to their back! They will have to withdraw! Take heart, young Major. Quebec is safe. Now leave me in peace. My humors are acting up, and I shall have to be bled. And I hate the surgeon's knife. A glass of port is far superior!" the disheveled Marquis smiled, as he poured himself a glass of dark wine from a dusty decanter. "Will you have some?"

"Thank you, sir! A walk in the night is my anodyne!"

"Ah! So Rousseau claims. I met him once, in Paris. Delightful man, but a dreamer, *mon vieux*! We should send him to your *sauvages*! That would nip his palaver about their gallant behavior. Not 'Man in a state of Nature,' but 'Man in a state of barbarism!' would be more like it! Take my word, de Robert. Be alert! Watch your end of the heights! But the battle will not come there.

"Wait! Stay a moment. Someone must understand! You are young and full of courage. Who knows what will happen here, but here is the truth. De Rigaud hates me. Yes. I swear before His Majesty and God, 'tis true. He's jealous and covetous of his own authority. He refuses to acknowledge mine. He fears if I fail Paris will disown him, and if I succeed, the same. He's a bitter and petty *intendent*! And Ramezay, Sir Major Jean-Baptiste, is scarcely better. To him alone belongs the defense of the city! That is, in his mind. I've pleaded with him countless times to mount cannon on the heights, but, *Non*! He needs them for the city! For Quebec!

He could care less about my troops. How do I fight a war like that? The indentant casts himself as the legitimate sovereign of New France, caters to the whims of his Canadian-born citizens, and disparages my role, save as Louis Quinze's Commander of the *French Army*, not, Monsieur—the General of all! Only my Louis-Antoine, the noble Captain Bougainville, supports me. No general could ask for a more loyal aide-de-camp. Now," he paused, vexed and perflexed all in the same breath, "*bonne nuit*, good man. Good-night!"

François listened as another shell hissed up and into the city. Its bright red burst sent showers of sparks across the night. Its white smoke formed a round cloud before drifting slowly to the east. "Whoosh!" came another one. A third behind it! François walked on. In the distance he could make out the dark outline of the outpost and the few tents Montcalm had permitted. He wondered if Captain Julien was enjoying the fireworks, or fearful that Wolfe's attack might soon be nigh!

Far to the west, a child's cry woke Hélène from her fretful sleep. Noël was crying, almost coughing, strangling in her sleep. Hélène rolled over and kissed her daughter—hers and François'. The child sniffled, stirred slightly, and fell back into quiet slumber. Hélène felt strangely alone, though a Chippewa family slept less than forty yards away in their own wigwam.

Returning to Frontenac had been difficult. Trappers heading uplake and into Ontario's interior were pressed for time. The season for furs was fast upon them. Still, a few came ashore to find shelter in the walled fort, and trade for what dried fish and pemmican the Chippewa made available.

Hélène could not fall back to sleep. She slipped out of her bed of furs, piled on pine boughs, and peeped into the dark. Stars pulsated overhead in the bright dome of the cool night. For a reason she could not fathom, yet fully feared, she remembered the night her father had been killed before the Seneca mutilated his body. Wounded and bleeding, he had looked into her young eyes. Her mother held his hand and, humming an Indian death song, rocked back and forth. On she sang, on she rocked, with quiet composure. It was her life. The way of her people! Why should it be otherwise? Suddenly, the Seneca tore her mother away and clubbed her father to death. Then they committed their atrocities! As his life ebbed away, her mother paused, bent forward, and threw herself on his body. Hélène could not dispel that horrible night from her mind. She walked toward the lake's edge, found a large rock, sat facing the east, and sang her mother's chant to herself. Her heart told her it was something she must do. She sat there a long time, weaving back and forth, singing to herself, until Noël's cry interrupted her private world.

As Philippe gazed across the Plain, a new set of flashes caught his eye, accompanied by the muttering clatter of distant musket fire. He turned and faced the cliffs. Tiny puffs of dim yellow smoke appeared, then fizzled at the end of the dark heights. Musket sounds emanated from the high brush near the outpost! As he stood midway between the citadel and the far end of the field, François realized that Julien's position was under attack. Quickly, he turned and began the long jog back to Montcalm's headquarters.

Standing outside his tent, Montcalm paced with his cavalry officer, Johnstone. The two had been watching the bombardment. Montcalm turned in François' direction as he approached.

"Sir!" François asserted, as he gasped for breath. "The British have ascended the heights! A great commotion has erupted there. Firing has broken out all along the bluffs. Please, sir, come and see for yourself."

"*Bon Dieu*, I don't believe it! It's a diversion I tell you. A diversion," the General grumbled, as he wielded about toward the area. "Johnstone, summon a regiment. No, two. Take one from the center and one from east of the city," he croaked, as he bent down to check his boots. "Join me in the Plains of Abraham! Major, have the livery bring up my horse, and one for you, *s'il vous plait*. Arouse the camp!" he ordered as he returned to his tent for his coat and hat. He sat briefly and buckled on his spurs. "What time is it?"

"Two a.m.," François replied.

Moments later, he and the General road out together and crossed the wooden bridge over the star-white Charles River. All was so calm and dreamlike. A light drizzle began to fall.

Chapter Thirty-Six

"Where are your savage friends?" the General asked suddenly.

"With the Canadian forces, I believe. That's where I saw them last."

"Then we should meet them soon," he said, as their horses clattered along the damp street and entered the bombarded city. Increasing number of British shells hissed up across the dark river into the misty night. With disconcerting chaos, they plummeted iron-hot into the heart of the town's ancient buildings. Montcalm said nothing but kicked his handsome bay's flanks with quickened spurs.

"*Alors!*" he called out as they neared Vaudreuil's stone and log-hewn maison. "The British have crossed the river!"

The *intendent* had come to the door. Still dressed in his nightgown and white stocking cap, he peered at them in apprehensive dismay. "I've heard the same and ordered our Canadians to take the field. They're forming up outside the gate."

"How many have you sent?"

"Enough!" de Rigaud insisted, with a tone of resentment in his reply. "Your army far outnumbers our own!"

"This is no time for jealousy!" Montcalm quipped. "I've sent for Bougainville to assemble them now. Time is not in our favor. I need Ramezay's guns."

"I'll do what I can!" the peeved Vaudreui rejoined. "But if Quebec is attacked, I need them here. The fate of the city lies in your hands! We've supplied you all we can."

Montcalm spun his horse around, glared with astonishment at his French "equal," and spurred his horse on. "*Viens, vitement!*" he called to François. "We've not a minute to spare."

As they rode out the gate and into the Plain, columns of troops in white stretched to their left and more to their right. Immediately in front of them, Vaudreuil's Canadian regiment waited as the two galloped up the rise. A mixture of *coureurs de bois*, Indians in scalplock, and Canadain Regulars turned as they came into view. Among them François spotted Joncaire, Tekacayah, and Yellow Hawk. They stood amid the others in the hazy drizzle and watched the horsemen approach. Montcalm's own soldiers recognized his gray bay and waved as he drew closer. Shouts of "hooray!" and huzzas of ardor greeted him as he waved his hat in return. "I will see you on the heights!" he called to François as he trotted toward the column to his left. The light rain began to lift as the morning light reflected off the army's raised bayonets. Just then, a shell exploded near the bluffs, sending a shower of spinning shrapnel toward François. He dodged the largest flying piece, but his horse caught a fragment of the jagged ball. The animal snorted in pain, lept crazily into the air, and hurtled Philippe to the ground. The great weight of the horse came down just shy of his leg. The blow stunned his senses; nonetheless, a surge of adrenaline rushed through his body, and, rolling forward, he picked his musket and himself up and raced toward Yellow Hawk and Joncaire. They reached for him and pulled him into line. "You, François!" ordered Yellow Hawk. "Stay behind me!" he mumbled in a garbled voice.

Loud huzzahs filled the air as Montcalm reviewed the troops. With raised sword in full command he galloped past his own men and in front of the Canadian line. He turned and rode back toward his regiment along the bluff. On the white tide marched up the Plain toward a narrow ridge. Abruptly they stopped. The entire army halted. François' heart thundered in his chest. As the mists cleared, an ominous formation of red troops topped the horizon. "*Mon Dieu!*" cries from the French line rose. "It's serious now," Joncaire said, as he paused beside Coup de Sang, with François and Yellow Hawk to his right. All eyes turned toward the proud rider near the bluff. His blue coat gleamed in the fresh morning light. His wide sleeves went up, like the arms of God. With sword raised, he brought it forward, and waved for his men to follow. Onward they marched, over the gentle rise. In nervous silence they swished through the wet grass toward the red line.

Still clad in Indian leggings, loincloth, and soft moccasins, William watched with the rest of Wolfe's regiments as the French wave crested the meadow's ridge. Though placed in the center of Murray's brigade, his view of Wolfe remained gratefully unobstructed. Since two a.m. they had responded with anxious hearts to all that Wolfe had commanded. Scaling the heights, one by one, they had amassed a force of thirty-five hundred red coats on the high bluff. The city lay in full view. The rain had ceased and the sun struggled to peep through the morning's band of bright pink clouds. "A glorious day!" someone whispered to his right. "Sure! For dyin'!" cursed another farther down. "No more of that!" a third man objected. "Check your powder! Be sure it's dry! An' keep your eyes on him!" he nodded toward an officer nearby.

William strained to hold the moving line before him in steady focus.

"They're comin' on!" the third man whispered. "Damn if they're not a ready target, banners an' all."

Suddenly, William jolted at the shrilling scream of the Highlanders' bagpipes to his left. Dressed in kilts with their tartans soughing slightly in a cool breeze, they stood in clan formation, with muskets up and broad swords buckled about their waists.

William brought his full attention to the long white line. In its center, strode the strange amalgam of French-Canadians, their copper allies of the Great Lakes, accompanied by fur trappers, woodsmen, and a knot of wily *coureurs de bois*. He wondered if François were among them, or Coup de Sang, or Joncaire, or Yellow Hawk. He squinted to make out each figure, but the mass of men blurred into a formless mob in the sunlight's haze. Without warning, they stopped, raised their muskets, and, at an officer's command, let loose with a cacophonous fusillade of lead and cheers. On they came. They paused, knelt in the grass, reloaded and ran on the double-quick fifty yards closer. Again, they halted, raised their guns, and peppered his line with a searing scream of lead.

"Steady! Steady!" ordered the British officer closest at hand. "The General's not given his nod! The poor bastards! I tell you, we'll be sending them all to Hell!"

On now rushed the men in white and deerskin gray. They reloaded as they ran. Without supervision, they charged. A desperate cry rose in hoarse chorus as on they came, firing individually, some kneeling, others standing with perfect calm to fire again.

"My God!" William groaned under his breath. Less than sixty yards in front of him raced Yellow Hawk with François just behind him. To his left loped Joncaire and Handsome Dog!

"Ah! Such bloody luck!" the man beside him uttered. "I've got 'em all dead in sight."

Suddenly, down the line came Wolfe's command. "Hold! Hold! Hold!" Then the horrible words: "Fire!"

The roar deafened Sir William's ears. The great white wall wavered! Reeled back! Man after man fell. The line broke, its charged collapsed. More men stumbled as their forward movement stalled. In sheer defense, he aimed his piece to fire. A savage had breached their line. The Indian fired point blank into William's side. At that same instant, William's bullet struck the large Indian in his jaw. The half-naked native's face exploded red with blood. It was Yellow Hawk! The soldier beside William shouted and bayoneted the Indian twice.

William looked down at his side, as he knelt to reload his gun. Blood gushed in a dark stream just below his chest. Joncaire's image wavered twenty yards before him. He too had stopped to reload. Without a second lost, the Frenchman hurled his hatchet toward William's head. The blade severed William's ear and opened a deadening gash from his skull to his neck. William collapsed in the wet bramble, still conscious but unable to fathom what had happened. Numb and startled he sought to sit up but couldn't. Joncaire rushed forward, smiled, brought up his knife, only to die in a volley of blasts. Behind him stumbled de Robert. He had been struck during the fusillade, but refused to fall. Back staggered the French line. Stragglers limped and hobbled in haste before the British could fire again. Coup de Sang caught François by the arm and raced with him down the field. Montcalm rode past horrified. The shattered French assault stopped; the broken ranks turned and stumbled in retreat toward Quebec's walls. Montcalm rode among them, attempting to stem their flight. Helplessly, he was being borne away by the momentum of the panicking troops.

"He's dead!" someone shouted. "He's dead! General Wolfe's dead!"

Someone raced past William. It was Monckton. "My God!" he shouted. "Don't buckle now! Fix your bayonets and charge!"

A roar went up from the British line. Boots and gaithered feet rushed forward. William listened as the bagpipes wailed. Blood had soaked his shirt. He lay back, groaned, and fought to remain conscious. He didn't want to faint or die. He wanted to hold on. The intermittent clattering of musketry grew weak, then distant, and slowly faded away.

Yellow Hawk's body lay less than an arm's reach before him. The big Algonquin's eyes stared open. His chest rose and fell with slight breathing. He was still alive. William pulled himself toward the dying savage and grasped his hand.

Yellow Hawk's disfigured face and mangled chin oozed with lymph. He blinked, stared at William, and tightened his grip in the bond of death. He stopped breathing and smiled with his eyes. From somewhere far away a semblance of recognition flitted momentarily in what remained of his face. The pupils of his eyes grew wide, their focus dim. He pressed William's hand once more, released it, and, expelling a long deep breath, died.

William's head began to throb; the pain in his chest caught his full attention. More than blood seeped through the black hole below his ribs. He knew what the sinewy bulge meant. He lay back in the grass and pressed his lips against its moist stems. He thought of Gray's *Elegy Written in a Country Graveyard*. He knew it too. What English schoolboy didn't? How strange the joy and solace its lines contained!

The curfew tolls the knell of parting day ...
And leaves the world to darkness and to me ...
The paths of glory lead but to the grave.

As he sought to reposition himself, an anesthetizing heaviness began to settle across his chest. It filled him with a pleasant feeling, a numbness that relieved all pain. No! He whispered to himself. No, no! No! But somewhere deep and dark the silence whispered "Yes!" William strained to raise himself, but his arms would not move, nor could they move, nor his hands nor legs. He thought of Anna. Of Pontiac! Of the dying Christ! His face rolled sideways, his breathing stopped. Light! Light! O precious light! Then all became dark.

As Tekacayah jogged slowly along, he paused to give François time to catch his breath. Handsome Dog could see the elongated wound in François' thigh. It ran diagonally from his hip to his knee. He shifted his arm to brace the panting Frenchman, hoisted his weight onto his own hip, and, half-carrying, half-supporting his pale co-warrior, struggled to keep abreast of the crumpled army. As he ran, he looked up to see a cannon ball streak across the field, bounce, and slice into the fleeing troops. It struck a rock, ricocheted up, and spilled Montcalm from his horse.

"Stop!" François pled. "Drop me, if you must! Help the Marquis. He needs our help!"

Handsome Dog paused, dragged François toward the writhing commander, and peered down at him.

Montcalm staggered to his feet and re-mounted his horse. The Marquis's side dripped with blood. A white bone protruded above his right knee. His shirt had filled with more blood, where coils of black intestines poked through. The General smiled, reached down for François' hand, touched it; then nudged his horse forward. "*C'est rien!*" he assured the wounded Major. "*C'est terrible! Terrible!*" he observed, as he glanced across the Plain toward the limping columns of his retreating army. "Who would have thought this could have happened? *Jamais! Jamais!* Never did I dream it so." He spurred his horse and, with head erect, turned to face the desperate horde. "Entrench! Entrench!" he called above the muttering of the mob in retreat. But on they came, eager for the safety of Quebec's walls. Weak and faltering, Montcalm yielded to the flow of the soldiers and entered the gates of the city with his head still proud but his eyes cast down and chest afire with pain. Handsome Dog swung in limping motion behind him, with François on his hip, and followed the General's horse. Crowds of townspeople watched as the procession passed. Church bells tolled. A bright sun peeped through the low clouds as the last drizzle of the morning sparkled in the wet streets. "This way!" someone called. It was as an officer on horseback, struggling to make his way to Montcalm. "Sir! The surgeon's house is this way," he pointed. "Bougainville is in the field now and will entrench the troops!" Montcalm did not reply. The officer reached for his horse's reins and led him through the crowd.

In a stone house with white curtains drawn across the windowsills, Montcalm was laid upon a table. With a great sigh he stretched out and gazed toward the doorway. There, Coup de Sang waited with François in his arms. The great general rose slightly on his elbows and waved for Handsome Dog to enter. "No, no!" a servant cried. "Ah, yes!" Montcalm replied. "*Ici, nous sommes tous égals!*" He laid his head back down and lost consciousness.

François watched as the surgeon lifted the Maquis's blouse and peered at Montclam's torso. Gently, he laid the blood-soaked cloth to one side, the better to examine Montclam's chest. The surgeon's head jerked back; his face twitched with nervous alarm. Without glancing further, he approached Handsome Dog and François. "Lay him here," he pointed to a sheet-covered couch. "Where does it hurt?" he asked.

"Everywhere!" François moaned.

"Where most? Your hip or breast?"

"Breast? I thought it was my hip and thigh!"

"Yes. But, this, this wound here," he probed François breast bone, "a ball's entered here. No? Can't you feel it? *Ici!*" he pressed the wound.

"Oh! *Mon Dieu!*" François groaned! Waves of nausea rolled hot and foul through his body. His upper stomach throbbed with a wrenching ache. "I didn't know."

"Well, You are!" the surgeon stated matter-of-factly. "Your hip I can treat, but, Monsieur, this wound," he touched his chest again. "It is in your lungs. If not your, your heart! And all this blood!" he held up his red-stained hands. "It is not so good. I will prepare an opiate gum for you and," he glanced toward Montcalm, "the poor Marquis. I wish it were not so."

Sweat collected on François' brow and trickled down the edges of his face. Its salty residue tainted his lips and dripped onto the couch. The surgeon bent forward and wiped François' face with a corner of his sweat-drenched shirt. A strange face appeared before him. The owner held a brown clay cup in his hand. Protruding from it were grape leaves, soaked in white opium. "Here," said the surgeon. "Chew this and rest." He motioned to the servant, stood up, and placed a similar leaf on Montcalm's lips. The weary man sat down and cupped his head between his hands. "What time is it?" he asked the servant. "Two p.m.!" the servant answered. "Come for me when darkness falls. I've done all that I can for now."

François felt a hand on his shoulder. He looked up. It was Coup de Sang's.

The big Indian had turned his face toward the window. Someone had drawn the curtains back. The light blinded François as he lay there in his semi-conscious, semi-opium induced slumber. Half-awake, half-cognizant of his senses and thoughs, he wondered if Hélène had made it to Frontenac. He blinked as he stared toward the window. Coup de Sang followed his gaze, rose, and, walking toward the window, drew the curtains closed.

To sleep, to dream, perchance to dream no more. Where had it gone? The tumbling waters of the rivers? The forests dark, with clear blue skies, and frozen lakes, and quiet snowfalls? A woman's touch? Her savage glances, their tender love? Somewhere he was with her. "Hélène! Hélène!" he mumbled aloud. "Noël!"

He looked up. Tecakayah had taken his seat again. François wanted to thank him. But to sleep, to sleep, to sleep! He felt his body drifting away: light, weightless, into silence and calm.

Suddenly François awakened, opened his eyes, and rolled sideways. Waves of hot, sickening pain throbbed through every part of his body. The gash in his thigh and the wound in his side ran wet with blood. He recognized Tekacayah, bent forward and beside him. "*Alors!*" he whispered. "*Mon bon sauvage ...* My coat pocket," he motioned with his limp right hand. He struggled for breath, coughing up globs of burning mucus as he spoke. "The brooch. Take it."

Handsome Dog placed his arms around François and raised him slightly. His eyes stared intently into the Frenchman's. Still holding François tightly in his arms, he reached into the Frenchman's pocket and removed the pin.

"Coup de Sang! Find Hélène. Give this to Noël. It is all I have to give her, now," his words drifted away.

"Tekacayah will not forget this," Coup de Sang said.

François swallowed the leaden obstruction in his throat. He couldn't breathe. Something was lodged there, hard, immovable. Somewhere he is running. His legs can't keep up with hers. "*Vite! Vite!*" she says, trying to get him to hurry. She stops, bends down, and lifts him into her arms. On they run, her Chippewa braids flopping against his soft cheek, as if to wipe away his tears. They reach the top of the hill and stop. "*Voie-tu?*

Là-bas? Oui?" She adjusts him on her hip. In front of them, a frightened deer bounds through the forest, over the ferns with a grace new to him. Kicking his legs, he tries to free himself from the cradle of her arms. She looks him in the eyes. "You are not fast enough, my little one. It is already gone." Out of her arms he slides, hitting the ground. His legs work in quick intervals, following the unmarked path of the deer. "François, come back!" the young woman commands as she chases after him. Deeper into the forest he runs, not looking back. Suddenly, from far off, he hears the heavy bay of hounds. *"Attention, François!"* she shouts. He hesitates, then laughs, running toward the dogs. He hears the voices of men. He recognizes his father's voice—deep and calm. Before he can run deeper into the woods, the Chippewa catches him and sweeps him up into her arms. From their horses, his father and the Sires of the King's party smile at them. The bay of the hounds grows dim and dimmer. His eyes click open. "Hélène, Hélène! Where are you?"

"Mon pauvre français!" said Tekacayah, as he laid him back on the surgeon's couch.

Chapter Thirty-Seven

THE ORANGE SUN slid slowly west behind the dusty curtain of that long September day. The dozen or so diggers that moved along the Plain stopped by each corpse to make certain the dead were truly dead. "Look at them two!" a sailor said, as he nudged the bodies of Joncaire and Yellow Hawk with his shovel. "Imagine the likes of us havin' to dig their graves. And this one here, look at 'im!" he pointed toward a third body. "The man's half savage, I believe. Warlock an' all! Whatta ya think?" he asked his comrade.

"Let him lie! Ain't fittin' to place him in no grave with our own. That's what I say. French or Indian!"

"Right and true," the first man said, as they passed on.

Hearing them mention the words 'savage' and 'Indian,' the Seneca who had rowed William across the river waited till the two men left. With somber curiosity he approached the dead man in the grass and looked down. "Um!" he grunted, recognizing Sir William's body. Half savage he did look, in his white shirt, deerskin leggings, loincloth, and moccasins. The Indian squatted to examine his knife in its fine sheath of beaded hide. He slipped both off William's waist and tucked the knife in his belt. Momentarily, he lifted his eyes toward the steep escarpment northwest of Quebec. A half-mile below its base began the shade of the deep woods. The Great Spirit within the Indian spoke to his wondering thoughts. He understood its silent voice. He needed nothing more. Shouldering William's stiffening corpse, he trudged toward the forest green and the white birch in the dying sun. There above the Plains of Abraham, he built a scaffold and, searching for an appropriate raiment, found a Frenchman's banner, blown by the wind as the day had passed. It bore the emblem of the Languedoc brigade. He wrapped it about William's body, tucked it firmly across his face, and sat beneath the wooden bier.

'*Häy, qua! Häy, qua! Hä-wen-né-yu!* Ho, Great Spirit! Listen to my words, O Spirit. What is Red-man that you see him? Like the wind in the reeds, your people come and leave. To You, *Hé-no*, our Grandfather, hear my chant, hear my song! To You Grandfather in the Thunder, I sing for this man's spirit. To You Mother of the Earth, of summer's heat and ripe corn's growth, to You, O You, great giver of life, I sing." Slowly he turned and faced north. "Hail to You, venerable Fathers, with heads of white and beards of ice! What to you is human life? We give it back! Why did you curse us with your white children? Were not your red children fair enough? *Háy, qua! Háy, qua! Häy-wen-né-yu*, O Great Spirit, hear my song. *Na-ho!*"

The Indian rose from where he had squatted and threw dust into the air. Surely he had done enough. Far off, he listened to a wolf's howl. It came across the lonely woods and down the steep escarpment. The hair on his neck quivered. He looked up at the stars. Good, he thought. The Fathers had come. *Ga-oh*, the Spirit of the Winds, had heard his song. What he had done was good.

As dawn's pale glow cast Quebec's shadows across its silent walls, Coup de Sang carried François' body in his arms. Already the meadows' grass lay heavy with dew. Up past the British sentries and over the gentle rise he strode, bearing the Frenchman's corpse with quiet resolve. Steadily he climbed toward the far-off woods that bordered Abraham's Plain. Midway, he paused to rest and glance back across the city. The Frenchmen loved it. The British would take it soon. What was there for him?

He climbed on up toward the gnarled birch, the tall spruce, and graceful maples red in the rising sun. As he drew closer, his eye caught the sight of a fresh burial grounds, or so its lone scaffold indicated to him. Yes! That would work. Better in the wind, where the Spirits live, than in the stone-hard ground! With nimble hands he created a second scaffold beside the first, entwined stout vines about it, and placed it high overhead, beyond the lunge of wolves and wild dogs. He lifted François' *fleur de lis* draped body into the scaffold, stood in silence for a time; then turned west, and began jogging toward the river. There I will find a canoe, he thought, and paddle toward home. But where was home? Frontenac! Came the answer. Go to Frontenac!

Chapter Thirty-Eight

THE FIRST LIGHT SNOWFALL of mid-October whispered past Tekacayah's ears as he paddled into the wind. Above, in the downy clouds, he could hear the last skeins of geese heading south. Their honking calls stirred a loneliness within that he had seldom experienced. Joncaire had been like a father, François-Philippe a distant brother or kin, the French his only family, Hélène alone now left to pique his primal soul. Plus, François' dying request. He would go to Frontenac.

The river's current buffeted his canoe, making it difficult to ply the freezing waters, but paddling along its northern bank propelled him forward in spite of the spray in his face. Behind where he knelt on his knees, lay two fat geese, killed an hour earlier, prior to the snowy gale. With each stroke of the worn paddle, he strained to catch sight of Frontenac's narrow point and quiet cove. The snow picked up and, falling heavily, forced him to cover his head with the badger cloak he had found with the canoe. All that had been west of Montreal.

Soon, he dragged his bark ashore and huddled in the birch and pine along the river's bank. Darkness fell, night descended, and the snow ceased. High above, a million stars scintillated brightly in heaven's black dome. He built a small fire and, hovering over it, munched on a twist of venison jerky he had retrieved from the battlefield. With early morning, he launched anew and paddled toward the distant point that glowed in the dawn's light. A woman had come down to the bay's shoreline.

He could see her outline and the child beside her. Smoke drifted purple in the frigid air behind her. The walls of Frontenac came into view. The woman looked up and stared in his direction.

Paddling slowly ashore, Handsome Dog lept out of the canoe and pulled the craft into the rocky pebbles along the water's edge. He paused, picked up his gun and geese and walked slowly toward the waiting woman. At the same time, he patted the pouch on his belt where he carried the shiny brooch.

Hélène clasped Noël's hand and stepped forward. She had recognized the Indian's silhouette the moment his canoe grated ashore. She had expected someone to come. That he was alone confirmed the spectral night of last month's dream and the memory of her father's death. Now her song's refrain stood before her, in the flesh! She waited in silence as Coup de Sang approached.

"Ojibwa woman, I have come for you," he said. "I bring this gift as food," he extended his arm, holding up the geese for her to see before laying them on the rocky coast. "François has passed into the realm of the Great Spirit. We will see him no more." He laid his musket beside the geese and glanced at Noël. "Come!" he said to her, as he bent down and opened his arms. "Tekacayah will not harm you," he enfolded the child, smiled, and lifted her as he rose again. He reached into his lead pouch and handed her François' mother's brooch. "For you," he said, placing it in her hands. "From your French father."

"Ma-ma! Look! From Daddy! Isn't it beautiful!"

Hélène took her daughter's hand in her own. "Yes, *ma petite*! As beautiful as your papa was!" She kissed the child's fingers and the delicate brooch. "*Ah, bon Dieu!*" she cried suddenly, as tears trickled hot down her proud face. Slowly, she brushed them aside. "Yes!" she whispered with excitement as she regained her poise and smiled at Coup de Sang.

"In the spring, let us go beyond the Lakes, to the forests of Wisconsin," he said to Hélène. "Will you come? Will you be my woman, my squaw?"

She stepped closer and looked into his grave, but manly face. "Yes! We will go with you," she answered. "But Tekacayah, I am not just 'Ojibwa.' I am French, too. One calls me 'Hélène,' a name I love." She studied his face for his reaction. "My fire is warm," she turned in the direction of the wigwam. "So is my heart," she stated, as she placed his hand on her chest.

"Good! Ojibwa Hélène! And I, I am Handsome Dog. Coup de Sang runs with Joncaire in the other life, the other world. I, Tekacayah, run with no one now. Only you!" He bent down, retrieved his musket, and, shifting Noël's weight on his hip, walked toward the walls of Frontenac's ruins.

Renwick's horse clopped warily along, crushing the icy puddles beneath its hooves. Its rider guided it down the bank to the frozen stream. Burke's house loomed cold and alone in the hoary mid-day air. Ice crackled in the nearby cedar boughs. Slowly it slid off in showers of sparkling crystals as the sun's glare turned the ice into mush. Renwick clapped his hands together and placed them to his lips, emitted a vaporous breath and shook his fingers to keep warm. With slipping hooves, his horse mounted the slick bank and trotted with renewed enthusiasm toward the log house on the hill. Renwick's face burned from the cold that stung his cheeks, lips, and chin. Coming down the lane, a horse-drawn sled jerked from side to side in the road's icy ruts. Behind it rode Blue Hatchet, mounted on a sorrel mare. Renwick could see his barehead and long braids. The youth had become a man. A wolfskin draped his shoulders. He was taller than Burke.

Langdon was steadying the single, horse-drawn sled as it drew closer. Beside him sat Sarah and, in her lap, Anna's cherry-red-nosed little boy, Ashby. All were bundled in heavy coats with silvery wolfskin furs tucked about their feet. A white glow of frosty mist encapsulated the horse's mouth and nostrils. Renwick reined up to watch the sled approach.

"Whoaaah!" Langdon called, as he pulled back on the reins. Slowly, the heavy sled creaked to a halt in the crunchy path.

Sarah lifted off the shiny furs and, stepping from the sled, slipped along the ice toward Renwick's horse. Quickly, he dismounted and caught her about the waist with his left arm. "Careful!" he smiled. "I've come too far ta watch ya fall now! I guess you've heard the news?"

"Yes!" she looked up at him. "A surveying party headed for the

Tennessee stopped to deliver Faquier's letter. I wasn't surprised. Just numbed. 'Missing,' he wrote, 'but dead. Last seen by a corporal on the line.' Colonel Washington urged him to send it, so he said." Sarah studied Renwick's eyes, nose, and chin. "We've missed you here," she added softly.

"Aye! And I thee! I've done a lot of thinkin', ya know. They say I've got a way with words, but deep inside, No. Sometimes ar human dreams are shorn away. An' we the livin' ar left in destiny's sad wake. Perhaps in part it's God great plan, some great eternal scheme. I dinna know. I'd be afraid ta say. But mostly, when I give it thought, it's best to fault poor mankind. Ya canna suffer tumultuous times without commensurate sorrow." He glanced away; then back at her. "Nor someone to love! I'm a askin' for your hand, I am. If you'll 'ave it, Sarah?" He bit his lips.

She rose to her tiptoes in the cold and kissed his chapped mouth. "Come! Louise will be excited to know."

"I was a hopin' you'd say that." He looked out across the frozen stubble, the distant tree line of the dark forest, and the mountains beyond. "It makes me feel at home, Sarah. It makes me feel like a man."

The wind picked up and snow began to fall. From far away a wolf's howl drifted across the hollows and dark coves. The horses neighed and stomped their feet.

"Aye!" said Renwick. "Aye!"

About the Author
BENJAMIN W. FARLEY

Born in the Philippine Islands, **Benjamin W. Farley** grew up on tobacco and cattle farms around Abingdon, VA. He is a graduate of Davidson College, (A.B.) and earned his master's degree and doctorate of philosophy from Union Theological Seminary in Richmond, VA. As an ordained minister, Farley served Presbyterian churches in Virginia from 1964 to 1973. Farley was Yount's Professor of Philosophy and Religion at Erskine College, Due West, SC, where he taught from 1974 to 2000. He served as adjunct professor at Presbyterian College in Clinton, SC, from 2000 to 2003. He is the author of seven scholarly works, two collections of short stories and four novels, set principally in the South.

Other books by the Author
Beyond Homer
Corbin's Rubi-Yacht
Of Time and Eternity
Quilly Hall
*The Hero of St. Lo: Stories
of South Carolina And Georgia*